SELL MONTANA

A NOVEL BY

STEVE GILREATH

Harpeth Corner Publishing
An Imprint of SGTV, Inc.

Identifiers: ISBN 978-1-7355271-0-9 (paperback)
978-1-7355271-1-6 (Ebook)

FIC037000   FICTION / Political
FIC016000   FICTION / Humorous / General
FIC019000   FICTION / Literary

Book Cover Design by Thom Schupp

Typesetting by David Prendergast.

Editorial Services by
Erin Young
Jared Sullivan
Barbara Carpenter

Printed in the United States of America
1 3 5 7 9 10 8 6 4 2

For Denise

And For
Alex, Hayden, Graham & Andi

Notes from Steve appear at the end of the book

Hi! I'M THE AUTHOR AND
ALSO A NEIGHBOR FROM COTTONWOOD.
I'M GLAD TO SHARE THIS NOVEL WITH
YOU. PLEASE ADD YOUR COMMENTS TO THE
FRONT OR BACK AND I WILL CHECK
BACK. I HOPE YOU ENJOY THIS
RIDS INTO THE FUTURE!

Steve
2-21

THE NEAR FUTURE

SUMMER

BITTERROOT RIVER, MONTANA

Cold water would help. Bullseye Magee squatted by the clear river and dipped her bandana for a quick rinse. She smiled a little as the frigid water splashed across her face, then retied the blue cotton triangle around her tan neck. Looking downstream, she gazed at Trapper Peak in the distance. That familiar mountain and the majestic lodgepole pines in the foreground allowed her to exhale. To her left, the small group that hired her to guide their trip fished, as they had before. These clients knew how to fish but were loud about it.

Bullseye—who had not been called by her given name of Laura Brennan in the forty years since middle school—watched a fly plop in the water a few yards in front of her. Within seconds a wide mouth propelled by a silvery muscle sliced the shimmering water and engulfed the lure whole. Her clients would eat well before flying back to Washington. She had earned her money by bringing them to the right spot to catch cutthroat trout, and that was a good thing. These politicians, especially the vice president of the United States, complained like toddlers who dropped their popsicles when they didn't catch anything on these expensive outings, regardless of how bad their fly rod technique had been.

Bullseye let it roll off her back and onto the invoice, which she added up in her head as she stood and ambled toward the Secret Service agents, standing back a few yards. Her formula was simple: Start with a figure that was equal to other high-dollar wilderness guide services in remote Montana, then add a steep entertainment fee because they liked her storytelling around the campfire on crisp, cool nights, plus a surcharge for keeping her mouth shut when they talked about secret stuff. Finally, she layered on a generous aggravation fee because all these men were idiots, making her wish she could head to the house the moment they arrived. She held her own during the back-and-forth ribbing that just came natural to a group of guys when they were out in the woods. But when the jokes went too far—and they always went too far—Bullseye shut down or got mean. And mean was funny to these guys. She had kicked a lot of coffeepots in campfires while she cut down their feeble efforts to hit on her.

It wasn't her fault she was hot, and it wasn't their fault that most of them conjured up haunting memories of her dad, but she added another zero to the invoice just because. She smiled at her own reflection in the rippling water as she walked along the river, wishing the panicked trout would spit out the VP's hook and swim away. He had brushed against her one too many times for her liking on this trip, so she had a thought to just keep raising their invoice until they complained. It may not be fair, but she had learned as a little girl that the world worked like that sometimes.

Net hoisted waist high, Vice President Bill Fowler goaded his fishing buddy, Secretary of the Interior Alan Stubblefield. "I'll need some help carrying all these fish. Good thing you don't have anything to weigh you down."

Stubblefield's answer came in the form of a small rock, pecking the VP on the thigh before glancing off his waders. "Catch this," trailed the warning, too late to help.

Bullseye stood chatting with the Secret Service agents. "I guess you don't consider a friend throwing a rock a serious attempt on the veep's life." Then turning in the general direction of the veep, she warned, "That dirt talk might work with your Washington buddies, Mr. Vice President, but you try that here in Montana and you're liable to catch a much bigger rock."

The veep was in good physical shape and inhaled in front of Bullseye. He chuckled until he noticed Bullseye was serious. Just then a walnut-sized rock flew over Bullseye and pinged off his rod.

The vice president wasn't smiling any longer after he overheard one of the Secret Service agents say, "He should have used a bigger rock."

VIRGINIA CITY, MONTANA

"You don't see this in Malibu," sighed Evan Morris, as his Tesla crossover parked itself on the near-empty Wallace Street, just across from the Placer Gold Café. By *this*, he meant that no one had bothered him for an autograph since he arrived in the tiny Montana town of Virginia City. *This* would be a nice change of pace for the gorgeous but seasoned actor even though, truth be told, he had not been besieged lately in Hollywood by the media or by work. Still, having a complete change of pace and meeting some real people might give him a respite from playing the same old Hollywood game.

That's the script he had created for his decision to relocate to Montana. The truth was more depressing. His phone had not slowed—it had stopped ringing. Out of habit, Evan tapped his phone to life, but saw no calls. Not one friend from Hollywood had checked in on him in the weeks since the move, adding to the sad scene. Being famous was one thing, but that was the ego and money part. Being a part of the Malibu culture, where his opinions mattered among important people, where his presence brought credibility, was the truly affirming part. Evan tapped his phone again and remembered days when calls from studios stacked up to discuss roles, buddies who wanted to partner on deals and the honorary charity chairmanships of this and that continually floated his way—all of which had dried up over the last decade, tracking with his acting career. Being off-screen was one thing. At least his movies would live on forever, somewhere. But getting excluded and erased from the elite Malibu social scene was the devasting part for Evan, who felt like a ghost, watching friends and peers roll the party past him. He didn't want to wither and drift into obscurity in front of fans and friends. If he could no longer contribute artistically, if he couldn't "matter," and if others just didn't include him near the epicenter of Malibu society then, like an injured wolf, he wanted to leave the pack and fade away on his own terms. He slid his phone down on the passenger seat and looked out the window. Being seventyish in Malibu was ancient. It felt like he had been embalmed prematurely. Montana seventyish looked different to aging Evan Morris.

Letting go of Hollywood would be tough. The main street in Virginia

City, Montana, looked dry and a little sleepy to Evan Morris on his first morning trip to town. He wondered if he would miss telling people he wanted to be left alone, if, in fact, he really was just left alone.

As his ostrich boots hit the dusty street in the morning sun, he noticed a couple in front of the county courthouse staring at him. He tipped his perfectly formed Stetson, to which they returned an annoyed half wave. Evan looked around and down and noticed that the only things in the entire town not covered in dust were his boots and his car. He hated sticking out. He wanted to get dirty.

Finding his way around wouldn't be hard. Wallace Street, the main drag through Virginia City, was only a few blocks long before the scrubby hills swallowed it up again. The town was about as deep as it was wide, with a slight tilt, so there was an uphill side to the east. Evan did a quick 360 to view the tiny town and sensed a downside as well.

After spotting the sign for the Madison County Offices in the courthouse building, Evan shuffled across the street, dragging his heels to kick up some dust. The real estate agent he had used from Big Sky, an hour to the east, was similar to the people he had left behind in his California circles—very similar—and had warned him about the locals in Virginia City. Even though they were in the same county as the chic resort of Big Sky, the Virginia City Montanans were a much more "salt of the down to earth" type people, as she had called them, combining her metaphors.

And that's what Evan wanted. Down to earth. And a ranch. That's where a wounded wolf would hide. Not in a ski resort condo at Big Sky. Big land on the Virginia City outskirts had been his choice.

Evan had listened to news reports on iHeart over the last two days, which helped override doubts of his decision to start a new life in Montana. He sat alone on the scenic front porch of his newly renovated post-and-beam ranch house with massive, twin river-stone fireplaces and imagined parts of LA crumbling in the riots. On long drives up into the foothills of Ramshorn Peak to scan the broad valley, he slid the windows down and cranked up Sirius to hear about the looting that had spread up the coast toward Malibu and believed he'd gotten out of California just in time. Rioting and burning had ignited in the larger cities across the country but had not yet percolated on the streets and the back hills in places like Virginia City of Madison County in Montana. He felt safe and lonely at the same time.

Looking around the main street in Virginia City, he was a little nervous

4

about meeting the locals in the county seat. As a wounded wolf, he wanted to hide from the eyes of the world, but as a new Montanan he pondered the opportunity to drop some stakes and dig in. The locals were the real deal. He didn't know what he'd have to change to show them he was genuine.

3

WASHINGTON, DC

The sudden summer thunderstorm soothed the angry mob, whose tempers had flared earlier in the midday sun. They had thrown the first bottle at police just before noon. Three separate crowds of seven thousand to over twenty thousand churned and twisted past the Marriott and Freedom Plaza on E Street NW, the Smithsonian's Renwick Gallery on Seventeenth Street NW, and the stores and restaurants of New York Avenue NW, converging and covering the White House on three sides. There were far too many protestors to assign individual blame for any of the violence and more difficult still to designate a leader for the insurgency. This mob, like a shoal of krill pursued by a gray whale, materialized from nowhere, without a front or an end.

Earlier in the morning—like many recent days—angry citizens from all walks of life flooded streets near the National Mall, ignited by posts on Twitter, Instagram, BuzzCutt, and Facebook. Today seemed to reach a critical mass, however, as more people than ever showed up. More "lost my job"; more "can't feed my kids"; more "Relief?" protesters, all pleading their cases on signs and in chants.

Their illicit assembly circled the Washington Monument. No permit— no protest. No matter to the citizenry. They were vocal about *The Budget Problem,* as the current administration (and the previous three) referred to it, and begged for relief. Real relief this time; not just lip service. Crowds churned their way toward the White House, but small, violent spin-ups erupted, and several hotheads fired shots into the air. The drone of ambulance sirens attested to devastation beyond a few broken windows.

For the last hour, the president had been slipping from room to room in the second-floor Residence, watching the crowds swarm the streets that bordered the White House. He clenched the curtain in the West Bedroom as he watched a mob flip a car upside down on the White House side of Lafayette Square, to become an impromptu stage for angry speakers to address the enraged crowds. A team of protesters with portable Wi-Fi repeaters in backpacks spread out among the crowds, allowing the passionate orator's inciteful words, streamed on Facebook and YouTube Live, to ripple through thousands of cell phones that combined to create an ominous, reverberating voice pulsing through the streets, which seemed to surround the White House. The president slammed the curtains shut, but then opened a small slit to spy on the horde. One angry spokesperson encouraged the mob to push toward the White House fences as she leaped off the dented Nissan Pathfinder and watched it get set ablaze to the cheers of the protesters.

The First Lady came up behind her husband as he peered through his surveillance slit. She slid her arms around his waist and stretched on her toes to rest her chin on his shoulder. He sighed and clasped her hands in his. His fingers caressed her wedding band and toggled the tiny diamond in the engagement ring he had placed there twenty-six years before. Success and a thriving career in politics called for an upgrade to something with more carats over the decades. He loved that she wouldn't hear of it. Her family had hated the ring from the beginning, telling her within easy earshot of then-poor grad student Dan Crowley that it was unfitting for their family image. She defended him as "having potential." Touching the tiny diamond made him wonder why being elected president of the greatest country in the world did not yet make him feel he had realized his full potential. Touching her tiny diamond grounded him, as did the thick smoke from burning buildings that marked the path of more protesters approaching the White House.

After absorbing signs in the crowd and hearing the president sigh, she pecked his neck and inhaled a slow sniff of his familiar flannel shirt—the favorite when stress levels were high. As they looked at the crowd, she whispered into his ear, "I can't tell, are these Democrats or Republicans?"

The president missed the sarcasm. "It's both. It's everybody. The White House is under siege by her own people, fueled by pure anger and frustration."

"I can't say I blame them, Crowley," Denise said. "They think they're under siege by the White House and Congress. They voted you in, hoping you can fix this thing and the clock is ticking." After a pause, she continued, "The name *Budget Problem* just doesn't seem big enough to cover this situation, does it? It's hard to remember how it got this bad."

The Budget Problem had united people of varied backgrounds in common protest. Decades ago, our government started gaining debt, outrunning common sense by spending much more than it should. Spending more than we generated by revenue created an annual deficit. At the end of the budget year, those deficits, plus the money Congress

7

borrowed from our citizens' retirement funds, were added to the national debt. Continued spending in the '90s, '00s, the teens, and into the '20s compounded the problem, and the '30s looked even more dire. The national debt curve was so steep it looked like a ski slope. There had been bright moments during some administrations, but Congress and most presidents found prosperity coupled to spending. In the '20s, unemployment had fallen, then risen—helping, then hurting. Pivotal issues had new champions on both sides, and the country split even further into a house divided.

The president said, "There's so much tension out there. The Gospel of Mark and Abraham Lincoln both mentioned the fate of a house divided and it wasn't good."

Trouble had amplified throughout the '20s when government grew almost unchecked and the presidency with Congress became a testing ground for wild economic theories, promoted by all parties. Revised tax laws claimed 50 percent of the salaries of most middle-income families. Discontent grew, with some insisting the only answer was more government intervention in every area of American life. They closed loopholes and raised the rate yet again on their favorite whipping boy, the top 5 percent, which heretofore paid a huge percentage of the overall tax bill—and that 5 percent became the target only after Congress had pummeled and bled the top 2 percent, but couldn't generate enough revenue to keep pace with the lawmakers' benevolence. As a result, they had moved their money offshore. Punitive taxation and a lack of incentives caused industry owners to stop hiring altogether. A robust jobs market for all Americans in the early '20s had evaporated, and a tidal wave of small businesses shuttered their doors. Corporate tax burdens increased as lucrative (some said crazy) exemptions were closed, and soon large corporations followed suit. Hardship and panic enveloped the nation.

"Rebuilding after two pandemics didn't help. It's almost impossible to see how our economy could have survived being turned upside down twice in a decade," said the First Lady. "It was important that government stepped up to lend a hand to our citizens and help them have jobs to go back to, but that was money that had to come from out of the blue."

The Covid-19 or "little pandemic," as it was renamed once the devasting Novido-virus pandemic swarmed the planet later in the decade, was a good primer to help us understand that government could help in time of crisis, but may serve people better by getting out of the way during the recovery effort. Novido had frozen the economy through '29 and into

'30, when the reality of widespread death matched the early grim models. The world shut down, but a thriving black market emerged as government seemed to have no answers except more layers of government.

Throughout the recoveries, the political parties tried to outgive each other as the House and the Senate doubled down on promises to make life easier for Americans, courtesy of more government programs. And promised. And promised. Getting re-elected was a strong opiate for politicians, who continued to talk change but spent dollars. Public dollars. These programs caused more division, pitting one segment of the population against another, even though both sides were well-intentioned.

Widespread public disenchantment reached a boiling point at the end of the 20s' when the president and Congress, while addressing the Novidovirus recovery, also had to pay the bills for programs offered years earlier by their predecessors, in exchange for election. They couldn't kick the cans any farther down the road. Free technology equity programs to equip all lower-income families with unlimited data access and mobile devices; government-assisted air-conditioning and heating for every dwelling; and staunch requirements for renewable resource reconstruction of all buildings (at a factor of eight times conventional cost); the free-ride policy (officially the "Get America Moving" program), where every American family could exercise their "right" to personal transportation, and accompanying programs for government-owned electric-car manufacturers driven by shrinking, but still powerful unions; and the massive GIP or "Guaranteed Income Program," where every citizen (and noncitizen) received a payout from the government just for being, whether or not they worked. GIP had become known as the "Great Inflation Prod" as it added to the downward economic spiral (not to mention another baby boom). The Democrats and Republicans each had their names for these programs and others that were compassionate, expensive, and created largely to help each party win a larger constituency. Congress could be very caring when using money that didn't exist and both parties had taken turns adding to the country's massive debt term after term.

And while programs for individuals had to be paid, Congress also had to craft support for small business and corporate bailouts that helped more than the stockholders to prevent life as we know it from grinding to a halt.

Splat! A balloon filled with red paint smeared across the portico driveway, after being launched from somewhere deep in the crowd with an improvised slingshot of surgical tubing and duct tape. "Mr. President, please stay away from the windows," said Kendall, the lead Secret Service agent, screaming into the room.

"It's paint. It's only paint. I'll be ok, Kendall. It's probably latex that will wash off easily." The president leaned back toward the window, peering out through the slit in the drapery.

The attempts to take care of the masses and the programs used as leverage to keep their faithful happy had motivated a majority of the citizens to lean on their government like never before. Receiving more income by staying home, not working, was an easy choice for most. But now there wasn't enough government money left to lean on and far too many leaned. Big corporations and small businesses were in the same boat, feeding off of stimulus program after program, then acting surprised when Congress implemented rules and quotas that affected their industries. Things soured when they bit the hand that fed them.

All these things—some necessary, some merciful, some frivolous—when tallied, required a bulkier government structure to implement and monitor.

"So, help me understand," the First Lady said. "What's the difference in the debt and the deficit?"

Dan Crowley looked slyly over his shoulder at his wife. "We both know you had better grades than I did in global economics. This is a trap."

"More like a refresher course. What are the differences?"

The president sighed and said, "The deficit is the amount of amount of money we spend every year that is over budget…"

"You mean the money we don't really have, and that starts with the budget you proposed as President?"

"Technically, yes but Congress actually spends it and we find ways…"

"And the national debt?"

"We keep a running total of those overages…"

"The money we didn't have every year but spent anyway," she said.

"Yes. Sure but sometimes there are surpluses. That total is the national debt."

"Isn't there more? I mean, don't we take those overages and have to pay interest every year on them? And I remember something about Congress borrowing on people's retirement funds from social security, so there's a cost to that right? All that gets added in the national debt total, I think."

The president's hands stroked the tops of his wife's fingers, still clasped in front of him. "So, the simple diagnosis is that we spend money we don't have and there is no sign of slowing down. You're right. Now keep going. I'm sure you are about to point out that government has to grow larger to manage all the debt, which just compounds the problem, right?"

Unchecked growth allowed our government to gobble up an increasing percentage of GDP, like a coal-burning furnace. Governments use GDP, or Gross Domestic Product, to measure what a country is good at producing and to determine their ability to repay their debt. It consists of, well, everything. They lumped it all into four components: personal consumption, business investment, government spending, and net exports, for standard comparisons.

Conventional economic wisdom held that lenders worried about being repaid when a country incurs debt greater than their entire economic output (GDP). The World Bank said a country reached a tipping point when the debt-to-GDP ratio exceeded a threshold of 77 percent, but the US started a troubling spiral in the second quarter of 2019, when their debt-to-GDP ratio soared to 103.2 percent. A decade later, in 2028, it swelled to 178.8 percent and tripped every alarm in 2030, when the US quadrupled the World Bank warning level of 77 percent, reaching a staggering 309 percent of GDP.

"Even high school economics students know we can't sustain this level of spending and borrowing. An unprecedented 21 percent of your annual fiscal budget will be consumed by debt service in 2030. Over one-fifth of our annual budget went toward paying the interest from past spending! We'll never dig out of this hole."

Dan Crowley was silent as he processed her comments and the situation through the window.

Previous administrations and other parts of government looked everywhere for answers. Overseas debt brought more intervention from China and others who secured large chunks of our country. They exercised leverage throughout the years, hampering exports and allowing cheap imports to stifle manufacturing, finally knocking the dollar out of the world standard in favor of China's yuan. The resurgence of bitcoin and the introduction of Libra and other strong crypto and digital currencies created an alternate economy, siphoning more wealth out of America.

In the ultimate move of desperation, Congress rescinded the GIP program, yanking the guaranteed salary many leaned on, finding it impossible to cover the costs. Pouring salt in the wounds of the masses, they recommended people return to work—to jobs that no longer existed.

And the people—everyone—rebelled in different proportions. Nothing had united the citizenry like this sweeping crisis. Paying an unfair share of taxes for others incensed some. Being asked to pay any tax at all upset those who had paid none in the past. But receiving money for nothing in the GIP and having it yanked away was the final straw. The target of frustration varied as all hell broke loose in every corner of the United States: at town hall meetings, rallies, and random civic events. And now people died in riots.

Denise sniffed his flannel shirt again. "You know, you were part of the problem when you were in Congress. Do you regret those bills you helped push through? The wasteful spending?"

"Hindsight is—of course I do. But a lot of those programs did good. In the middle of campaigns, I made promises that I didn't even think about. All politicians are guilty of the same thing. We all want to help those most in need, so it was hard to vote no on programs that fed people or helped with jobs in the short term. We ignored the long-term damage or just assumed they'll get fixed down the road."

Denise added for him, "And you discuss budgets in the trillions, and so a little bitty million-dollar amendment comes along, you stick it in, knowing no one even has time to read the bill. Who cares, right?" She nibbled his ear, then spoke right into it. "I've always heard that politicians get elected for creating jobs and growing the economy. They lose elections when unemployment and taxes increase. So, remind me, what's the incentive for Congress to ever reduce the deficit?"

Dan Crowley realized he didn't need to answer or agree. He never dreamed a budget crisis could lead to such widespread civil disobedience and violence in America. "Do you remember me talking about my Haiti mission project in college? I was only there for a summer, but I saw firsthand what grassroots protests look like. Three people got killed right in front of me, just for trying to improve their lives. I swore I'd never forget it."

Denise relaxed her grip and came off her tiptoes to circle around in front of her husband, never taking her eyes off his. He loved and hated that maneuver. The intimacy excited him, but he knew she would get him to admit something already obvious but unspoken. She slid under his left arm to complete the circle and tightened her grip as he drew her closer.

"The question is, Crowley, are you ready to do what it takes to fix this mess? People are dying—not just from financial crap but from the protests about the financial crap. We could be headed into another civil war."

"An *uncivil* war, I'd say."

Spot protests had cropped up for a decade, however, the demand for

12

the government to let go of their money sounded more threatening today. The mob was louder and closer to home—his home, at least, for the time being. Even the Rose Garden couldn't filter the angry insults as the protests strangled the streets nearby.

And that's when the next bottle flew over the fence toward the White House. This one was on fire.

4

DAVIS, CALIFORNIA

At first it wobbled a little, then hovered in place. As promised, the flying car hung in the air like a UFO. After the programmed pause, the Hock Industries team put the noisy flying car through the paces.

As part of the final phase of certification, the AFV-22 (the unimaginative project name assigned to the twenty-second version of their Autonomous Flying Vehicle by a Hock Industries scientist) had to achieve several levels of proficiency unwitnessed over the thirty-plus years of its development. This exercise, if successful, would allow the team to take the vehicle for a real shakedown at the Yuma Proving Ground.

There had never been a successful flying car for a true urban application (*Jetsons* and *Chitty Chitty Bang Bang* notwithstanding). Twenty-five other manufacturers had prototypes that flew, but all required short runways, created too much wind to land in urban settings, or faced other limitations. The AFV-22, nicknamed the Magic Carpet, had taken off vertically with a bit of wind and noise, but vertical nonetheless. After a few wobbles, it shifted forward when louvered panels tilted behind 150 small, electric high-speed fans and zoomed ahead in a straight path. After a return trip from just a quarter mile away, the flight team shut it down right on the marked landing zone.

The FAA had assigned General Amy Starnes (US Army, retired, but still called "General" out of respect and fear by everyone, from her staff to her husband and kids) to evaluate the autonomous flying car technology and the massive infrastructure recommendation for approval by Congress. The general growled under her breath, "Gall-durn-it! They just may have figured this flying car thing out."

"General, this could change the way everything works," exclaimed an aide trailing one step behind.

"Flying is one thing, Son. Lots of companies do that. Flying through downtown with a thousand more of these things whizzing by is another. But this is one to keep our eye on. Our world needs this right now."

5

WASHINGTON, DC

The Roosevelt Room in the West Wing of the White House was large for a four-person meeting. It got small fast. "I don't care how we got in this mess," yelled President Crowley, throwing volume one of an old Tax Code across the table, slamming it against a shelf, taking out a Civil War–era lamp on its way. The other three assembled jumped. "Let's remember what we did wrong, but not waste time trying to place blame," he said, calmer. "In case you haven't noticed, this country is on the verge of falling—no, ripping itself apart unless we can figure something out. So, let's hear your best ideas."

"We have to raise taxes again," offered VP Bill Fowler, arriving late the previous night from his fishing trip out West. Raising taxes was the default position of every administration, despite party, and the only quick answer.

"No!" Crowley yelled again, seeking volume two of the Code that contained eleven times more words than the Bible. "Don't you know what those protests are about? People have had enough. And it's not just here. There are protests in Phoenix, Chicago . . ." He snapped his fingers, looking for help to fill in the blanks.

"Phoenix, Chicago, LA, New York, what's left of Detroit, Twin Cities, Miami, Atlanta . . . and lots of smaller cities. There're online effigy-burnings, 'hate-fests' on Facebook, and a massive demonstration in San Antonio this morning," rifled off Secretary of Commerce Wayne Redmond, scrolling through his phone.

"We need drastic answers," pleaded the president, with empty hands outstretched. "Answers that are bigger than anything we've discussed before. Something to produce incredible revenue, and I mean in short order. And to make it harder, we need to raise revenue, while we cut taxes. If we don't deliver relief to the people right away, we'll lose this country."

"We should hire Randy's think tank full of white guys," offered Chief of Staff Graham Blair as he straightened the perfect knot on his R. Hanauer cobalt Carlisle bow tie. His knack for breaking the tension was legendary. In intimate circles, he sometimes called the president "white guy," who in turn referred to him as "black guy," a long-standing routine from one of their

15

first visits to a *Washington Insider* interview, where a commentator had identified them as such over a mic thought to be turned off. They had been close friends for years, through local, state, and national campaigns. The two were always together but found it funny that a commentator couldn't tell them apart, except for color. Crowley had been out front as the affable candidate; Blair behind the scenes as the pensive strategist, the handler. Crowley's attire was usually disheveled, in need of attention; Blair, impeccable in a suit and bow tie and five inches shorter than candidate Crowley. Blair had shaved his head since high school, while Crowley had longish locks for a white candidate. Both had stunning intellects and yet, some commentator could only see "black and white" and got caught saying it.

Blair often provided the politically savvy angle for a discussion, giving the president perspective and freedom to think beyond the expected. Blair pursued the Beltway solution and said, "His think tank helped create some wild scenarios for healthcare back in the teens. They might inspire some fresh thinking."

"No, no," the president countered, expanding the sloppy knot on his "Caffeine Molecule" tie, a Christmas present from his son that he was only allowed to wear on internal days in the Oval Office. "This is too big for one company to handle, and we don't have time for a big study. Our country's— and our—butts depend on coming up with something revolutionary."

After staring off at the ceiling, the president said, "We need to get a bunch of smart folks—maybe thirty or forty and lock them in a room so we can suss out every scenario—stuff we never dreamed. There has to be a solution."

Blair said, "We'll put together a list of recommendations and try to expedite this thing. I'll speak to some senators who still want to rub elbows with the White House. I think a good target is to have the first meeting by the end of the month."

"Three o'clock," said the president, ignoring Blair. He turned and looked at the astonished faces around the table. "Three o'clock today. Each of you grab three or five people and get them ready to head to Camp David to work awhile. We are going to make a run at this, even if we sequester ourselves for a week—me included. I want to meet some smart, creative folks—so let's reach outside the normal group of butt-kissers. We have to save this country."

"But, Mr. Pres—"

"And don't tell these folks what's going on. Just tell them that a matter of utmost security to the United States is at hand, and we need their help. This has to be a secret—I mean a *real secret*—not one of those *DC secrets* where you tell everyone you tell that it's confidential. No press—hear me, everyone? No press. We have to keep this quiet until we come up with some answers. The country can't think we're grasping at straws . . . even if we are. Blair will coordinate. See you at Camp David in"—he glanced at his watch—"five and a half hours."

He flew out of the room over a chorus of "buts" and "can'ts."

6

VIRGINIA CITY, MONTANA

"Well, here comes ole what's his name," said Bullseye Magee, peeking through the dented metal blinds of the Madison County Courthouse. The dusty blinds weren't original to the 1875 construction but must have been added soon after. She said, between bites of an apple that slid off the blade of her fishing knife, "Oh, and would you look at those shiny new boots? I bet they're fresh from Brooks Fifth Avenue." She smiled at her own joke, since her rancher friends Hitch Jenkins and County Commissioner Morris Evans didn't track with her humor.

"Who's his name?" Morris Evans poked from behind the *Madison County News* app on his iPad.

"That rich Hollywood actor guy, that's who. The one that bought the Tucker 'n Bachman ranches." To herself, she said, "Dang, he's a looker. That's quite a bumper on the back of that chassis." Turning to the guys, she added, "Shoot, you oughta know his name better'n anyone else, Morris."

Hitch Jenkins leaned over from his regular chair in the corner and looked out of the window nearest to the door. "Yep, you should know his name, Morris."

"Bullseye, you're the gal who takes the vice president and all them muckety-mucks fishing and hunting. I don't care to know them folks," said Morris.

"Those are politicians, not celebrities; and, believe me, there's a big difference, but I'm telling you, Morris Evans, this is one celebrity name you should remember," added Bullseye.

Morris Evans leaned forward just in time to see has-been-leading-man and action-movie-hero Evan Morris flatten his nose as he tried to push the door clearly marked "Pull."

"Hey, fellas . . . ma'am. You should get that door fixed," joked Evan Morris, to a semisilent reaction as he stepped up to the worn wooden countertop. He pushed aside the jellybean holder / World's Greatest Golfer paperweight to make room for his elbows. "How we doin' today?"

"OK," said Hitch Jenkins over his glasses and under his cap. "You?"

Morris Evans watched from his chair behind the desk and harrumphed, "I'd be better if people read the Pull sign."

Evan laughed, then said, "I'm just getting settled up on my new ranch . . ."

Bullseye felt him pause for a "Welcome to town" or a question about which ranch he had bought. The three locals just glared.

"I just bought the old Tucker and Bachman places . . ."

Bullseye knew how this little tug of war worked: in equal parts, her two friends stayed silent, and the new guy squirmed and continued to offer more details, thinking something might spark a conversation. She had seen these painful exchanges play out with other people who moved to the area. There was a slight mistrust of anyone moving to the sparser areas of Montana by the locals, which was amplified for anyone of celebrity status. Her group had taken it on themselves to front the vetting process with newcomers, in hopes of cultivating appreciation for becoming a Montanan, or at least chafing a little as part of the entry ceremony.

" . . . and I wondered if I need a permit or an environmental impact study to drill a well and cut some trees," Evan finally finished.

"Don't need one for cutting timber if it's just for your house or barn, but there's some paperwork for drilling the well," Morris said as if he had pressing county business. His wooden chair groaned as he leaned back and plucked a copy of form mt-e9907 from a credenza stacked high with various papers and pamphlets.

Evan looked around, as if the paparazzi may swarm, then pulled out some tiny, foldable reading glasses to help investigate the form. "Hmmm . . . last name first . . . Morris, Evan."

"Yep?" said Morris Evans, now back behind the tablet.

"Excuse me?" said Evan Morris.

"I thought you called me," said the commissioner.

"I was just reading the form as I filled it out. I said, 'Morris, Evan.'"

"I know—that's my name."

"Your name is Evan Morris too?" said the actor.

"Naw, it's Morris Evans. That is what you said," bellowed the commissioner, holding up the nameplate from his desk, sounding more perturbed.

"I was reading the form—it says, 'last name first.' I'm Evan Morris," he said, offering a friendly handshake. "That's interesting that we have the same name."

The commissioner leaned over his desk to the counter, tentatively accepting the handshake. "Too bad you got it in the wrong order."

Evan continued begging a welcome. "It's so beautiful up here. This land has more than its share of stars at night."

"We got a few more stars than we need in the daytime too," mumbled Morris. Bullseye laughed at first and then tried to cover it with a cough. Hitch reeled her in with a disapproving stare and stepped in as referee.

"Don't you pay him no never mind, Mr. Morris. Our Morris is as crusty as they come and wears his County Commissionership like a halo. I'm Hitch Jenkins and over there is our friend Bullseye Magee. I'm sure she's laughing because she just thought of some new scam to separate a group of tourists from their money."

"Hey now!" protested Bullseye, almost enough to stand.

"You all live here in Virginia City?"

"Bullseye has a nice spread outside town and is a hunting and fishing guide, and she also owns the old Lame Horse Creek tourist trap over in Idaho. If you got twenty dollars, she can help you dig for gems in her mine shaft, spend the night in a real authentic ghost town . . ."

Morris Evans put his tablet down and piled on, "Which features all new fresh ghosts since she just built this old ghost town six years ago."

Bullseye rose to defend herself. "OK, that's enough. You fellers have hung out with me long enough to know that's just not true."

Hitch and Morris recoiled, obviously not expecting a fight.

Bullseye let a sliver of a smile slip into the corner of her mouth as she sliced off another section of apple. "Now, you know that if you want to dig for a world famous Bitterroot Valley sapphire or sleep in the haunted hotel room practically certified as the spot occupied by Lewis *and* Clark *and* Sacagawea . . . it will cost a lot more than twenty bucks!"

Hitch said, "And now you know the real Bullseye Magee, Mr. Morris."

"What they won't tell you, Mr. Morris is that I have discovered a few sapphires and even some genuine diamonds on my place on the border in Idaho. And when I find a few bigger ones, it'll shut them up for keeps."

Morris Evans shot back, "Diamond flakes, you mean. You'd have to glue a few of those together just to see them without reading glasses."

"They're there, fellas—I can smell 'em," added Bullseye, as she tilted her head back like she was savoring a diamond aroma at that very moment.

"And what exactly does a diamond smell like, Bullseye?" asked Hitch.

Bullseye rolled her head sideways to face Hitch. "Like money, boys. Like husbands lined up with hands full of hunnerds, just waiting to shove it in my pockets."

"So, diamond mining is your full-time occupation, Bullseye?"

"No," interrupted Morris. "To be fair, when Bullseye ain't mining

20

money from unsuspecting tourists in her sapphire operation, she makes a real living as a wilderness guide for those high-dollar political types from Warshington. And she's pretty good at it. She had the vice president of the whole United States out last week. He's a regular of hers."

"If I can help that poor man catch a fish, I can help anyone," said Bullseye.

After a short laugh, Evan said, "So you cater your hunting and fishing trips to the stars, Ms. Magee?"

She slipped the slice of apple off her knife blade and spoke while she chewed, "Everybody calls me Bullseye, and naw, there's always a camera nearby when you star types come sniffing around. The politicians think it's cute that a woman spearheads a guiding service, and those old guys think I'm hot, which helps, but it's privacy that I offer my clients. Those politicians and big corporate types are always trying to hide something—I'm not talking about nothing major illegal, don't get the wrong idea, Mr. Morris, but if they want to stretch the bighorn season by a day or so while they talk about something secret, and it's private land, who says that's a problem?"

"I understand, Bullseye, and please, call me Evan," he said, tipping his hat again. "So, the mining and ghost town stuff is just a hobby. Is that around here?"

Bullseye smiled and shifted her weight, tipping her hand that there was more of a backstory required in her answer. "Well, it's somewhere between a hobby and a total pain in the butt. I inherited it a while back from a worthless uncle that wanted to make certain he left as big a stain on the rest of my life as he did when I was a little girl. So, I make OK money with the guiding service, and I got more land to hunt on from my uncle. Either way, it keeps me from having to work on my ranch, which is a whole nother story, Evan. Someday we'll line up some shots, and I'll tell you about that."

"Well, how about that? I just moved to town, and I already have a drinking date," Evan Morris boasted as he turned back to his form.

Bullseye watched him lean over the counter to write. Evan was on the seasoned side of extremely good looking—she remembered seeing him on those old magazine covers. He was older and weathered a bit, but the years had been kind. He had a Malibu weathering that textured and defined a person; not a Montana winter-after-winter-work-in-the-cold weathering that chiseled and broke a man. She liked the Malibu weathering to look at but had been around enough famous people to see through their thin veneer. Like a trout at noon, she wasn't easy to catch.

"OK, Mr. Backwards-Name-with-the-Stars, we need to finish up so we can get to lunch," said Morris Evans. The others rose to leave.

"Nice to meet you all. I hope to see you around," offered Evan as his last first chance at connecting.

"You planning on putting up any fences?" asked Morris.

Evan took off his glasses and stammered for a second, looking to give the answer he wanted to hear. "Well . . . I . . . you bet. As soon as I get horses or cows, I'll make sure they get penned in."

"Told you," said Morris to Bullseye and Hitch. "All of you Hollywooders swoop in and buy up these big ranches all around the county. Most of you hardly even stay here more than a few weeks out of the year, but you think the first thing you have to do is put up fencing. We like these open spaces. Besides, you got enough land that your horses will wear out before they ever find the edge of your place."

"Well, that's good advice. I guess I won't be fencing then. Thanks for the tip," surrendered Evan Morris. "And by the way, I'm not just out here for a few weeks. I'm hoping to ride into the sunset years on my ranch here."

"Well, I've heard that before. I hope you find your way around all right. I'll let you know when the drilling application is approved," directed Commissioner Evans. "It just has to clear the County Board."

Evan paused, then said, "Well, back in Malibu I could get things fast-tracked by the codes department in about a month because of my connections. Is that possible here? I know it's asking a lot."

"Oh, Son, this ain't Malibu, and we don't care about that status stuff. The County Board is just Hitch, Bullseye, 'n me, so we'll kick it around over lunch and you can pick up the approved permit this afternoon. But it's Meatloaf Monday over at the Placer Café, so don't expect anything before two p.m."

Over her shoulder, Bullseye offered, "Sorry for the rush, Evan, but there is some risk of missing out on a slab of meatloaf if you don't get to the Placer in time."

The ex-Hollywooder slid out of the courthouse behind the trio and had just defrosted from the cold reception when he ran smack into April Lear.

DAVIS, CALIFORNIA

The long, twisting driveway to Hock Aviation, narrowed by a lack of attention to the vines and other overgrowth, disguised the innovative aero-technical development facility from the main road. General Starnes wondered how an independent scientist had created one of the first potentially successful autonomous flying cars—without the help of the government or the military. This Hock guy wasn't even a military contractor. It was common to see guys parlay their armed forces contacts into something marketable. Hock didn't have any of these advantages.

A quirky contingency of scientists and mechanics approached the car as Starnes arrived. Dr. Hock greeted her with, "Welcome back, General. It's exciting to have you here for the next level of testing." He offered a timid handshake but was out-squeezed by the five-foot-nothing Starnes.

The general was overdressed in a navy-blue suit, cut to look like one of her old military uniforms. There was an order that came with military life, a sameness that she missed, especially as she gazed across the oddity of young scientists, all clad in jeans and every pattern of plaid possible. She adjusted her suit collar and brushed her sleeve after interacting with these creative *flightrepreneurs*, as they called the category, acting as though they might have fleas.

Starnes smiled after the first successful test, showing she wasn't skeptical of Dr. Hock's accomplishments. These folks had reached for the stars and darn near grabbed one. But there was more to the process, and she was the gatekeeper they had to convince in order for the government to commit the infrastructure required, including the public-safety aspects of the flying-car technology. "Well, it doesn't look like it should work, but dang if y'all didn't figure it out," she conceded, exposing a gentler side. "Son, I will be amazed if that thing can thread the needle from here to the first target without killing anyone."

"Excuse me, General, but we refer to the destination marker as the 'bearing site.' We've eliminated all offensive and violent words of destruction like 'aim' and 'target' from our company's jargon," preached one of Dr. Hock's assistants with peace-sign bone plugs inserted as ear gauges.

Starnes didn't even try to hide her expression, which shifted from

You're kidding, right? to *Don't piss me off, kid.* Their progress in relations prior to the dove comments was erased as a noticeable chill fell.

"Well then, missy," Starnes said, rubbing her chin, "we'll see about that. You just get that thing to fly, on course and 100 percent safe, and we'll call it whatever the fat you want."

General Starnes glared at Dr. Hock, clarifying that she was not accustomed to dissension in the ranks. He said, "Let's look at the new paint job. We'll be ready to fly here at o–two–thirty–hundred–o'clock–p.m."

Starnes chuckled and said, "Alrighty, let's look at this thing."

Dr. Hock shuffled along, with shoulders slumped, likely from carrying an entirely new category of technology on his back for more than thirty years. He'd suffered through all design phases, including retractable wings, helo-prop hybrids, and others before his multi-mini-fan configuration took off. He kept his long silver hair swept back in a ponytail and constantly pushed his small wire-frame glasses up on his nose. Each lab coat he wore had huge pockets that he could "stuff with lots of, well, stuff," as he liked to say, and different nicknames embroidered on them, to suit his mood. Dr. Grumpy, Fly By July 20??, Doc Can Do!, Doctor Getouttamyway, and others were amusing to General Starnes.

The whole entourage moved to a rough metal shed, with an interior they had scrubbed, painted, and meticulously organized. It smelled like hot flux and hard work, with the look of a leading-edge electronics lab. Thirty years of pictures along the west wall told the development story for AFVs 1 through 22.

Three prototype AFV-22 Magic Carpets rested under dramatic halogen downlighting, their shiny epoxy skins shimmering. The vehicle looked to Starnes like a Camry or the newer Ford Stellaris resting on a bed of 150 small, but powerful fans, each about ten inches wide by fifteen inches long. There were servos and cams hidden inside the Kevlar housing on each fan.

"You folks think these things'll fly right from someone's backyard, through rush hour and a sky full of drones delivering pizza, and not crash into anything or anyone, right?" asked General Starnes.

"Yes, General. Yes, we believe they will and no, this is definitely not drone technology," said Hock, pushing up his glasses. There are some big differences needed to transport people safely in an AFV. Our cargo is human, so we have to factor in traffic, weather, and yes, even drones with collision avoidance."

After more discussion about the additional burdens of cabin comfort for the passengers in an AFV, traffic rerouting, and the government's role in creating highways in the sky to limit AFV patterns, noise, and other hazards, Starnes reiterated why the upcoming tests were so important.

Wendell, one of Hock's most trusted assistants, beckoned the group to come over to the "Safety Logistics Station," as identified by an acrylic-and-metal sign flapping in the breeze. The presentation included a brief history of autonomous vehicle movement on land. It highlighted the achievements of Tesla, Toyota, Amazon, Mercedes, and FedEx, among others, but also what they had done wrong during years of development, with a video of vehicle crashes into storefronts and parking lots and other catastrophes on the roads. The country could not afford the same slow learning curve with vehicles overhead.

The country had accepted a new paradigm since autonomous and driverless cars, trucks, and delivery vehicles began operating on roads all over the country in the mid-'20s. Wendell stepped forward and delivered the jumping-off point for the flying autonomous vehicles, as the lights oscillated and created an intense, warm glow around him.

"But a car is operated by the driver or the fleet owner. There is collision avoidance, but no central source for data or capability to have all cars directed into specific traffic patterns, for mass evacuations, say, or just general efficiencies. We tolerate traffic jams on the ground as each vehicle works in isolation, but if they extend the same capabilities to the autonomous flying vehicles, chaos would be unavoidable. Quiet or privacy sacrificed. It would be impossible to avoid collisions, once you factor in rush hours, drone traffic, and weather. Our years of R and D included not only the safe and comfortable transport of our passengers but recommendations for standards to preserve order and safety in our skies."

Cued by an illuminated spotlight, Dr. Hock stepped forward. "General, imagine thousands of AFVs in the air, heading to an urban area, like downtown Manhattan. The sky can handle an unlimited number of vehicles, yet what happens on the receiving end when they all have to land? What is the protocol with limited space on the ground and a fixed length of hover time before they plummet to the ground as their batteries die? We must calculate each of these elements before a car even takes off. It's like creating new mini-airports and managing air traffic control and parking garages concurrently. And with Uber, Bezos, FedEx, Domino's, and all the others trying to launch delivery vehicles into the air, safety is key."

The pool of light widened as Hock Industries navigation expert Andi

Calton stepped up and said, "But we're still in the lead, General, and that brings us to radar and traffic control. You know that we program the craft to follow LiDAR signals. By using a flight plan from the point cloud, we have a view in the onboard nav system that is centimeters accurate, even though it was created from miles up with the help of the GPS grid. LiDAR uses two hundred thousand pulses a second from a photon laser to reflect off the surface to map not just topography, but buildings, trees, towers, you name it."

The nav expert continued, while the detailed wire-frame image of a cityscape swooped and weaved behind her. "General, a flight plan based on LiDAR provides an accurate picture of where an autonomous vehicle is flying, in great detail. But what about all the other vehicles flying in the same space?"

Andi Calton moved forward a little, to regain her spotlight. "So, what all that means is that every vehicle must interface with a robust traffic-control system that we affectionately call NORM. The NORM system accounts for every flying object, routes them, and controls the flight window so we don't stack cars up in the air. It continually revises that plan with point-service system updates—LiDAR—along the way, so the latest data on all those factors reaches the vehicle's nav system in flight. It can even read the power levels in every car in the air, rerouting those that are getting critically low on battery."

The general rested her chin in her hand as if she were studying the entire physics of flight. "This NORM traffic control system must be massive."

Dr. Hock said, "It is, but it's localized. Transponders installed in each car emit a signal that feeds the traffic data. It's pretty cool technology. For example, it factors in surrounding weather and the altitude, since there will be layers of cars flying over each other." At that moment, a whirring sound rose from outside the building, as shutters shook, then opened along the entire side of the building. Four AFV-22s sat side by side on a concrete pad with their fans spinning. Calton eased a lever forward on a small controller, and all four cars lifted four feet off the pad and hovered in the air. The edges of the cars were almost touching, yet still holding their own space. After fifteen seconds, Calton eased the cars back down to earth.

"We know we can't fly them above ten feet prior to the official test, General, but we wanted to have the cars say hello and show how tight a formation they can hold."

The shutters closed as the fans on the cars spun down. Hock added the final navigation element and said, "And, as a backup, as you've requested, General, we've installed some of these GCTs on the way to the target." He smiled slyly at the peacenik assistant.

Starnes smirked, acknowledging the comment, but then reassumed her stern, you-better-impress-me grimace.

"The GCT, or Ground Coordinate Transmitter, is this small disc, used to triangulate bearings with the craft and two other land-based beacon points as it flies by," he said, holding up a Frisbee-sized disc, with a small antenna attached. "We mount this piece in the craft and larger beacons on mountaintops, cell towers, in tall trees, wherever. It's old-school navigation, but it still works."

Starnes flipped the disc over and passed it down the line to get it out of the way. "And by 'we' you mean the Army, right? I authorized the expense item for an Army team to deploy and install these transmitters, since it was our insistence that you include them in the test."

Dr. Hock stepped in. "That's correct, ma'am. The Army will install a trail of the transmitter beacons along the entire test course, as requested."

Calton continued, "And you pair the transmitter beacon with a support pod, for power and protection." An assistant rolled the cart holding a three-foot diameter, drab-green metal housing, with chasing blue LED lights around the entire circumference, into the space in front of the FAA visitors. "The small disc is the brain that fits into this larger orb."

"And that's the thing that will make sure this car doesn't fly off course, right?" bellowed Starnes. "I feel much better about a test knowing that there's some land-based conventional technology factored in each vehicle, while your NORM system is playing LiDAR chess with all those vehicles."

"Well, that lets the car know precisely where it is in relation to the beacons on the ground. We are prepared," Dr. Hock interrupted, "to employ all technologies for this first long-range test if required, but we still believe in our NORM system and LiDAR technology as completely reliable. We will have your system on board for the test, as requested. While it works by triangulating between two towers and the vehicle, it's just too slow to be completely reliable for flying vehicles, and it doesn't address other traffic. But if you want it—"

"Very well. I haven't decided on long-term use, but it's promising that you will be ready to use the backup system if we need it. I realize that LiDAR has been around a while and you have full confidence in this new air traffic control system, but I'm the one that has to protect the public," warned Starnes. "This GCT thing could help this flying car know its location at all times, by triangulating with two of these beacons, even if it does nothing to help with traffic jams."

"Yes, ma'am. Just so you'll know, we're being as careful as Google and Mercedes when they tested their driverless cars," said Hock, "although, our technology is much more advanced."

"And a flying car over a city is much more demanding than taking a blind guy down the road to a 7-Eleven." Starnes grunted, signaling caution.

8

VIRGINIA CITY, MONTANA

Once upon a time, running into a star of April Lear's caliber would be a dream come true for a man. She assumed another Hollywooder like Evan Morris would be pleased to see a familiar face. On his rapid exit from the county commissioner's office, he had smacked into her, and now had no escape.

"Well, what a gift this is, delivered directly into my very open arms, right here in tiny Virginia City, Montana," she said.

April Lear had captured the hearts of American audiences four decades earlier as the precocious daughter with the syrupy southern voice in the *Family Workz* TV series. Her teen star had faded fast, so she honed her target to guys everywhere with her extra-revealing role as the blonde serial killer in *Tami Romps* and the sequels, *Tami Runs*, and *Tami's Run Back—The Revenge*, all to lukewarm acclaim.

Now, most any guy could describe more detail about her body than they could their fantasy football lineup, but with less enthusiasm. No matter to her. She had been careful to put away a significant portion of the money she made early on, and as her body parts drifted south, she headed north to the mountains of Montana to escape the chase of LA.

At a charity event, April had overheard a *People Online* reporter mention that Montana was the new hideaway hot spot for stars. She bought a small place on the outskirts of Virginia City, in Madison County, wedged between two mega-ranches owned by film legends. Her first year in Montana had been spent decorating and redecorating her hundred-year-old farmhouse and the small pole barn.

After the decorating grew too lonely, April spent her spare time as champion for any cause, feeling that she could fix most issues "with a lovely little soirée," as she was fond of saying. In Madison County, however, there were too few issues that needed her help. At sixty-something, April felt very alone in Montana. She was better at being alone if there were a few people sprinkled around. That's what "Hollywood alone" had always been. "Montana alone" helped her realize how afraid of most things she had become with age.

"Hello, April. Sorry for the crash. It's good to see you again," he said.

She believed his level of sincerity, seeing he had just left the locals.

"I haven't seen you since the Squash the K-Cup rally at my house last May in Malibu. Oh, all those little plastic coffee cups being washed out in the ocean . . . my goodness. That was a lovely little soirée, wasn't it?" she mused, stroking the tiny chandelier of an earring shimmering and spinning as she tilted her head, then continued, "Are you settled in yet? How's everyone treating you?"

Evan glimpsed at his phone. "It's been great. Nice and quiet, which is why we all come up here, right? I've had a few cold shoulders from the locals, but it's better than them chasing after me, I guess. It'll just take some time to get comfortable."

"I know the perfect way to help you and Janet—"

Evan cut her off with, "Uh, Janet and I aren't 'Janet and I' anymore."

"Oh, that's too bad. Even though she was so young," April dug, "I really liked her."

Evan missed it and laughed nervously. "She couldn't see herself living in Montana, and I couldn't see myself living with her."

"Oh well, I hope she's OK with all the trouble back in Malibu. It's just horrible what's happened to our hometown, with the riots everywhere," April said. "I'll just have to throw a lovely little soirée, to raise awareness of the trouble back home. Evan, it can be in your honor." April took out a small notepad and scribbled a note furiously with a jewel-encrusted pen. "It'll be a great way to introduce you to all these Montanans and make your transition here a little gentler. They're nice folks once you get to know them."

"Thanks, April," Evan said. "There's nothing like one of your parties. I'll call you next week, and we'll figure it out." He retreated and side-stepped her. "Hope I'll see you around town," which meant, *I hope I don't*.

"Don't mention it," she sang, which meant, *Please do!*

Evan touched his watch, which caused his Tesla to purr and pull around to meet him in front of the café. He'd parked only twenty feet away, but old habits die hard.

CAMP DAVID 1:00 PM

President Crowley discussed his hope for the meetings with "Mrs. President," as he called Denise, on the helicopter ride over to Camp David. She sensed a new resolve. He dropped his head to make some notes while she said, "This is your chance to actually move your agenda forward. You've been complaining since the inauguration about the daily tasks and formalities that come with the job, so I'm glad you get to dig in and take this crisis head-on."

Dan Crowley nodded while devising the plan for the brainstorming session, but put his pen down and leaned over, kissing Denise warmly on the cheek.

Although Denise loved the formality of the White House, she looked forward to any time spent at Camp David with her husband, away from the spotlight.

The WPA (Work Projects Administration) created the area in the late 1930s as a camp for federal government folks to "recreate." Denise could see why FDR chose Camp David as an official presidential retreat to escape the stress, not to mention the heat and humidity of the nation's capital. A fan of James Hilton's *Lost Horizon*, Roosevelt had dubbed the place "Shangri-La." It truly felt miles and days away from the Oval Office. The current First Lady wondered if Roosevelt's First Lady had been the one to push him to establish Camp David.

But this was no vacation. The country needed crisis leadership. Denise Crowley could tell her husband was primed for the task. His excitement— both palpable and relentless—reminded her of his first day of Princeton grad school, when he planned to change the world—only this time he had the power to do it.

To break through his cloud of clutter, the First Lady simply said, "Dan." She rarely called him by his first name. He had just been "Crowley" when they were alone, ever since undergrad, because she hated the way an old University of Illinois girlfriend had stretched and dragged the name Da-an out to two syllables. Denise had chosen a sterner use of his last name for contrast. He confessed her choice made him feel powerful, and so she had called him Crowley for decades. Denise Crowley said, "I know this will be an intense couple of days, but I want you to know that I believe in you. I know you can find answers."

As they walked into the Aspen Lodge, she hugged her husband, mostly to encourage him, but also to get close enough to straighten out his collar in the back. He had smuggled his comfortable plaid-flannel work shirt and swore it helped him be creative. She thought it looked worn out, but she adored the way he relaxed when wearing it. With the collar in place, she hugged him tighter, pulling him close.

Chief of Staff Blair barged in on the moment shared between the First Lady and the president.

"Dan, I thought you should know; riots in Miami and LA have flared up again—and are much worse this afternoon. Early estimates are thirty dead rioters and a dozen from our side."

"Our side? Aren't we talking about citizens, Graham?" asked the president. "Isn't everyone here on our side?"

CAMP DAVID 3:00 PM

"Keep your seats, ladies and gentlemen," said President Dan Crowley. They didn't. "Thanks for getting up here so fast—especially those of you who have no idea why I've called you here." The Laurel Lodge conference room at Camp David was too small for the fifty folks assembled. The president didn't seem to mind.

Logistics and stories of lives topsy-turvied would have been a captivating way to start the meeting, but the president was ready to move ahead. He took his seat at the center of the polished wooden conference table while the crowd on the second row of seating away from the table began sliding and shuffling chairs and stools, trying to secure his eyeline.

"So, why are you here? Look around. Why would you, or the person next to you, be sitting in this room right now? I can tell you it's not because of a position you hold, something you think you've earned, any of that. And you're not in trouble." There were nervous laughs around the table. "You're here because one of my close advisors believes you are a good thinker—that you have the potential to help us create a path to save our country."

The president stopped to take a sip of water and to monitor the expressions around the monolithic table. The senator across from the president looked down to survey her nails. Two different cabinet members closed their eyes a bit as they smirked and tilted their heads, while nodding. Hearing they were smart was apparently no surprise to this group.

"Here're the rules. You've been invited here to accomplish an unthinkable task. We are not leaving until we stumble upon some viable options to solve *The Budget Problem*. We need to generate new income, without raising taxes, and trim the current budget and size of government debt by twenty-one trillion dollars." He spun around to activate the light panel on the large wall-mounted digital display board, revealing the amount written with a 21 and a parade of zeroes following, in glowing orange marker. "We have to lower taxes and take pressure off our people. We have to create real growth and employment. You will figure out the steps required to allow the government to help its people, while reducing its scope and size to an unrecognizable sliver of its former self—"

"Twenty-one trillion dollars? Did you say cut twenty-one trillion, sir?" queried three or four attendees at the same time in almost the same words.

"Yesterday afternoon, eight citizens died within twelve blocks of the White House, and the only thing they did wrong was attempt to make their voices heard in protest. They were trampled or shot in crowds that had nowhere else to turn for answers. Outside of DC in the last thirty days, we have witnessed three hundred violent deaths. How much is each of these lives worth? Can we contemplate the impact on their families? This will not stop, for sure, but one thing I will guarantee you: if we don't fix this, and I mean soon, it will cost the country much more than twenty-one trillion to extinguish the flames and mend our nation."

A few of the members leaned forward against the table, expressing positive body language. A few others leaned back, to hide behind the person next to them. The tech assist activated the monitor at each end of the room, and live scenes on CNN showed rioting in Miami and LA, with a lower-third crawl recapping how many deaths in each city, suspected motivations, and other grim news. A panel of experts came on-screen and assigned blame, using the names of some of the people in the room. President Crowley turned off the screens as everyone in the room pivoted back toward him. He hoped that the reality of the scene was enough for them to take off their "Beltway goggles" and see Washington's responsibility for the problem.

"We need to figure out how to transform this country's finances. Now I want some radical ideas to reduce the deficit from this year's budget and carve a massive piece off our debt," pressed the president, "invent things from the ground up. It will take that kind of action to get us out of this jam."

After a short silence, the vice president sought to prime the idea pump with, "Twenty-one trillion? It took us two hundred fifty years to get in that much debt, and you want to solve that in a day, Mr. President?"

"It was a lot quicker than that, Bill. Let me remind you that sixty years into our life as a nation, Andrew Jackson paid off our entire debt. We had no debt at all! A hundred years later, we had the equivalent of a trillion in today's dollars in debt, during World War II, but it went back down after that and we didn't hit our first real trillion in debt again until the '80s. The 1980's. So remember, it took two hundred years as a nation to reach our first trillion in debt. Just twenty years later, in 2000, we were over five trillion dollars in debt. That's a five hundred percent increase in just twenty years! And it didn't stop. We started 2020 over twenty-one trillion in debt and now, just ten years after that . . . we have just crossed thirty-five trillion dollars in debt."

Some attendees scowled, as if they had no knowledge of our catastrophic debt accumulation. A few heads dropped down to avoid eye contact.

"Do you get it?" the president continued. "Can you see what that means? Our rate of increase is unstoppable. I know we've suffered through two pandemics that crippled our economy, but that's not the only reason we are in this condition. Congress, well, all of us, have raised our debt another ten trillion in less than a decade! Can't you see where this is going? Nothing less than radical policy changes and a twenty-one-trillion-dollar bump will start to get us out of this mess," said the president, raising his voice.

One senator tried to interject, "Well some of the old concepts for budget cuts worked reasonably well . . ."

"No, *none* have worked! How do you think we got in this quagmire?" fired Crowley, who wished he had a copy of the Tax Code to throw. "Think about the implications of this. We will cease to exist as a society, as a country, if we let this debt increase. I'm not just being dramatic. If we spend a huge portion of our budget each year on debt service, we won't have any money left for roads and bridges. If we just print more money, inflation kicks in and our money becomes worthless. The way we're going, all public services will eventually shut down. And what do think will happen when people are told they will not be receiving the social security payments that they've paid into their entire lives? We are not far from that reality, people." Stunned and scared expressions crept across the faces around the table. "Today we will clean the slate and come up with a whole new way to raise money and cut the budgets in all of your departments. And by cuts, I don't mean reduce the rate of increase. I mean slash or cancel. Congress has never been able to trim a budget. Ever."

The president tilted his head back and spoke with a little whimsy, to ease the tension he had just created. "Listen . . . there's no way that the government—all of us—has gotten everything right. We all know that there's fat in every department. Well, here's some more history—for almost two hundred years, our government cost just a couple of percent of our GDP. In the last fifty, it has ballooned to almost fifty percent! We just can't maintain that level."

Eyes worked upward, connecting with the president. A few scribbled notes.

"We are called to reinvent many aspects of government. I want to hear crazy ideas—stuff that people would've laughed at a few years ago because it was too unlikely. Now's the time to be bold, creative, different."

After a brief silence, Interior Secretary Stubblefield offered, "We could sell advertising space on the Washington Monument." He leaned forward, trying to begin the sell. "It's got a lot of square footage, and it's our third most photographed landmark." No one challenged his ranking system or the two locations above it.

"Yeah, but maybe only sell one side, so as not to deface the whole monument," added someone from the corner, with a little enthusiasm.

Is this idea building steam? thought the president.

An angry-looking woman whom the president didn't recognize raised a hand from the far-left corner of the room and said, "You know, we could do it with lasers or holographs, so we don't have to hang anything directly on the monument . . ."

President Crowley knew this would be a staggering task, but he had hoped a crowd of this caliber would offer something inspired. When someone suggested the hanging of a huge screen from the Arch in St. Louis to premiere Hollywood blockbusters, he could see revolution was surely at hand.

11

MADISON COUNTY, MONTANA

The wind blows the smell of them dirty ole cattle,
Right past the pen and the barn where I rattle . . .
. . . around.

"Bullseye, answer your dang phone, girl!" yelled the ringer on her phone, in her own voice, interrupting her poem. She had recorded the ringer to mock her friends who always screamed at her when she let her phone ring endlessly. If she didn't feel like talking, she just let it ring. She didn't feel like talking often.

Despite the name and the reddish-darkish hair, there wasn't a hint of a brogue when she did speak, now several generations removed from Ireland. She had returned to her ranch from town and headed straight out to the fence line on horseback, where she often came to look for her future or bury her past. The future was stark; her past—more depressing still. The prior week's take of $25,400 in cash from Stubblefield and Fowler (or actually a tagalong supporter because those guys never paid for anything) made the present a little more tolerable. Not a bad wage for showing a few purebreds where the fish were hiding, then looking the other way when they went over the limit. Taking the risk was better than working, but the money wasn't the deal. The deal for her was pushing the guys around, and a vice president at that, on her fishing trip and then heading to town and messing with a bona fide good-looking man to boot, even if he was a has-been movie star. Not a bad week at all.

The trail behind her barn was steep, so Bullseye leaned forward in the saddle as her horse picked its way through the gravel and fist-sized rocks on the climb up the ridge. Bullseye fancied herself as a cowgirl-poet. She loved to romanticize the rancher's life in verse: the hard work of herding cattle, the test of wills in breaking a horse, riding the fence line for days on end. There were only two problems: She wasn't a cowgirl, and she certainly wasn't a poet.

"So, Bullseye grabbed that snake by the head,
And peeled off the skin to wallpaper her shed . . ."
She liked to ride, but that was recreation. She'd been around ranchin'

all her life and grew up helping her father, who was known far and wide for the quality Shorthorn cattle he'd raised. Like his father before him and his before him—back until the first of the Irish immigrants learned what a Shorthorn was, working their way west from Ellis Island.

Daddy Magee was gone now. Dead thirty years—struck by lightning atop a hill sitting on his horse, so everything had fallen to Bullseye. But years of him calling her worthless and lazy had become self-fulfilling, and she couldn't care less about ranching. Her dad had clearly wished for a boy, and she could never do enough to cancel that disappointment, so she had checked out long ago.

She crested the ridge and stopped to take in the view, or just to be still. Time slowed when she rode around the ranch, but her horse, shaking the flies out of its eyes, reminded Bullseye to ride a little farther along the ridge. She was near the spot where her dad had died, which she could see across the fence line. Bullseye had written her very first poem at ten years old and still recited it every time she rode the ridge, almost forty years later:

"My life is a-waitin' just over that ridge,
Soon as my daddy jumps off of a bridge . . ."

She would later try to substitute *lightning* for *bridge* to match his fate but never quite arranged the words to fit; but she got close with *ride* and *fried*.

To hear her tell it in a song (you couldn't call it "singing"), one would have thought Bullseye got her name from being a crack shot, a fearless hunter who could stare down a charging bison. Every single hunter and fisherman who used her services asked where the Bullseye name came from, and she found it easy to be a legend when she was crafting her own story line.

Truth was that Laura Brennan Magee had a chance to be all that as a child—until her father beat her down day after day. It was her dad's form of encouragement. It did anything but inspire.

But her young life had been much more tragic than discouraging. On the worst nights, after long pulls on a bottle and a "session," as he called it, between him and his wife that left her sobbing or bleeding or both, Daddy Magee would come after Laura Brennan. She ran or tried to fight, but she was young and rarely escaped. Her mom helped cover her fat lip in school with ice and a story about wrestling a steer. The worse stuff—the sweaty embraces and drool, the grip on her throat while he ripped her clothes, the unspeakable, the unthinkable—all that had become her reality, got pressed behind a veil she created in her mind, an unfocused blur, until he freed her or passed out. She and her mom spoke of escape or worse options, but fear prevented those thoughts from taking root.

The defining moment came late one steamy Sunday afternoon. Since before sunup, LB, as he called her, had done all that he demanded. She'd fed, herded, mended, baled, and rode until she could barely stand. She just had a little trouble with one stubborn bull who balked, snorting and scratching up dust instead of following her lead.

"Pa, he's not gonna go. He's gonna charge me," confessed a shaking ten-year-old Laura Brennan.

"Aww, I didn't know you was wearing a skirt today," chided her pa. "If you wuz a real ranch hand, you'd just pop that ole bull in the butt with a rock. That'd get him moving. But I bet you couldn't even hit the ground with your cap."

In response to his ridicule, LB hurled a fist-sized stone at the bull, missing by enough to confirm her father's comment. The second miss prompted a slap to the back of her head.

"LB, you're about as useful as a saddle on a sow. I'll bet your momma puts your britches on for you. I'm going to the house to wash up. Don't you come in until you get that bull in the pen, hear me?"

The sun headed for Idaho, and LB wanted to complete her task in the light, or she'd have to deal with a stubborn Shorthorn in the dark. She remembered her trusty slingshot hanging in the hay barn and raced to it, stopping only long enough to find a perfect, bullet-sized rock. She loaded her ammo and snuck around behind the bull, within twelve feet, took sight on his hindquarters, pulled those old inner-tube straps back as far as her arms would allow, and let fly.

LB's stone pellet whizzed wide right, missing the bull's rump, once again affirming her dad's assessment of her aiming skills. Although her aim was off by just inches, the bull looked around just in time for the stone to smack him right in the eye, which exploded in a cloud of red goo! LB and the bull both shook their heads. One was mad. One was scared. They both ran.

LB jumped the fence to the pen, hoping to find safety. The incensed bull bucked and then crashed right through, shattering a section and the gate. LB scrambled over the opposite fence and headed west.

Three fences, two hay wagons, and a half mile later, that bull was still chasing LB. Pain from the exploded eye slowed the mammoth animal by sending him in circles now and then, offering the terrified girl just enough of a lead to head toward the next hiding spot. The chase ended when LB vaulted up an apple tree right next to the crossroads, about a mile and a half from her house.

Mad as he was, the bull couldn't climb. Scared as she was, LB could cling to that tree for hours. And that's just what she did since the bull spent the next nine hours circling, charging, and butting the base of the tree throughout the night.

LB figured that Old Man Magee wouldn't assist, and he certainly wasn't going to let the girl's mother intercede. LB loved the safety of the tree, away from her sweaty, throat-clutching father, during the dark, star-filled night, but worried about the price her mother would pay for her poor aim. Including the bull, the night proved sleepless for all four of them.

Dawn revealed an exhausted, but alert LB nesting in the tree. The bull remained angry and persistent. Then the school bus drove by. LB's few friends and many tormentors saw the girl treed by a bull circling below her. The driver didn't bother to stop at the crossroads; instead, the bus rambled out of sight, leaving a trail of dust and laughter.

It wasn't until the next evening that her father finally shot the bull, but didn't say a word to LB. He let her crawl down and retreat to the house alone.

Those twenty-four hours of hiding out, eating apples, and being tormented by the bull, plus the ensuing weeks of ridicule at school and the period of disgusted looks and silence from her father, hardened her disdain. Everyone greeted her with "Hey, Bull's Eye," which later became the one-word moniker "Bullseye" that followed her the rest of her life. Her poems were the only place the name was hers, grown from a legend and not shame.

During that period, she'd decided that she was done with ranchin' and done with her father. At ten years old, however, she was only tough enough to leave home in her songs. He chased her now and then, sometimes caught her. She fought but was still young and so small. She lowered the veil in her mind, and let it pass, out of focus. She just did her time until Daddy Magee died. Those were her forgotten years, behind her veil. She was seventeen when he died, and there were no tears.

Too bad it had been lightning that got him. She wanted to be the one. She inherited the whole place by the time she was eighteen, right after cancer got her mom. On one very sober night, she burned the house, then sold that piece of the ranch where the house had been, and left Montana for Seattle, LA, and eventually San Diego, to try school and to leave bits of herself spread across the West Coast, all to scrub her father's memory from every part of her body and mind. Those few years stretched across two decades. When she couldn't lose the past, she'd headed back to Montana to live on the remaining part of her haunted ranch. She buried most of the bad stuff deep under the surface. The memories were there, just buried, deep. She rode every chance she got, sometimes for work, sometimes just to not be anywhere else.

Once she reached the highest point on the ridge, Bullseye swung her leg around the back of her horse and dropped the reins, allowing Girl, as Bullseye had always called her horse, without officially naming her, to graze in the tall grass. After kicking a heart-sized rock loose from the dirt with her foot, she picked it up and threw it over the fence toward the spot where her dad had died, hoping to bury his memory a little deeper. And that helped her exhale enough to get on with the business of the day. She flipped up the worn leather flap on the saddlebag and lifted out a pair of Zeiss binoculars to scan the twelve hundred acres in the two valleys on the backside of her ranch for signs of life. A group of hunters was coming to this property in a week, and she needed to see what the elk were planning. An impatient scan revealed only one coyote about a mile away, chewing on the remnants of a hare. Thin hunting meant she had to up the ante on her storytelling in order for her clients to walk away satisfied with the experience.

Without really working, Bullseye scratched out a living by leasing the land rights to the oil and mineral companies and by accommodating parties of big-game enthusiasts. She hung around the fire at night with the hunters and their guides, mostly out of boredom. They liked the stories she made up since she wouldn't talk about her actual past. A few years in, she started guiding the trips herself and polished her stories to a folklore level. Word spread that she was a good hunt in Montana.

Then an attorney had called about a will from a dead uncle and a deed to a run-down tourist trap on the Idaho border. She learned that she had become the proprietor of a worn-out ghost town with a dig-your-own-gems mining operation for tourists, south and west just across the Idaho border— all from an uncle she had hated just as much as her father because he looked at her just like her father did and told her she was worthless, just like he did. But the land gave her a little more hunting property and something to do, and she could prove to her uncle's ghost that she could succeed in something, so screw him. That was the joke. The place actually *was* haunted, by the ghosts of her throat-grabbing dad and nay-saying uncle, who she hoped were both sizzling in hell. Anyway, when she tired of people, the border was a good place to hide, not dealing with anything real.

Girl sauntered back over to Bullseye and nuzzled her arm, rocking Bullseye back into the present. If the elk weren't running on her ranch in Montana, she would take a run down to her land in Idaho and see what was stirring down there. Some of her clients preferred the steep, wooded area and the river over the rolling hills of her Montana spread anyway. She swung up on Girl and started the slow ride back down the hill, while she thought through her Idaho operation and her situation.

Her Lame Horse Creek Ghost Town and Mining Operation was unique, located at the southern end of a soaring alpine meadow that flattened out for a few miles, allowing runoff from the surrounding peaks of the Continental Divide to fill a creek bed and run out of Montana, into Idaho. The Nez Perce was shallow, except during the spring runoff, when it swelled to become a fast-moving river. The picturesque valley that held the meadow and the river, just west of Lost Trail Pass Ski Area where Highway 93 crossed over the divide, was remote and reachable only by a tiny country road. The little town of Lorae sat across the border on the Montana side, just a slingshot pop from her place. After going through a gorge right at the border, the river slowed on her land, where she could offer great fishing and hunting, with little interference from game officials.

The more money she made off her tourist scams, the more she became convinced that not only was her uncle wrong, but there was an idea out there that would allow her to get the best of some men—some very powerful men, even if it was one guy at a time. That would show 'em, and in her mind, help her get even—whatever that meant.

Bullseye split her time between the Lame Horse Creek tourist trap in Idaho and her ranch in Virginia City, Montana. When she felt like talking a little, she joined the gang down at the County Commission office in Virginia City or at the town's only diner, the Placer Gold Café. Even though she was a "she" and twenty years younger than those old farts, they had always treated her like "one of the guys" and loved to hear her stories from her guiding trips—what she could legally talk about—and the ghost town. Bullseye often wondered if these guys knew how sad she was on her silent days or if they knew anything about her old man's compulsions and her crap growing up, since they had known him. They had never said anything nice about him she could recall. She looked forward to seeing them on her mornings in town, even when they didn't talk at all. Ranchers didn't mind just being together, without gluing it shut with a bunch of chatter. Sometimes proximity was enough for old friends.

Bullseye was dark and pretty. Worn a bit maybe, but striking, with little effort. She wasn't gingered and freckled Irish; she was a bit darker, with a mysterious smile and a firm upper lip that gave away nothing, hooded eyes that could easily convey disinterest, and just a hint of freckles.

She had tried love a few times, but it never stuck. They all reminded her of Daddy Magee, and so she showed them the door and circled back to her friends or life alone. Bullseye enjoyed her privacy and loved hanging with her old friends Morris and Hitch, who gave her room.

But when she was home or in the truck driving down to Idaho, she still gazed into the future, dreaming of the day when she would rake in her "whatfer." And whatfer with zeroes on it.

Girl circled the house and wandered into the barn while Bullseye hopped off her back to fill the water bucket and slide off her saddle. During a quick brushing, she gave more thought to her whatfer.

Evan Morris and other stars had always seemed like small potatoes to her. They could afford big ranches, but she already had a big ranch, thanks to that throat-grabber Daddy Magee. No, her large score would be something unlikely, perhaps the result of a deal with one of those high-octane politicos, like Stubblefield- and Fowler-type characters from Washington that could net her a few million worth of walking-away money. She had overheard enough talk over their trips to know that those gentlemen were too much like her—which meant there was a deal in the offing somewhere. But more important to her was control. It was the joy she would get from dragging some men around and leaving them in her wake. She just had to bide her time until the opportunity presented itself.

12

CAMP DAVID

54 HOURS LATER

A slight breeze flowed across the patio. Naval Support Facility Thurmont, better known as Camp David, sat just high enough above the plains to catch any wind rattling around the northern Maryland woods. The president kept the group engaged by changing locations around Camp David, from the conference room at Laurel Lodge, to the casual lobby around the fireplace at Aspen Lodge, and intermittently breaking into small groups in kitchens and other rooms down the hall.

One group met in the south wing, which had hosted strange bedfellows back in the mid-twentieth century during the Camp David Conference with President Dwight Eisenhower; the ruler of the Union of Soviet Socialist Republics, Nikita Khrushchev; Soviet Foreign Minister Andrei Gromyko; and US Ambassador to the United Nations Henry Cabot Lodge, among others, all sleeping just a few feet apart. Today's discussion was no less surreal than the one that had taken place three-quarters of a century earlier, during the first years of the Cold War.

A group of eight, including two senators, a cabinet member, two advisors, and three others moved into Holly Cabin. Jimmy Carter had used this very cabin to corral Menachem Begin and Anwar Sadat to talk peace in the '70s, yielding the historic Camp David Accords treaty between Israel and Egypt.

The impact of their historic setting was not lost on the president. As the sun set on the third day, they moved to the patio, hoping to refresh their tired brains.

Two days of straight sessions with just a few short breaks and a six-hour nap each night showed in the red and blurry eyes. They ate meals at the meeting table and scattered notepads, etablets with doodles, diagrams, dollar signs, half-thoughts, and many, many scratch-outs around their plates. They pulled various apps up to help with calculations, legal questions, and the search for a miracle. Chargers for a myriad of devices snaked across the floor.

Crowley rose to his feet and headed back to the portable Promethean display board, digital marker in hand. "All right, here's what we've decided so far: we can't just cut the government in half. Selling part of our naval fleet to our allies looks like a possibility that could generate a significant amount of cash and continuing revenue for maintenance and training support—"

"And we hope they don't turn around and blow us up with our own weapons," said Fowler, met by silence.

"We agree that something like the Citizens to Mars program is a great idea—if private industry hadn't gotten it off the ground first."

"Thank you, Elon Musk," Fowler said with a smirk.

The president said, "And I've made notes on the enhanced national lottery with massive ticket prizes, but even if we did all that, it would still leave us radically short. I know we don't think about this often in Washington, but let me help you with the math. Those millions we're talking about . . . it takes a thousand of them to get to just one billion. And a billion doesn't even pay the ante in this game. Part of the problem is that we can't even conceive of how big those numbers are.

"I can help, Mr. President," said a plump figure from behind a big belt buckle, leaning against one of the stools across from the president. Harlin Sage had been invited by the vice president, specifically for his ability to state things plainly—and to repay a favor with some presidential facetime. His lobbying position with the Pork Purveyors Council was a fun entre to any conversation.

"You have a solution? Great, let's hear it."

"Well, I don't have an answer to this budget quandary, but I can help folks understand how big those numbers are. Over at the PPC—that's the Pork Purveyors Council—we use an illustration that everyone can understand: bacon." Sleepy eyes opened wide. "Yessir, bacon. Now, imagine a nice, thick slab of bacon. I'm talking about a piece so thick that after you cook it, you're still looking at almost a quarter-inch-thick slice of pure pork perfection laying in front of you. Now, start stacking those pieces, not end to end, lay 'em flat on top of each other. You with me?"

"I can almost smell 'em, Harlin," said the president, enjoying the engagement.

"Now, if you had a million pieces of bacon stacked up like that, can you guess how tall that stack would be? I'll tell you—nearly four miles high! Or you could lay it down and go from the Lincoln Memorial over to Capitol Hill and back again."

Somebody licked their lips.

The president could see the illustration coming and asked, "So, how far could a billion pieces reach?"

"Now a billion stacked up and laid down, would reach from the Lincoln Memorial to, get this, Paris, France."

There was an audible reaction from the table at the increase from a million to a billion and many heads turned, sharing surprised looks left and right.

"Wait for it. That was a big jump but wait until you hear about a trillion. That's a thousand billion, right? If your bacon-stackers got this put together, you could go from here, to Paris, then go to all the way to the moon and back. . . eight times!"

The room was silent. A couple of mouths sprang open, but no sounds escaped.

"Thanks, Harlin. You really drove that home for us. So, a few million in cuts won't help because we have to reach over twenty trillion. There has to be some stone we haven't looked under yet . . . something we can sell, invent . . . what haven't we considered?"

A few folks leaned forward in their chairs as the president worked his way around the group and glared into each set of tired eyes. Chief of Staff Blair, in an obvious attempt to deflect the president's stare, turned to the far end of the table and offered, "We haven't heard much from the group at that end of the table. Secretary Redmond, you're in charge of commerce. What's been going through your mind?"

"Well . . . ," he stammered behind a possum-in-the-headlights look, "I have one idea, but I don't know how viable it is."

The president encouraged Redmond, "Just come out with it. Your idea has to be at least as good as anything Fowler has offered."

Redmond sank in his chair as if he were preparing to hide. "Well, I was thinking . . . maybe we oughta . . . sell Montana?"

Giggles started, first with Fowler, and worked their way around the table. "Did he just recommend we sell Montana?" the junior senator from Ohio, Tyberius Wright, asked with a laugh. Heads tilted. The president stared, not sure what he had heard.

"What was that?"

Redmond sank a little lower. "Sir, I suggest we sell Montana."

"You can't just sell a whole state!" and "That's ludicrous!" were among other protests erupted from every corner of the room.

"I know it sounds crazy when you first hear it, but think about it . . . why couldn't we sell Montana? We're not really using most of it," countered Redmond.

"Well, what about Mount Rushmore? That's a national treasure," asked Wright.

Redmond, emboldened by Wright's misfire, sat up straight and declared, "I believe you'll find the faces of our presidents huddled together safe and sound next door . . . in South Dakota." There was more laughter, but it was no longer targeted exclusively at Redmond and his eccentric idea. "You said come up with something radical. Montana is a great state, but it has a sparse population. Why couldn't we sell it?"

"Why not sell Alaska back to Russia? I bet they'd love to buy it," said Senator Wright, finally getting the history correct.

Redmond answered boldly, "Because Alaska has more natural resources, including oil, and offers a significant strategic military advantage. Wyoming actually has fewer residents than Montana, but it's landlocked within other states. We could separate Montana more easily because it's on the border."

Several questioned Redmond's seriosity. When the veep said state boundaries had been "set in stone" since our nation's founding, Redmond gave him a history lesson about Congress changing the shape and size of many states over the years—radically, as a matter of fact, well into the twenty-first century—in the 1990s with parts of Ellis Island changing hands from New York to New Jersey and recently with the massive shift in '28 when half of the conservative rural counties in Oregon and Washington fought tooth and nail to jettison their western urban counties (and lawmakers) to become part of Idaho, tripling the size of that state. Someone at the other end, near the president, brought up the imminent court ruling due in the Georgia/Tennessee squabble over water rights that would change both states' boundaries any day.

The discussion shattered into side banter, comments, and jokes. President Crowley emerged from his bystander position, stepped to the side of the digital display board, and swiped open a clean panel. He picked up the digital stylus and began writing:

Sell Montana: Potential Buyers/Potential Price:

Everyone in the room froze. There was a strange look in the president's eye. He saw something that others could not. "Montana is huge. I bet it's more than a hundred thousand square miles . . ."

Secretary Redmond belted out, "Sir, it's 147,046 square miles, with 1,492 of those miles covered in water." He smirked. Flummoxed stares swiveled from his end of the group back to the president's.

"At current real estate values, we couldn't get enough money to make a difference. I mean, we'd have to factor in something for existing private landowners, so that wouldn't leave enough to make it worthwhile." The president's mind was whirling.

Shaking the stylus at the assembled, he said, "But if we could package something with this land that no one else can offer, no one in the world, we might be on to something." He wrote one word across the glass panel, overlapping from the "Potential Buyers" column, all the way through "Potential Price," and activated the glow command, which caused the word to light up in orange:

Sovereignty!!!

The expressions softened, but confusion still owned the day. Senator Wright started to say something, but the president muted him with a wave of his hand.

"What's the most valuable thing in the world? Freedom. It's freedom." Crowley put down the stylus and became a cheerleader. "If we could sell Montana to a large group of people without freedom, without a country, someone who hopes to create their own nation, like the Christian Kurds in Iraq, or the Palestinians—who knows—we could demand a huge asking price. I mean, where can someone go who wants to become a sovereign nation?"

The entire assemblage reacted but didn't dare offer an answer.

"For the right price . . . say twenty trillion, we could offer someone a new country, a new land that's rich in resources, while we bail ourselves out of trouble."

Everyone scrutinized the president now. Several leaned forward to listen more closely. No one smiled.

"It would have to be a people group with a wealthy heritage. I guess it would have to be rich people. Someone that made money from oil revenue, most likely, or had gold reserves in ancient treasures or something," interjected Kim Laughlin, seated next to Redmond, who smiled at his idea being validated.

"Yes," said Crowley. "A neighbor of poor refugees wouldn't help us any, so it would have to be a cash-rich but land-poor people group to even consider this." The president reached down for a handful of almonds and popped a couple in his mouth, then said, "Take the Somali population. There are what, about five million of them settled in Minnesota now? They apparently like it here even though it's cold, which says something about the concept, but they're not land poor and not rich enough as a people group to help the US. The richer and more oppressed, the better. I bet Israel

48

would kick in ten trillion just to move the Palestinians halfway around the world!"

The president stopped himself, took the stylus, and wrote "#1 Palestine" below "Potential Buyers." A few nods bobbed around the table. The president, still ahead of the crowd, shifted away from the economics of the situation.

"Ladies and gentlemen, Americans are rioting and killing each other because there is a crisis with starvation and shelter—right here in America. And we have only given them empty promises to lean on and divided them further. Our country will continue to deteriorate unless we do something radical. Selling an entire state is crazy and a painful process even to consider—but at its core, it's just land. We have expanded our borders before and just maybe it's time to contract." The president looked at several shocked expressions and retreated. "OK, it's not just land. There are people who are citizens who live on that land, and it will be almost impossible to consider relocating them to somewhere else. But if we don't act, thousands, maybe hundreds of thousands of Americans will die in a new civil war of sorts, under our watch. And that is far, far worse."

Exhaustion and the weight of this idea allowed silence to engulf the group.

"I'd be willing," whispered the president, then proclaimed to the whole room, "I'd be willing to cash in one star from our great flag if that's what it takes to save the other forty-nine."

Fowler looked across at Stubblefield. Timid heads turned. The president's willingness to state a specific formula of sacrifice had astonished the audience.

The weight of the topic seemed to make the walls of the Laurel Lodge conference room lean in, threatening to collapse on the weary attendees. The president called for a short break and directed everyone to walk around a bit, then reassemble on the upper terrace at Aspen Lodge.

After thirty minutes of leg stretching and side conversations, the team gathered, settling into chairs clumped into an informal configuration to shake up the hierarchy of the conference table. Blankets lay folded on the backs of each chair, and trays of snacks peppered small tables within reach of every seat. The First Lady encouraged everyone to settle, making sure every need was met. As the president approached his seat near the firepit, Graham Blair raised a hand and stood to speak.

"Mr. President, I just don't see how you would even consider this. I mean, in a long list of crazy ideas, this seems like the most un-American idea ever," said Chief of Pragmatism Blair. "How . . . why would you expect the country, much less Montana, to go along with it?"

"Thanks for doing your job, Graham, to help me see both sides. Montana is the challenging part. They will have to sacrifice everything," said Crowley as he circled the group, popping a few more almonds and connecting person-to-person. "While I don't know if this can work, I do know this for certain: forty-nine other states will be appalled at the suggestion, then relieved that I haven't come looking to their land for answers. For decades, Congress has turned ninety-eight percent of the country against the two percent, forcing the wealthiest to carry a heavier tax burden—just for being more successful, more fortunate, wealthier. This is the same thing, if you think about it. I don't think it's correct, but I think it's worth looking at."

A few more nods signaled open-mindedness—even if some were appalled at the suggestion and his statement. Darkness enveloped the group on the upper terrace at the Aspen Lodge of Camp David as President Crowley made a formal declaration:

"So, based on everything I've heard over the last three days from this group of very smart people, the best idea we can come up with to save the United States of America is to sell Montana."

13

VIRGINIA CITY, MONTANA

"Yeah, I'll call—" was all Evan Morris got in before the "Signal Faded / Call Lost" message came up on his phone. *Frustrating and peaceful at the same time.* The first three weeks on his new ranch had been nice, but the solitude was already growing thin. He didn't want to admit that he missed seeing people, and he sure didn't want to admit that he missed people seeing him.

The Placer Gold Café was only open for breakfast and lunch three days a week, and Evan had made most of those in his first two weeks. As Highway 287 turned to Wallace Street, a few tourists slowed down just long enough to drink in the seven blocks of downtown Virginia City and a few authentic buildings preserved from the short-lived gold rush of 1863. Mona, the owner and only server, was an aisle wide, with an attitude larger than that. She wore a "word of the day" button that never changed, reading "tip!" A coffeepot was always in her right hand, and two or three pencils dangled precipitously from the left side of a messy bun, within easy reach.

Mona had kissed Evan on the cheek the first time she had met him, without even putting down the coffeepot. He had advanced the ritual on the next visit, kissing her first on one cheek before she kissed him. A double-kiss greeting was routine among Evan's Malibu aristocracy.

Earlier in the day, Mona brought him the check and said, "You will show up tonight, right? I think it's nice that April put this together, and it's a good chance for you to get to know everyone." Evan was so lonely that he'd even agreed to attend April's "lovely little soirée" in his honor. He thought about the cold side of the locals he kept sliding into and second-guessed his answer, now that his car was taking him toward the party at April's farmhouse. He wondered if anyone would notice if he didn't show. Mona had advised him to suck it up and attend.

The drive along 287 climbed in altitude north and west from Virginia City. His Tesla crossover could take him anywhere, but he enjoyed reclaiming the wheel in these open spaces, and navigated the twists and turns along the Ruby River, shimmering in the sunset on his left. "Gotta get in some trout fishing," he said aloud, but thinking what that really meant: *I'll need to buy a pole, a hat, a vest, take some lessons, find out if there even are trout in Montana, and figure out how to clean anything I might catch . . .*

The word "Malibu" on his Sirius NewsTalk station interrupted his thoughts. He heard enough to realize that the riots had spread to his old hometown, as desperate gangs decided some of the kind-hearted and fabulously wealthy celebrities should share with the less fortunate, like they had asked everyone else to do for various charities on TV. Looting had reached a block south of his second ex's house.

Sad and mad, Evan realized he would never return home. Normal life continued around most of the country, but violence had erupted in pockets of most large cities and now touched his old, protected hometown. His life would never be the same and he was sad about that, even though it had been his choice. He was mad that the world was changing for so many others without their choosing. Jobs were vaporizing, and he was hearing about the desperation in communities in Los Angeles where he had helped raise money and awareness over the years. Evan yelled at his car dashboard, "Call Yvonne," hoping to connect with the hardworking director of the inner-city ministry that had shepherded him through several community workdays in past years. His relationship with her had started off rough, as she demanded he actually meet people in the neighborhood and work, instead of just showing up to smile for the cameras. Those days and the relationships he built had put him in touch with the need of others and ignited the best parts of him. When Yvonne's message beeped, Evan said, "Hey, Vonnie, it's Evan. I'm thinking about you and all the kids down there, girl. I'm sure you have your hands full with these riots, and I hope you're safe. I'm sending you something to help. I know you can find the best use for it—you always do. Protect yourself, so you can help others, OK?" Evan hit "end call" and said, "Venmo five thousand dollars to Yvonne." He drove on through the hills, smiling like he only did when his emotions were ignited. Leaving his friends at Help Our LA had been the one regret Evan had about moving away from California. The HOLA bunch valued him for his heart, and he doubted he would ever find anything in Montana to plug the hole he felt from missing them.

After twenty more minutes, Evan maneuvered up to the front of April's cute farmhouse, festooned in pastel colors. An interesting array of pickup trucks and SUVs crowded the driveway and most of the front yard. Evan sensed which belonged to the local ranchers and which were celebrity owned, which prepared him for the cold stares that would come from at least half the room.

14

VIRGINIA CITY, MONTANA

Evan entered the front door of the quaint farmhouse, overdecorated in "frontier chic" and noticed that April waited until he stood in the center of the room before she squealed, "The guest of honor has arrived." Her shoes clicked on the wide-plank ponderosa pine flooring as she tiptoed across the foyer to greet Evan. The clicking ceased as she stepped on the oversized, red Lakota Sioux–woven rug centered in the entryway.

"My dear friend, Evan Morris," she said dramatically. "I am so glad you finally made it. You know you don't have to be an hour late for parties up here. You're not in Malibu anymore."

Evan couldn't help but think she had strategically timed her walk and opening remarks to land in the center of the room, punctuating her "scolding" of him with a loud peck of a kiss on the lips, while Evan felt the stare of the locals.

Mona came around the corner, clearing a path with her laugh. She held two small plates loaded with fancy canapés and treats from April's soirée spread. She dipped in for a kiss and a re-kiss and as he noticed her multiple plates, encouraged him to "Take two, sweetie, they're small."

April swirled around her guest of honor, introducing him to a few different locals, then landed in front of Hitch, Bullseye, and Morris. Shaking hands, Evan said, "I've met Hitch, April. We've run into each other at the café a time or two. And I remember . . . Bullseye, right?" He stepped a little closer and offered a hand. "I think I passed your place on the way out here, didn't I?" He remembered how firm her shake had been at the Commission office the week before, and she outgripped him again. "That was quite a beautiful pasture full of purple flowers. Looks like a lavender carpet."

"It may look pretty from afar, but that's spotted knapweed," Bullseye said, taking a large step back as Mona squeezed in the circle.

Her green eyes welcomed him as she pulled her hair back behind her ear. Evan had seen her with only a tight ponytail under a hat, and this wilder, air-dried style captivated him.

"I'll tell you, Mr. Morris, nothing gets a bunch of ranchers talking like noxious weeds, and you have stepped right into a conversation ripe for the picking. Those purple weeds you mentioned are cute but deadly . . ."

"And that's not her ranch. That's the Parker place next door, and they ain't doing much to keep it in check since Old Man Parker is getting on," said Hitch, joining the fray and handing Evan a bottle of Big Sky IPA.

County Commissioner Morris Evans took over the conversation. "Leafy spurge, Canadian thistle, hound's-tongue, field scabious, Dalmatian toadflax—they's all bad around here. Weeds are the devil, Evan Morris, and it's up to you to keep them in check on your land," he warned, while pointing a finger in Evan's general vicinity to add emphasis.

"But that knapweed is the worst. It'll choke off the good stuff and make a pasture death for livestock," said Bullseye, continuing the lecture. "We've lost a lot of ranch land to bad weed control."

Evan, pleased to be engaged in a local conversation with the entire County Commission, took a sip of his beer and pressed on. "That's got to take a lot of time. How do you keep ahead of it?"

"It's just time and the right equipment," offered Hitch.

"Or you take the easy way out and do what them other rich fellers from Hollywood do and just hire some of the locals to manage your ranch for you," Bullseye bragged, on behalf of her fellow Montanans.

"So, you manage ranches for some other folks, Bullseye?" asked Evan, impressed. Hitch and Morris smiled and turned to see Bullseye's response.

"No, sir, I just hired a new guy myself to handle the weeds, so I can spend most of my time down at my other spread in Idaho. I stay pretty busy with my business ventures, and I don't mind getting help."

Evan said, "Oh yeah, the ghost town and mining operation, right?"

"Nice of you to remember, Evan. I spend a lot of time down there keeping all of that running," bragged Bullseye as she leaned against a tall wooden stool that matched the live-edge-cedar bar top. She used the back of her hand to push a wild sprig of hair back off her face while blowing a soft puff of air out of the corner of her mouth to aid in the movement.

Her manicure surprised Evan. No polish, nails trimmed very short, natural and attractive. She looked strong too. He noticed people's hands.

Commissioner Morris took over, forgetting where Evan had come from. "A lot of those high-dollar California folks that move up here hire us locals to take the worry out of running their ranches. That's the best thing they can do since we know how to run 'em right. Bullseye here just doesn't like the day-to-day stuff that's needed with a ranch, so she can be off digging for dollars."

"How far is it to Idaho? Where do you fly in to?"

"It's only a few hours' drive, Evan. Fact is, I've got a burgeoning enterprise with a new sapphire vein in the mine. Now, that takes some work."

"Yeah, work to separate them suckers from their wallets," chided Hitch. "Bullseye can squeeze a nickel out of anyone walking by her place. It's one-part dude ranch and one-part mining scam."

"Now, here we go again, Hitch. I don't want to give Mr. Morris here the wrong impression. He's from Hollywood and he understands what I mean when I say I am in the entertainment business, not the 'authentic' business." She flicked a flirtatious little wink his way. "But that's what people want to hear. That's show biz. Right, Evan?"

Evan backed her up. "It just takes a great script, Bullseye."

April latched onto Evan's arm and said to the crowd, "Gentlemen, and lady, you will just have to continue your rancher talk without the actor Evan Morris. He has not seen my spectacular succulent display in the atrium."

As April guided Evan away, Hitch reached out and grabbed Evan's hand with a hard squeeze and told him he was available if he needed any help on the ranch. Evan noticed Hitch was missing half his ring finger and the other nails were permanently impregnated with grease. His index fingernail resembled a claw, likely the result of an ancient injury, torn in half but long since healed over. Hitch's palm felt like sandpaper, leaving Evan embarrassed at the contrast of his own soft palm to that of a real rancher's hand. He dropped the grip and let April guide him away. He overheard Hitch say, "I was just starting to like the guy."

Bullseye said, "*Actor* Evan . . . that's got a good ring to it." She turned to Morris Evans and said, "Since your names are almost the same, we can call him 'Actor Evan' and you can stay just plain old Morris, or I can still shout 'Evans' when I'm trying to shut you both up. There, simple as can be."

"*Actor* Evan," mused Evan Morris. It felt appropriate because someone in these cinema-starved hills had finally acknowledged his connection to the craft. Over his shoulder, he cast a warm smile and a wink at Bullseye, who touched her cheek, like it was getting warm for the first time in a long while.

Morris Evans grunted loud enough for Evan to hear, "Hhmmpppfff. His horses'll never make it through the winter."

15

CAMP DAVID

The entire cast of visionaries reassembled in Laurel Lodge after a short break. Sleep had not factored in for most of the attendees, but the excitement and adrenaline of transforming their country filled the energy gap. Blurry-eyed, they rose to greet the president, back from a two-hour meeting on other matters. He passed the coffeepot down the table, after pouring a cup for himself.

"Thanks for your hard work these last few days. I know you're all exhausted, but the result was worth your sacrifice. We have the skeleton of a radical, but effective plan here that involves the abolition of numerous government departments, slashing budgets and resources in others, and of course, the sale of one of our states. And you each have your committee assignments to see how in the world we can approach the reclamation of land from the folks in Montana, the PR effort with the rest of the country, the economic impact of departmental cuts, prospective buyers and so on. "

A few heads nodded while he blew across the top of his coffee cup. This time, fatigue drove the slow response more than skepticism.

"And just to underscore the importance of this work, I want Blair to give you an update on events in the rest of the country. Graham?"

"Sir." The chief of staff nodded with a dour expression to the president before he turned to the assembled group. "The riots have continued in Miami, LA, Chicago, and many other major cities. But today violent protests with fighting—and some shooting—have erupted in Kansas City, Memphis, Flagstaff, Montgomery, and an assortment of smaller towns. The protests have killed twenty people just this morning. A store owner shot six teenagers while they looted his electronics store in Memphis; and in Rochester, four children were shot in the crossfire as tension escalated between the local police and protesters. All four have died."

A somber pall filled the room, causing some to look down while others focused on the president. He could tell they craved some assurance that the wild scenarios they were exploring could somehow stop this madness.

"These are Americans killing Americans. They died because they didn't have enough to eat, or a job, or just ran out of hope. Our work here is crucial. You all have your marching orders. I have to rush back to the White House, so we need to wrap up. Keep in touch with your committee. I want quick results on these questions."

The newly formed teammates exchanged glances as somberness melded to resolve.

"But," Crowley cautioned, "this has to remain top secret. I mean it! No spouses. No aides. No boys at the club." He assumed the women present knew that this included them. "And no press of any kind. I don't care who you owe a favor to. If I hear of any leaks, I will find out where they came from and fire your ass before you know what hit you. Even if you don't work for me, I'll make sure there are repercussions by violating the NDA you signed. Do you understand what I'm saying?"

Mumbles of affirmation reverberated from the crowd. Some attendees were convinced and hopeful while others doubted whether they could keep a plan of this magnitude quiet.

"Seriously," the president continued, softening his tone, "one little leak could cause widespread panic with all the departmental cuts we're talking about, and economic disaster in Montana. There's a ton of legal groundwork to do before we know if this has a snowball's chance. Let's see if, just for once, we can keep a secret in this town. I expect reports to come through Blair, and I want to hear from each of your groups every three days."

As the parade of limos and black SUVs loaded their weary cargo, the president walked onto the circular gravel drive, re-rolled the sleeves on his flannel shirt, and shouted, "No one hears about this. *No one!*"

He waved a menacing finger at the cars driving away but dropped his arm when a disagreeable odor wafted toward his nose. After wearing his favorite shirt for three of the five days, he wondered if Denise would still like the way it smelled.

* * *

It took about ninety seconds for the first call to leak from a limo, heading down Highway 15 back to DC, having just left Camp David. "We need to meet. I'm onto something boiling hot. Meet me at the club in two hours," the tired figure said. Without waiting for an answer, he hung up and settled in for a short nap.

The same call took place from six identical vehicles, all with different meeting locations and times. The first text read:
>U gone yet? Need to meet ASAP!!!!

>>On the runway
>Turn around. Now.

One mile ahead, in a black SUV with opaque windows, Vice President Fowler stared across at Interior Secretary Stubblefield and said, "I don't think there's any chance this could happen . . ."

"I don't know," said Stubblefield, rubbing his chin. "He'll probably get run out of office just for mentioning it—which wouldn't be all bad," he added, wondering if he was looking at the future president of the United States. "But I tell you, once people in other states hear it can help cut their taxes without causing them any heartache, they won't care what happens to Montana." The two rode in silence for a few miles, torn between sleep and opportunity.

Fowler blurted, "I'll tell you what, Alan, you might be right about this sell Montana thing happening. Everything I've worked for all these years, kissing the party's butt, doing time waiting for my turn, investments for the future—everything is going down the crapper. I imagine you've heard the whispers that the committee has taken away my shot at the White House so the party can run a younger horse? It's enough to make a good man do some terrible things. And I wasn't all that good to begin with."

Many opportunities for graft and corruption had been dangled in front of Vice President Bill Fowler during his years of public service by a wide variety of characters. Most of the deeds didn't feel like he was breaking the law. Most of them had felt like doing favors for well-deserving citizens who had a compelling case and just needed help. Sometimes, they would swing something his way for gratitude. As the political offices got higher, the dollars reached unfathomable levels, while the circles expanded to "friends of friends." He was locked deeper in the game than ever imagined. The darker side of politics had engulfed him without ever making a conscious decision to head down that path.

And that's why this day was different. After spending half a week with the president trying to solve an unsolvable crisis, the vice president could put his finger on the calendar and say, *This was the day that I made a straight-up decision to jack the system for as much money as I could, before it all fell apart.* He would do whatever it took, short of murder. No amount of love for his country or respect for his office or even admiration for the presidency would save the US, and if by some miracle it survived, how would all that help Bill Fowler in the long run? He was being jettisoned by the party, so it was time for him to seize this narrow window of opportunity and grab his portion on the way out.

A sinister smile snuck onto each man's face. "Might be a good time for a little hunting trip out West. I know a very industrious guide who would love to help us figure out a better use of Montana's resources before Crowley sells the place. I can only imagine what the retail value of the parts of Montana would be . . ."

16

DAVIS, CALIFORNIA

Test teams pushed the AFV-22 Magic Carpet further during the five days that Starnes had been on-site at Hock Industries than in any of the previous twelve months. The short, untethered tests provided proof of concept as the flying car swooped around the mock landscape and tight quarters as prescribed.

Dr. Hock scurried around the test facility like a nervous wedding host, pointing out final touch-ups to his staff. The track included a one-square-block urban landscape, with four-story building facades, flat trees constructed out of plywood and rebar roots, a bridge made from aluminum concert-lighting truss, streetlights, and other typical downtown features. A forklift dropped the last old junk car on the painted roads for scale, in front of the one building that had enough steel in the frame to support a rooftop landing pad. The plan called for multiple flights each day, with different objectives and durations.

The tests started with a few gasps by the Hock staff. General Starnes raised concerns and eyebrows, after a few bobbles here and there, and one hard bounce off a fake power pole structure. Several of the Hock team members sent laser-eyed messages of blame at other team members across the room but kept their mouths shut. The margin for error in the navigation of a flying car carrying live passengers was close to zero, and the early flight demonstrations, while impressive, were still far from perfect.

"I'm glad I insisted that you include that backup onboard navigation system," crowed Starnes, trying to out-shout the engines of a landing vehicle. "You might have taken out that pole altogether."

Dr. Hock had prepared his staff for the comment and explained the backup navigation system installed on each test vehicle may have actually generated interference with the NORM traffic control program, causing the collision with the pole. "General, the Point Cloud system from LiDAR gives us a flight plan that is accurate within a few centimeters."

"Maybe, Son," said General Starnes, "you might convince me to try a couple of these things without the backup in a short-range test; and then, we'll see about the long-range deal. You just keep your flaps up."

Dr. Hock had no idea what the last part of the general's statement meant but asked her about the overall likelihood of government funding for a program as large as the autonomous flying vehicle program.

"That's for folks to decide who fly higher than I do, Son. I'm not here to figure out the finances. I just make sure they can fly safely and confirm the infrastructure that's needed. This project is huge, but it doesn't look too crazy compared to some of the other programs we spend money on." She slurped her coffee and leaned on the edge of the flight control console.

"Well, General," said Hock, "there are a lot of elements. I think it will be like building a new air traffic control system and highway system all at once because of the charging stations, inspection locations, and volume control elements, not to mention rolling out the massive NORM flight navigation computers. With so much trouble in the country, we're a little worried about where the president sees this program ranking."

"I can tell you they've got their hands full, but I believe what you've got here can transform our culture—our whole way of life. I can see these vehicles saving lives in times of evacuations from hurricanes or forest fires—no more gridlock for hours. They will help people get to hospitals minutes quicker. I can see EMTs or police having special lanes carved out in the air that truly can't be accessed by anyone else. And I think if you want to get started soon, I could make a case to let private industry and vehicle owners pay for the whole thing, sorta like the government uses oil leases. The scale of this just may help save our economy."

General Starnes's vision riveted the entire Hock team. Her flip from adversary to champion had been swift but wonderfully positive. Dr. Hock pushed the vision further. "Imagine, General, that there's a Broncos game on a Sunday afternoon. The FAA can certify a plan that instantly activates new air lanes to the stadium, so there's no traffic jam in downtown Denver, automatically diverting any AFV programmed for the stadium from regular lanes to those special areas. So, an event drawing a hundred thousand people at one time could have zero impact on existing traffic."

"If you get this thing to do everything you say and if Congress doesn't screw it up by adding a bunch of needless hoops to the process, and a bunch of other ifs all fall in place, I think you folks just might change the world. There're a lot of other big-name companies trying to jump ahead of you, but you've done the homework to get this far. I'm cheering for you all," said Starnes, adding a bit of a smile.

Hock said, "Thanks for shooting us straight, General. We'll keep our flaps up and try not to screw it up."

Starnes's smile grew a little larger.

17

VIRGINIA CITY, MONTANA

The Ole Gold Rush Days were a big deal in Virginia City. The locals talked about the event for a month, to take a break from discussing weeds and the weather. Mona convinced Evan to join the town's big event, and they met at the Placer Café to walk over together. The violence in other parts of the country laid a depressing shroud over the Ole Gold Rush Days, but the town leaders decided it wise to continue the event and offer everyone a respite.

History held that as they worked their way west, the Skeffington clan had discovered gold in the streams near what would become Virginia City. By the time Madison County was in full-on gold fever, word had spread that miners were pushing aside the smaller pieces of gold to retrieve the bigger nuggets.

As a cute nine-year-old, Bullseye Magee had dressed up as the ghost of Pappy Skeffington and rode one of her mules down Wallace Street to declare the "Ole Gold Rush Days officially open." Mona filled April in on the genesis of Bullseye's ride: she had first performed the role for a school project and got so much love and affirmation from the townspeople—both such unfamiliar ground for the poor neglected and abused girl—that she asked to ride again the next year and the next. By the time she wasn't a "cute little girl" any longer, the ceremony had become a tradition, and Bullseye was just tough enough to prevent any challengers from taking her spot on the mule. Around thirteen, her dad had told her to stop dressing up, which was all the impetus she needed to stay on the mule for life.

Morris Evans punctuated the annual mule ride of Pappy Skeffington by firing a replica Civil War cannon. No one had challenged Morris about the connection between the gold rush and the Civil War either, so he kept on firing year after year. The ritual had happened for enough years now to be a tradition unto itself, and no one dared miss it, if only to see if this would be the year that Morris blew himself to smithereens.

The smell of funnel cake was like an oversweet cologne to carb-averse Evan Morris as he weaved through the tiny festival. The miniscule layout of booths and a flatbed stage did not match up to the hype he registered from the locals over the previous month. His new friends and neighbors were all in attendance, and the prospect of being "spotted" by fans kept his attention high, but the smattering of people in attendance was sobering. At least it was something to do in quiet Montana.

18

WASHINGTON, DC

President Crowley was fond of looking out of the Oval Office window toward the Washington Monument and often thought he could have constructed it out of sugar cubes. He had built one in just that fashion thirty-something years prior for a social studies project and would have won first place had it not been for that smarmy Volcano Kid next to him whose reenactment sent corrosive vinegar drops gushing toward the western face of his sculpture, dissolving it into a Leaning Tower of Pisa. That kid, Rhett, was always under his skin. Like one nail scraping on a blackboard, back when they had blackboards. Crowley reigned victorious that year by winning the class presidency, leaving Rhett relegated to the VP slot. He had learned to get along with those one-nailers when life bound them alongside, which turned out to be a skill that would serve him until current day. Even this day.

The president swiveled his chair away from the window and started the meeting with his core staff. "Graham, I know it's only been a few days since we left Camp David, but I want an update from all the committees we formed. Trouble is escalating, and I've only heard from one group so far."

Fowler said, "We'll goose them up, Dan, but you know it's a huge long shot."

President Crowley was used to the vice president's pushback on just about every issue. Secretly, he called him "Rhett" under his breath as a tribute to the Volcano Kid. He could almost smell the vinegar drops spewing his way this morning. Choosing Fowler as vice president had been a payback to the party for pushing him up to the presidential slot, but one that was hard to swallow. Fowler had brought a stream of donors along for the ride, but once the election was over, the president realized that he just didn't like the guy.

"There won't be a civil war over this Montana thing, but there might be if we don't do something," countered the president. "I mean it, guys. We have to move, and the more I think about it, we may have a few months—not years—before the country implodes."

Chief of Staff Blair offered one final gut check. "So, Mr. President, you are serious about this sell Montana concept?"

"Unless you have a better idea, Blair, but I've asked a big room full of smart folks. No one had anything better to offer. We will make those drastic cuts in the departments, and I'm moving ahead as if this is the best idea we have."

"Or something breaks us," said Fowler, pausing the conversation.

"Maybe," said Crowley, "but I'm less worried about us than the country. I've spoken with a group of Kurds, and they'll be the first to give me a read on the viability of this thing. I don't know if they have the money we need, but it will provide proof of concept."

Blair looked at Fowler with surprise. "When did they contact you, sir, and how did they even know we were thinking about this?"

"I called an old grad-school buddy who has become a Kurdish tribal leader with a lot of clout. Remember, we've educated a lot of royalty from all over this world, and we can use those relationships. Some of them even like us. I told you guys that I'm moving ahead, and I mean it."

Crowley revealed his plans for a secret meeting with Azwar Zinar, whose group of Christian Kurds had been overrun, first by ISIS forces, then by the Sunni Kurds. They had some money, little power, and no land. The Syrian segment of their tribe was in even worse circumstance. The resources in their coffers contained ancient treasures, stockpiled from trade and thievery along the Silk Road, coupled with oil revenue from modern times. The president's hurried briefs led him to believe it could be time for a change of venue for this group of Kurds to survive, if they still had enough money.

"Would they be good neighbors, Dan?" asked Blair.

"Is Mexico a good neighbor?" Before they tried to answer, he filled in the blanks. "They are, but not because we agree with everything they do. They have tremendous problems with poverty, drugs, corruption, immigration—you name it. And yet, they're good neighbors because they don't attack us, and we trade back and forth. By that definition, I think the Kurds could be amazing neighbors."

Before adjourning the meeting, the president was asked his thoughts on ousting our citizens and sweeping their land away. He put his hands behind his head and said, "Let's refer to this act as 'saving the country' and 'sacrifice,' instead of taking anything away from anyone and see if that positioning will help our efforts. We need to keep the country's prosperity in mind here, not the sacrifice by the locals, painful as it is."

Nods and sly smiles worked their way around the office.

"But to answer your question, we have to treat everybody fairly, somehow. They won't like it, but we still have to try to do what's right."

19

VIRGINIA CITY, MONTANA

Ole Gold Rush Days had not been the treasure that Actor Evan Morris had hoped, but a joy, nonetheless. Mona asked him to anchor the celebrity judges' panel for the pie-baking contest. He arrived to find the other two "celebrity" judges were the county's top-selling Farm Bureau insurance agent and Scratches the Clown.

Decades back in California, Evan had rejected the judging gig on the Miss Universe pageant, even though The Donald had called personally. His term as a guest adjudicator on the Sundance Documentaries Panel was more befitting his career, according to his agent—even if he couldn't stand to watch most of the entries. *Those little films were always so horribly depressing or confusing.* But that was years ago. Now he had spent the last two hours sitting next to a clown named Scratches, eating pies that tasted like crow.

The shiny part of the Ole Gold Rush Days for Evan had been the time with his new circle of friends. Evan enjoyed the visit and easy conversation: asking Morris about the dangers in firing the cannon, telling Bullseye that she "looked good in a beard" as Pappy Skeffington, eating half a funnel cake, and then circling back to Bullseye. Her confidence and her chaps attracted him.

The long drive back to his ranch allowed time for Evan to think about his move to Montana. There was something to this place and he wanted to fit in, maybe even make some friends. But, parts of this transition would be a stretch. He wasn't a small-group guy and wondered if people who got together all the time ran out of things to talk about.

The pasture full of purple flowers that appeared around a long, slow bend cleared his mind. "Spotted knapweed," he whispered and slowed to look at the beautiful, menacing weeds Bullseye had introduced to him. "Stunning," he whispered again, but realized he was no longer talking about the weeds. Bullseye had settled into his mind, just as he had settled into Montana. She was unlike any woman he had dated, messed with, or married in California. He let the car drive again and moved the rearview mirror, so he could look at his eyes close-up, while speaking out loud. "Is it her confidence, or her candor when she laughs at herself, or is it the way she acts like she doesn't need anyone in her life that's so appealing? It's definitely not the beard . . . but it could be the chaps."

20

WASHINGTON, DC

The Capitol Hunt Club was a fake hunting lodge hidden down K Street in DC, two blocks north of The George Washington University campus. The rustic entry facade stood in contrast to most entrants dressed in coat and tie. Very curt hosts with earpieces escorted nonmembers who wandered in not just to the door, but outside, well beyond the lobby.

The hosts allowed members who passed the first visual test access to a cherry-paneled waiting chamber with ornate woodwork—a holding tank, with several surreptitious cameras peering out from holes in the exquisite, dark molding. Once escorted inside, members wandered through rough-hewn cedar posts and beams, and into the Safari Room, a cavernous area adorned with various stuffed bodies, from oryx, elephant, lion, and leopard—all posed to attack. Two taxidermied hyenas at the end of the bar shared one last laugh at the patrons' expense.

A left turn from the lobby allowed the members to enter The Swamp— a darker room, lit only by rusty lanterns, featuring Spanish moss dripping off the walls and acrylic-covered cypress knee tables. A snarling alligator next to the doorway held a tray of mints, while a Stephen Foster soundtrack tinkled throughout.

Vice President Bill Fowler and Secretary of the Interior Alan Stubblefield loved to meet at The Hunt Club. It was reminiscent of being outdoors and, by Washington standards, was private. No one noted who met with whom within these dark rooms. Fowler relaxed in The Hunt Club.

Their favorite corner of the club was the spacious Montana Room, with one wall plastered floor to ceiling with a mural of the Madison River Valley and its fabled Big Sky, and the rest of the room packed with mounted trophies of mule deer and American elk. Like all serious hunters, Fowler imagined his name on one of these massive animals. They both loved hunting but couldn't have come to it from more different directions.

Stubblefield grew up in West Texas, son of an oil-patch dad who crewed production rigs around Midland and traveled long 21/7 stints in the Gulf of Mexico on a drilling rig and sometimes months, not days, in Alaska and Montana on the pipelines. His dad didn't have much use for his mom or being around people either—so between long weeks away, he spent the time at home hunting with his son in the West Texas scrub, talking only when mandatory and loving the outdoors with no one telling him what to do.

Left to his own devices while Dad was away, Alan would grab his .22 or his .270 rifle for more punch and tell his mom he was going hunting. He dropped his first doe by ten, collected enough squirrel tails and hare pelts to pad his entire bedroom wall, and learned to clean and eat most of what he shot. Boredom set in, and the sheriff suspected Alan (accurately) of shooting two neighborhood cats, along with some of the town's neon signs, which taught him to be better at being bad. School got tougher as he treated his teachers like his dad treated his mom, until he finally realized it was easier to con the faculty and classmates than to fight them. Baylor seemed like the best choice for college, to follow the pretty girls from his church. Along the way, he'd managed not to shoot anybody and turned from a rough loner into a leader. The Texas hunting and gun lobbies picked him as their guy and boosted him up the political machine until landing as Secretary of the Interior. He spent more time talking about hunting than getting out with the rifle since coming to Washington, but kept one long, scraggly rabbit's foot in his pocket from the first hare he had snared at seven. It reminded him of the best parts of home.

Bill Fowler, on the other hand, didn't know which end of a rifle the bullet came out of until he married into a well-to-do San Angelo, Texas, family who owned a deer ranch, among other enterprises, including timber, oil, and shipping. The marriage was a big score for the son of an insurance salesman. His mom taught him the value of social skills while his dad tried to teach him selling techniques. He ended up focusing less on skills and more on the shortcuts to life. A quick study who understood everything had to have an angle, Bill worked hard enough to get into Vanderbilt in Nashville, with significant financial aid to compensate for his dad's economic fluctuations. Regardless, he made it in, and good grades came easy. He was an extracurricular guy, and coordinating social activities became his trademark, so he parlayed his fraternity party skills to the political party, which eventually led to the number two job in the country. Vice presidents often were the guys who knew how to throw great parties.

The path to the vice presidency was pretty simple for Fowler. Make some deals. Swap this for that. Trade now for something down the road. Most of his deals helped his position and were not for money. The results had boosted his stature, but Fowler could see the end to his political ride coming and did not want to exit with just a VP's pension as his only means of retirement income.

His "pension at home," as he used to call his years of marriage, was in jeopardy. His marriage had survived solely because of her massive family fortune and his political potential. They had drifted apart as the years went by, and when party leaders hinted that he could rise no further politically than VP, the need for her money, her family connections, and her affection diminished, became unimportant. During more grounded moments, Fowler admitted that neither his wife nor her family had any interest in keeping him around once a presidential run was taken off the table. Fowler's vision of the future included a fat reward for all the butts he had kissed on the way up, but he no longer factored in a wife, her money, or the party to fund that future. He was still working on Plan B.

"Alan, there's a lot of these record-breaking animals out in Montana, and the president wants to sell them to some Kurdistani? What's the most valuable trophy for hunters in Montana?"

Stubblefield started the roll call. "Well, there's elk, bighorn sheep—"

"I'll tell you what it is—it's whatever the hell you, me, and our buddies want to hunt at the time—that's what's most valuable," interjected Fowler.

"Bill, I think Crowley just might be serious about this sale, and if it looks like it will go through, we ought to head up to Montana for one helluva shoot-out before they shut it down. I mean blast anything that moves. No limits!"

"Better than that," raised Fowler, "we need to cook up a plan to relocate a few of the biggest animals we can find somewhere secret, outside of the state, so we can hunt them whenever we want."

A frightened look crossed Stubblefield's face. "You mean like start a forest fire to scare them out?"

"No, that's a little dramatic. Flames would be effective, I grant you, but hard to stop. No, I think we need to catch a bunch of big animals or explore a stampede of some sort and see what mischief we can create in the Montana woods. If we get the right guys involved, we could make a lot of money."

They discussed his wife's private big-game ranch in Texas. Investors and enthusiasts who owned ranches like hers maintained herds of American deer and elk or imported exotic animals from all over the world for wealthy hunters to get a guaranteed shot at something, netting millions a year.

"All we need is a bunch of guys making some noise, and every animal within a mile would hightail it out of the way. If we could set up a pen on some land in Wyoming or Idaho and they run right inside, we'd be set."

Stubblefield smiled and raised his glass.

21

AIR FORCE ONE

JOINT BASE AL-HARIR, IRAQ

The president rarely looked out the window while on Air Force One because restless assistants and hectic briefings provided constant distractions. Today was no different. The approach to Joint Base Al-Harir in northern Iraq had been extra busy, given the short preparation time for the trip and the small support group to help cram. The press secretary had made excuses for excluding the press corps, but only after the president snuck onto Air Force One, saying he "needed some time to work on a high-level plan regarding the current budget crisis."

This was an unprecedented trip to Iraq, and others would view meeting with a Kurdish tribal leader on very short notice well beneath the office of president. The Kurds had achieved autonomy across Turkey, Syria, Iraq, and Iran, but had not forged their own physical country or gained a voice in any significant global conversation. This trip included many unknowns, which encouraged the president to risk a scorching from the press over the secrecy of the trip versus exposing the reality of his desperation. He had chosen Al-Harir as a newer, smaller base away from the main press hubs in Iraq.

Two government Middle East experts had scrambled to assemble a complete profile of Tribal Leader Azwar Zinar and the Kurdish-Christian situation in time to join the president on Air Force One for a briefing. The Kurdish Security Force, called the Peshmerga, had distinguished itself over the last few decades as fierce defenders of Kurdish freedom. The Christian Kurds, however, were allowed to join only as small civic groups and not as a recognized force within the Peshmerga. In their nation of thirty-five million, the Christian segment of Kurds was still a minority and had lost ground.

"Twenty years ago, I had a lot of late-night coffee-shop study sessions with Azwar. We spent hours talking about the situation all around the world, and I sort of remember his ranting about the Sunnis and somebody else. I wish I had listened closer. I know he was always pissed off, but I don't remember at who, exactly," said President Crowley as he read the brief.

Azwar's tribe had pushed back the resurgent ISIS to help recapture Kirkuk, which had ping-ponged back and forth since World War II to

Saddam Hussein, ISIS, and back again to the Kurds. The Kurds referred to Kirkuk as the "holy city," hosting Islamic, Christian, and Jewish religious sites, including the Green Dome mosque, the Red Church, and a tomb considered being that of the Jewish prophet Daniel. The oil-rich land under the sites made it more valuable to some than the religious significance above ground, which kept it contested until the Kurds had established the latest tenuous control.

As Air Force One descended toward the desert into the base at Al-Harir, recaptured and secured during one of the recent insurgencies, the president scratched some notes on the back of a beverage napkin:

-long shot leaving homeland with religious sites
-the chance to start a new heritage and own it
-no conflict. peace.

It didn't seem like much to bargain with. *Have I flown halfway around the world, only to equip myself with three points on a napkin?*

He was lost in that thought when the wheels touched down and rocked him back to his senses. It was a long shot, but that's all they had right now. A soft prayer leaked out loud enough for the two Middle East experts to hear. They added their own version of *amen* when the president concluded. Crowley looked at them and wondered if they had any idea how big a Hail Mary they were just praying for—and what was the equivalent of a Hail Mary in Islam or the other faiths he was about to encounter?

22

MADISON COUNTY, MONTANA

Bullseye hit "end call" harder than needed. She wasn't desperate, but the VP had told her to call in a month to set up the next trip; and so she'd done it. Her short fuse lit anytime a man with authority controlled the situation.

Business was slow, and she couldn't shake the feeling that she could make money off the vice president and that fellow Stubblefield. They knew all sorts of bigwigs in DC and could easily send some hunting buddies her way.

With the summer holding on so hot and the economy growing so cold, the tourist mining and ghost town business had been slower than moss growing and made her curse her uncle for leaving her the place and curse her dad for being his brother and curse him some more for all the other stuff.

All the other stuff. That sounded so benign. Sometimes she pushed it farther back and could drop the veil to blur the horrible memories. Sometimes those bad moments wouldn't dim, and everything got tougher. Heavier. More depressing. *Depressinger.* That was her word for the moments when misery crashed in from all sides. She would ask herself, *What's after depressing? When things get worse? Depressinger.* That used to make her laugh and help avoid *depressingest.* She couldn't imagine life at level 3, so she just slapped her chaps on and rode through a good depressinger wallow.

But the cost of a past like hers, with a demon-like dad that would tear up a little girl now and then, showed up in places that didn't look like hurt to others. When it was depressinger, she looked tired, quiet. She hid. She rode her horse, stared. Sometimes she disappeared down her mine shaft in Idaho, scratching around for sapphires. She hid right in front of the hunters she was guiding. The key to hiding in a group was to adopt a role—pretend to be the hero in the stories she crafted and make sure all the talk was surface chitchat, where anything said made them laugh but carried no weight, lasting value, or commitment. She became skilled at hiding in plain view.

At the end of a depressinger morning, she rode close to the house, slid the saddle off in the yard, and let Girl find her way to the barn. She walked inside, kicked a cat, maybe by accident. The screen door hammered its frame behind her as the linoleum floor squeaked a bit under her boots and the couch sucked her in. Anything bingeable on TV worked as a sleep catalyst.

Netflix> Popular>Snore before her boots hit the floor.

23

WASHINGTON, DC

Fowler looked down at his phone. Over the noise in the Capitol Hunt Club and the intensity of their conversation, he had not felt it buzz. He peered through his reading glasses.

"Well, speak of the devil. Jen says Bullseye called the office and left a message. I tell you she's the one to help us execute the plan on the ground in Montana."

"You think she's got the stuff to run a stampede, Bill?"

"I don't see her getting on a horse and running a bunch of elk through the woods, no. But she's about the toughest person I know in Montana, and she likes money more than she cares about most laws. I guarantee she can find the right bunch to do the actual dirty work, and that will keep us insulated by one more layer from anything happening on the ground. We just help them find a spot to funnel the game and handle the money," said Fowler, with a half smile. "Besides, we know she can take care of herself with guys at our level and not get into trouble, and she's never sold a story to the press or let anything leak out. She's solid."

The two discussed the resources needed to construct a world-class hunting resort, with a series of gargantuan lodges, thousands of acres of land with perimeter protection, and hundreds of thousands of prize animals worth tens of millions of dollars. Bill Fowler started compiling his list of acquaintances that would pony up the millions they would need to get it done.

Stubblefield closed the heavy wooden door to the Montana Room while Fowler punched up Bullseye's number.

24

AIR FORCE ONE

JOINT BASE AL HARIR, IRAQ

The tarmac at Joint Base Al-Harir was lined with troops to welcome the president, along with a small delegation for the Christian Kurds, led by Azwar Zinar. The pomp and circumstance was kept to a minimum, as the president's presence had been a secret until the last minute and time on the ground would be brief. The base commander saluted, then walked down the line, introducing the president to key staff, then worked his way around the brass to greet some of the other soldiers and airmen standing on the perimeter. Cheering from the ranks answered the president's waves to all.

Crowley then rushed, actually hitting a quick stride, over to greet Kurdish leader, and former roommate, Azwar Zinar, in front of his delegation. They shook hands briskly and hugged, while the president covered his mouth and whispered in Azwar's ear, "Good to see you, Az-hole."

The Kurdish leader didn't flinch, whispering back, "You too, Dan-hole." They continued the hug for a few moments and then repeated the introduction routine down the line with Azwar's group. While the secret meeting would scald the president in the American press, the pictures would boost Azwar's profile among the other Kurd segments, helping his people.

Azwar whistled as he stepped on board Air Force One. "Somebody in study group has done well for themselves," he said, nodding with a smirk.

"We're a long way from Princeton and that little coffee shop . . ."

"Small World Jitters," said Azwar. "Now we're on to large-world jitters, right, friend? I seem to remember making a lot of plans back then about changing the world. It's not quite so easy, now that it's in our grasp, is it?"

"It was supposed to take a few months, right, to straighten everyone out, make hunger and everything that sucked just go away, and peace would spread like a warm blanket because everyone across the world would join hands?" Both men laughed and Crowley added, "I'm not sure how things are over here, but it's going to take me a few extra months to figure it all out on my end."

The good friends reminisced about who was better with the women, who sucked more at basketball, and who got left on the short end of the twenty dollars they used to loan back and forth. They asked about family, "whatever happened to's" of old classmates, and some job comparisons.

The mood in the small room on Air Force One changed rapidly once Crowley swerved into the actual agenda for the meeting. Az had not envisioned the disastrous situation Crowley faced. "Dan, I'd love to be your neighbor, but there is no way this can happen. Are you completely out of your mind?"

"I'm just trying to be a good leader. I have to find some amazing solution to save my country, and yes, I may be out of my mind."

"And that's wonderful, but what kind of leader would I be if I moved all my people halfway around the world, taking them away from all they loved? And if we did, we are a small number compared to the total Kurd population . . . we could never populate a place the size of Montana and certainly couldn't come up with the money. I'm flattered, but even if we had a fabled Ali Baba–sized treasure tucked away from our Persian past, finding peace may not be worth the price of abandoning our culture's heritage and cherished holy sites. This would be insurmountable for any people group, and I think you are underestimating that, just as you did with our discussions about the Sunnis in grad school."

"Well, I know more about the Sunnis today and that's a different topic, but what about the Somalis? They have embraced the United States as a new home far from their traditional land."

Azwar rubbed his chin. "OK, good point, although their struggles are different than many of us in the Middle East. But you are right, that is some sort of proof that your theory has legs, but they are wobbly, skinny legs like that girl you set me up with our first week of grad school."

"I seem to recall you talking about marrying that wobbly legged girl after two dates, but your family wouldn't hear of it. I get your point, my friend. And now I have to consider the negatives but take the few positive comments and weave them into a storyline that could warm my talks with others."

Azwar rose, sensing the reunion was over by the activity rising around the plane. "Find a people group with more money, and motivation to leave their home, and somehow arrange visitation rights—like a pilgrimage for the faithful in their culture to visit the holiest sites from time to time. I don't think they are out there, Dan, at least not the ones with as much money as you are talking about, but I know you'll keep looking. And, here," he said as he handed his old roommate a twenty-dollar bill. "I don't know if it's my turn but sounds like you need to borrow this, Dan-hole."

The president rested his head in the deep executive chair as the enormous jet left Iraqi air space. Christians and Jews make trips to Israel. Muslims make their hajj to Mecca once in their lifetime. Why couldn't others settle down to a peaceful existence in Montana and make a pilgrimage when they felt called? Everybody wins.

When an aid interrupted his contemplation, he leaned back and swiveled away from the window. "Mr. President, the First Lady is trying to reach you."

"Hi, dear. No, it didn't last long, and we're on the way back. Seeing Azwar made me appreciate my younger days. You won't believe his family. I kinda expected to see the same Az we left behind at Princeton. I guess we're all getting old fast these days." He paused, listening. "Speak for yourself. And yes, since I know you'll ask, he called me Dan-hole when we first hugged." He listened. "Yes, of course I did."

Denise laughed, then told her husband about headlines that condemned the president for hiding from the riots by jetting off to parts unknown. CNN had been the hardest on him.

"They're just bitter because I didn't let them on the plane. It's hard to be working on this solution when we can't tell anyone the details about how this will help Americans at home—"

The First Lady cut him off. "Or tell them about this whole concept of taking part of our country away. I still haven't heard how you'll approach that announcement."

"Working on it, dear. I just need to know there's a chance I'll find a buyer, and it'll help make it more real or at least a little clearer." The president told her that Az's tribe did not have deep enough pockets, but he didn't get laughed at and Az helped him make the deal more attractive to other potential buyers. He just had to work his way down the list—as soon as he created a list.

They talked a little longer, and Crowley tried to sound awake while they discussed their schedule for the next few days. It was college orientation week for his son, Keaton, and Denise said for the fourteenth time that they should try to make his college experience as normal as possible. Dan agreed and somewhere over the Atlantic they defined "normal" parental involvement at the orientation of Keaton Crowley at Auburn University as Mom and a small contingent of four Secret Service agents. Before saying goodnight, Denise repeated her promise to tell anyone who asked that "Keaton's dad had to work this week and couldn't get away," hoping to sound like a normal American family.

Dan added, "And it's OK if you introduce the two guys following him to class as Uncle Secret and Cousin Service. They'll love it."

They swapped "love yous" and then Dan promised to nap, right after one more call, to the prime minister of Israel.

25

WASHINGTON, DC/OUTSIDE CONNOR, MONTANA VIA SLACK

Stubblefield excused two lower-ranking Capitol Hunt Club members from the Montana Room, closed the doors, and punched in Bullseye's contact name. Fowler was on his right, just out of camera range when Bullseye popped up on Slack, sitting up on her couch, roused from her nap.

"Bullseye, Secretary Alan Stubblefield calling. How are you ma'am?" he asked, not caring.

"I'm all right, Alan. I was resting but hoping to hear from you boys. You told me to call you about the next trip, so I left a message or two for your boss. How's the herd over in the Capitol?" said Bullseye, before she pulled her shirt closed over her tank top and ran her fingers through her hair.

"Same ole stampede," drawled Alan, slipping back into his West Texas accent.

"Well, that's too bad."

"Now, Bullseye. We loved being up there and have always valued your wisdom and expertise. It just gets busy down here, crazy busy, you know?"

"To be honest, Alan, I see what's going on in the country and it doesn't look like you guys are doing too much of anything. Things are pretty bad, aren't they?"

Dropping the accent, Stubblefield replied, "Well they are, Bullseye, and that's the reason I'm calling."

"You and the vice need a place to hide out?"

"No, Bullseye, we're not looking for a hideout." He glanced at a grinning Fowler, who had moved across the room. "But we want to have one of those conversations where no one else can hear any details."

Bullseye paused, and said, "Alan I don't talk to no one else nohow, so you don't have to worry about things on this end. Our business is *our* business." She walked out on her back porch and circled with her phone in front of her to show miles and miles of an empty landscape to emphasize her point.

"I know that, Bullseye, but just thought I'd mention it on the front end," Fowler said, nodding his approval. "We need to discuss something that goes a little beyond stretching some big-game license infractions."

Bullseye didn't flinch at stretching the law. "Assuming there's enough money involved, I'm in. How can I help you fellas?"

Fowler thrust his palm up in a "stop" motion, but Stubblefield was ahead of him. "Let's not talk about any details over video, Ms. Magee. How about the vp and I head up to your place in Idaho for a little fishing this weekend, and we talk in person?"

"Yeah, I think I can squeeze you in," Bullseye said. "Just come on up— I'm sure they'll be biting."

"There might be a little more ruckus with all the protests going on. They're keeping more protection around us now."

"No problem, long as the lodge at the Lame Horse suits them. They won't bother me none." Bullseye paused, then added, "Alan, do me a favor—lean over and tell the veep that the answer is still no and will always be no, will you? Maybe that will save a little rejection time when he thinks about hitting on me. See you soon, fellas."

"All right, we'll see you Saturday . . . ," said Stubblefield, before he realized that Bullseye had disconnected on her end.

Fowler, after being silent the entire Slack call said, "Looks like we need to attend to some of the people's business in Montana this weekend. I think we're on to something enormous here, Alan. The president may yank the rug out from under us in Montana, but when I think about how much our buddies will pay to hunt a prize elk, I mean, what's ten thousand times ten thousand? We can make millions and have a lifetime of great hunting."

Stubblefield said, "We sure can, but sounds like you need to find your prom date somewhere else. Let's not push her, Bill."

"Go line up the trip, Alan," said the vice president as he dismissed Stubblefield and his comment. "I've got to make a couple more calls."

26

AIR FORCE ONE

OVER THE ATLANTIC

The prime minister of Israel hung up first after a long, positive conversation. The PM had affirmed Israel's commitment to the US as a good ally, while delivering a slight scolding about the financial situation.

Crowley knew one quick way to stop a lecture from any Israeli: "What would it be worth to have the United States remove the Palestinians from the Middle East?" The PM said Israel would be indebted to the United States for all time.

President Crowley was less concerned with all-time gratitude and more with a $15 trillion payday. The PM had hinted that Israel could generate "any price" the US felt it needed for a scenario to relocate their number one nemesis. The Palestinians had gold storehouses and allies who would offer substantive support toward the trillions the president needed, in exchange for peace. He would just have to move citizens of our country off their land and hand their keys to a terrorist-friendly group. *How would that speech start?*

Air Force One descended into Thule Air Base in Greenland. The president's staff designed the stop as a press smokescreen, but Crowley was sincere about the meet and greet for the military personnel. He was surprised by what he found.

The airmen, when given permission to speak freely, did just that. One first lieutenant said, "Sir, how's the battle going in Detroit? My family says it's pretty rough and, well, so bad, sir, that my wife has been called in to work the ER all weekend during these protests. We live in a pretty nice area, sir, and don't see stuff like that."

A pilot, holding a picture of his family in front of a car with a broken windshield, said, "It's hard to imagine we are safer, tucked away on a foreign military base than on home soil, sir."

The group wasn't complaining, just venting. "Any chance we can redeploy, Mr. President, and help restore the peace in the Lower 48?"

The president sensed desperation from the airmen. *Defend the country from itself?* "Thank you for sharing honestly with me. We've never seen anything like this, and we will let you know if the military can help closer to home. Until then, I ask that you pray for the country and for me. You will soon hear about some plans that are radical, and I will need your support. My prayer is that God's will be done. It's so much bigger than what I want."

79

27

VIRGINIA CITY, MONTANA

The centerpiece of the Placer Gold Café was the Community Table, which comprised three folding tables placed end to end and covered with heavy vinyl, nearly matching flowered tablecloths, surrounded by twenty-two chairs. Anyone could grab a seat and join the conversation, with separate checks. A stained white coffee mug with a spoon sticking out and a knife/fork/napkin mummy marked each spot at the table. Mona kept everything and everyone in line.

The Community Table gang shared gossip, tossed out opinions, and solved the problems of the world daily. Topics drifted from weed control to fencing to crazy news events, but always circled back to the weather. Ranchers always talked about the weather.

There was a hierarchy, with the end of the table anchored by the county commissioners—Morris Evans, flanked by Hitch Jenkins and Bullseye Magee—not because of their county political standing, but because of their unparalleled tenure at the Placer. Mona bumped her way around the long table and used her own hierarchy for coffee refills, based on who tipped well. Hitch had a sweet smile and often said nice things about her hair, but his cup always got refilled last. Mona referred to him as "Rockefeller," "Trump," and "Sheik," but he continued to drop a dollar after every meal like he was doing her a favor.

Evan Morris had become a regular at the café over the last few weeks but still sat alone at a two-top booth. Mona could tell by his frequent glances toward the Community Table that Evan wanted an invitation to join. Mona worked to mix the Hollywooders with the locals, thinking it would be good for business, and between refills, urged Evan to "just go on over" and Morris to "invite that nice movie star to the big table," both to no avail. The male ego, not to mention the male ego through a rancher filter or a Hollywood anything, was thicker than Placer Café oatmeal. There were cordial "hiyas" as they passed in or out, but nothing in between. These men just didn't mix their worlds, unless pushed.

"Hiya, Actor Evan," said Bullseye, patting his shoulder as she strode past Evan Morris on the way to her spot at the Community Table to join the rest of the Madison County regulars who had already finished their breakfast.

"Hi, Bullseye," Evan said as Bullseye scooted by. Evan leaned over to watch her confident stride, while Mona noticed that he noticed that sort of thing. She poured Bullseye's coffee without asking and wrote her order before she said a word.

"Oversleep, did you, Bullseye?" teased Hitch.

"I guess I'm the only one at the table this morning talking with the vice president of the whole United States about a fishing trip this weekend. Or did you fellers take care of your Washington DC business on the way here?"

From across the restaurant, Mona watched Evan perk up at the mention of the vice president.

"You ought to bring them here to the Placer, so we can straighten 'em out," said Hitch. "But I guess you'll be squirreling them away down at your place in Idaho. Who else is coming with them—the pope?"

"You never know with this crowd. All I know is that I get my money in cash, and I get paid pretty darn well not to ask questions. And we don't lose any fish, because those guys couldn't catch a tissue with a Velcro mitt." Laughs all around.

Evan made a restroom stop down the hall, past the gallery of the classic gold rush photos and on the return route circled the Community Table, bumping into the back of Bullseye's chair accidentally on purpose and said, "Say Bullseye, I heard you say something about meeting up with Bill Fowler. Please tell him I said hi, will you?"

"Will do. I should've known you two were friends."

Evan smiled and returned to his booth. Mona grinned as she refilled his coffee. This poor, gorgeous man looked so alone. And worse, she knew how nasty Bullseye had intended her comment to be, but this one didn't have a clue. Mona started making a list of things she could teach this sweet man and grinned again when she imagined how fun class would be. The first thing she could school him on was that Bullseye was never impressed by rich, famous, or powerful people. Never. And especially men. Never ever. But she did like to mess with them and take them down a notch . . . or six. Mona wanted to warn him, but Bullseye was her fave and, in a way, was getting even for all of them.

28

DAVIS, CALIFORNIA

Hock absorbed the phone call from Starnes, who insisted on the land-based transmitters to track the AFV, besides NORM and the LiDAR system. After a short wallow in group misery, he shifted gears back to mentor and chief problem-solver. "Look, team, we can make this GCT navigational thing work. This is a little setback, but it's not like we didn't see it coming. Our earlier prototypes all had the older navigation, anyway."

Hock pulled Wendell aside and told him to get the battery group to lighten up. "The general was smart," he continued, "to have dual nav systems on board, just to be safe. Society would not let cars fly anywhere they wanted. The noise and safety would be a nightmare." They had to design, program, track, and monitor travel lanes in the air, express lanes for long-distance travel, emergency lanes to various public safety sites, clearance for airports, and many overhead clearance issues for schools and more. The computer system managing every single flying car had to make sure they had a clear path to fly and a place to land before they even launched. It also, and maybe more importantly, had to have control to tell them where not to fly. Hock Industries' future was not to sell a few million autonomous flying vehicles. The future was to design and support the entire system that managed autonomous-vehicle flight safety for the government.

The team always responded well to Dr. Hock's vision casting, and the gloominess lifted. He waited until they all looked up at him to add another morsel, "and this news just flew in . . ." to groans. "It seems our friend General Starnes has been lobbying a few folks hard on the Hill, spreading the word that our NORM program and Magic Carpets may be a big part of the answer to rescue the economy. She is mapping out a broad plan of public/private partnerships that will bring jobs and commerce back in place. And she's trying to help them understand that any infrastructure costs will be more than offset by the savings of wear and tear on our aging highways and bridges. After a cheer, the team rolled up their sleeves and reheated the coffee.

29

VIRGINIA CITY, MONTANA

The Community Table thinned out as the ranchers headed off toward the busy late-summer day on their ranches or those they managed. Mona topped off Evan's coffee cup after every three or four sips, a by-product of his generous tipping. He felt more remote than ever at his table for one, except those three or four times when Mona tried to squeeze by and bumped his shoulder with her ample rear end, which he took as a sign of affection. She turned to smile before she entered the kitchen on every trip.

As the last couple of folks stepped away, Bullseye turned and walked toward him. Without asking, she slid into his booth and their knees bumped.

"I'll tell the vice pres you said hey, Evan. He's a tough bird to figure out. So, you guys are pals?"

"Well, sure. I've been to several events to help raise money for him. We're more public about the Earth Party guys back in Malibu, but I've played both sides of the fence with the major party candidates, so I'm in good shape no matter who wins. I mean, the goal is to get invited to all the parties, right?"

He could tell from Bullseye's face that she didn't care much about the party circuit in Malibu or anywhere, most likely, but she understood getting along with both sides of political parties.

Bullseye slid deeper into the booth, making an embarrassing noise on the dark-red vinyl seat covering. The sound didn't faze her one bit as she asked about the VP: Was he honest? Or was he just out to make a buck? Did Evan trust him?

Evan wasn't comfortable with the line of questioning since Bullseye was probing deeply into the man's character, and that meant he had to admit that he didn't know the vice president very well. He explained that "being friends" in Hollywood meant that he had been to several events but, in reality, had only met once. Could the VP be out for money? Sure— what politician didn't crave power or money? What else was there?

Bullseye said, "That's OK, Evan. I don't want to make you feel creepy or anything. I'm just trying to get a read on the guy since we're hanging out more often with money changing hands. That man likes his fishing trips, and he's good at finding other people to pay for it."

"Say, Bullseye, I could join you on your next fishing trip and check out the VP for you. I haven't seen him in a while, but I know he'd be jazzed to hang out. Those guys always enjoy having celebrities around, and I speak his language. I'm not the best fisherman, but you could help me figure it out, right?"

"I'll be glad to help you brush up on your fishing sometime, Evan, but we better not plan on this one. The VP and his boys want some alone time. They were specific about that. I'll mention you to him, and we can hook that up for next time."

Mona arrived with the check and a coffee to go, so Evan did not have to answer. She took his credit card and walked to the front. He moved "learn to fish" to the top of his mental to-do list.

Bullseye straightened her well-worn hat, glanced at her phone, then turned and stepped back next to Evan's booth. He was getting up to leave, and they came eye to eye, facing each other, which neither moved to correct. Bullseye spoke softly, and never took her deep-green eyes off of Evan's bright blues.

"You know, you seem like a decent guy, Evan, and I've enjoyed bumping into you here and there. I'm just wondering how long you're going to keep sitting over here, all by yourself for breakfast. I can't tell if you're just hiding and don't want to make friends, or you just don't know how."

Evan smiled nervously. He shifted his weight but did not take his eyes off of Bullseye's tan face. "That is a great question, Bullseye, and I have to admit you're the only person smart enough to ever ask me that. I think I know the answer—"

She cut him off. "No, sir, I'm not smart, but I am intuitive. I know people, well, men inside and out, and I can read them like an ad in a bathroom stall. Anyway, go on, I cut you off and I think you were going to say something straight from your heart, something I'm going to like hearing because it's your truth."

"OK, first of all, I could grab a beer and just watch you go at people all day long. 'Cause that's what you do; I've seen it at your table. You lunge at people and won't let up until you get an answer you like, and they love to come right back at you. That is, if it's a day you want to talk. I've seen you on other days when you just sit in your own bubble and let it all roll by. You are a fantastic woman; I can see that from over here, and that's regardless of which version of you shows up at the table. Second, I don't know what I want because there's a chance I'm just now trying to figure it out after six-plus decades. Everything I was used to has gone. People used to stop me in the street, and my opinion used to matter on things around town."

Evan spit a little bit on "town" and wiped it gently off of Bullseye's cheek. He continued, softer, "Look, it's deeper than that, but let me say, I came here to hide. Boy, did I pick the right place to disappear." They both looked around at the empty café. But, now that I'm here, I think I want to hide from my old life in Malibu . . . maybe . . . but settle in here and start something new, with different friends and have my voice matter somehow."

"Well, Evan, I can see deep inside you and there's work to do, but I like what I see, so much more than just some spoiled rich dude with the most magnificent eyes I've ever been lost in."

They both blushed and both reacted like they were surprised by being able to blush.

"You do have a way of slashing and loving on somebody at the same time, Bullseye. That's what I see in you with the guys at breakfast."

"Those guys at the big table are keeping you at arm's length because no one knows what you're about. What are you looking to get done? We get a lot of stars roll into the county and disrupt our peaceful patterns, then take off. Some people move up here to hide out, and that's OK. Others are looking to make some dream come true or make a difference. I'm glad to hear you ain't happy just sitting around all day looking gorgeous—and I must admit, Mr. Movie Star Guy, you are very good at that." Bullseye smiled and lowered her eyes to confirm that her statement applied head to toe.

"You said my eyes, right," commented Evan, which caused her to refocus on his eyes.

"Uh, sure, Evan. I hope you figure it out. You seem a little lonely sitting all by yourself every day, so why not glue together a plan of things you want to accomplish, then come join us at the big-boy table some morning. Don't wait for an invite from those hardheads. I'm inviting you. I'll make sure you're comfortable, and I'll make those guys behave."

"That's very nice, Bullseye, and it means a lot coming from a natural beauty like yourself," said Evan.

"See, there's that surface crap that none of us here in Montana have time for, Evan. What do my looks have to do with anything?"

Evan recoiled a little. "I was talking about your 'I do gorgeous so well' comment a minute ago. Seems fair for me to compliment you back. And you *do* happen to be a stunning woman. You may not hear it enough or be comfortable with it, but let me tell you, *stunning* is the right word.

85

Captivating would do as well. And as far as the rest of your little diatribe goes, what do *you* want, Bullseye? What's *your* driving force?"

After taking a second to carefully organize a few words, Bullseye leaned even closer to Evan and whispered, "My turn, Evan. That's what I want. I've waited a long time and worked hard for my turn at . . . well, exactly what, I can't tell you, but I'll know it when I see it. You're not the only one trying to figure it out. I've been bored my whole life. My little ghost town and the mining thing, even my ranch here, are just placeholders until I get in the big game. And when I do, when it's my turn . . . every good thing will collide. I see a beach, a bunch of money, some cool drinks, and a man who's smart enough to keep life interesting when he talks—a man so hot that he keeps it even more interesting when he doesn't speak. My turn is coming, all right, and I can smell it the same way I can smell diamonds. Mark my words, Mr. Gorgeous Actor Evan Morris."

And with "Morris" still forming with her mouth, Bullseye slipped two fingers inside the front of his belt, right behind the buckle and pulled him firmly against her. She tilted her head, leaned forward slightly, then kissed Evan softly on the lips. Their contact was caring and relaxed and ended with a slight quiver that left Evan speechless.

The crash from the kitchen door rocked Evan back to awareness. As Bullseye released his belt and turned to leave, Evan saw Mona's empty right hand and the spinning remnants of a broken coffeepot on the floor by her feet. Mona's mouth was open, but no words escaped as she swapped her attention from Evan to the coffee crisis and back again.

Evan watched Bullseye stride out of the diner and knew that little kiss they had just shared would rank on his "Top 5 All-Time Off-Screen Kisses"—a list he kept in his head and debated from time to time for fun. He had never expected a Top 5 contender to come from a fiftyish, gorgeous nonblonde Montana rancher. This was a serious new entry, he told himself, since he couldn't remember the other four top contenders at that moment.

30

BITTERROOT RIVER, MONTANA

Two hundred miles was a long way to smile, but the color and warmth never left Bullseye's cheeks during the entire drive from Evan Morris's gorgeous lips to the Bitterroot Valley, where she would meet the vice president for their fishing trip. She said what was on her mind and loved leaving a beautiful, powerful man speechless. The Evan episode not only warmed her but boosted her confidence while she prepped her mind for her next guests. Telling Evan how to handle himself with the other men was her gift to him—the kiss was her dessert.

Secretary of the Interior Alan Stubblefield ducked as he ran beneath the rotors toward Bullseye to shake her hand as though she were a dignitary. The vice president of the United States followed and took her hand, while holding his cap. *If only Daddy Magee could see me now*, thought Bullseye.

"Thanks for meeting us, Bullseye," yelled Stubblefield as Marine Two's rotors powered back up for takeoff to head up to Malmstrom Air Force Base for fuel and some show-and-tell for the local forces.

"Welcome back, Alan, Bill. You boys ready for some fishing?" She thought the vice president's handshake was still a little wimpy.

"Oh, we're definitely fishing on this trip," said Bill Fowler.

"Mountain whitefish. I'd like to latch onto a five pounder," prebragged Stubblefield. "If you can show us one of your secret spots."

The small parade, with Bullseye alone in her truck, followed by two black SUVs holding the Secret Service and the politicians, took off toward the higher elevation of the Bitterroot Valley, to one of Bullseye's private locations on the West Fork of the Bitterroot River. The speakers in her truck blasted "Check Yes or No" from George Strait as Bullseye joked out loud, "Now, where did I put those five-pound whitefish?"

31

WASHINGTON, DC

Peace and serenity blanketed the north and south lawns of the White House. The calamity started just outside the double-fence perimeter, where a throbbing mob gathered and pushed against the barriers. A National Guard presence had been active for the last two days, after two protest-related murders had taken place in front of the White House. The Guard, the DC Police, and the Secret Service had coordinated their command, with the directive to stop the protestors from going over the fence at all costs—a complicated mission because the protest had no official leadership or organizing body. It was a mass of individuals from all parts of society, making their angst known, but their actions hard to predict.

Darkening clouds gathered over the White House, setting the stage for a clash. The central theme was relief from suffering. The unprecedented financial crisis coupled with a modern sense of entitlement ingrained over decades by a willing Congress had created a very dependent public. Impromptu spokespeople, foisted on top of cars and looped into the Twitter and Periscope live feeds that echoed across the ominous sea of mobile phones, torqued up the crowd's intensity with each incendiary point. They pounded home the growing resentment for "the haves" and no additional patience for suffering by the "have-nots." Social media—and hunger—had a way of fanning the flames of unrest, sparking action.

Whistles, cheers, then alarms and tear gas heralded the disturbance on the west side of the fence, near the Rose Garden. Two of the protesters, dressed in business suits and black eye masks, yelled, "Here we go," and produced two collapsible ladders to lean against the barricades and the fence. Others yelled loudly as a gang of bold protesters traversed the ladders and attempted to hop the fence. As the Guard and police focused on that breach, three other areas were hit, with a waterfall of citizens approaching the fences on ladders. The SWAT team positioned closest to the White House radioed the command to "clear fence line in 3-2-1 . . ."

A tremendous bolt of electricity cycled through the barriers protecting the White House, scaring, shocking, and even burning anyone touching one of the fences or metal ladders. An immediate hush fell over the crowd as they surveyed the wounded, followed instantly by a loud roar from the northeast corner. One guy, about twenty years old, carrying an American flag, had cleared the fence on a wooden ladder just in time and raced across the lawn toward the White House portico entrance.

President Crowley had watched the entire event unfold from the second-floor Residence window of the White House, checking in with multiple departments and key personnel across the country via a variety of devices. He charged down the small spiral staircase to get to the portico door as quickly as possible once he saw the kid hop over the fence, and ran onto the lawn, yelling, "Don't shoot him, hold your fire, don't shoot!" A swarm of agents blanketed the president, just as two SWAT team members tackled the intruder. "Bring him inside. Safely!" shouted the president, which was repeated instantly by the Secret Service contingency. Quietly, he prayed for a solution to this madness, for calm, and then he prayed for rain.

The president slid inside just as a flash of lightning struck, followed by a deafening percussive clap of thunder. The crowd stopped chanting for a second, and the scattered glow of cell phones extinguished as the rain pelted the gathering. The protesters didn't completely disperse, but the driving late-summer storm dampened their enthusiasm and decimated their numbers.

Whoa, I usually don't get my prayers answered that fast, thought Crowley.

The agents delivered the wet, scared fence-vaulter, in handcuffs, to the president in the foyer of the White House. The president offered his towel to Ken Seger, as he was introduced by the Secret Service, taking over the arrest. Noticing the handcuffs behind him, Crowley took the towel and wiped some blood from his face and rain off his hair and jacket. "Ken, what were you thinking? You were about to die, do you know that? Are you an idiot, Son?"

The trembling college kid raised his head and said, "No, sir, I'm not an idiot. I'm a senior economics major with the highest GPA at Clemson, and I don't care if I die today, because you know as well as I do that if not today, it's going to be soon. There's no hope for us, for any of us, Mr. Crowley. I hope you have some spectacular secret plan that can fix this mess, because if not, they'll be a lot more guys like me coming over that fence."

The president clenched his jaw and turned a slow circle as he asked Ken a series of questions about his motivation and understanding of the problem. Ken's thoughtful, passionate answers to the president's questions forced Crowley to take him seriously. "Who's got his phone?" asked the president to the agents. "Uncuff him, now!" he yelled over their objections. "Kid, if you try to hurt me, *I* will kill you, got it? But let's see if we can work together to help the world out a little."

Ken stood dumbfounded as his cuffs were removed and his phone was presented in front of him by the president. "Unlock it. What's your favorite platform on social media, Instagram? How many followers do you have?"

"BuzzCutt," Ken replied nervously. "But I only have about a hundred friends."

"Not anymore," said the president, holding the phone up and activating the live video function. "This is President Crowley and I've just finished a meeting with Ken Seger from Clemson, one of my new economic advisors. That's a little bit of a joke, because earlier today, Ken was one of the protesters who nearly got killed trying to deliver his message of doom and gloom to me personally. I want you all to know that Ken Seger will now have a seat at every single one of our financial discussions on how we are going to reshape the financial future of this country. He's the ultimate pessimist and he represents thousands of you gathered in protests today. He will be the one to listen to your demands, your worries, and make certain you are all represented in those meetings. You will see him near me when I announce some radical new programs in the very near future. While I don't like his tactics and I don't want anyone killed in these protests, I value your right to speak. I'm praying and working on a 'spectacular solution,' to use Ken's phrase. You can reach him through his BuzzCutt account. It may take him a while to get back to you."

The foyer broke into a brawl. The president's team from the West Wing had filtered in and jumped up and down, high-fiving at the genius of the live announcement and new addition to the staff. The security side of the crowd shouted and clawed at Ken, begging the president to let them arrest him or just tear him apart on the spot.

The crowd quieted when the president held his hand up to speak. "First of all, Ken, are you in?"

"I . . . I don't know what 'in' means, but you bet I am. As long as this can count for my senior project." The thin college kid rapidly wiped his blond hair, teasing it into place with the towel the president gave him. He pulled the towel down and noticed the embroidered seal of the President of the United States of America. "And can I keep the towel, you know, to seal the deal?"

"You need to work on your negotiating, kid. OK, Graham, get Ken cleaned up, walk him around the shop, and then let's figure out some parameters. I want you to stay outside, Ken, so people can have access to you. You'll be in here for a lot of meetings, but I meant what I said. I'm counting on you to give it to me straight." He nodded and Crowley continued, "Two things: secrets are secrets and you can't blurt out just anything you hear. We talk about stuff that's life-and-death for a lot of people. And second, bring an open mind, not that college-why-can't-the-world-just-work thing. I used to have that, and it's just uglier in real life. We are solving very real problems."

"You bet, Mr. President. And thanks for not killing me," he said as he wrapped the towel around his neck, making sure the presidential seal was showing.

Chief of Staff Blair ushered the new college-aged advisor away, after alerting the president that he had an update on the "Orlando Situation" inside the East Room. The president entered and found, standing in the middle of the large rug, handwoven by Betsy Ross and her circle of friends, a petite end table holding a spoon and a small silver saucer brimming with raw chocolate-chip cookie dough. The president had alerted the kitchen that the "stress-level was high," which was code for Chef Orlando to intervene. On day one of his administration, Chef Orlando had asked the president about his cookie preference, and he replied, "Chocolate chip, baked in my tummy-oven, at 98 degrees." From then on, the chef saw it as his patriotic duty to supply a small tub of raw cookie dough during the most stressful situations.

With the spoon dangling from his mouth, Dan Crowley wandered to the Oval Office, processing all that had transpired. Some challenges are clear-cut, like curing cancer. The president thought about that list—*find a gene or a drug that kills cancer cells, then make a bunch of them, then you have cured cancer*. It seemed so much easier for somebody to tackle that than to solve the problems that were facing him: *Get people to stop depending on the government for everything. Get the government to stop promising everything to people so they will work for themselves. Get jobs, so there is money flowing. Get money flowing, so there are jobs. Fix everything that's broken or unsafe. Borrow no more money and don't sink us deeper in the hole while you fix it. Help people believe in America again. And sell part of it out from under them to help in the meantime.* The ideas spiraled like a vortex.

There was so much to love about America, yet right now and right in front of his window, everything seemed wrong. Could he save the country, or had it slid too far down? What could *not* saving the country look like? Where was the bottom?

32

BITTERROOT RIVER, MONTANA

Bullseye shook her head at their horrible fly technique and had a hard time deciding whose was worse. She landed on Vice President Bill Fowler as hands down the worst fly fisherman she'd ever guided. Their minds didn't appear to be on the fishing, however. The VP pulled his lead agent aside and requested more distance.

Stubblefield started with a little foreshadowing, saying, "Bullseye, this conversation may leave your head spinning. There's some high-level stuff shaking in DC that involves Montana and some other countries."

"I know there's some bad stuff happening all over the country—lots of violence and such." She kicked a small rock, rolling it in the river.

Stubblefield shook his head. "Yes, there is, but we're talking about a whole different level. We're talking about something that may take away your lifestyle forever."

They had Bullseye's attention as she circled up and sat on a large boulder near the river's edge. Bullseye dredged water bottles out of the Yeti and tossed one each to Fowler and Stubblefield. Fowler took two hands to catch his and dropped his fly rod in the process. "That's a lot of drama for a fishing trip, fellas. How about you fill in some of the details?"

Stubblefield yielded to Fowler, who took the lead. "It's top secret, but my boss wants to sell Montana to another country to raise a bunch of money." They each silently took a seat on a nearby rock, to let the news sink in.

Bullseye sank to the ground, sliding off the front edge of the boulder, pushing her hat over her eyes. From under her hat, she said, "But how . . . who would . . . I mean, did you say 'sell Montana'? I own part of it."

"You know the country is falling apart. You've heard of all the protests and crazy stuff going on in Washington—"

"And everywhere else," interrupted Fowler, with urgency.

Stubblefield continued, "And the president has cooked up this crazy plot to sacrifice Montana to save the rest of the country. He wants to claim, then sell the entire state to some foreigners who need a home. We hated the idea and didn't think in a million years it would have a chance of passing, but now it looks as if it's gaining steam. The president won't announce it for six months, but it's in the works. They're figuring out how to compensate you folks for the land you own and how to move everyone somewhere else."

Bullseye didn't know where to start with the long list of questions that popped into her head. She rolled to her right, straight into the shallow, cold river, lying there face down for as long as she could hold her breath. She gasped as she emerged from the water, trying to find her breath, stolen by the cold water and the crazy talk.

Stubblefield interrupted the self-baptism. "I know it's unheard of, Bullseye. But don't worry . . . we have a plan to help you through this."

"Slow down. Slow way down, fellas. You gotta be messing with me. Has the president come right out and said he believes he can bail out the entire country by taking away our land in Montana and selling it to someone else? And that makes sense in what world? And he thinks that will make enough money to help the rest of the US? Aren't we gazillions in debt?" said Bullseye, perplexed in several directions at once.

"He's looking at some Iranians or other Middle Eastern people as potential buyers, and they're loaded," said Stubblefield, adding fuel. "I know it's a lot to drink in, but trust us, things are so bad around the country that the president is all in on this idea. But before the president can sell off this land, we believe we could help you stake your claim. We think you should reposition some trophy-sized game to a place we're buying across the border in Idaho."

Bullseye sat down on the boulder, squeezing water from her jeans, then sprang right back up to pace in a small circle. She kicked her Yeti cooler into the river and watched it float away as she sorted it out. "So, this is happening—our whole state is going away, and you think it's a good idea to talk to me about helping you find a few elk and get them to Idaho? And then I lose my ranch? That's what's important to you?" Bullseye said, almost spitting fire.

"No ma'am," Fowler said, taking control. "We want to help you get what you deserve. We want to help you get settled before all hell breaks loose here and to do that, we want you to stampede thousands of prize game to our preserve before they take away this beautiful land. You'd start up in the northern part of the Bitterroot Valley and run a herd of elk or white tail about ten or twenty miles down to Idaho, somewhere near your Lame Horse Creek spread. That will not only give us a lifetime of trophies and good eating, but it will give you enough money to rebuild your dream ranch anywhere you want. And that's on top of however the government will compensate you."

Bullseye was still too overwhelmed to answer, so Stubblefield added, "And you could manage the new preserve and hunting lodge as long as you want. Live out the rest of your life with no worries, doing what you do well, telling stories, guiding trips for our friends. We're talking about millions of dollars coming your way, Bullseye."

Millions caught her attention. Bullseye sat back down on her rock and pondered whether our country could sell a state out from under its residents. "Stampede? A real stampede, with lots of critters?"

Thoughts collided, although not one of them included whether this was, at the least illegal and, at the worst, deadly. Her honest-to-God first thought was whether this could be the one final way to prove she was a rancher worth her salt, a rancher who could wrangle any animal. She could take away the shameful context of her name and rebrand herself as a "real" Bullseye and get rich doing it. She could *become* the legend in her stories—a cattle rustler, engineering a stampede, outsmarting the US government . . . . A breeze whipped her hair in front of her eyes, so she grabbed it back into a tight ponytail, taking a band from her wrist to secure it. The pause gave her a few seconds to process the situation.

Fowler helped. "A drive like this will take planning and a bunch of tough ranch hands. Some boys who aren't afraid of breaking some laws, cutting fences, and even starting a few fires here and there."

Stubblefield piled on, saying, "They could ride four-wheelers from somewhere in the Bitterroot National Forest down the valley to the Idaho border. Maybe fifteen to twenty of them. Or a hundred. It'd be like an old cattle drive . . ."

"I think you mean old-fashioned cattle rustling," said Bullseye, with more inspiration than hesitation. "There's federal land between here and there—like most of the Bitterroot National Forest. You fellas would have to help keep the rangers and the BLM folks looking the other way so we could slide through. It'll kick up a little dust to get this done. And it won't be cheap . . ."

Bullseye was proud of herself for predicting Fowler's shyster profile. If a stampede of hunting animals was the opportunity to get hers, she wouldn't hesitate. They could have her farm and plow under the memories of her dead father. If the money was right, she wouldn't even need to pack. Everything Bullseye Magee needed for a new life was waiting somewhere on a beach.

"We got a few things to figure out before you boys pick out curtains for the new lodge . . ."

33

SOUTHWEST MONTANA

Evan drove the hybrid SUV instead of the Tesla because it had a range of six hundred miles. He wasn't sure how much of that six-hundred-mile range he would eat up as he blitzed across southwestern Montana headed toward—well, he wasn't sure where he was going.

There were things to sort out, and his therapist once told him to take a long drive on the PCH to clear his head. *Five hundred bucks an hour and she prescribed the Pacific Coast Highway.* He could see why people made fun of Californians.

Seek wisdom. That sounded like something else his therapist would say. Like Proverbs or a Buddhist thing, but Bullseye had mentioned it as she described her drive down to Idaho, listing the little towns she drove through, like Sula, Twin Bridges, and Wisdom, Montana. Evan took off through the southwestern part of the state seeking wisdom—and perhaps to rub shoulders with the vice president—but the real reason was to see Bullseye in her element.

It made little sense to just drop in on Bullseye after a four-hour drive. He rehearsed an excuse, even though it was spandex-thin. But there was the kiss. In a moist-lipped moment, that woman had grabbed hold of something inside of him. Her challenge, the call to stand up and find some meaning, made him want to rally. She could see where he was weak, and she still liked him despite his frailty. And she stamped her thoughts with that kiss.

"If you're stuck in between two worlds, maybe you should plant a foot in one of them and see if it grows roots . . . ," Evan whispered, in his movie-cowboy accent.

That line had drawn snickers during the Hollywood preview of his third-to-last movie and was one of the first signs that his time on the coast might be over. He couldn't blame them for laughing and feared that whatever he said to Bullseye after the long drive would sound like that pathetic movie line, but that was a risk he would take. This was step one of carving out a new life, with deeper relationships than the ones he left behind. He wasn't just hiding, he was building. "That sounds a whole lot better," Evan said as he stopped to stretch and pee. The view from the floor of the Bitterroot Valley was stunning, and the signs for the West Fork of the Bitterroot River rang a bell. He took a left, heading west and south, following the old travel brochure for the Lame Horse Creek Ghost Town and Mining Operation he had picked up from the rest stop, which showed the attraction in its heyday.

The two-lane road bounced right along the river on the narrow valley floor, and about twenty miles up in hills, Evan glanced through the gigantic lodgepole pines to his right and caught a glimpse of Bullseye's truck and two large all-black SUVs parked about a hundred yards off-road, next to the river. He pulled off on the dirt road that headed back toward the river and stopped in a cloud of dust to collect his thoughts. He rolled his windows down to take in the late-summer air and to hang his arm outside, trying to look casual. Forty yards from the cars, a Secret Service agent jumped out from behind a tree, gun drawn, and yelled, "Halt, hands on the wheel." Before Evan could say anything, another agent appeared at his window and grabbed his arm, twisting it back, outside the door. "State your business, stranger."

Evan screamed like a bingo winner at the surprise attack. After he collected enough oxygen, he said, "It's OK, fellas, I'm Evan Morris, the actor. I'm here to see Bullseye . . . and the vice president, of course."

Bullseye came running up from the riverside, still dripping wet. "Evan, what in the hell are you doing here? It's OK, boys, he's a friend."

The agents relaxed their stance and backed away, moving toward the river, closer to the vice president. Evan rubbed his arm and climbed out of the hybrid SUV and hugged Bullseye, not caring that she was soaking wet.

"What the heck are you doing here, Evan?"

"I wanted to see you, Bullseye. I thought it would be a nice surprise to see where you worked and to say hi to Bill Fowler. You seem surprised all right. Did you fall in or something?" Evan shuffled while he tucked his tapered plaid ranch shirt deeper into his jeans.

After taking off her hat and mussing with her hair, Bullseye stared at Evan with pleading eyes. "Look, there's no time to explain, but I promise you that this is the absolute worst possible time for you to drop in on me. We're at a critical point in some negotiations, and I mean critical. We can't be interrupted. Evan, remember how I said these guys value their privacy?"

Evan tried to hug Bullseye again, but she backstepped a foot or two, leaving his arms hanging. "I'm sorry, Bullseye. I wasn't thinking about right or wrong, I just trusted my heart for once. I wanted to see you, plain and simple."

The wind rustled the pine needles for a moment while Bullseye stared down Evan's beautiful blues. "OK, star boy, you get credit for making a move, but I don't need a man shoving his way in on my business world. This is where I work, and gorgeous or not, you could ruin everything. So, head out and let's pick this up in a few days when I clear my head."

The long, lonely drive back to Virginia City allowed Evan time to replay the failed afternoon and take stock of his situation. He had no friends, unless he counted April Lear and Mona. He was an acclaimed movie idol, and yet couldn't get invited fifteen feet to join a few crusty old locals at their table. He owned a ranch half the size of Malibu but didn't know how to drive his tractor, set up his fishing rig, or even build an outdoor fire without an "on" switch.

In Malibu, he had left behind a few friends who didn't even care enough to check in on him, two ex-wives, and a crime wave.

"Virginia City—two hundred thirty miles," said the syrupy voice from his car's Garmin navigation system.

More miles helped him sort out the options: His celebrity status would not define him. It would always be a part of him, and he would be glad to acknowledge it, but his new goal was to use the wisdom and resources he had gained from being an actor, well, a celebrity, which is bigger than an actor, and build a platform to change some part of this planet. Evan could see himself coming to the rescue of those in need. He knew he would never cure cancer, but he could motivate a bunch of others to help fund a cure. As a connector, he could make an impact. He wanted to become a bigger part of something he believed in.

But what to do about Bullseye? He had misread that situation completely, driving all that way to sweep her off her feet and instead, got punched in the gut. Her parting words still stung, and he didn't fully understand them. From six feet away, she had said, "Get your hand off my throat, Evan." It was clear that this one needed plenty of room.

34

WASHINGTON, DC

THE WHITE HOUSE RESIDENCE

Denise Crowley sat up against the headboard and absentmindedly dangled a large spoonful of raw cookie dough—his favorite bedtime snack—in front of her husband and said, "Can this even happen?"

"Sure, you just make the airplane noise or whatever game you want to play to get me to beg for that cookie dough, and I'll jump for it."

"Sorry," she said, handing him the spoon. "I mean, can you really just take homes away from people? Is it legal to *sell* a state?"

Crowley cleaned the spoon with his top lip as he pulled it out of his mouth, not wasting a speck of the sweet treat. After a quick swallow, he said, "It's confusing, but looks like it's legal. We've done it for decades for railroads, utilities, all sorts of zoning regulations, and who knows what else."

"But this is different. This is an entire state."

"Worlds different. It'll have to go to the Supreme Court, but I'm told it will pass, given precedents in our 'takings' rulings in the '90s and the teens. The more I've studied this, the more amazed I am at the number and scope of actions our federal government has taken against private, state, or city property, and won. They based most of the cases on economic problems— either new development needed or financial disparity that the government sought to remedy by seizing land. This is a much larger scale, but the premise is the same, and boy, do we have an economic problem."

"But Montana didn't cause the problem, right? Doesn't that make this different from, say, an abandoned district in downtown Detroit? When officials seized and sold that, it was to fix that problem."

"It's never easy and you're right, my dear. So, we're looking at the nation as a whole, and this becomes part of the equation. I'm counting on the wisdom of the Supreme Court to help figure this out."

"Not to mention the political sensibilities of the Court?" Denise asked and declared.

The president smirked a little and said, "Now you know as well as I do that the highest court in the land is above political persuasion." His laugh was just as loud as "Mrs. President's" but both faded fast.

"But I think the justices realize it may be the only way to save the country, and that's gotta buy us some favor."

"As long as you figure out how to compensate all those people who get moved out of Montana. That will go a long way toward winning approval," said Denise.

Dan walked to his closet, giving the spoon one more going over and took off his robe, then moved to his sink to brush his teeth. Between the foam, he said, "Of course, dear, but that's the hard part. There're a lot of Montanans who won't think any amount of money is fair for the resources they are being asked to give up. And there will be lots of people in the public at large who think they should get something for the sale of the national park land up there. We're still running the numbers because it has to make sense. If it costs us ten trillion to compensate all the Montana claims and we can only sell it for twelve trillion, then it won't be worth the trouble. It's just not enough to help solve our problems. We'll figure something out."

Denise took her robe off and climbed under the covers. Dan switched off the light, climbed in his side, and said, "Now, if I promise to compensate them fairly, would you sneak back down to the kitchen tomorrow and authorize Chef Orlando to serve up a spoonful of cookie dough, at least during high stress situations? *Somebody* told him it was a matter of national security that he no longer provides any to the president."

35

BITTERROOT VALLEY, MONTANA

Bullseye woke up early and reran yesterday in her head. She had sent Evan off with his tail between his legs, finished the meeting with the DC boys, watched their helicopter take off, tossed the fishing gear into the bed of her truck, and ran a few minutes up the valley from where they had fished off Highway 473 to spend the night in her mine shaft at her Lame Horse Creek tourist trap. There was a lot to sort out, but she had been too tired or too overwhelmed to make the run back to Virginia City. She checked her rearview once or twice to make sure Evan wasn't following her. Part of her was livid that he showed up uninvited, and part of her wished he was still back there, trying to catch her. Between the hammer that Fowler had dropped and the intrusion by Evan, Bullseye had a fitful night of sleep.

Her hideaway in the mine shaft was sparse but comfortable. She had a small trailer topside but found it too hot to sleep in during the summer and noisy from all the animals roaming around, so she retreated to a makeshift bed in her cave, falling into an intermittent, nervous sleep, in the cool fifty-seven-degree climate and the sound of trickling water, just a few yards inside the front entrance.

She awoke with focus after just a few hours, splashed off her face in the little creek that ran through the cave, dressed, and hopped in the truck for her therapy session back to Madison County. Leaving bright and early for the four-plus-hour trip back to the ranch in Madison County was easy, with so much on her mind. She always did her best thinking on the road—it didn't take a therapist to help her figure that out.

Could they sell Montana? They sure acted like it, and this was the vice president talking—he should know. *Could this be a setup?* Maybe, but why go through all this with the vice president just to catch a small fry like Bullseye Magee doing some poaching? No. *Could this moneymaking scam be big enough to pad my dreams for life?* Abso-dang-lutely, and the trick was to recognize an opportunity like this when it slapped you in the face.

The downside? If they were right, she would lose her ranch anyway. Her father had sown the ranch with rows and rows of hurt. They were welcome to it, and she hoped they put a camel pen right over his grave. If

100

NOVEL BY STEVE GILREATH

the president was going to sell their state, there was nothing she could do to stop it, so she might as well make some money to help soften the blow. And a little extra cash for running some animals out of the state would not hurt anyone anyway. Whoever might get mad would be losing their ranch too and would have bigger worries on their mind. If this did really happen to her state, she wouldn't be stepping on anyone she knew. They were all being squashed.

Can I do this? Hell, yeah. You're a rancher, right? It's about time you proved it. Have some backbone, woman! Do I have the energy to do this? How much energy does it take to hire some thugs that can do the actual dirty stuff? Use your head, girl.

The sun was high overhead by the time Bullseye rounded the last turn into her ranch, but her moment was just dawning. It was her turn.

Whatfer? I'll show 'em whatfer.

She filled the afternoon with schemes for stampedes and wild game. Bullseye scratched out specs on everything from frag grenades to live animal traps. She researched Aboriginal herding techniques with fire and drums in the outback and fifteen other approaches that all sounded too small, too drastic, too expensive, or too illegal. She needed more ideas to make this work.

And then the phone sizzled three times in her pocket. On the screen appeared a picture of the rear end of Morris Evans's horse, which Bullseye used as his caller ID:

>Get you carkas over here right now!!

Two exclamation points from Morris Evans indicated a crisis. Bullseye hopped back in the truck and tore off toward town.

101

36

VIRGINIA CITY, MONTANA

Hitch parked his Ram in a rush in front of the courthouse and hurried up the creaky wooden steps. The blinds inside the window of the courthouse snapped shut. He turned to look down the street. No one had followed him. "What's with all the cloak-and-dagger nonsense, Morris?" Hitch asked as he entered the office.

"Quick, get in here," whispered Morris as he took Hitch by the forearm to usher him into the office.

"What the . . . ?" was all Hitch had time to mutter before Bullseye, who blew on her coffee as she was just sitting down in her regular chair in the corner, motioned him to grab his seat.

She said, "Hurry in here, Hitch. I'm sure ISIS is coming up the valley right now. Morris is on level Orange about something." She smiled while taking a big sip of coffee.

Morris ignored her sarcasm and jumped right into the story. "I just got off the phone with Hayden Schupp, and he—"

"Hayden from Senator Hepburn's office? What the heck did he—"

"Yes, yes, from our senator's office, but don't interrupt me!" Morris shouted, holding up his hand. "You won't believe this. They want to sell Montana."

Morris had delivered the message like a punch line. Bullseye looked surprised, and Hitch didn't move or react at all. The news hung there like a fart in a space suit. Bullseye cleared her throat before looking down into her coffee, then up at the guys. After a few looks back and forth Hitch said, "Who is 'they' and what do you mean 'sell Montana'?"

"I don't know all the details—let's hope it's just a rumor, but those eggheads in the government are cooking up a plot to sell our state to Iraq or Mexico or something to make a bunch of money. Hayden heard it firsthand from the girl that cuts his hair, who was told by the guy she's been seeing, who's a driver for a vice something-or-other at the State Department, who overheard his boss on a call being asked to look into recruiting a foreign buyer for *our* land!" stammered Morris, in a manner that suggested this was an airtight source.

"But . . ."

"How in the hell . . ."

"There's no way in hell . . ."

Hitch said, "Morris, you gotta have something mixed up here. He must have overheard someone talking about buying some land here or something."

Morris eased himself into his groaning wooden chair but leaned forward, hands folded on his desk. "No, I got Hepburn himself on the phone. He wouldn't full-on own up but said he had heard part of that scenario whispered about and he was not being allowed in certain meetings around the Capitol. What they're talking about is selling our entire state to another country. The boys in Warshington have been brainstorming ways to make up the deficit, and this is the one idea that made the most sense."

"I can't imagine the ideas that seemed too crazy to consider," said Hitch.

They both looked at Bullseye, who stared down at her coffee. Hitch said, "Bullseye, you just took a few of them hunting. The vice president must have said something."

"Well, as a matter of a fact, I overheard something about a land sale, but didn't believe what I heard. It just sounded like crazy talk, and I thought nothing solid would come out of it."

"I hate Warshington," repeated Morris, who punched his desk on "Warsh."

"So, you heard about this, Bullseye? Why didn't you say anything to us?"

Bullseye paused for a second and looked at her friends. She squirmed in her chair and said, "Fellas, I don't know what I heard. Those political guys stack up more crap than my Shorthorns. I can't sift what's real and what's smoke. When they were talking about doing something with Montana, it sounded, well, just lunacy. I mean, they talk about sawing off California and floating it out to sea, and I don't give that a second thought. They talk about bombing the snot out of all sorts of countries and poisoning their opponents before a debate, and it makes them all laugh, and then they get on with their trip. It's just not real, and so when I heard this, I just tossed it on the same trash pile as that other garbage."

Hitch shook his head slowly while Bullseye sipped her coffee and Morris exhaled a guttural, "I hate Warshington."

37

YUMA PROVING GROUND, ARIZONA

The base at Yuma Proving Ground was one of the world's largest military facilities, with thirteen hundred square miles wedged between Interstate 10 and the Mexican border, bisected by the Colorado River. The military had certified most every US weapons system in the last century at Yuma, so wringing out a flying car was easier and less noisy than most of the projects that come through their hangars.

Earlier prototypes of the Autonomous Flying Vehicle accommodated four adults, yet the FAA banned any human participation with a full car until certification was complete. Their latest version of test cars contained tricked-out interiors with plush seating, reading lights, Wi-Fi entertainment center, and more for the press to conduct ground-based interviews during the testing periods.

Inside YPG (the name used for Yuma Proving Ground by those in the area) were several testing ranges, including the most instrumented helicopter test course in the world, the Cibola Range. They equipped Cibola for just about anything that involved flight tracking, telemetry, flight dynamics, and precision navigation systems. The AH-64 Apache helicopter was just one system wrung out on this course during decades of operation.

There were over two thousand square miles of restricted airspace around YPG. The Army would know if the AFV was worth its salt by the time it had traversed that much area. They had to know with confidence that this new technology could navigate within inches of its programmed path before they'd turn it loose cross-country.

"Morning, everyone. Just like in our backyard, right?" said Dr. Hock as he entered the control tower and tapped Andi Calton, the programmer who had assembled the day's flight test for the AFV, on the back to initiate the flight. "OK, Andi, everyone, here we go."

The electric engine whirled to life with a bump and a metallic scraping sound but purred as it kicked up dust off the concrete pad just outside the hangar. It blocked the view from inside the control tower until the thickest part of the dust cloud parted and the AFV-22 Magic Carpet came into view, hovering a foot off the pad. Hock would always come up on his toes during takeoffs.

"OK, let's run the sequence. Twice around the park," said Andi, to no one in particular, while the assembled team from the FAA and the military watched through the large acrylic window. The flight path had been pre-programmed just as a future AFV owner would program a trip to the store. They analyzed the takeoff on a wall of monitors fed by forty-eight cameras around the immediate area. The craft rose above the dust cloud as if floating on air, with just the tiniest of wobbles. The candy-apple finish glistened in the early Arizona sun and shimmered as the vehicle rotated in a 360-degree pattern, all part of the test. It paused with a slight shimmy and then descended to a perfect landing.

After tapping the ground, it ascended to seventy-five feet elevation, spun ninety degrees to aim due west, while the small fan housings rotated horizontally to urge the craft off in a forward direction. Six onboard cameras verified the smooth rotation of the louvered doors on the fans, along with a stable cabin ride. And then it disappeared from eyesight.

The test was near perfect. In real time, the assembled tech contingent monitored and commented on the dashboard readout of all test flight analytics. Some watched the drive point-of-view camera to imagine the ride as a passenger. Fast speeds, low altitudes, and all very exciting!

After the twenty-nine-minute test that ran the car over twelve miles and included several touchdown landings, simulated slow traffic congestion, and a high-speed stretch at 110-plus miles per hour, they returned to the pad next to the control tower. Dr. Hock beamed with pride and worked through the crowd to get in front of General Starnes as she walked around the dusty AFV. "Well, General, that was a good run, wasn't it?"

Amy Starnes looked at him with a tight smile. "You bet it was, Hock. I knew your little buggy here could fly like a demon. You're a smart guy and you've invested a lot of years into this. The hard part will come tomorrow when we fly with other traffic."

"We'll be ready, General," said Hock, wondering if they'd be ready.

38

WASHINGTON, DC

The First Lady tiptoed into her husband's private study attached to the Oval Office and found him head in hands, rubbing his eyes. "More bad news?"

"I've just heard the Montana buyout estimate from the secret committee at the OMB, and it is steeper than we thought. Three trillion. So now I have to find a buyer with at least fifteen trillion—more money than some nations have generated in their entire history—and spend three trillion of that to displace the rightful American owners of the land I've just sold out from under them. It's so surreal, so in the middle of these details, I step back and remind myself that this was the best idea a bunch of smart people could come up with to save our country. There doesn't seem to be any other option, at least that's not on this scale, but I don't know how to work this out."

"I don't know either," said Denise Crowley as she moved her husband's hands from his eyes and snuggled into his lap, "but I know who will if anyone can. You know what they say when things aren't easy, that's when the tough—"

"When the tough makes an ass out of you and me," said Dan Crowley, with a tired smile.

For years, Denise made fun of the metaphors her husband had used in speeches and loved to butcher and spit them right back at him. The cliché game had become sport for her and guaranteed to make him smile—even with the world crumbling around them.

"You know, there is no 'ass' in team," she said, smiling.

39

VIRGINIA CITY, MONTANA

The team spiraled through two hours of discussion about the sale of their homeland from the close confines of Madison County Commissioner Morris Evans's rustic office. Bullseye had glared right in the eyes of the vice president as he warned of Montana's impending demise, yet debating it with Morris and Hitch made her think she had imagined the whole thing. A call to Allen Yoneyama, County Commissioner from Missoula, with closer ties to one of Idaho's senators, confirmed the rumor but provided no added details.

They paused the conversation, stood, stretched, paced, then switched chairs and launched in again to consider the possibility, probability, and logistics of *their government* betraying her own citizens.

Bullseye searched the faces of her friends and realized the impact of the event on them. She was not sorry for considering the scam that the VP had offered, given the fact that the land was going away. But she realized now that she had to stand with her friends somehow, to help them through this chaos. Recruiting them for the cattle drive scam wasn't a good option, but something compelled her to consider their fate carefully. After scattered periods of puzzled silence, Bullseye rose from the desk chair with a finger pointed in the air and declared, "Gentleman, our path is clear. We were born here. Our families settled this land. It is time for us to claim that birthright. Since the United States of America has abandoned and betrayed our great state, we must secede and become our own country."

A call for secession typically carried as much weight as a Sasquatch sighting, but in this confusion-filled morning it was a plausible response to a perplexing problem. The Montanans allowed Bullseye's idea to steep in the gravity of the moment: *The United Nation of Montana . . .*

40

WASHINGTON, DC

THE WHITE HOUSE/ROOSEVELT ROOM

The video with protestor Ken Seger and his appointment to the economic advisory board had not quelled the stress of the mob and security outside the gates of the White House. The unrest intensified, and just getting to work proved difficult for the weary-looking group assembled by the president around the large conference table inside the Roosevelt Room, named after President Theodore Roosevelt, who first built the West Wing, and his fifth cousin once removed, Franklin Delano Roosevelt. The West Wing underwent a renovation in 1933 under FDR, with a shuffling of the Oval Office and others, partially to help hide Franklin Roosevelt's paralysis from public view. The president realized his council was meeting in the Roosevelt Room to hide their paralysis, this time resulting from *The Budget Problem*. The major agenda item became a scolding by the president for not moving faster on the Montana solution. He delivered the details of his overseas trip to meet with Azwar and told the attendees in clear terms how serious he was. If they couldn't stumble on answers to the crisis, this nation would soon have a flag with only forty-nine stars.

"About that," said Interior Secretary Alan Stubblefield, stretching to keep his elbows on the table. "I've been thinking about our flag, and I wonder if we'd be smarter to preserve all fifty stars on the flag, by moving Montana inside another state. We could lessen the trauma if we carved out a few hundred square miles of Texas, or the corner of Utah and Colorado, and redraw the boundaries to make a smaller Montana. We could squeeze all the citizens of Montana in a space half the size of Manhattan without pushing very hard."

"If we lose a star for Montana, we'll gain one when Washington, DC, becomes a state. Or Puerto Rico. It won't be long," said Wayne Redmond.

The president watched, then said, "OK, set that aside for now. It may turn more states against the proposition."

President Crowley presented the financial overview, with a minimum fifteen trillion price tag, to stunned silence. Fowler looked around the room and could tell that the astronomical number the president had just mentioned presented an impossible goal for anyone to grasp. And that was on top of the six or seven trillion in departmental cuts discussed. The discussion led to a roll call of the same plausible countries who could be buyers, followed by the same firm reasons each wouldn't work. Vice President Fowler smiled as the meeting broke up, and slid out to avoid the escalating tension between the participants and the president.

The vice president scurried out to the West Wing Colonnade, catching up to Stubblefield. "Do you think there's any chance this will stay a secret?" asked Fowler.

"Hard to imagine, but all hell will break loose when it gets out," said Stubblefield. He paused and added, "I wonder what it will be like in Montana when they get the word? I know if that were West Texas, where I grew up, people would grab anything they could carry and steal the place blind."

Fowler looked at Stubblefield. "What do you know about the timber industry, Alan?" Without waiting for an answer, he continued, "Did you know that a single large tree can sell for more than $25,000 at today's timber prices? And Montana is full of old trees that we have no business leaving to whatever Tom, Dick, or Assad comes in to buy our state."

"I've got a little homework to do, Bill," said Stubblefield, "but I'm assuming that all we have to do is move some of those trees out of Montana and whittle them down to cash, right? Sort of like the animal stampede."

Fowler explained an opportunity to intercede for an old Montana logger named Humphrey Mankin. Hump had run into trouble with the Bureau of Land Management, and all Stubblefield had to do was flex some cabinet-level muscle to get Hump out of hot water. Hump would be in their pocket for life, and millions could start rolling in while the chaos of the state sale ensued.

* * *

By eleven a.m. the next morning, Interior Secretary Alan Stubblefield had intervened with the BLM on behalf of "solid citizen and critical link in a secret government program" Humphrey Mankin and reported back to Fowler that it was easier than expected to get his case set aside. Fowler told him the rest of the opportunity would need more work, but the return would outweigh the effort and risk.

"Isn't that how we evaluate everything?" asked Stubblefield.

"It sure is, Alan. It sure is."

41

YUMA PROVING GROUND, ARIZONA

The AFV took off from the concrete pad near the control tower for the last test of the last day. During the previous three days, Hock's AFVs had proven their airworthiness and navigational prowess by negotiating the distance courses set up by the Army, of up to eighty-five miles. Analytics on all metrics were near perfect. The craft could do everything Dr. Hock had promised.

For the next leg of the test General Amy Starnes stood behind a first lieutenant who had assumed the controlling position at a sinister looking console in the back row, away from the one used by Hock's crew. She leaned in and said, "OK, let's see how they can handle a crowd." The first lieutenant pushed a button labeled "launch" and two dark monitors blinked to life. A twelve-foot drone ignited and took off from across the Yuma Proving Ground, hit an altitude of seventy-five feet, and turned, screaming toward the AFV.

Dr. Hock shouted, "General, what's going on here?"

The general smiled as she picked up a headset and commanded, while replacing her hat, "Scramble Black Dog." Another two monitors sprang to life, showing an older Apache helicopter taking off from the desert. "I'm just trying to see how your little project plays with others."

"Don't shoot us down, General!" pleaded Hock.

"Target acquired," said the first lieutenant.

"Just crowding you a little, Hock," said the general, and the images on the drone's monitors tilted sideways, then leveled out, as a tiny dot in the distance became the Hock AFV. The drone buzzed within three feet of the car, which shook and spun off course for a few seconds before righting itself.

As the AFV got back on track, Hock nearly cried, "General, is this necessary?"

"Sure as heck fire is, Hock. What happens if you do a great job selling these things? The skies will be choked up with these darlings, and then you toss in a million drones delivering Amazon goodies and who knows what else." She turned to her man and said, "I guess that's the cue for who knows what else."

The Apache helicopter swooped into frame and caught up to the AFV Magic Carpet in a second. It matched the velocity but picked a flight line just thirty feet above the flying car. The blade wash caused the AFV to start a gyration that amplified with each revolution.

"OK, you can back it off," said General Starnes. The Apache pulled up, just as the drone came back around for one closer pass. As it pulled very near the AFV, the gyrations widened, and the flying car spun off its axis. There was no warning. All monitors from onboard cameras went black. The long-range cameras from the tower brought the fiery crash so close-up that Starnes thought she could feel the heat.

"What . . . what the hell did you do to my car? To my life?" cried Dr. Hock, sinking to the floor.

"First regulation recommendation. Keep a hundred feet of headroom minimum from other rotor traffic. Tomorrow we'll test our side clearance with other AFVs. We need to know the tolerance minimums, if these things need to fly in tight proximity, Hock," said Starnes

"General, do you understand the significance of this crash?" said Hock.

"You've got plenty of cars, Hock. You knew we would crash a few."

"That crash is different. We're on your test range. That video can never be released to the press or out in the wild. Without full explanation, that crash could scare off every investor we've ever talked to and sink our program from ever having a future. Please, General, can you guarantee confidentiality on that crash?"

Starnes sighed heavily. "I get your fix, Hock, and I'll squash this for now. We have a long way to go, so you should be more worried about what's coming."

42

VIRGINIA CITY, MONTANA

For the third night in a row, the lights shone from the windows of the County Commission offices upstairs in the old courthouse. Morris, Hitch, and Bullseye had widened their circle of those in the know about the government's plot to rip their homeland away. They now included about thirty-five community business leaders and big ranchers, from the mid- and southwestern parts of the state. A few extras had shown up, proving how difficult a secret this would be to keep. There were about as many sport coats as Carhartt jackets in the room

"Look, there's just no way around it," said one of the big ranchers, commanding everyone's attention. "We all agree that we will not let Washington sell our land to anyone," he continued, to an affirming chorus, "and we all agree that the best way—the only way, at this point, for us to legally keep our land is to secede and become our own country. We need to meet crazy with crazy."

He coaxed a little dip-spit into his coke bottle as he took his seat, then raised a hand to acknowledge the scattered applause. The details of secession were daunting—and unfathomable should the US flex a large military effort against its own citizenry. It would be over before it even started. A general in the Montana National Guard assured everyone that there would be no military intervention, at least while he was alive.

Next up was the celebrity partnership question. Could the lifelong Montanans trust the California-come-latelies to stand shoulder to shoulder with them? Morris rose from his chair, Bullseye noted, to begin his President of Montana campaign. "The only shot at secession is to join forces with every citizen of Montana—and that includes them celebrity folks."

Most heads nodded, but some had slowed to a very noncommittal wobble. Morris continued, "We need their money and influence to help build sympathy in the other states." Morris uncrossed his arms and added, palms open, "I know it will shock you to hear me say this, but them celebs ain't so hard to get along with, if you feed 'em right."

Laughter peppered the room—a welcome event in the face of such dire decisions. One of the big ranchers said, "At least they'll be good at putting up fences all around the state." There was more laughter, which this time sounded like consensus. A few longnecks clanked.

Bullseye leaned her chair back against the back wall near the corner and balanced the enthusiasm for secession with the reality of challenging the US government—which included the military. Morris asked the attendees to give Bullseye a hand for being the "mother of the revolution" and suggested they use her face on the poster.

Bullseye stood, with her back to the wall. "Whoa now, Morris. You all just pump the brakes on that 'mother' stuff." Laughter floated around the room. "I'm glad to give that idea to the people of this state, but I'm not your poster child. You all know that I'm more comfortable around a campfire stretching stories than fanning the flames of discontent. I'm behind you all the way, which literally means I won't be up front. Ever."

More laughs peppered the room as Bullseye sank into her seat and her smile faded away. Picking a fight with the US military was a losing proposition—worse than a battle with one mean bull, which her name never let her forget, she had lost once upon a time. While she listened to the Secession talk from her corner, Bullseye worked through details of the big-game stampede the VP had dangled in front of her. Her childhood taught her that if things got ugly, if someone had you by the throat, it was important to have an escape.

The cattle rustling thing feels more like a crime wave than an escape, thought Bullseye as she rolled through the pros and cons in her mind.

43

SULA, MONTANA

Any day in the woods was a good one for Secretary of the Interior Alan Stubblefield, but this day did not include his rifle or hunting . . . for animals at least.

Vice President Fowler had done his part to connect Stubblefield deep in the timber world, who, in turn, arranged a pardon of convicted timber poacher Hump Mankin with just a mention of a "secret commission, involving Montana and the current financial crisis." The rumors about the "Montana solution" were rampant in DC, and just a whisper brought tremendous latitude; now it was time to reap the reward for his intervention on behalf of Mankin.

He exited the rental SUV at the top of a hill near the end of the dirt road. A hazy trail of blue/gray smoke hung in the still air, pointing to a small cabin, surrounded by a rusty stockade of old logging vehicles and random machines, all frozen in place by time and neglect. He yelled, "Mr. Mankin—it's Alan Stubblefield. I'm coming in . . . OK?"

Two bright-blue Steller's jays traded sarcastic squawks, but that was it. Otherwise silence. The secretary took a few steps forward, cupped his hands, and yelled, "Hump, I said it's Alan Stubblefield. We've got business to—"

"I hear you. Come on in, Mr. Secretary," echoed Hump Mankin through the thick woods down from behind his cabin. "You're all right." He leaned on a shovel, while he squinted to see if anyone was with the secretary.

Stubblefield breathed easier once inside the cabin. He had not expected to find the beautiful woodworking projects that overwhelmed the room. An entire couch carved from a single log glowed with a hand-rubbed tung-oil finish and served as the centerpiece. Stubblefield made a quick guess that a hundred rings ran up the back of the couch, making the tree a century old.

"Can you guess how many? One thousand seven hundred and forty. That's how many rings are in that log. That's an old log, all right, and a beautiful piece of furniture. Everybody asks that. Pull up a log and have a seat," offered Hump Mankin. "Good to see you face-to-face, Mr. Secretary. I didn't expect a house call. I've met a few big shots during my timber lobby days, but never way out here."

Stubblefield selected the biggest and tallest chair in the room and mounted it. His legs dangled above the floor. "Hump, I just wanted to make sure you didn't have any repercussions after your last little tangle with the National Park guys. Those rangers can be very serious about their work, and the vice president himself told me about the trouble you'd been in."

"You ain't lying, Mr. Secretary," said Mankin after spitting in a cup. "I appreciate you intervenin' like you did. I don't know how my family could have made it if I was sitting in prison for the next ten to fifteen years." Hump pulled off his cap and scratched his head as if it helped him think. "What's happened to this country and free enterprise? I'm sure gonna watch my step."

"Well, Hump, I'm glad to hear that you're on the straight and narrow. And I'm glad that my efforts earlier this week, in some small way, helped you stay out of prison. It was a risk to put my name on the line with the BLM guys like that, but I know it was worth it to have them drop the charges. I know you'll do the same for me someday," added the secretary in one long breath, clarifying that there was an outstanding debt.

"Straight and narrow, yessir, Mr. Secretary," said Hump. "That is what you want to hear from me, right?"

"Sure thing, Hump. I hope that nothing can sway you from that old straight and narrow path. Not even, say fifty thousand dollars," Stubblefield said.

Hump kept scratching and glanced over at the secretary, slipped his hat back on, and said, "You know, Mr. Secretary, a man could take a step or two off that path for fifty thousand dollars."

"I guess that means he'd go down the river and through the woods for, say, seventy-five thousand?"

"And around the corner for an even one hundred thousand. You know I owe you one, Mr. Stubblefield, so just let me know . . . ," fished Hump, "who do I need to slice up for you?"

"*Through the woods* will be enough, Mr. Mankin. No one said anything about killing anyone. Here's what I'm thinking . . ."

44

VIRGINIA CITY, MONTANA

Morris Evans didn't see Actor Evan coming down the sidewalk before he swung open the heavy court house door. The wooden edge of the door just missed Evan's nose, but knocked his hat off and scattered the pile of papers he was holding across the plank sidewalk. Actor Evan scrambled. "It's OK, Morris, I've got this." He continued to scoop as fast as he could, without organizing.

After Morris Evans stooped to help, he noticed that the embarrassment on Actor Evan's face wasn't about walking into a door, as much as having dropped a large pile of pictures and newspaper articles about himself.

"You makin' a scrapbook or something?"

"I just received a press packet from my agent, and I was sifting through it—you know—looking at the old days in Hollywood."

Morris let it go. "Yeah, I know what you mean," and continued, "you got time for a quick gab? I've got something I've been meaning to kick around with you."

The ex-Hollywooder acted glad not to have to deflect any insults about the pictures and said, "Sure."

"Oh, boys!" shouted April, as she tiptoed along the wooden walkway outside the courthouse building. "Gentlemen, I might say that all the Evans and the Morrises are looking wonderful this morning."

The men looked at each other, trying to sort out that one.

"We was just headin' up to my office for a little chat. Would you care to join us, April?" invited Morris.

Morris tossed his hat into its regular spot on top of the wooden cactus cutout and slid into his seat behind his desk. April had talked the entire trip up the stairs, to the coffeepot, and a minute after they sat down. Eventually, she had to breathe, and Morris jumped in to transition the casual gathering into a more serious mode.

"I've called you both up here to discuss something very secret."

Evan tossed a quick glance at April and whispered, "We've been called?"

"Can I count on you both to keep this a complete secret?" He looked at April and said, "It's important that no one find out about this."

The committee had decided they needed to tell a bunch of the California transplants in short order, but not in the press. He was sure they could count on April to spread the word to most of them, but only if she thought it was a secret.

"Of course, Commissioner Morris, cross my heart," April offered with choreography. Evan nodded his consent.

"Let's drop the commissioner and just think of me as an average citizen," said Morris, maximizing his role in the room and in life. "We have become aware of a situation in Warshington, and we need your help."

Without knowing the cause, April leaned farther forward, as if already on board. "It sounds important, Comm . . . Morris. I'll do whatever I can to help. Um, do you mind if I take notes? I just want to jot down some thoughts as we move forward, so if I can just borrow some paper . . ."

Morris handed over a notepad and a pen from his desk, and April scribbled:

Lapel ribbon color . . .

Any situation or cause worth its salt required a fabulous color-coordinated ribbon and banner accoutrements, in order to make a proper statement.

"April, did you hear what I just said? The government—*our* government—of the blessed United States will seize our state and take it away from us, to sell to some foreigners. Doesn't that bother you?" questioned Morris.

"Why Morris, of course it does. I'm taken aback, and my silence is only because I'm pondering the gravity of the situation," countered April.

More notes:

Maybe we don't need a color for the ribbons—maybe it should be bolder— a metallic texture . . . like rusty steel or gold? Maybe copper . . .

45

YUMA PROVING GROUND, ARIZONA

The discussion levels elevated to a bona fide argument. Hock's Magic Carpet prototype lay in a crumpled pile of charred metal spars and fan blades, after the prior day's crash. General Starnes seemed to enjoy the bickering and said that they didn't mind crashing a few vehicles in the name of safety.

"You destroyed my freakin' car," was all Wendell could say aloud to anyone in uniform. The conversation had taken off in the morning right where it had landed the evening prior, with liability talk, the blame game, and questions about whether the crash had incinerated the entire program. The metal hangar caused the yelling to echo, forming a mash of words that bounced off the walls into a din of indistinguishable jibber-jabber.

After two hours of fighting, Dr. Hock slid outside of the hangar to breathe some fresh air. General Starnes had beaten him outside and just finished a call.

"It's nice and quiet out here, Hock. I hope you didn't come out here to yell."

"My guess is, General, that you've made up your mind about any changes going forward, and we may as well just get on with our plan if we hope to get this thing certified, right?" said Leroy Hock, almost waving a white flag.

"Right on both counts, Hock. Listen. I'm sorry about the crash, but that happens in these situations. You've crashed cars before; I've seen the videos. Let's get over it and work on that NORM computer system to see if we can sharpen the air traffic collision avoidance part of your deal. Everybody wins. You do this my way, and you won't have a bigger fan in front of Congress when you're looking for special privileges for landing zones, charging depots, whatever. I want to get this thing moving and create some jobs to dig our country out of this mess."

"OK, General. I'll load it up. You'll get all the data from both nav systems, and you can see every little wiggle and bobble this thing makes. I just hope the data will stay confidential when we pass."

Starnes snuck a small flask out of her jacket and unscrewed the cap. She proposed a toast to seal their truce over the muffled yelling from inside the building.

46

WASHINGTON, DC, TO LANGLEY, VA

Marine One, carrying the president and Graham Blair, lifted off the south lawn of the White House. The short helicopter ride off of the White House grounds to CIA Headquarters at Langley offered the president an astonishing view of the pulsing horde of protesters surrounding his home. The propeller noise outside plus cabin soundproofing erased the angry chants, drumbeats, and whistles that haunted him inside sections of the White House and nearly repainted the silent, arm-waving scene below as a peaceful group of well-wishers.

Langley was even more secure as a meeting site than the White House for the room full of dark suits who represented the alphabet agencies that performed clandestine duties for the United States government. The CIA had extensive monitoring capabilities for events worldwide and tragic domestic events filled the screens during this meeting deep underground.

President Crowley did not know everyone assembled in the large room but hoped that someone in this dour group met his qualification to have back-channel connections to groups interested in securing a homeland. There were many disenfranchised people groups—the tricky part was finding the right one with access to enough money, but no interest in obliterating the United States. Casting a wide net among his agency heads had been straightforward.

"This may seem like a new tactic, but the US has bought and sold large areas for military bases around the world. I don't feel this is much different," said Crowley.

"Beg your president's pardon, but this seems very, very different," said the head of the CIA. Others indicated agreement as the director continued, "But I think we can find the right folks to talk with. For years, we've supplied aid and weapons to many groups around the globe, hoping they would recapture their country from the bad guys. It didn't always work out. We'll start with those folks, and it's a long list. We know who's got the need."

"But they also must have the money," reminded VP Fowler. "An ideal buyer for Montana would be an existing country or people group with ample resources, like gold or oil; likewise, they must also have formidable conflict at home, so it motivates them to look for peace."

"And maybe the right buyer will have sympathetic friends in other nations who will help fund the purchase," said Crowley.

After a few "what ifs," one of the ranking members in the meeting tapped her pen and interrupted with a somber comment, "You are kidding, right? I've known most of you a long time, and I know we go through drills from time to time, so this is a joke, *right*? Dan, you're not serious, are you? This whole thing that we pursue selling a part of our own country?"

The room chilled. He had the benefit of time to sort out the crazy from the potential of this scenario, but still, he couldn't blame his old friend and trusted security advisor Alexandra Woods for calling him on it.

"Allie, I wish it were a joke," started Crowley. "I'll tell you what—name a city. Any city, maybe a hundred thousand population or more."

Alexandra said, "Grand Rapids?"

"You grew up there, right?" guessed Crowley, remembering the interview with Allie before her agency appointment. "How many people live there?"

"About a quarter million."

"The economic situation, as we sit here, has caused over two thousand deaths from rioting—that's from violence during protests and looting deaths in just the last few months. Add the complications of real starvation from no work and it's conceivable that within a few short years, we could see enough Americans die to equal a city the size of Grand Rapids. We are powerless to stop the violence if we don't fix these problems. If just moving a state's worth of people will save the lives of hundreds of thousands, not to mention save our way of life, I'm willing to try it. To be honest, I don't know what else to do," added the president.

A few sighs later, the president brought the committee up to speed on the discussions with Azwar's Kurdish tribe, highlighting the tribe's inability to fund a venture of this size and their reluctance to leave a homeland of religious significance. He also recounted the call with Israel.

"China?" said Alexandra. They had become the richest country in the world, and the yuan had become the top global reserve currency. Years of securing acquisitions in the US had positioned them as a partner of sorts with America. The committee discussion equated a sale to China as a step toward their world domination and surrender for the United States. China was out.

"OK, we'll work behind the scenes for a few months. This still has to remain quiet—which will be tough as we look for a buyer." Crowley wiped his brow. "By the way, how many of you heard about this concept before you walked in today?" Every hand in the room lifted. The president dropped his head in his hands.

VIRGINIA CITY, MONTANA

Silence and *people* do not mix in April Lear's book of etiquette. When two or more gathered, conversation should fill every crevice, just as a sweet, chilled *panna cotta*, adorned with a blushing ripe strawberry, should punctuate a fine meal. They had endured hours of agonizing discussion with elongated periods of torturous silence, causing her to twitch and shift regularly.

The core group of Secessionists, minus Bullseye, had gathered in the commissioner's office in the courthouse building, filling all six seats. When asked if anyone had ever confronted the government, Evan mentioned that he had taken on the Malibu Zoning Commission over a permit for a kid's tree house, which, April pointed out, he had slept in after wife number two tossed him out. "Is there legal precedent for this?" Evan asked, deflecting attention from his past.

Morris Evans said, "There is. Over twenty groups have tried to secede from our country since the Civil War, even though the Supreme Court ruled about a hundred fifty years ago that it wasn't legal to secede. Now, that doesn't mean we shouldn't try. Our situation is different. The Court said that 'unilateral secession' was unconstitutional, but also commented that 'revolution or consent of the states *could* lead to a successful secession.'"

"So, that means, what?" Hitch and April asked, together.

"That means the Supreme Court left the door open for a legitimate secession with a vote of the state's people. Let's face it; we joined the Union by ratifying the Constitution at a convention. We should be able to '*un*-ratify.'"

"But didn't the others try?" asked April.

"April, there hasn't been a state get behind a legitimate movement yet, so those efforts don't compare to ours. Parts of California, Michigan's Upper Peninsula, Long Island, and others have tried to secede—some with good reasons but never good enough to drive a whole state behind the cause."

"There's always a secession movement underway in Texas, at least on bumper stickers," added Actor Evan Morris.

"And then there are the Conch Republic crackpots in the Keys, the Pot Republic in Oregon before it was legal everywhere, and a cluster of other mostly single-issue folks. Those rebellions never worked because they were just a group of fringe citizens barking at the government. In our case, the United States is the aggressor, so the sympathies of the court *and* the people should be with us."

Evan picked up the cause and said, "So the key is to get all our legal ducks in a row, sign up as many Montanans as possible, including the governor and current representatives, draw up a constitution and other key documents of secession—and try to do it all out of the media's eye? That's a tall order."

"It sure is," affirmed the commissioner. "And it will take money. We need to get local lawyers, convert our US currency to gold, and a whole lot more, I imagine."

He had broadcast the earlier order of events to the entire room. Commissioner Morris Evans turned to Evan Morris and changed his voice to an uncharacteristic softer tone. "And we need someone with your influence to put a face on the PR campaign when we tell the world what's going on. Someone the entire United States will rally behind with Montana as the underdog. Can you do that, Evan? Will you do it for our new Montana homeland . . . *your* homeland? Will you be the face of the Secession movement to the rest of the world?"

48

WASHINGTON, DC/MADISON COUNTY, MONTANA BY PHONE

"Five hundred a head seems a little rich," bargained Interior Secretary Alan Stubblefield. There was a pause on Bullseye's end of the phone. Stubblefield had told Fowler he was worried since she had not called in the days since their proposal to put together a wild-game stampede to their new hunting compound. They figured she'd be all over them wanting details and deposits.

The longer she remained silent, the more Stubblefield fidgeted. After allowing adequate squirm time, Bullseye said, "I can stampede all the prize game you want, to Idaho or anywhere else. I know the land up here, I can find the guys who won't mind handling this business, and I have the gear. Alan, your huntin' buddies will pay ten thousand dollars or more for a shot at a huge elk. You'll have more than you can handle for the rest of your life, and you know it."

"I don't know, Bullseye." Alan knew it. Elk can live on about a half acre each, or about half as much as a dairy cow. If the food supply was ample and there were enough watering holes, the herd would breed and grow like crazy. Stubblefield had his eye on about nine thousand acres, so he could handle upwards of fifteen thousand deer and elk.

If Bullseye was as good as she promised and her boys could wrangle at least forty-five hundred head of elk and white tail down to their new reserve, it would cost him a little over two million, along with another two mil for the lodge. He could easily turn that into twenty or thirty million and still have a lifetime of uninterrupted trophy hunting. With some luck, he could double that amount.

Stubblefield looked down at the list he had assembled of partners willing to fund their project. The consortium included well-connected lobbyists, two senators, several very wealthy corporate higher-ups, and a pro-football-team owner. They were all avid hunters and would recruit more buddies for a lifetime of trophy gathering. He rechecked each name on the list, confirming that not one of them had balked at a "buy-in of a half million" to cover the upfront costs.

"You don't have to tell me right now, Alan. But don't doubt that people up here are already talking about the government selling the state, and it won't be long before they're panties are on fire. They didn't hear it from me; I promise you that. So, call me back in a year, and we'll see where the price is then," twisted Bullseye.

"OK, Bullseye, I get your point," said Alan, knowing Montana would vanish from the map in a year or two.

"You just get the deposit ready and drop it in the same account you normally send the payment for your fishing trips. Nothing to worry about, Alan. This will run like snot on glass."

Bullseye's confidence comforted Stubblefield, but he hadn't risen to a cabinet-level position by trusting someone on word alone. Before the call ended, he wrestled control back from Bullseye. "Listen, we're going to need to test this concept, and we mean soon, before the snow flies, so we can learn what equipment would be best to get a few hundred large animals running the same direction through the forest. The test will have to involve a couple dozen ATVs or bikers and last a few days so we can watch the animals' behavior in a guarded perimeter overnight."

Bullseye had given some pushback about tossing together a test in a couple of weeks but quieted down once Stubblefield agreed he would pony up a fat fee for the task and a deposit for the spring drive.

49

NEZ PERCE RIVER, MONTANA

Hump's crew required little prep time to get ready for a fall and winter-long session of stealing old-growth trees from public land. Redge's banged-up flatbed remained stocked with saws, chains, wire rope/slings, chokers, gas cans, chain oil, climbing gear, pulleys, cant hooks, and axes all year long.

Provisions and camping gear for the harsh, snowy Montana winter were jammed on Hump's truck. They would have to stay mobile with a small footprint, in case anyone was snooping around.

Four days after Hump Mankin's hardwood summit with Secretary Stubblefield, the crew rolled up Highway 473, high into the Bitterroot National Forest, then rumbled down old logging roads near the Nez Perce River and settled in their base camp. It had been a snap to recruit the team, once Hump revealed the details from the meeting with Stubblefield: "He'll pay two million if we can stage seven thousand logs in the Nez Perce River bed, so the spring melt can carry them over into Idaho, and more if we add to that number. We just cut 'em into twenty-foot lengths and float 'em, then pull them out to dry down in Idaho. Easy-treesy, boys." Once Hump added the details about the "damn gubment" selling their state out from under them, what little hesitation there was disappeared.

The trucks ended up all catawampus along a hillside so steep that the logging gear almost unloaded itself. Redge pitched his tent first and had a fire blazing in the crisp night air by the time all four one-man tents circled the pit.

The men ate their dinner in silence. Redge watched the glow of the fire dance on the branches of the massive ponderosa pines all around them. Shadows played on the next layer of the branches above those and added an ominous dimension. "You think anyone can see us down here, Hump?"

"Naw. We're tucked in deep. Chances are if anyone found us down here, they're not supposed to be here either. At night we're just campers. We'll keep our eyes open from the trees during the day to see anything coming."

The others nodded. Redge slurped the last remnant from a can of Dinty Moore Beef Stew that he had warmed up over the fire. "Sounds good, Hump. That's it for me, boys. I'm going to pay the water bill and head to my tent. There's a lot of climbing ahead of us tomorrow." Redge staggered off into the night to pee into the Nez Perce, before tucking himself in.

50

VIRGINIA CITY, MONTANA

The courthouse lights spilled into the evening once again. Virginia City had not seen this much nighttime activity since the '60s—the 1860s, during the town's gold rush crush. Around that time, the Vigilantes of Montana, one of the most controversial organizations in the territory's history, had formed to bring justice to the area by hanging bandits they referred to as "road agents." Folks came from miles around to hear the pleading of the robbers, who were set free after telling a particularly emotional tale or hanged right on the spot.

The vigilante spirit was alive during the hastily organized meeting to discuss the rumors. The room was at capacity, with late arrivals squeezing around the perimeter, filling the windowsills. Folks had driven from surrounding counties, with a few flying down from Missoula and Great Falls, including a rumored visitor from the governor's office. Morris warned that the core crew should exercise caution since there were government workers in Montana. *Federal* government workers, who's bosses were in Washington. This apprehension was worth addressing right up front.

The crowd rumbled as Bullseye arrived late, slipping in the back of the room, just as Hitch Jenkins weaved his way up to the front. "Looks like a good crowd," fumbled Hitch Jenkins, with an attempt to kick off the program. "Thanks for making the drive folks. This is a big deal, and I'm glad you came out. I say 'me,' but I mean a bunch of me's on the core committee that helped get this thing going . . ."

The core group had mapped out who would say what, and Hitch's only role was to say "Hello" and "Here's Patriot and Madison County Commissioner Morris Evans." The roar of the chatter dulled by the time he finished his first two words, and the instant hush seemed to spook Hitch. Actor Evan spotted Hitch's sweat-beaded forehead and red-splotched neck. He turned side to side to see if anyone else sniffed out Hitch's predicament.

Hitch continued, "We think, well, we hope some . . . er, most . . . well, all . . ."

Everyone stared at Hitch as he stammered and exchanged glances with other faces around the room. Evan Morris sat up taller and moved his lips, prompting, hoping to pull Hitch along to the end of his sentence.

Evan had seen panic before, often from studio execs at award shows. Hitch had full-on stage fright and was shutting down in front of this crowd. The Malibu Movie Star–turned Montanan rose out of his seat a little higher, hoping to catch Hitch's focus and help him exhale, but his awkwardness was spreading to the crowd. They shifted in their seats.

Five more uneasy seconds passed before Evan grabbed Hitch's eye by pointing to his mouth with an exaggerated *Introduce Morris*. Hitch nodded, a blank slate, and said the first thing that popped in his mind, "You all know Actor Evan Morris, don't you? Well, here he is!"

There were a few excited gasps and cheers, along with applause, coming from the women in attendance. His presence was a novelty to those folks who lived a county away and didn't realize that Actor Evan was available for gawping at the café most any day it was open.

Evan jumped up front and noticed a grumpy Morris Evans, the unofficial leader of the movement and planned next speaker, with arms folded in disgust at being passed over by Hitch.

Actor Evan loved a crowd, but realized he was working without a net. That very afternoon, the guys had discussed the liabilities of telling the wrong folks too soon. He decided to be safe and throw to Morris, but not before his dramatic take on the gravity of the evening's events.

"Hitch, you didn't have to go on so . . . ," started Evan, to a titter of giggles, all in the female register. "Before I turn this meeting over to Madison County Commissioner Morris Evans—I know, coincidental with our names—I just wanted to make something clear. The events that stand before us tonight will mark a turning point in history . . . in *our* history."

To add emphasis, Evan leaned forward and gripped the worn wooden lectern with both hands. He scanned the crowd to make sure they were tuned in. They were with him, riveted after just one dramatic gesture.

Morris Evans smiled, having received the nod from Actor Evan.

"And I say *our* history because we are Montanans. I am now a Montanan." Actor Evan built with the intensity of a Southern Church of Christ preacher. "I may be new to the state, but I'm *all in*. I left everything behind in California to come here and carve out a new life—just as many of you and your ancestors did"—heads nodded—"and tonight just may go down in history as the night we leave behind petty arguments between *big-*

city Montanans and *rancher Montanans*. We can no longer afford to be separate. We *must* stand together as proud caretakers of our heritage and our state."

Actor Evan barely finished the sentence before April jumped to her feet with a torrent of rapid little claps, made as if her hands were hinged at the base of her palms. A few other women stood to get a better look at Evan Morris in person. Some husbands rose, responding to elbows thrown from their wives.

After savoring the moment, Actor Evan moved on to the business at hand. "Please, take your seats. Thanks—I didn't mean to get so wound up. I know you've all heard rumors of impending events or you wouldn't have invested the time to be here. I want you to hear the course of action that we are planning, so let's welcome Madison County Commissioner Morris Evans."

The commissioner strode up to the lectern to a wave of applause, still directed toward Actor Evan, who waded through the crowd of well-wishers and back-patters on the way to a fifth-row seat, saved for him by the beckoning April Lear. Actor Evan turned back toward the front and raised a hand to deflect attention over to Morris, beseeching his new fan base, "Thank you again. Now let's hear the details. Commissioner Evans?"

"What you've heard is true. The government of the United States of America is plotting to take our land away and sell it to a foreign concern. They are planning this to answer the insane debt problem that has been festering in Warshington for decades," delivered Morris, in a calm but stern cadence, with emphasis on *Warsh*. He allowed a beat between sentences, for impact.

"This has been in the works for more than a year and, as implausible as it sounds, they plan to evict all of us within eighteen months . . . that's right, less than eighteen months," he repeated, to address the gasps in the crowd, "and sell our land to a foreign group as soon as the screen door hits us on the way out."

Renee Riggins, sitting in the second row, rose to her feet and yelled, "That's outrageous!" then, spun around to face the fifth row and pleaded to Actor Evan, "What can we do about it, Evan?"

Evan looked a little mystified why the question came back to him. Not wanting to disappoint his public, he stood and responded, "Well, we have a plan in place. Morris will tell you more about it," and flashed a smile that made Renee glow with her decision to direct her query to him.

Up front, Morris Evans wrestled back control by tapping the podium with the palm of his hand mildly and said, "Fellow Montanans, before the US comes to take our land away, they need to know it's ours for keeps. We've paid for it. Our families have bled over it. And now to hold onto it, they've given us no choice but to claim Montana as our own country."

Morris paused again for dramatic impact as the words settled on the stern, weather-worn faces of those in the room.

"You mean, actually secede?" said someone way in the back, jumping his pause. A few people were already nodding.

"I proclaim that Montana secede from the other United States of America," Morris said, striking his hand, loudly this time, on the podium. "There, it's official. Secession is the only way we can see to hang onto our homeland. I will say, now that we all know what we're talking about, we need to make sure we know who we're talking to. The federal government has become our adversary, but some of you work for them. Soon, you'll have to pick sides. For now, we ask that you remember you are here because you are first a Montanan." He struck a more sympathetic tone and added, "One way or the other, you will lose your land or your job, so we ask that you keep this quiet to anyone outside the state until we declare, and that will mean keeping it from your boss if you're a federal employee."

Looks of mistrust rolled through the audience. There were federal employees all over Montana and some in the room that evening, including post office employees, BLM and forestry people, homeland security and military, transportation regulation officials, and more. A couple had even worn their National Guard uniforms that very night and tried to sink in their seats, covering the patches on their uniforms. They affirmed their loyalty to Montana loud enough for those a few rows away to hear, and all eyes refocused on the podium.

"But how can this even happen? How could one state take on the entire US government?" questioned Howie Costello, a man Morris saw get nervous even at county weed-control meetings.

Hitch snuck back toward the front, having mined some confidence from the performances by Evan and Morris. "Without giving too much away, I can tell you that preparations are underway. This was Bullseye Magee's idea. Bullseye, say something."

Bullseye rose with a slight blush from her back-corner seat. "Well, I'm not one for public speaking. I'd rather be doing anything than standing here right now, but when I heard about this travesty, it just seemed fair to me we should get to keep what was ours. And keeping our homes meant that we had to secede. That's how America started right? Look up *despotism*. The Declaration of Independence uses that word and says when your government treats you crazy bad, it's your *duty* to abolish it. What could be more despotistical—if that's the right way to say that—than the government stealing our entire state? It's just that simple. My friends have put legs on this thing and that's why they're talking with you all tonight. We need your help, and now I'm drifting back to my corner where I feel more comfortable, so someone else can talk." She blushed even brighter as she scooted to her seat.

"It won't be easy, but we're not talking about a bunch of farmers grabbing rakes and rifles to fight our way out of the country," interjected Actor Evan. "It must be more strategic." Every female nodded.

Morris stepped in. "So, here's the plan. We will win on the battlefield of public opinion. The idea is to appeal to the citizens of the United States—by making sure they realize this could happen to their state next—and enlist their help in letting us secede. We think we can create such a public outcry that the government will have no choice but to let us go or stop talking about selling Montana."

Hitch added, "And we don't believe the public will stand for any military intervention against its own citizens. We aren't telling them we don't love the US. We're just reminding them that the US came to grab something that's not theirs to begin with."

"That's what started the Boston Tea Party!" shouted someone from the far-right side, over by the snack table, to a chorus of "hell yeahs" and "you betchas." Evan Morris thought about jumping in over the inaccuracy of the statement but decided against it. The sentiment was correct.

"Remember Kent State?" added Morris Evans. The blank facial expressions betrayed most had lost the lessons from that day on a little knoll in the middle of a college campus in Ohio during the Vietnam era. "Soldiers in *our* National Guard opened fire on *our* own citizens and killed four—just for protesting a war that most found unjust. That act of aggression transformed our society. The military became the adversary, fomented by cover pictures on *Life* magazine, and the chasm between the establishment and citizens cracked open. That day changed America."

Evan Morris felt anchored. He felt involved with the movement. "Let's look at what's happening in the rest of the country. People are being killed in riots because of the terrible condition our government has gotten us in. We can manage our affairs better than they can, and I think *that* alone is enough reason to secede." Cheers erupted from the crowd as Evan snapped his head in a series of "yeahs" while heading back to his seat.

After more inquiries and lots of buzzing side conversations, Morris stood up and called the first part of the question with the assembly: "OK, we realize you don't know all the details—and we don't either, but you all know what we're discussing now. Before we go any further, we need to know who thinks this is crazy and wants no part." A nervous tension permeated the room. "We know you're scared, but based on what you know so far, if this isn't for you, there's the door. It would be best if you left now, and all we ask is that you don't tell anyone."

Whispers rippled. Evan assumed no one would dare leave in front of their neighbors, even if they could not stand with the cause. There was a quiet scuffle in the fourth row when Blake Nelson grabbed his coat, stood up, and scooted out from the sixth chair in the section. Every eye locked on him.

"OK, Blake, we understand," said Morris.

"Oh, I'm with you boys, Morris. Go ahead and have your battle. I'll be there. I'm not about to give up my land to the government or anyone. No, sir, they'll have to shoot me and my wife to get me off my place. But I promised Betty I wouldn't miss the last episode of *Amazing Race*. We been watching that show for decades and what with the big finale tonight, Betty says we have to watch it live, because her sister is always tweeting spoilers. I doubt you'll figure it all out at this gathering, so you just let me know where to meet up next. I'll be ready."

A nervous laugh rolled across the crowd, but no one else moved.

"Sounds like most everyone is on board or has their DVRs set. Let's take a few last questions; then we'll map out the next steps," said Morris.

From just off the center aisle, a hand shot up. "I'm Bernie VanZee from up near Bozeman, and it's nice to meet you fellas," he said, then turned toward Evan Morris and added, "My wife says you're a great actor," which earned him an elbow to the thigh. He turned back to the front and asked Morris Evans, "So how do we go about getting the whole country to feel sorry for a bunch of ranchers way up here in Montana? They can barely find us on Google Maps."

"Great question, Bernie, and you're not far off," answered Morris. "We intend to put a warm, friendly face on Montana. A face that everyone is familiar with and couldn't imagine leaving out in the cold or pulling the land out from under. We plan to start a 'Montana's Our home' campaign and have one spokesman familiar to everyone introduce the entire world to our situation."

Evan sat a little taller in his chair and felt his face warm as Morris continued, "And you're wondering who could fit the bill and carry that immense responsibility, aren't you?" Heads turned, many with puzzled expressions. "I'm glad to introduce you to the new face of Montana: Evan Morris."

Applause erupted across the room from more than just the women. The plan made sense. As Evan rose to acknowledge the burden being placed on him, those in the room showed they could imagine citizens reacting in the other states. How *could* they take this man's home away?

Evan tipped his hat and then rested it back a little farther on his head—so the light would hit him just right. Shadows could not obscure the new face of the Great Nation of Montana. Evan was home. It was clear that he mattered in Montana and was being embraced by a large cross section of citizens for more than his film career. His new life was dawning.

As the meeting disbanded, most of the women squeezed their way toward Evan Morris—letting him know they were ready to stand by his side.

Others mingled, kicked around questions, raised doubts, put fears to bed, and experienced an entire gamut of emotions. Evan noticed Bullseye Magee slide around the perimeter of the room. He caught her eye and smiled over the heads of several fans waiting for pictures. She stopped and looked at Evan, who still looked at her, and the double take helped her warm smile erupt into a full-on, schoolgirl blush.

51

VIRGINIA CITY, MONTANA

Bullseye watched the reaction to her secession idea from the edges of the courthouse, believing it would fail. While the rest of the state figured that out, she would make millions from the boys in Washington by stealing a herd of prize game in her stampede scam, as the state was torn apart.

She wanted to believe Evan could get it together and be the leader they were setting him up to be. Oh, sweet Evan and the way he looked in front of that crowd . . . . And she hoped her friends could pull off secession and peaceably separate from one of the most powerful countries in the world. She paused and replayed that sentence again . . . . *Separate from one of the most powerful countries in the world . . .*

Bullseye shook her head, causing her ponytail to loosen up. She combed through her hair with her fingers, drew it tight and wound the band on a few times while she affirmed in a whisper, "This is crazy. For-real crazy." Remembering the lessons from her childhood, she thought about creating an escape route in her mind. *You always need an escape,* she told herself, and that's when her idea hit:

I own the Lame Horse Creek mine shaft in Idaho that points toward Montana. With a little more digging, I could have a secret pathway out of Montana — or even back into Montana, should someone want to escape — or smuggle contraband back and forth between there and the good ole US of A! And I could set up a tollbooth of sorts to charge these folks a ton of money or gold or whatever . . .

While the others gathered their thoughts on recruiting celebrities, Bullseye made a list of excavating gear to expand her mine shaft into an escape tunnel.

Conflicting ideas raced through her mind. A secret tunnel under the border could be her moneymaker. All she had to do was dig. People would pay tons to use this smugglers' route. It was dangerous. She would have to play with some rough individuals—but Bullseye had tangled with bad dudes most of her life. When she was ten years old, she couldn't fight back. As a woman, she was equipped and ready to take on anything. She could always shut down the whole stupid idea if things got too dangerous.

Bullseye was itching to get started as the meeting broke up, and was two steps toward the door during the final admonition about secrecy.

52

DETROIT, MICHIGAN

Two thousand five hundred thirteen citizens, some of them law enforcement and National Guard, had died in clashes that had flared up in the summer's heat. That number was about to rise precipitously.

It started small, when a group of ten looters tried a smash-and-grab at an upscale electronics store on Woodward Avenue in downtown Detroit while a crowd was still milling about in the aftermath of a protest rally about the economy. Police, on-site for the rally, responded instantly, trapping several of the looters inside the store. Shots were fired from both sides, sending the crowd into a panicked scatter. The looters set the store on fire as a diversion, which quickly raged out of control, engulfing the entire block of ancient three- to five-story brick buildings. Flames licked the window frames of every floor, shattering glass and quickly melting the rooftops, sending plumes of black smoke skyward, visible for miles around.

Sirens wailed from police and fire units responding to the fires and reports of more looters taking advantage of the chaos. Gang generals sent their lieutenants into adjoining blocks to bust into stores and reap the harvest while the police were occupied on Woodward. These blocks were set on fire as well, as the looters escaped, to create more hysteria. Within minutes, rival gangs appeared, wanting to share in the bounty, and the confusion.

Many of the innocent protesters, surrounded by burning structures, had scurried to parking garages and other nooks and crannies to hide from the random shooting between the gangs. An abandoned building across the street from the Shinola Hotel on Grand River Avenue collapsed, most likely because of the rush of people seeking shelter on the rickety scaffolding that supported the front wall of bricks on the six-story structure. The block-long waterfall of bricks killed more than a hundred and buried many others, while the domino effect of the falling wall crashing into nearby burned-out structures pushed them over in different directions, crushing many more victims who were trying to escape. Sniper-style fire from other abandoned buildings executed eleven firefighters during rescue attempts.

Within two hours, the governor ordered the National Guard to intervene, which arrived quickly and erected a thirty-block perimeter to contain the "war zone," as one commander called it. They created limited exit paths, which citizens could crawl through, be photographed and searched, then sent on for medical treatment as needed. An intense gun battle followed between armed citizens, various gangs, police, and the National Guard. When the smoke cleared and the bricks were removed from collapsed structures to rescue the injured, more than thirty blocks of downtown Detroit had been destroyed, with six hundred fatalities and hundreds wounded, filling local hospitals and morgues.

The nation mourned and all eyes turned to Washington, DC, for answers.

53

WASHINGTON, DC

"Take your seats," said President Crowley as he strode into the Situation Room, catching the tail end of a discussion between two attendees about their kids' soccer games the previous day. This curious contrast between the normal course of life in the White House and the crisis outside echoed around the country. A majority of people still maintained normal life—going to work or school, avoiding pockets of tension, but the tension varied house to house, not area to area. Unemployment skyrocketed and most feared there was no bottom in sight with the Detroit Massacre, as the press dubbed the catastrophe, being the first in a series to come. Three thousand one hundred thirteen citizens was the new score after the debacle in Detroit.

Monitors in the Situation Room carried images of the Detroit Massacre, intercut with tearful memories of those departed and curses for gang members, the military, police, and politicians, with the president at the top of the list.

The president had reunited a small contingency of key committee heads for the fourth time in the five months since the Camp David meeting. "I'd like everyone to welcome Ken Seger to our midst. You know his story, and he's been briefed on the Montana concept and sworn to secrecy. Welcome to the fire, Ken. How has your life changed so far?"

Ken squirmed from his corner seat and said, "Thank you for allowing me to join you, Mr. President." He turned to the rest of the group gathered and said, "I'm still absorbing the magnitude of this challenge and the lunacy of the Montana thing, but so far, I don't have a better idea and I promised the president I won't just sit here and complain without adding my own ideas. One important update for you all: I now have four-point-six million friends on BuzzCutt, so that's cool. I've read a lot of stupid ideas so far, but nothing I can report as helpful." A few smiles popped up.

"Good for you, Ken. I hope you keep digging through their thoughts and I know you will represent them well when you're more caught up. Moving on . . ." Each meeting had brought discussion but little firm progress to the nation's problems. As a result, this meeting grew very intense.

Crowley leaned on the back of his leather chair and picked up a file to give a quick look through, then peered at Fowler and Stubblefield. "Looks like you two have taken trips to Montana this month. Got anything to report?"

Secretary Stubblefield was the first to speak. "Mr. President, I'm very excited to report that the transition committee has made great progress toward the resettlement plan for the citizens of Montana." Several surprised expressions crossed the faces of those flanking the secretary, some of whom were members of that committee.

"Can you tell us what that progress looks like, Alan?"

Shifting forward in his seat, Stubblefield began, "Mr. President, we've established a legal committee with some of the top minds from Justice and have coordinated future meetings with the judge advocate general, so the legal side of the military will be ready to jump in, should things get rough."

"And which of those meetings did you hold up in Montana?" pushed the president.

Stubblefield sank back in his chair a bit, dropping his swagger for the moment. "Well, sir, we held most of those meetings here in DC. I took a site survey to Idaho and Montana to help understand the lay of the land and get in touch with some of the people firsthand. I felt it was important to get to see those people in their homeland, so I can better understand them."

The president looked from face-to-face, amidst tightening silence. Fowler and Stubblefield glared at each other.

"Ladies and gentlemen—that's what I'm talking about," said President Crowley, proudly. "Thank you, Alan, for hitting the nail on the head." Turning with a nod, he rose from his lean on the chair and paced around the room. "This transition will not be easy. We are pulling the rug out from under our own citizens. To do it peacefully, we'll need their cooperation, not a fight. Thanks, Mr. Secretary, for striking the right chord with them—keep it up."

Fowler and Stubblefield gawked at each other and smirked. Over the next hour, the president pried reports from the various committees and assigned more tasks. Progress fell well short of the president's liking, and voices crescendoed at multiple points, some still arguing whether the entire concept was legal or ethical. Crowley was long past those decisions and tried to remain encouraging, but the net result was frustration with the lack of movement for the impending catastrophe staring them down.

As the meeting adjourned, the VP crossed the room to find Stubblefield and whispered, "It appears that we were just handed a free pass to visit Montana anytime we'd like. Set up the next trip."

The president barricaded the doorway of the Situation Room after Chief of Staff Blair handed off some bad news. "Ladies and gentlemen,

Blair has alerted me to a new situation in Denver, where a protest has involved gunfire and more casualties."

Blair switched the large screens in the Sit Room to the imagery from various news organizations covering what appeared to be a mass shooting. "Four white gunmen in black coats with signs on their backs proclaiming 'No future for us, no future for you' shot up the Sixteenth Street Mall in downtown Denver just a few minutes ago, in a grizzly, premeditated attack on a protest rally." Police had killed all four perpetrators, but not before they had slaughtered over twenty innocent protesters and bystanders. One victim was a baby, still sitting upright in her stroller.

Everyone stiffened, watching the images on the screens, barely breathing. The murdered baby in her stroller produced gasps across the room. Ken Seger vomited into a beautiful antique vase in the corner.

"I've heard that quote just recently. Where did that quote come from?" asked the president.

Seger wretched again, then sheepishly said, "Sir, I can explain that. Those are the words that I screamed, or close to them, when I jumped the fence to the White House the day we met. Several people videoed my leap, and the scream has been picked up by radicals here and there as a rallying cry. I hate it and don't really know what it means, sir. And now, this?" He started sobbing as he heaved into the vase again.

"So, fix it. I don't know what that means either, Ken, but see if you can talk it down or diffuse it somehow, since those are your words." The room settled during a long pause, with all eyes focused on the sobbing college kid. "Ken, let me explain how these meetings work. You're jumping in at a high level here and seeing how powerful words and actions are, not to mention how fragile and crazy our world is right now. I don't have to say much more. When I say 'fix it,' I assume you'll figure out all the ways to take the sting out of that slogan, and I mean soon. I'm going to move on, confident that you will do your job to help our country restore hope, which is the thing that's really needed here. I don't want to spend any more time on this now or in the future, hear me?"

Ken swallowed and wiped a remnant of his nervousness off the corner of his mouth. "Yessir."

Turning to the entire group, Crowley said, "If this doesn't drive home . . . this crisis won't pass, and the country will not heal itself. If you won't help me solve this, I will find someone who will," then spun on his heels and rushed back upstairs to the Oval Office.

54

SOUTHWEST MONTANA

Bullseye careened through the Big Hole Valley and across the southwest corner of Montana to her tourist trap of a ranch, Lame Horse Creek, just across the Idaho border. The entire jaunt took just under four hours, depending on the number of tractors and horse trailers she got behind on 287 and 41, and "rush hour" in the little towns of Twin Bridges and Wisdom. Huge snows in the early winter could double the travel time required, but this early-fall trip was all clear and she made good progress. The sun was up for her early start, after only a few hours' sleep following the meeting in town late last night.

The drive gave Bullseye plenty of time to question her scheming. At her core, she loved her country and she loved Montana, but now those two would be on different sides of the argument. She could tell that the vice president, who held the number two office in the whole dang country, was a no-count guy, just in it for the quick grab. An elected official running a game on the entire country—by stealing a bunch of prize animals just before he helped the president carve off her state from the rest of the country—felt dirty even to her.

They were taking her land—no, this was her throat-grabbing father's land. *They can have it.*

The second hour of her drive found her composing a cowboy poem, dedicated to Vice President Fowler:
The VP is coming, you know by the stench,
Maybe ole Fowler will fall in a trench
And clobber himself in the head with a wrench . . .

She would be glad to put together their stampede, a perfect scenario for her to jack their money as ransom for stealing her home. It would cost them millions. And while she ran that game above ground, millions more would pass through her tunnel. If her Montana friends could convince the other states to rally around the Secession, she'd run the tollgate on a secret trade route back into America. They would not catch Bullseye Magee flat-footed. *Keep his hand off my throat,* she told herself, and "he" came to mean every man who could possibly mess with her. *Every stinkin' one of 'em.*

After she crossed Gibbons Pass and screamed up Highway 93 into the Bitterroot Valley, Bullseye took a fast left. She paralleled the West Fork of the Bitterroot River into the hills, turned south through the little town of Lorae on the Idaho border, and skirted past the faded wooden entrance sign to *Bullseye's Lame Horse Ghost Town — Trail Rides, Mining for Famous Montana Sapphires and Gold Panning.*

The dirty F-150 truck barely had time to stop before she hopped out and, repeating, "String, string," bolted toward her shack/gift shop to dig through an old trunk for some string and topographical maps. Subterranean measurements were a little tricky since her GPS devices failed underground in her cave, but she could figure them out with the right maps, a line level, and a long piece of twine.

After grabbing her supplies, Bullseye darted down toward the end of the tunnel and rolled out her maps while adjusting her headlamp. "OK, let's figure this out. The tunnel entrance to my mining operation is about a hundred and fifty yards from the border on the Idaho side, right about here." She drew an X on her map. She continued to scrawl a jagged line, mimicking the path of her tunnel as it existed. "The exit on the Montana side should be about three times that distance inside the state. Four football fields from the border should create the perfect smuggling route for my clients to sneak contraband between the new country and the US. If this sale goes through, securing the border will consume years, and they will start with the big roads, anyway. By the time they discover my entrance a few hundred yards in and away from any town, I'll be a few million dollars down a beach somewhere."

She studied the map to help decipher the most prudent path. Backing up and going around Lorae would take too much effort, so Bullseye continued her operation right under the edge of the little town and planned to exit on the hillside or the banks of the Nez Perce River somewhere upstream. Lorae comprised only a couple of buildings anyway, with few people around. The MooseTracks Diner was the busiest, but it only attracted a small lunch crowd.

She flipped her maps over and scribbled a list of even more gear she would need. At the bottom of her to-do list, in large letters, she wrote "How and where in the world will I find some desperado to pay me a bucket of cash to use this dang tunnel?"

Her mind wandered while she headed to the surface, to do her thinking in the sunshine.

WASHINGTON, DC/LAME HORSE CREEK, IDAHO BY PHONE

Alan Stubblefield sealed his office and told his iPhone to call Bullseye. "Hey there, we're all set. I've closed on ninety-two hundred acres of land right down the Nez Perce River, in Idaho. It's right across the river from your Lame Horse place. I've ordered the deer fence—"

"You know those rascals can jump eight feet high."

"I'm well aware of that, Bullseye," said Stubblefield, as he thought, *I am the secretary of the dang Interior.* "We've gone up ten feet, and we're doing two runs with a twenty-six-foot chase in between, just in case a tree falls on one of them. I don't want to lose any of these jewels."

"Well, speaking of jewels—is my deposit on the way?"

Straight to the money. That is why he knew she was right for the project. Before Stubblefield could let go of the money, however, he had to confirm a few more logistics. Her answers satisfied Stubblefield that she had the plan, resources, and backbone to pull off the test stampede with just a few weeks of prep.

"The first half million should hit your account in about an hour. This will more than cover your team through the test and over the winter, until the drive. I'm eager for an update."

"Oh, no worries there, Alan. Just one thing. That little test you want us to run? With gas, ATVs, horses, food, and who knows what else, it's gonna cost upwards of fifty thousand. I hope you realize that."

Alan grinned to himself. "I put seventy-five grand extra in the deposit to take care of the test and still leave the half mil in place as a down payment on the spring stampede, so you should be set and ready Bullseye. Sounds like we understand each other just fine."

"Yessir, we sure do. We certainly do," Bullseye affirmed.

56

WASHINGTON, DC

The White House Residence was often cold but rarely lonely. Privacy was in short supply for a president in the time of crisis. Dan Crowley walked upstairs, saying goodnight along the way to those who would watch out for him until morning, closed the door to the Residence on the second floor, and loosened his tie before he kissed Denise.

"Long day running the world?"

"Feels like it's running me. There's this weird dichotomy—normal life, with some people getting along just fine and celebrating all the things we love, like high school football games and going to movies—then there're reports of tragedy and misery a few blocks away in the same cities."

Denise listened and added as the president looked over her shoulder toward the window, "Or right outside the gates of your house. If we look out across the South Lawn, we see people heading to Smithsonian buildings and others driving to their jobs. But if we look out the north windows, we can see burn marks on a building where they set a car on fire and two different groups with protest signs. It's only getting worse, isn't it?"

They spoke about the protests and the progress of the "Montana solution," as their team now referred to it. The First Lady had stopped questioning whether this was a good idea and agreed that the sale was the best option on the table.

"You know, the secret is getting out. I greeted a school tour by Skype this morning, and a student—a second grader, mind you—asked if it were true that we're in so much trouble that we need to sell some of our states so we can survive? And before I could answer, he asked if he could give me a list of the states he doesn't like so you would know where to start."

"Did he show you the list?"

"He said we should sell Texas first, because the Cowboys were his least favorite team."

"It's hard to argue with logic like that."

"That's not funny, Dan."

"Hey, you hate the Cowboys as much as I do. It's a little bit funny."

NEZ PERCE RIVER, MONTANA

Hump engineered a very productive flow with his small crew. Trees were taken down by two of the guys and lay scattered along the hillside until they could come back to cut them into twenty-foot sections. The other guys hummed along, using the motor and sling to drag trees down the slope to create small stacks near the creek bed. Between the belching diesel engine and the yelling, the crew made too much noise to notice the small platoon of Army personnel that had settled on the ridge opposite the one where they were working.

Redge spied them from the top of the tree he had cut, prompting him to toss one of his smaller chainsaws to grab the other guys' attention. They cut the motor and cussed him for almost hitting them with the saw but shut up when they saw him fly down the rope toward them. Something had to be wrong.

"They's on to us, you idiots! The Army's coming over the ridge, setting up a base camp," screamed Redge to his team.

He clued them in to the invasion by a few military trucks and a small group of personnel across the gorge and led the team upstream a ways to throw the soldiers off the trail. They watched into the afternoon as the platoon sent two men up the tallest fir on the ridge to build a small platform about the size of a bald eagle's nest. Redge knew this size relationship for a fact, since he'd cut down a few eagles' nests in the past, to protect their timber business.

Redge didn't blink as the light faded, and the Army men hoisted a disc about four feet in diameter, with a pulsing blue ring of LED lights. They were dim but still easy to see against the approaching night sky. They secured the disc to the platform, then lowered themselves to the ground, hopped in the truck, and scrambled down the other side of the ridge.

The boys stared at the disc, then at each other, from the security of their hiding places. Redge ventured the first question. "What in tarnation you reckon that thing is?"

Hump's decision for the group to take a week off to let things cool down, just in case the Army guys suspected something, seemed like a good idea to Redge. They left most of their gear and headed off upstream, wading in the shallow river to cover their tracks.

58

YUMA PROVING GROUND, ARIZONA, TO BITTERROOT VALLEY, MONTANA

The Army vacillated between peak efficiency and wasteful busy work. The tasks at hand were clear: To prepare for the Autonomous Flying Vehicle navigational distance test flights, the squad was to test the tracking beacons' frequency settings; calibrate the solar panels for greatest exposure to the sun, based on latitude of deployment; apply the crisp black stencil declaring the expensive beacons as "Property of the US Army," and ready the four-foot green pods to ship out in their custom suspension crates.

The pyramid of forty-six GCT units, or Ground Coordinate Transmitter pods, towered over the hangar floor and would cover the entire route, or roughly one every thirty or thirty-five miles between the Yuma Proving Ground base in the Sonoran Desert, midway between Phoenix and Palm Springs, all the way to Malmstrom Air Force Base in Great Falls, Montana.

The rough terrain the Army would cover with the base units would push the deployment squads to their limits. The logic of wanting to test a new, self-navigating flying car over a long distance, but not over the heads of many people, was sound, but the route over the western edge of the Wasatch mountains, through deserts and across the Continental Divide, seemed a lot more treacherous than a nice flat beach.

Five crews struck out in beige camouflaged trucks, carving a path toward Canada, with the goal of installing seven to ten of the beacons each within the next two months.

Baker Crew drove into the Bitterroot Valley in Montana, and on to the little town called Darby. They set up their camp in the valley on the edge of the Bitterroot National Forest. Half the crew would work the valley floor, while the other half worked along the Continental Divide. The first install was on a ridge above the Nez Perce River about four miles northwest of a little dot on the map called Lorae. The mission for each team on the first day was to prep the site for a beacon and rush to pinpoint a rowdy roadhouse to rendezvous later that evening. They had enough nights to try each team's selection, and the team who picked the rowdiest joint won free wings.

The Continental Divide team took off uphill and found an old fire watch lookout road near the ridge that saved hours of carving through the countryside. It took less than an afternoon to build the mounting platform high in a Douglas fir, install the solar panel, attach and test the beacon unit, pack up, and leave.

The Army platoon had talked about visiting the logging crew across the gorge to learn more about the local roadhouse situation, but the crew vaporized as soon as the Army arrived. Once the Army crew saw the blue LEDs of the unit glowing in a circular pattern, proving the orb was ready for a navigational test, they took off down the hill to a little roadhouse near Sula that they had Yelped.

59

CORVALLIS, MONTANA

"Real Ranchers Wanted for Old-Fashioned Cattle Drive" read the post on the Sturgis Online board. Sturgis, South Dakota, was the spot where bikers rallied, and the online board was one of the spots where they checked in, while roaring around the country. The subhead read, "Tats, rockers, and prison record a must." Some readers may have wondered if that requirement was a joke, but it would have been music to the ears of those with all three.

After false starts from some flaky dude-ranch types and a couple of pseudo-cowboys, Bullseye heard from a serious biker gang. The concept of a gaggle of recreational ATVs cruising around the forest had faded early in her thought process. A well-organized biker gang with the proper motivation would be perfect for wrecking fences and tearing across the countryside to stampede animals. The gang could provide their own diversion in nearby towns while the rest of the group wrangled the herd around the outskirts.

There was no hesitation by the Driven Gang to kick up a few fights or break some stuff while others pushed some wild game along. This motorcycle gang, based out of Minneapolis, wasn't a bunch of sightseers. They were the real deal, and their rocker, or banner below the gang logo on their jackets, declared it to the world. The middle word "Driven" was huge and easy to read. The words above (Never) and below (Past) were small but issued the challenge to other gangs to stay back.

Bullseye had texted and spoken by phone twice with Shank, the leader of the Driven Gang, and agreed to meet up in Corvallis, farther up Montana's Bitterroot Valley. That would deflect suspicions away from her hometown and position the gang a little closer to the Bitterroot National Forest—the starting point for the stampede preliminary test. As a bonus, it wasn't too far out of the way for the Driven Gang, as they headed to Seattle for the winter, just for the hell of it. Bullseye pulled into the meeting spot, along with the season's first spit of snow.

The Dud Ranch—no one recalled when the *e* had fallen off the sign, but the owner liked the revision and never fixed it—was a favorite biker bar and roadside motel, tucked way off Highway 93, back toward the east side of the valley. The owner was a withered-up, salty-mouthed guy named Chaz who didn't like to

NOVEL BY STEVE GILREATH

work much, happy scraping by on memories and an old pension from the Anaconda Copper Mine. Chaz didn't mind having guests at the bar, as long as they didn't order anything fancier than a beer and left when he got tired.

All bikers looked—or at least dressed—alike to Bullseye. A few of the bikers gathered around a guy on a chopper, clearly in charge. Despite the light snow, he wore only a leather vest, exposing his arms to the elements. A little pinstriping on his tank matched the tattoo on his bicep that read "Shank."

Shank waved his gang to the sides of the parking lot and directed Bullseye, to follow him inside the bar. He was tan or windburned and had a few holes where piercings or bullets had passed. His blue eyes were no match for her green eyes. Bullseye stuck out her hand with confidence. She had dealt with a lot of tough ranchers and more than a few jerks in her lifetime and knew that she could handle one more, if that's how he wanted to play it.

After very brief introductory comments they jumped to the details of the stampede. Fifteen bikers, tearing across the countryside, making as much noise as possible? Scare some big animals in the process? No worries for Shank and his team. Why did she want to do this? Didn't matter.

"All right, you guys are what I want for this little scandal. The first dusting of snow is on the ground, but we need to run a little test for three or four days next month before we kick off this venture for real next spring. So, here's the deal: twenty thousand dollars cash now . . . ," said Bullseye, her voice wavering just a little. She had done her research, but it hurt to spend that much money with someone she had just met. She laid the envelope on the table.

Shank took it and tore off the end with his teeth, then thumbed through the contents, as if he could count that fast. The left corner of his mouth turned up just as he spit out the piece of the envelope. It would be a good winter, but he acted like it could get warmer.

Bullseye smiled. "And I've got another thirty thousand tucked away somewhere safe. You hold that twenty K for now and get fifteen of your toughest riders back here on November first for our test run. It'll last only a few days, but it's got to be great," added Bullseye. "I'll have that envelope waiting here when we start the test and even more at the end a few days later if you hold up your end of the deal. If everything works out, I'll need more of your guys in the spring for a much bigger drive, with a couple zeros on it."

Turning to look at his lieutenants, Shank broke into a full-on smile and nodded. "Don't worry, ace. We'll be here with the list of gear you say we'll need, ready to get it on. It'll be a blast." To seal the deal, he picked up a beer bottle and clanked the one he ordered for Bullseye.

147

60

LAME HORSE CREEK, IDAHO

Back in her tunnel, Bullseye ceased digging long enough to wipe her brow. *Hard. Harder. How can the rocks be getting harder?* she thought as she scratched her way deeper through the mountain. It was the same granite, same limestone that she had worked at the mouth of the tunnel, but the rocks seemed much tougher now. *Because I'm in a hurry*, she thought. Occasional veins of softer volcanic material brought bits and pieces of relief here and there, but it was tough going.

Tight corners or places with flaky roof sections required Bullseye to use a pickaxe to work the rock by hand, to make sure the ceiling would hold together. Her big excavator would tear apart the half mile needed to bring her tunnel entrance back into the new nation of Montana, but the hand work was a smart way to test the rock and a spectacular method for heavy thinking as she expended the physical energy. She pulled up her gloves, picked up the pick, finished her back swing, and held while thinking:

How can I trust a bunch of badass bikers who don't give a crap about anything—maybe not even money—to do what I need? They have to break laws the right way to get good results and not get killed in the process . . . clank went the pickaxe.

As it smashed into the rock, the pickaxe flaked off a small section, along with a few sparks. The clank sound echoed down the tunnel and died out.

Are those dang animals even gonna run when those bikes . . . clank . . . *come charging, or will they bed down and let 'em run past? Nobody knows if this will work, but it's a bet worth a couple million* . . . clank.

And speaking of nobody knows if this will work, I've got to dig and blast an absurdly long hole through solid rock or else find a bunch of cracks; then, I get to figure out how to find some jackass Bandito to pay me a fortune to use the place and remember . . . clank . . . *not to get killed in the process* . . . clank.

Oh, and yes, the best part . . . clank. *The best part is that all my closest, dearest friends are counting on me to help execute my own stupid idea of carving out a brand-new country, assuming we can get the frickin' United States government to roll over and beg for mercy* . . . clank . . . clank . . . clank.

Oh, don't worry, LB, that should be no problem. Among our assets, we got one mean Irish chick, a few wrinkled-up ranchers who think they're pirates, and a genuine drop-dead-gorgeous movie star . . . clank. *That should be enough for the battle, right?*

She parked her pickaxe and unthreaded her bandana to wipe her brow again. This deeper part of the cave contained natural hot springs and evidence of geothermal activity, creating a mild sauna. The effort from a few swings with a pickaxe caused her core temp to rise, so she stripped off her flannel shirt and grinned her subtle Irish grin. This grotto was her domain, and no one else was nearby.

The grin wasn't for parading around topless—she often walked around without a stitch on when secluded in the warmest parts of the tunnel. No, this grin was courtesy of Evan Morris and the memory of that kiss. She hoisted her pickaxe to her shoulder and got even warmer as she dwelled on Evan.

He is indeed stop-the-truck gorgeous all right. I don't know what to do with that man. He just about ruined my deal with the vice president, just showing up like that. I was pretty hard on him. Yes, I was. But after all, he did drive four hours and didn't even know if he would find us. That's saying something, right, girl? I quit looking for "the one" a while ago, but he sure is fun to look at while I figure this out . . . clank.

61

BIG SKY, MONTANA

When Evan Morris's boots hit the street in the Big Sky Town Center on Lone Peak Drive, the contrast again struck him. Jewelry, cars, high heels—everything around the posh resort was spotless and shiny, except his dust-covered boots. He had been shuffling around Wallace Street, trying to kick up a little dust, and now Evan realized he didn't really want to sparkle. That was different. He preferred dragging a little dirt and enjoyed becoming a meaningful part of the Virginia City political landscape. There, he just wanted to fit in. But this was Big Sky.

Mona didn't serve warm brie and quail eggs like his favorite Big Sky haunt. But then again, Virginia City had Bullseye. Evan got out of his car and sent it to park, thinking through the Bullseye situation while he took his first steps back into Big Sky. *She is a challenge, fun and frustrating to think about, in equal parts. She drew me in with the right chatter and questions, not to mention the kiss, then stiff-armed me and shut me down cold during the fishing thing. And she still hasn't explained what that was all about.* The tinkle of a bell on a door opening brought Evan back to his Big Sky mission.

While he was growing used to Virginia City, Evan admitted his affinity for high-end boutiques. Being catered to and fussed over were familiar routines that Evan missed from his days living on the coast. A little recognition by someone—anyone—added to the white-glove treatment from shop owners in Big Sky would make a nice break from anonymity for Actor Evan Morris.

Retailers displayed anticipation for ski season in the windows of the Big Sky. The economy muted this year's splash, but shop owners still dangled their best efforts forward to lure buyers. Evan loved to shop. No, Evan loved to buy.

On the third stop, the Burton Store, Evan leaned a mosaiced snowboard away from a mannequin in the window to run his hand along the edge. Two women stopped outside the store and pointed at him through the window. One of them covered her mouth while the other one giggled. Evan returned their wave with a tip of his hat.

The bell on the door signaled their entry and after just two minutes,

150

Evan had posed for pictures and signed autographs. Both women were younger than Evan, maybe in their forties, he told himself. Any younger and they wouldn't have known who he was. Maybe they were in their fifties and had just rearranged some of their parts. Age didn't matter to Evan, since they had recognized him. After posing for another picture, the sleeve on his expensive silk shirt snagged the bejeweled jean jacket of the taller one and made it difficult for them to separate, which gave them more to laugh about.

As he put his other arm around the tall one to free himself, she looked him in the eye, reached around to caress his butt, pulled him close, tilted her head, and initiated a long, wet kiss. Her forwardness caught Evan a little by surprise, but it didn't scare him away. His hat fell off in the process, which the short one caught in midair.

"Now that was nice," said Evan as he freed his sleeve, his lips, and his mind all at once. He leaned back just a little with a satisfied smile, his butt still in the grips of the tall one.

The short one pulled Evan's arm away from her and handed back the hat, then said, "Evan, if you think that was good, wait 'til you try this."

She stood on the edge of the display to get a four-inch boost as she cut in front of the other woman to face Evan, practically climbing him while reaching up to comb through his thick, blond hair, then guiding his head to hers, teasing him with a tiny peck of a kiss, followed by a supple, inviting kiss that left Evan a little weak-kneed. He came up for air, then closed his eyes and dove for another. They swirled around, knocking the snowboard and mannequin over, which fell forward and shattered the store window while the boutique owners just watched.

Evan walked through town, after offering to clean up the broken glass and taking a few more pics with the short/tall twins, but had lost his desire to shop any longer. He touched his watch for his Tesla to come take him back to Virginia City. Riding west, toward the sunset, a thought occurred that he would no longer need his Top 5 Kiss List. From that point forward, he would only have to evaluate each kiss against the one from Bullseye. He firmed up his bottom lip and said, "And those were no Bullseyes."

62

CORVALLIS, MONTANA

Bullseye itched. Whenever she was around this much leather, the cows were still wearing it. After a few days preparing for the kickoff of the stampede test and carving her cave walls, she had hopped up to Corvallis and found herself surrounded by a horde of bikers from the Driven Gang, who had showed up en masse on November first, as expected, just when the snow blanketed the valley. Although she asked for fifteen "herders" to stampede the game south for a one-week test, they insisted on bringing all 147 members, wives, concubines, and hangers-on. Masking any intimidation, she tried to stretch a little taller as she strode toward the leather-clad clan.

Shank lay back, one foot propped up on the handlebars, and pulled a fourteen-inch blade from a sheath strapped to his right calf. After a little gabbing, he used the blade to reflect a slice of the beam from his headlight through the dingy, snowy morning, onto a topographic map, illuminating the part with the Bitterroot Valley. He twisted the metal to make it shimmer. "It ain't no problem, Bullseye. Half of us will stay down in town and keep the cops and Feds busy, and the others will ride through the woods to scare up some trophy deer for you folks."

Bullseye tried to stay in charge. "Move fast to keep ahead of the law and angry ranchers. It should be easy to look like a riot with this bunch, but no one can figure out what you're doing, right? I don't care if you have to smoke out a few canyons to move 'em forward, but I'd hate to see you burn down the entire state."

"You just get that envelope out and have the rest of the money ready. I know this first little rodeo is a flat rate, but you said there was a bonus if we get good numbers, right? We're on it, and that extra ten K will buy us one helluva Christmas party."

Bullseye cautioned, "And I hope you earn the bonus because that would mean that everyone walked away happy. Here's the other thirty-thousand-dollar deposit, so that's fifty K upfront, and you'll get the other fifty, plus the bonus after a good test next week. And hey, don't run us down a buncha babies. I want to know you can get something big enough for me to shoot at. That's what the bonus will be for."

Shank scraped under one arm with his knife blade. "Even them little ones will grow up to be big ones someday. Don't you worry about what we'll get." And at that he signaled for the others to mount up, and engines roared. Dust mushroomed as the first few bikes pulled out, waiting for their leader.

"I assume you won't get wound up if a few other items go missing here and there, right?" Shank boomed over the other bikes as he grabbed his throttle. "I mean, as long as we're tearing things up, we may just collect a few souvenirs along the way—something to remember the trip by."

Bullseye considered protesting but figured her voice would be drowned out by the thunder of the bikes. She didn't care anyway. Her payday was the only thing that mattered at this point.

A long line of bikes slithered up the Eastside Highway, into the foggy morning, toward the Bitterroot National Forest for a night of partying before the stampede test run.

Bullseye watched them fade away, then turned to head back to Virginia City. A little nagging corner of her mind wondered if it were even possible to herd wild game like cattle.

63

VIRGINIA CITY, MONTANA

Meatloaf Monday at the Placer Gold Café was Mona's busiest day of the week. Now that secession was being kicked about, folks turned to the Placer as the hub for news about the movement, filling up the joint daily. Mona bumped her way through crowded aisles and clutched a coffeepot in each hand to save trips.

Smaller splinter groups had convened at the four-tops, but the juiciest discussion took place at the Community Table in the middle of the restaurant.

Tensions had increased over secession issues but flashed whenever a visitor attempted to occupy one of the regular's seats at the Community Table. The hierarchy held fast, with the end of the table anchored by the county commissioners—Morris Evans, flanked by Hitch Jenkins and Bullseye Magee.

Actor Evan Morris took the next seat in rotation but moved even closer to Morris to the seat vacated by Bullseye, who was spending more time at her Lame Horse Creek mine. Curious fans of Evan Morris agitated Morris Evans to no end by coming up to speak with the actor but ignoring the commissioner. They confessed their love for him, repeated a favorite movie line, and requested an autograph or a picture. Even worse, several asked Morris Evans to take their picture with Evan Morris.

Morris Evans could yield his end seat to the "face of the nation," and people wouldn't have to squeeze in to get their picture taken—but the thought never crossed his mind. When Mona suggested a swap, Morris proclaimed the brains behind the Secession movement demanded more respect, and therefore the end seat. Despite some laughter from Hitch and Mona, Evan understood he was not kidding, so the "face of the nation" stuck to his assigned seat. But the truth was that Morris's train had left the station, once current Governor McLemore made it known he would stay in control as they grappled with nationhood.

The protected Vimeo message arrived by email to the whole team on the same morning and showed the governor in his office, talking directly to a camera. "Hey Evan, Morris, Hitch, April, and of course, Bullseye. I've seen videos of the movement you've started down in Madison County, and I wanted you to know that we have a secession plan underway here in the

154

state capital as well. Secession is our only way forward and of course we'll be stronger when we join efforts, and, Evan, we love the idea of you being the face of the new nation. Great idea, friend. I'll keep you posted on the effort up here and you do the same. God bless you folks and bless Montana!" The governor's leadership skills and Actor Evan's face seemed to be the most powerful one-two punch to launch Montana into the future.

Everyone sat in their proper place on this day, and Morris Evans began, "I think it's critical that we—"

"Evan, aren't you afraid of losing your movie career if you step up to defend our homeland?" asked Kelsey, one of three college girls down from Missoula, standing across the table while her two friends crowded behind the actor. There was a semiserious mix of furrowed brows and giggles from the girls.

Evan decided not to point out that his movie career had ended at least three movies ago and sought the high road of a patriot. "Well, I'll tell you . . . what is your name, darling?"

"Kelsey B," she said, to more nervous giggles by her friends. Evan thought she may have added the B on the fly, to sound more exotic or mysterious.

"Well, Miss B, sometimes we have to put country above all else. I may face retribution back in California, but I hope that citizens of the United States will rally to our cause and stand with us."

Evan seized the moment, using the perfect timbre in his voice as he stood and circled round the long Community Table. He stopped right next to Kelsey B, making sure the full length of his leg pressed against the side of hers and laid his hand on her shoulder.

"Kels, we all have to stand for something. The fact is everyone in this state will lose everything if we don't bind together to birth our own nation."

The word *birth* gripped the girls. He leaned a little closer to Kelsey and slid his hand from her shoulder to the small of her back. "And you girls are the future of Montana. Your new country needs your energy right now."

Evan gauged the effect of his delivery. While his speech had pushed Morris close to nausea, the girls had been won over. They would do whatever it would take to give birth to his Montana-shaped baby. A few visitors at other tables added to the smattering of applause. Kelsey B did not take her eyes off Evan's face as he scanned the adoring crowd.

The girls headed back to Missoula with a few more pictures of Evan and one that Evan took, after encouraging the three girls to drape themselves all over Morris Evans, who let a shard of a smile slip in the shot. Evan got in his car and made some notes on the talking points that seemed to work, for later use.

64

NEZ PERCE RIVER, MONTANA

Hump and his guys monitored both sides of the ridge as they snuck along the edge of the Nez Perce River and approached the Army gear stash. A little over a week had elapsed since the Army had evacuated, and there was still no sign of the troops. They gawked at the pulsing blue lights of the disc mounted by the gomers at the top of a ponderosa pine high on the ridge. The tree under the disc had to be 150 years old and worth a fortune and a half to Hump's patrons.

"What d'ya reckon it is, Hump?" said Redge, with a fearful eye toward the ridge. "You think it's trying to sniff us out?"

Both guys looked at Hump as he took off his cap, scratched his head, and stared at the glowing item up the hill. "Sure 'nuff they're trying to find us—figurin' out what we're up to. Got one of them solar homing devices, a camera, and a GPS thing in it," offered Hump, with a mix of caution and daring. "I think we'll just have to make them work a little harder, if you get my drift."

All three men laughed for a few seconds until Redge stopped to ask, "Uh, Hump, I don't get your drift. What're we gonna do to them?"

"We're just gonna have to relocate that thingamabob and see how they like it. Boys, we're gonna need that big tree that's sitting under their little platform. That'll be the next one we cut. We'll see if that dealie is waterproof when we send it downstream."

Redge caught up to the plan and said, "So, if they want to find that thing, they can look ten miles west of here. That's a helluva plan, boss."

Hump drove the truck back to the campsite, and the guys set up their tents around the firepit. Redge got the fire blazing quickly with a small propane torch, while the others broke out a series of canned items for dinner. They spent the evening discussing the plan of attack on the Army's massive tree.

65

LOLO NATIONAL FOREST, MONTANA

Shank felt like a king, posed high on a ridge in the morning sun, watching over his subjects as they tore off into the hills. They had zoomed south from Corvallis, down 93, through Darby, and turned west on Conner Cutoff Road, then up the valley toward the Bitterroot National Forest, where the bikers veered into the woods.

It was a rough start. Kip from Daytona Beach went down right away, trying to run his Harley through a barbed-wire fence. *Figures it would happen to a dude named Kip*, thought Shank, who suggested they invest a little more time cutting the fences, instead of driving through them. The goal was to penetrate the deep forest as soon as possible while seeking their prey and avoiding ranchers. They scattered their tracks through the light snow.

Nikki and Lauren cruised down the road about four miles and then atop a small bluff overlooking the valley. They hoped to see an elk or deer or any other animal scamper out of the woods. Anything moving ahead of the noisy group would signal success to the women scouts.

A huge dust cloud rose to the girls' left, a mile or two away. Wisps of snow swirled, picked up off the ground and from the trees by the stiff breeze, which made it hard to discern just what was happening. The dust-and-snow cloud inched closer, but no animals emerged from the underbrush. Nikki raised her bandana from her neck, tightened it over her nose, and covered her mouth while she dismounted. "Those guys don't know nothing about stampedes."
>Nothing yet. Go up on the edges.
>>K.

Nikki texted another update to Shank from her vantage point above the valley. The two girl scouts pulled up their collars, then left their perch and dove ahead another mile.

An hour later, the yelling and screaming had stopped. This didn't feel like fun anymore as Nikki took reports from the gang about how impossible it was to penetrate the thick undergrowth—especially on a Harley hardtail. They had only scared up some squirrels and rabbits—not the prize catch they had hoped for. Nikki zipped her coat up higher and said to Lauren, "A week full of this is gonna suck."

Nikki got off her bike and bent over the edge of Trapper Creek to resoak her bandana to cut the dust. "I think I see them coming down the hill. Man are they flying," she supposed through a cloud of smoke, as her warm words worked through the wet bandana and took shape in the freezing air.

Lauren twisted on her bike to look up the valley. "They need to spread out more. We'll never find . . . hey, Nikki, look!"

Nikki squinted and gasped. Up the roadway about a hundred yards, a dozen or more of the biggest animals she had ever seen rushed out of the woods and careened down the valley and into Trapper Creek. Just as fast, they vanished into the woods on the other side.

Shank and the gang cleared the woods a little farther up the road and stopped, looking bummed about not having seen anything bigger than a coyote. Someone pointed down the road where Lauren and Nikki now jumped and pointed like they were guiding a plane on the tarmac.

"Go!" Nikki shouted as they drove up. "There's a whole herd up the hill, giant deer or elk or whatever! You got 'em going! Don't stop!" Shank looked up the hill in time to see a huge elk turn tail and sprint into the woods.

The bikes fired to life, then ripped through Trapper Creek and up into woods. The forest floor was surprisingly smooth to ride across, with the ground between the large lodgepole pines trimmed short by grazing animals, making it easy to dodge the rocks scattered about and the occasional huckleberry bush. The girls high-fived as they watched the cloud of dust resume on the opposite side of the creek. *This is gonna be a cool week!*

66

NEZ PERCE RIVER, MONTANA

The loggers crawled out early to start as the sun rose across the new fallen snow. Each had dozed off the previous night discussing the pulsing Army orb, from their individual tents, pitched right across the stream. Hump couldn't take his eyes off the blinking blue hue of the tent illuminated by the blue lights. He swore it was sending some sort of code and felt close to deciphering it as his own eyes blinked, then closed for the night.

They grabbed their gear and waded the creek before climbing to the top of the opposing ridge. Hump snuck up to the base of the enormous tree as if it were a guard tower and craned his neck to see the top. They could still see the blinking blue LEDs chasing around the disc, at the top of the huge ponderosa pine, right where the Army boys had placed it.

Redge fired up his sixty-inch chainsaw. In less than a minute, he'd carved a huge horizontal *V* in the downhill side of the tree. He then swung around and made a slice through the uphill side, on a downward angle. He only made it a quarter of the way through before the huge tree cracked.

"Run for it!" yelled Hump. He never tired of seeing one of these monster trees crack and spit as it tore a path to the forest floor. "Timber!"

The length of the tree, with the help of a few thunderous downhill bounces, landed the tip on the stream's edge. As a bonus, the huge pine dragged down five other sizeable trees in its path.

The boys scurried downhill to see if the UFO was still blinking. They couldn't find it, until Redge slid his way down the soft clay bank into the creek. There it was, submerged in two feet of water and blinking like a bad aquarium bulb.

They cobbled together a raft from the limbs of the massive tree, fished out the Army's device, and strapped it to the top.

The weight of the blinking Army orb made the raft too heavy for the shallow pre-winter water level of the Nez Perce, and it bottomed out on the big rocks after just a few yards. They sectioned the huge tree, which they added to the pile of logs on the edge of the creek, waiting for the melt to carry them and the orb away to Cashville, as they now referred to their location downstream.

Redge asked the other guys again if they thought it was sending signals. He swore he was picking up something, through the fillings in his teeth.

67

BITTERROOT NATIONAL FOREST, MONTANA

Busting up other biker clubs was nothing compared to the animal wrangling the Driven Gang had undertaken in the foothills of the Bitterroot National Forest. Shank and his troops screamed and skidded as they traversed the forests, scaring animals forward. The bikers caught a glimpse of the beasts jumping out of the brush every now and then and yelled louder with each sighting.

The prey turned back on the bikers once or twice during the roundup. Kip from Daytona suffered another blow to his ego when a pissed-off squirrel dropped from a tree, down the neck of his thick leather jacket, causing him to ram into a Douglas fir. He suffered a nasty rip in one shoulder, and the squirrel jokes stacked up immediately. The other came when a buck charged one bike, locking antlers with handlebars. The kill cost the driver a new front end for his Harley but produced fresh protein for a delicious barbeque for the gang.

On that first evening, Shank set up a test containment area for the animals. While some enjoyed the barbeque, the rest circled the bikes to pen the animals in the middle. By their best count, they had trapped about thirty head of deer, two elk, and some other furry beasts built lower to the ground that looked fast and mean, snarling while they ran. They revved an engine here and there throughout the night, only to have a bunch of the animals run between or jump over their bikes within the first hour of darkness before heading off into the night. By midnight, all the big animals had charged out of the circle, to freedom.

Shank had the gang break out the beer, anyway. They completed the first full day of wrangling, had harvested some fresh venison for the barbeque, and had proved it was possible to stampede wild animals; and no one got killed in the process—not even Kip. They celebrated late into the night and would start again in the morning.

68

YUMA PROVING GROUND, ARIZONA

The monitor screens blinked as the Army diagnostic team booted up the test pattern for the beacons installed on the course from Arizona to Montana. A topographic map showed blips for beacon locations, coupled with analytics relating to signal strength and other data next to each blip. The data returned a positive message about the working condition of most of the radar beacons.

A few anomalies surfaced, which the crew attributed to poor focus on solar panels and one or two structural questions about the actual mounting. The failures could be snowpack related or even animal intervention from a large bird of prey.

The team's recommendation was to do a full on-site inspection of the problem locations in the spring. They would run the whole line of GCTs from Arizona to Montana before the flying car test to make certain everything was sitting pretty and beaming back the right data.

They filed their report to General Starnes that all systems were online and ready for a final wring out in the spring.

69

BITTERROOT NATIONAL FOREST, MONTANA

After a rough start and the exchange of some hardware—swapping the stiffer hardtail bikes for something with a little more bounce—the Driven Gang did what it was born to do: ride. And what Bullseye paid them to do: herd animals. The eight-mile test stampede seemed to work.

There was not much resistance along the way. No one got too wound up over some rogue bikers stealing a few chickens. Shank had been smart to leave cows, horses, and ranchers' daughters alone. The bikers sent a majority of the force into small towns more than thirty minutes away to stay in hotels, so they didn't make a big fuss camping in the woods. Good communication and some topographical planning allowed them to work in shifts and bring in more riders when they needed to fan out over a large expanse of broad or steep terrain.

Shank's longtime running buddy, Fleet, had upped the tech ante with some handlebar-mounted infrared lights and night-vision goggles, which helped them confirm when the pack strayed close to the edges at night. Fleet had announced that after big losses the first night, the overnight "leakage" rate was low for the hundreds of animals wrangled during their test on the following nights.

They had more proof when Kip launched his small drone and captured the stampede on camera. After counting over eight hundred animals on video by the third day, they knew they could send thousands of animals across the border to Stubblefield's little game playpen during the real run in the spring.

Shank convinced Bullseye that the whole stampede concept would work, once he forwarded the drone footage and the infrared images of the animals charging ahead of the bikes. She called off the test two days early so they wouldn't blow the whole scheme by alerting authorities and rendezvoused with Shank to drop off the bonus money.

Bullseye pulled into the Dud Ranch parking lot just in time to see a naked biker zoom by on his chopper, wearing only a pair of antlers harvested from a recent roadkill, with some of the animal's meat and fur hanging down his back like a cape. "I can only stay an hour or two, Shank.

I don't have anything to wear to this kind of party," said Bullseye, looking at the antler guy.

"Bullseye, you're the guest of honor. After all, you're paying for everything," said Shank. When Bullseye didn't laugh but only smiled, Shank reeled in his banter and said, "Listen, this stampede business was a blast and just what we needed for the winter. We'll be ready to go whenever you are—no limits. You just let us know."

"Will do. Don't go getting yourselves killed over the winter. I need you."

Shank grabbed two bottles of beer and walked Bullseye over to the firepit, handing one bottle to her as they sat down on a log. "So, what's your winter look like, Bullseye? What are you chasing after? Or are you hiding out?"

"Those are the only two speeds, right? I'm not sure, Shank. You've been on the road a while now. I bet you understand me when I say that there are things that pull me backward, just cause me to sit and deal with the devils from the past and then there's this thing that pulls me forward, calling me out to do something big. You know, take a once-in-a-lifetime shot." Shank nodded and took a slug of his beer. "Well, this feels like I'm on the front edge of that big thing. I just need to figure out which big thing to grab and hope I can hold on for the ride when I latch onto it."

Shank stared at Bullseye and nodded slowly, then sighed. "So, is this quandary a dude or a money thing?"

"A dude? God, no. Well, sort of, I guess that's part of it. I'm old, Shank—"

"Yeah, but you're still hot, girl."

She tipped her beer toward him and continued, "And haven't had the best luck with men, starting with my dad. I gave up on someone riding up on horseback to sweep me away a long time ago. But all of sudden, there's this guy who is not at all the type I ever saw myself with, and he's got eyes I can swim in . . . ," Bullseye trailed off, staring in the distance and exhaled, while Shank let her sit in the thought. "But no, I'm talking about money and a lot of it. When I bug out, I want a few million to take with me. I'm getting tired of snow and tired of memories haunting me and tired of this country's situation, and I may just have found a way to scratch out enough to go build a dream somewhere warmer."

"And if he behaves, just maybe you'll take the dude along for the ride?"

"They never behave, Shank, I know that for a fact. They all end up like the antler guy over there, in some form or fashion. But that would be nice, just this once."

They tapped bottlenecks, just as a small drone with a squirrel tail hanging on it zoomed down in front of them. Kip followed it in, shared a few stories, and ended up showing Bullseye his squirrel scars. After some cheers, high fives, and a long, caring hug from Shank, Bullseye hopped in the truck and tore out of the parking lot, leaving the gang to their celebration. The last image in her rearview was the naked antler guy doing a donut and the grimace he made when he tried to stand, only to find his business had frozen to the seat.

* * *

The gathering that evening at the Dud Ranch was a raucous celebration! Chaz, the Dud Ranch owner, slaughtered and roasted an elk that someone had shot from their bike, adding even more meat to the feast. Shank toasted the gang: to Kip and his squirrel scars, to the elk someone shot from the bike, to the bike destroyed by the charging buck, and to Chaz, ordained that very night as the best chef ever, to the *e* that had fallen off the Dud Ranch sign, to the naked antler guy with the deerskin diaper to help stop the bleeding, and on and on into the wee hours.

Shank made a private toast to Bullseye and the dude on horseback.

70

SOUTHWESTERN, MONTANA

Bullseye tore down highway 93, back toward Virginia City. It was late in DC, but she figured Stubblefield would want to hear her update on the test. With her forearm looped over the steering wheel, she scrolled through her contacts until she found "Stubb DC."

"Well, it was a good one," said Bullseye, before saying hello. "Those bikers kicked up a lot of dust, but sure enough, they put together a bona fide stampede of a thousand animals." Before Stubblefield could ask for any details, she directed him to look at the pics she had just sent, including the infrared shots from the nighttime corral with a few hundred pairs of eyes looking back at the camera. The killer shots were the two drone photos from high overhead, which revealed hundreds of animals, all facing the same direction—without question seeking their escape from a pursuer. The front edge of the bikers' assault team just barely made the frame to the left before a cloud of snow and dust swallowed their bikes.

"I know what you're thinking there, Alan. This will work in spades, setting you and your hunting buddies up for several lifetimes," Bullseye reassured him. "Those big-game ranches in Texas take years and millions to build a prize population. You'll be getting a trophy herd all at once, with no disease or breeding problems from limited gene pools. But, just to help with the math, that means you will pay an awful lot of money. I assume there are no limits here, right?" Bullseye smiled when he affirmed their deal.

"My guys will be ready when the snow breaks in March, but I'm going to lie low until then and hope this state holds together that long. Maybe you should focus on that. Everybody knows what's going on up here."

Bullseye hung up. She loved lecturing the secretary of the Interior on how he should spend his time, with no argument from his end of the phone.

She smacked the wheel with her right palm three times, making each strike progressively harder. This was a huge score, and to hammer home the moment, she yelled, "Yes, I am the man!"

71

VIRGINIA CITY, MONTANA

Stroganoff Friday was no Meatloaf Monday at the Placer Gold Café. A handful of regulars dotted the place alongside a few others from nearby counties who had stopped by for updated news on the Secession.

Morris Evans was on his throne at the head of the Community Table, waiting on his friends. He had news from the last twelve hours, about a biker gang causing some ruckus in the Bitterroot Valley. He often gathered intel from early visitors and dispersed it later as his own proprietary information.

Bullseye pulled into her regular spot, tired from the late-night drive from her biker party and a short nap at home. She crossed the boardwalk toward the café and caught up to April and Hitch.

"Lady and gentleman," April cooed. Bullseye mock-curtsied and Hitch raised his cap. "What a lovely day shining on our new countryside!"

With that, all three paused as Actor Evan Morris's Tesla slowed to let Evan exit, then parked itself, while April, Bullseye and Hitch said, "Morning" while entering the café.

Hitch said, "Hey, Evan, that was some performance with those three college girls yesterday. You really had them eating out of your hand."

Bullseye turned to Evan and raised an eyebrow.

Evan flashed a guilty look, then said, "I'm just trying to mobilize and motivate the grass roots, Hitch."

"I guess you'll make more progress reaching out three at a time like that," sneered Bullseye as she took her customary seat to Morris's right. She turned away from Evan as soon as she finished speaking, and reached for a biscuit.

Mona brought coffee all around, but Actor Evan fanned his hand over his mug and stopped her. "None for me, Mona. I'm headed out with Governor McLemore on a blitz tour with some key influencers in a few minutes. I'll have coffee on his plane. Can I get an English muffin and some juice to go?"

"I didn't hear about this," said Morris Evans, acting perturbed. "When did this come up?"

"He left a message for me this morning, and he wants to leave right away," said the actor. "I think we're meeting with small groups in twelve cities and on a few ranches. We need to get them on board with the Secession. I'm sure he's looking at a few of them for cabinet positions in his new administration."

"So, Governor McLemore will be the president and not you, Morris?" inquired April.

Morris Evans wouldn't concede without a fight. "I think the people would prefer an election."

"That's only fair," said Hitch, somewhat rallying to his side.

"You bet," said Evan, "in good time. We have to come out of the chute with Governor McLemore in place as president, so we can preserve the current state government structure as best we can. The new constitution being drafted in Missoula calls for elections four years after secession. He convinced most of the current senators and representatives to stay in office as we move forward."

The news of a constitution being drafted in Missoula drained some of the color out of Morris's face. Hearing that the rest of the government— even on an interim basis—had already been decided siphoned what little color was left.

Mona slid a Styrofoam box and cup in front of Evan, crowned with his bill. He grabbed his box and cup, dropped a twenty on the table, which was more than a ten-dollar tip, swapped cheek kisses with Mona, and headed for the door.

72

ACROSS THE STATE OF MONTANA

This being-the-face-of-a-new-nation business was much more difficult than the Liberty Life Reverse Mortgage campaign Evan Morris had shot as his farewell to Hollywood. In their meetings with key Montanans, Evan and the governor asked people to commit to something far more serious than a mortgage, and they expected him to have answers to very difficult questions. He felt stupid for not knowing about the process of secession or the administration of the new country.

It helped that the audiences for the first round of events had been restricted to an inner circle of trusted Montanans to mobilize a critical mass of influence and funding. The governor's staff had strictly forbidden the press, to prevent news leaking out for as long as possible.

Station owners squelched their reporters from covering the Secession until it was approved from the top. Some stories leaked out on independent outlets, but pressure from friends about protecting Montana's chances brought those reporters in line as well.

After the first four stops, Evan got the hang of the gig. These were not the typical movie-junket events that he could bail out of once he got bored. These were emotional, stress-filled tugs-of-war that persisted for hours. His role as adopted outsider was valuable, and he became effective at voicing his point of view.

The rumors of secession preceded the team in every setting. Their plan spread like a bad cold throughout these upper circles, which made the governor and Evan focus on damage control and rumor management as much as mobilizing resources. "There are some hot spots bubbling up, but nothing that's going to tear the state into pieces," said the governor to each small group gathering.

Sporadic violence and looting erupted in Missoula, Billings, and Bozeman as well, which added urgency to the discussions. Few details were available in the rural areas, but random thieves, mobs, and bikers had pillaged large ranchlands in so many directions that local sheriffs' departments with as few as six deputies countywide couldn't come close to controlling their actions. By the time they called the adjacent county for support, the bikers had scattered into the woods or down the road, making them impossible to catch.

This was clear evidence of the state's demise. What would happen once the president announced his intention to the public?

Evan was the closer in the campaign, calling for people to sign on to the cause, declare allegiance to their state—which soon would no longer include their country—and give lots of money and resources to support the effort. It was an emotional task that included several very long days traversing the state and as close to real work as he'd come in years, but Evan found it rejuvenating.

The favorite setting by far was in a living room of someone's enormous private home, with about twenty people in attendance. Evan sensed the powerful resources these small groups represented, and he could connect on a very personal level. He spoke from the heart but leaned on note cards he had cobbled together for the first few stops. As the week went on, he relied less and less on the script. "I am a Montanan now, and Montana is my home" became powerful statements for him to lean on. People listened intently. They latched onto his words and responded with serious questions and thoughts. When he could reply with authority, "From what I'm hearing across the state," Evan felt connected to the cause and empowered. The exchanges spurred him on to the next stop. And the next.

73

NEZ PERCE RIVER, MONTANA

>Pigs is in the pool...

Mankin looked at his phone for a moment after sending the text, half expecting an immediate response from Secretary Stubblefield. *I wonder if he'll figure out the code.*

The first serious snow of the fall had descended on the Bitterroot Valley, covering all the trees they'd cut and staged until spring. Hump didn't expect anyone to stumble on them in the winter. The narrow gorge was even harder to access with a couple feet of snow on the steep banks.

Hump had lined up about $1 million worth of logs in two months. The winter would make their production more challenging, but the blanket of quiet protection it afforded made working through the cold worthwhile.

Redge tossed the last chainsaw into the truck as they finished packing the gear to head upstream about a mile to set up a new camp. He had spent the last week running the numbers, scribbling his math on the inside of an empty ramen noodle package. His share, after conversion, rounded up to three lifetimes' worth of tall, cold brews.

* * *

The Brotherhood of the South Militia commander dropped his field glasses and crawled back down the ridge. He reported on the activities of the loggers in the gulch below, noting their progress had been steady over the four days they had been under observation.

The men talked a little, then vaporized into the woods, heading downstream toward Lorae. They didn't want to be late for their meeting with the governor.

74

WASHINGTON, DC

Stubblefield deleted the text the instant it came up on his phone screen. How could Mankin think a US cabinet member would answer texts about something as nefarious as stealing old-growth lumber?

Their potential success caused him to smile, just a little. If Mankin and his boys had collected anywhere close to the quantity of trees he'd bragged about, Stubblefield was set for life—as if his government pension wasn't cushy enough. He'd make $20 million off the trees that only cost him $2 million with Mankin.

The Senate floor hushed as the voice vote started. Stubblefield slid his phone into his briefcase before looking around. His report to the Senate Committee on water rights in Georgia had gone well. He ran his hand over the smooth wooden desk and noticed that each station in the Senate Chamber was unique. He looked closely at the wood under his notebook and traced his finger along the fine grain pattern—something he had never taken time to notice. The finish was rich and translucent. He wondered if the trees Hump was smuggling out of Montana would end up as furniture this beautiful someday.

Stubblefield continued his woodworking admiration session when he heard the majority leader slam the wooden gavel on the wooden base to announce the bill's passage. There was wood all around him, and he took the time to explore the paneling and intricate scrollwork that framed the Senate Chamber. "Impressive," he whispered, as the call for adjournment came.

75

KALISPELL TO LORAE, MONTANA

The last morning of the governor's statewide swing started like the final day of summer camp for Evan Morris. It had been an emotional few days, and the team had formed deep new bonds. Evan stretched and studied the private airstrip south of Kalispell pointed toward Flathead Lake before he boarded the governor's Super King Air and took his now customary mid-cabin seat. He pushed the button to release the swivel on the plush leather chair and spun around to face the governor across the aisle.

"Home stretch, everybody! What's on tap for today, guys?" asked Evan.

Head down in her iPad, the governor's chief of staff answered, "Our last stop will be interesting. A group of militias who are dead set on helping with the Secession have contacted us. We don't know how close we can snuggle up to these groups—we just know we can't work against them."

The governor added, "Truth is, if there were any rough spots during this process, it would have to employ guerilla tactics, not a mass assault. We'd never win on a level battlefield against the US Army, so these militia guys could come in useful as disruptors."

Evan asked about the groups and came to learn that well-organized area militias in Idaho, Washington, Oregon, and Montana could mobilize faster than anyone imagined. Although each group held different priorities, beliefs, and morals, their mistrust of the central government united them— so much so they were even willing to work with a state government to "slice the head off the snake that is the United States government."

The plane touched down on a private airstrip on the floor of the Bitterroot Valley near Darby, where the entourage jumped in an SUV and drove west into the hills, then south. The chief of staff explained that the meeting location was at a small restaurant called the MooseTracks Diner on the Montana/Idaho border. Only one small road accessed the area, and the militia scouts would see any unwanted guests.

"But that means only one road out for us, right?" Evan cautioned.

The governor smiled. "No need to worry, Evan. Nothing will happen today. I've met these groups for years off the record and it's always somewhere way off the beaten path. We try to stay in touch and hear their concerns since they're citizens too. We could meet on the Capitol steps, but I don't think that would serve our interests or theirs. It'll be all right."

The entourage pulled into the MooseTracks gravel parking lot about eleven a.m. Their SUV was the only vehicle in the area, except an old Ford that Evan hoped belonged to a cook, and an even older pickup half over the edge of the riverbank, missing two tires.

An aide, followed by the governor's chief of staff, walked in first, trailed by the executives on the committee. Eric Clapton sang "Change the World" overhead as Claudia the waitress slid around the counter and waved them to the other side of the restaurant.

Before they could even look at the menu, the front door swung open and a group of ten people—six men, two women, and two undetermined because of the large amount of hair, hats, and camo—sauntered inside. They introduced themselves with mystic organizational tags like *brotherhood* and *heritage*, followed by a region identifier like *southwest* or *Idaho* or *worldwide*. No one in Evan's group understood the tags, other than to acknowledge that this council represented a lot of different groups from a very large area and likely a diverse group of people.

The MooseTracks had served as a meeting house in the past for a couple of the organizations. "I'm just gonna start bringing some food out family-style, since we're all just one big happy group, and you can get about your business. Trust me, you don't want to order anything Reuben don't feel like making, so stick with our plates du jour."

Claudia's words were enough of an icebreaker to get the teams milling about, looking for chairs. They shook hands and continued the introductions along the way. The seating arrangement settled out along organization lines, with the militias on one side and the governor's team on the other.

The governor opened with a warm and inclusive speech for the new attendees. He turned their attention to Evan, who confirmed what he knew about the president's plan, while different militia members echoed the point with their own twists:

—Yes, those thievin' rascals in Washington are trying to steal the land right out from under us Montanans . . .

—Yes, those hypocritical snakes think they can buy us off with a little payment that's just pennies on the dollar for what our land is worth . . .

—Yes, those short-sighted cowards think they can pull the rug out from under us without a fight . . .

–Hell yeah (almost chanted), Montanans are being joined by other brave folks
around the country to rise up and set things right . . .
–Yes, there's an important role for your organizations in our fight . . .
–Um, sure, when it's all said and done, there'll be room for you to live free in the
new country of Montana. We'll set aside some land for your group to live as you
want — with no interference from the new government.

The governor's entourage pulled out of the MooseTracks lot after the
meeting dissolved and headed down the mountain toward Darby. He
looked out the window and tried to understand the full magnitude of what
had transpired during the previous two hours. He confirmed that everyone
believed they should align with the militias, a powerful and politically
potent segment, but still, there was something . . . . Evan captured the
sentiment of the group: "They feel dangerous. I know we can trust them to
do what they say, and they'll be present when we need them. I just don't
know how much of their own agendas they'll bring along for the ride."

The governor affirmed Evan's statement and added, "We need them,
plain and simple. We need every sympathetic person and organization we
can find if we're going to have a chance of separating from the US. It's like
a knife blade. We have the thick, strong part to provide the organizational
and legal strength with our legal team and passionate citizens. The folks
we just left are the sharp edge. They have a purpose and I'm glad they're
with us."

"I sure wouldn't want them against us," Evan said.

The group boarded the plane for a swing through the Ennis Airport in
Madison County to drop off Evan, and the discussion centered on the solid
week of work they had accomplished, along with the relationships formed
for the cause. The militia involvement had a sobering effect. Secession was
a daunting task from the very beginning. So, what was *daunting* with a
thick layer of surreal on top?

76

LAME HORSE CREEK, IDAHO

Bullseye unearthed some good luck in her mine shaft for a change. In the week since her successful stampede test, three runs back and forth between Montana and Idaho for supplies, two late nights in the tunnel scratching around, jacking some large boulders, the detonation of two low-grade charges, and a full night wallowing in depression thinking she had failed again and should just give up while her dad laughed at her, looking up from where he was roasting, she finally blasted through a wall to reveal segments of two other abandoned mines and a forgotten cave with a collapsed entrance that she could now connect into one long cavern. She added about ninety-two yards of progress in no time, albeit in a rather serpentine pattern. Bullseye now saw a possibility that she could actually carve this tunnel by herself, proving something to, well, herself in the process. Besides the money, no power-pushing man was ever going to tell her where she could and couldn't live, ever again.

Bullseye named the areas in the cavern to occupy her mind and to exact a little payback on the long, lonely hours of digging. The Daddy Magee chute, a dark foreboding trail, wasn't good enough to be a real tunnel because there was a choke spot at the end. It felt cold near the opening of the Daddy Magee chute, and Bullseye always buttoned her shirt all the way to the top whenever she had to walk past. After a few days of feeling creepy every time she was near, Bullseye decided to make a radical change. She hid behind a rock column thirty yards away, dropped down her ear protection, raised her .270 deer rifle, while sighting in a tiny little target on the face of a clay-like voodoo doll that semiresembled her throat-grabbing father. The bullet was the first half of the binary explosive combination; Tannerite was the other half, a moldable demolition explosive that farmers kept around to take care of stumps or rocks in the field. Once the bullet struck the Tannerite doll, a powerful explosion rocked the cavern, raising a cloud of dust and debris that rushed past Bullseye, ducked behind the rock column. For the second time in her life, she had buried Daddy Magee. She shed no tears this time either.

According to local iconography—a word April had left with her a few days earlier at the Placer—mineral mines permeated this area, under and around Lorae. Miners abandoned some old shafts because there was too much water leaking through the walls from the Nez Perce River or they just didn't bear any gold.

On the third day of cutting through her new cavern route, Bullseye broke through a thin shale wall and accessed a dome room, where the limestone ceiling had flaked off layer by layer over thousands of years (she hoped) and dropped to the floor, creating an expansive area the size of five tennis courts joined at weird angles.

Bullseye grew concerned at the distance to the surface in the dome room. The ceiling rose eighty feet, and by her estimation, could be right under the MooseTracks Diner, which was just over the hill from her place. In one corner of the large rock ceiling, she could see the bottom of a concrete footer from a building in a muddy section between rock segments. She couldn't hear any noise but knew she'd have to work quietly in this part of the tunnel. The concrete footer tip meant she was close to the surface in this area and that the MooseTracks was likely ten to fifteen feet overhead. The room that nature had carved was spectacularly large, but the pile of flaked rock on the floor was evidence that it had gotten that way by the steady collapse of the roof over time. She could tell by the imprint that the section under the concrete footer had to have fallen after they poured the concrete, or they would not have built there. The concrete now served as the ceiling in that far corner of the room. It was a risk to use this section, but no worse than the entire proposition she had undertaken.

A thin ribbon of water seeped through the walls and flowed steadily along the eastern side of the dome room. Bullseye reckoned this entire wall ran parallel to the Nez Perce River. The water coming in was only a trickle now in November, but she worried that the spring melt might bring a torrent if she broke through the wrong wall. To be safe, she dug westward and uphill, so she could get past the threat of both the river busting in on her and of being discovered by whatever building was right above her dome room.

This room she imagined would serve as her main staging area for "Smuggler Operations." She would hold her hands up and narrate the vision out loud: "So, let's say that some bad actors buy Montana and then move in. Say they use the tunnel to smuggle illegal stuff into the US without customs knowing anything about it. But say that secession works, and Montana becomes the country. Then this could become a smuggler route for people trying to move contraband into the US or from the United States back into Montana." She paced a few times around the big dome room and thought, *There's room in here for camels, tanks, drugs—whatever. I have to figure out how to get someone to pay me for it. You better get organized, girl, if you're going to show these men who's boss!*

77

BILLINGS, MONTANA/MALIBU, CALIFORNIA BY PHONE

"Hey, Morty, just checking in with things down there in Holly-weird," Evan Morris said to his ex-agent, with an inflection he had not used in a few months and realized how outside of himself he sounded. "I've got a question for you." The tour around Montana with the governor had been long, but informative. He wanted to look beyond the state boundaries to see what the rest of the world knew about their plight.

"Evan, long time no talk. Listen, I can't gab right now—it's crazy down here. There's rioting, carjackings everywhere . . . well, at least by our Whole Foods. Evan, they stole Missy's little Mercedes—just threw her right out of the car. They just take what they want. I'm buying a gun, I swear."

Evan waited until Morty took a breath and jumped in with, "So sorry to hear that, Morty. Buy a gun. A big one so you can protect yourself and Missy. I hope she's all right. Listen, I know it's crazy, and it's worse up here. This may sound random, but have you heard anything about Montana being sold off to another country?"

"I think I heard something about it, Evan, but I didn't give it a second thought. There's so much weird talk and I mean, Evan, they're right down at the Whole Foods, stealing cars from us. They knocked Missy down to the ground and took the Gucci bag to boot. My wife can't go to the market without fearing for her own safety. Why would I worry about what's happening way up in Canada?"

"Thanks for that Morty. It's Montana. I live in Montana now," was all he could muster.

Morty's tone changed, and he dropped down a couple of gears on his show-biz voice. "Evan, I heard about it at a fundraising dinner for that schmuck senator that's always got his hand out. He told us on the very down low that they were thinking about selling Montana, like it was the worst thing ever, but then said if they sell Montana, they could stop all the looting down here because that would fix the budget for the whole country. Sorry if that sounds bad, but you understand, right? It's all so crazy, but I'm in if it will help save our butts here in Malibu. You would too, right?" Leaving no time for a response, Morty continued. "So, listen—I have to run, Evan. Missy has a migraine, and I need to heat her head wrap. Let's hit the club sometime," he said out of habit, then added, "I'm really sorry about what's going on up there, but I'm scared, Evan. I mean, they're stealing stuff here, right from the Whole Foods, gangs of white guys with masks, and all the political stuff written everywhere, and it's just not right."

Evan hung up and realized he was leaning much heavier on his Montana foot. It was perhaps the first time he didn't really have his toes in the sand, even in his mind. Morty's words left a vile aftertaste.

The Placer Gold Café was down the road, and Evan wished it were open late so he could check in with the gang and update them on their abandonment by California. This would be bad news, and he wondered if they would leave Montana to fend for itself or if others in the Remaining 49 would have a more empathetic focus than his ex-friend Morty. He turned west and headed to his ranch for an early night's sleep, hoping to be in his seat at the Community Table right after Mona opened in the morning.

78

LAME HORSE CREEK, IDAHO

Bullseye was covered in rock dust and wet up to her ankles from slogging through the mine for days on end. She had stayed hard at it, blasting, scratching, and stretching her tunnel through the mountain, stopping only to grab an occasional power bar or to soak her aching muscles in one of the small pools that formed a natural hot tub near a geothermal crack in the side tunnel she named Evan because it made her warm. The water ran steamy and clear, albeit a little sulfurous. A towel lay coiled on a rock table with one end poking through the middle like a rattlesnake poised to lunge. Bullseye preferred to drip-dry, so she slipped back into her boots and jumped right back to work after each soaking.

Four shipping pallets and two wool blankets served as her bed for naps between rock-chipping sessions and, with some snacks, she saw no need to surface for days. Her underground lifestyle had already affected her internal clock, and she found working about six hours, then napping for two or three round the clock was most efficient.

After that week of chipping and hauling rock, Bullseye emerged, squinting, from her subterranean lair and slipped back to Virginia City to check on the farm and load up on more supplies. Breakfast at the Placer Gold Café to gather some intel from her friends felt a bit strange. The gang peppered her with questions, which caused Bullseye to squirm and dodge the details of her last couple of weeks. Hitch convinced the others to leave her alone after Bullseye offered her fifth version of "just trying to spruce up the old mining operation to make it more fun for the tourists." Evan wasn't at the table, and Bullseye tossed in, "Oh, I hadn't even noticed he wasn't here" just to add to the smoke screen. It appeared to work, as the table backed off the inquisition and returned to the forecast for snow. She ate and ran.

After escaping the interrogation, Bullseye made a swing back by the ranch to tag up with the UPS truck who off-loaded a colorful palette of goods from World Markets, Pier 1, and Amazon that included fabric, beads, pillows, and the final touches she needed to finish her cave in high style.

Taking her first above-ground nap in a week felt like a luxury. She grabbed a small twin mattress from her guest room, tucked it in the truck, and headed back toward Idaho.

179

79

VIRGINIA CITY, MONTANA

Evan could not get to sleep after talking with Morty in Malibu and then overslept with the help of some medication. By the time he arrived at the Placer Gold Café, some local luminaries, including Bullseye, had been and gone, but Morris Evans still held court over the Community Table. Mona rumped her way by with a coffeepot and dropped off a kiss, kiss.

While the other Community Tablers patted Evan on the back, April seized the conversation, which prevented him from launching into his agenda.

"Now, everybody, everybody! I must say the face of our new nation is looking a little road-weary this a.m. Are they running you too hard, Evan?" said April, adding, "I mean you've covered the entire state in just a few days."

All eyes shifted from April to Evan, including the folks at surrounding tables, who leaned toward the Community Table. He didn't disappoint with a detailed and colorful description of the interior of the governor's plane, the difficult questions heard in some lush homes where they had gathered with groups of rich ranchers, and the excitement and unity that he enjoyed at every gathering. Montanans appeared to be ready for action.

When asked by Hitch about a government structure, Evan confirmed that the Montanans he spoke with wanted to stick with the existing state government pretty much intact for a few years before pursuing fair and free elections. Governor McLemore was the right man for the job, affirmed Evan to the nods of everyone listening, save Morris Evans.

Morris said, "I'm still not one hundred percent on that, Evan. What does that man know about weed-control issues?"

"Weeds don't matter, Morris," Evan said, with his voice elevated. "We're fighting for our lives, and we have to focus on the main things that will mobilize the nation and set us free."

Morris leaned back, reacting to Evan's terse response.

"Sorry, Morris. I have an important update that I want to share with everyone . . ."

Every patron in the Placer Gold Café locked onto Evan's words as he described his phone call with Morty, the increased lawlessness in Malibu, and even more surprising, the awareness by people as far away as California that there was a deal in the offing for the sale of Montana.

"And here's the worst part. The president's decision to sell Montana—as repulsive an idea as that should be to other states—was not objectionable to everybody. Morty would trade Montana for peace back home at the Whole Foods in a Malibu minute. And their senator was the one telling everyone that if the country sold Montana, they would all be off the hook, all the violence would stop."

The only sound heard throughout the Placer were the dishes that clanked in the kitchen. April voiced the obvious question: "So, you mean the rest of the country may not line up to help us once we declare our new country?"

Mona hipped her way in the conversation with a coffeepot swinging in each hand. "Well, at least not that Morty twerp, right, Evan? We have got to get you a new agent, hon, and let him and Cissy, or whatever her name is, have their own little soap opera down at the Whole Foods. I know you can do better than that man." She looked around the room and the sea of sullen faces. "And that goes for all of us. We're not going to let Mr. Malibu Morty destroy our mojo. He obviously doesn't know anything about Montana, so you can all just park your poutiness and we'll get on with our plan. *We* have long lists of things to do, and they don't include feeling sorry for ourselves."

Evan jumped up and hugged Mona, to a smattering of applause.

80

LAME HORSE CREEK, IDAHO

Bullseye's entrance facade appeared typical of any old-timey ghost town—with a few special touches she had added over the years. Visitors expected the gold mine section to have a rustic mine cart and some kerosene lanterns. Rusty buckets, a pickaxe, and some fake dynamite helped round out the tableau. As her guests left ground level and descended further into the cave, they noticed some embellishments to indulge their fantasies. She hoped to lure them into digging her tunnel farther into Montana while they sought their fortune in gems. It wasn't cheap labor—it was a labor force that would pay her and do the work for a little fantasy role-playing.

In just a few days, using the mail-order resources that had filled half a UPS truck, she had transformed her underground bunker into a palace suitable for a sheik—or at least a cheap movie-version of a palace. Yards and yards of fine silk-like fabric hung down to form a sweeping entryway and walls. Bullseye overlapped Persianesque rugs and a variety of beanbag chairs draped with cheap, soft fabric all around the room. It was just dark enough in the cavern for a visitor to confuse the cheap décor with lush.

Bullseye scattered about old steamer trunks filled with Mardi Gras beads, rhinestones, marbles, and other shiny objects garish enough to insult anyone who should stop to think about it—which few who came this far ever did. This sultan's retreat was just tacky enough in the shimmering lamplight to excite the tourists-turned-miners.

This grand entryway was Bullseye's innovation to disguise the access to her smuggling route. She designed the fabric to baffle the sound of her continued digging. In the back of her mind, Bullseye dreamed that her tunnel tenant would be a sultan or prince impressed with her decorating efforts and offer to up the ante for the whole package.

The passage looked impassable, and no one would suspect it as the route entrance. Severe turns and dead ends caused by large boulders or rock faces too stubborn to give way seemed to block the path. The shaft was dark and wet—until she flipped on the lights.

A trail of bare bulbs in yellow plastic safety cages lined the cave's ceiling and swerved between the stalactites dripping from above. The lights spooked some small bats, who buzzed by Bullseye's ears to fly deeper down the cavern.

81

WASHINGTON, DC

Thanksgiving at the White House was subdued, at the request of the First Lady. Denise and Dan Crowley ate alone with their son Keaton, home from Auburn, and gave as much of the staff the day off as possible. Denise told her son that some peace would do his dad and the country good.

For years, Keaton had been encouraged to follow in his dad's footsteps at Princeton, where he had completed his graduate work. Keaton's mom took some pressure off by recounting the wide path his dad had trampled in his undergrad fraternity life at the University of Illinois. Despite the input, Keaton landed at Auburn to enjoy SEC sports, a passionate social life, a quality education, and some distance between him and the White House.

When Denise passed around the s'more pie, as was the Crowley family tradition, Keaton asked his dad about plans for the country. He had understated the pressure his classmates put on him about the condition of the nation and wanted to have a few answers ready for his return to school.

"I have lots of help, Keat, but I won't lie to you, Son—this situation is a lot worse than anyone imagined. Our problems cut deep and I'm looking at some radical answers."

Keaton weighed the serious tone of his father against the attempted marshmallow-licking of a s'more remnant clinging to the corner of his mouth, then said, "They must be. Students demonstrate everything on campus, and half the time I don't think they even know what they're protesting. Discussions in my economics class say the government is so desperate that they are considering selling ads on the Washington Monument or even selling off some of our national parks. Where does that stuff come from?"

Denise Crowley gagged a little on her s'more pie, then reached for her milk. She took her time with the sip, allowing her big eyes to peer out from behind the glass and dart from her son to her husband. Keaton could tell she was hiding behind her milk.

"That's not real, is it? Dad, please tell me you're not looking at selling ads on the Washington Monument as a possible solution to save our country," said Keaton.

"Keaton, I told you this situation is crazy and worse than you can imagine, but no, I am not recommending we sell ads. I will be honest and say that it came up as one of the bad ideas in our brainstorming sessions. I should fire every single person at our Camp David session. We classified those ideas—especially the horrible ones."

Dan helped Keaton grasp just how large the debt crisis had grown. Other than on-campus protests, Auburn was insulated from the real problems of the world. Fans still scattered toilet paper at Toomer's Corner after a big win, and the line at Big Blue Bagel still reached the door on Saturdays. Life at Auburn rolled along as normal, until most departments had been told to cut staff positions.

"So, about selling the national parks—that can't be true, can it? Who could afford to buy Yellowstone for enough money to help solve the crisis?" asked Keaton, trying to perceive and dismiss the concept.

Denise hid behind another long gulp, leaving her husband alone to answer.

"About that. We're not looking at selling the national parks, but there are some other options being discussed."

"That's good to hear. I didn't think it made any sense. So, there was this one rumor about selling an entire state or something. Can you believe that? How could people be so stupid?"

"I'm getting more milk. Would anyone like anything?" said Denise as she disappeared from the room.

Dan squirmed a bit and told him that the secrets were getting out faster than he could plug the holes, so he might as well share the realities with his own son. He admitted that he was about to sell Montana. Keaton was at first stunned, then loud. He gyrated, returned to the table, shifted in his seat, shook his head, and rubbed his eyes in disbelief. They discussed the logic behind selling Montana, Dan's discussion with Azwar and other people groups as potential suitors, and potential conflicts. The yelling finally calmed.

"Dad, you gotta let people know what you're thinking," Keaton said, while his mom listened from behind a third glass of milk.

"I know, Keat. I know. I keep hoping something will change and I won't have to. Like a miracle will revive the economy somehow or a buyer will come forward and we'll get a deal sewn up so I can present this as a real solution," the president said.

"Instead of the Hail Mary that it is, right?" Keaton added. "I get it, Dad, but think about it from the average dude's angle. The rumors I'm hearing are way worse than the actual news, and that's at Auburn. Imagine what they're talking about in Montana, Dad."

82

WASHINGTON, DC

Thanksgiving Day melted into Thanksgiving night at the White House. The West Coast football game was on in the background, but the president and First Lady focused on the "First Son," who listened, protested, burbled, shook, and paced around the room.

"Sell Montana is a thing. Just sell one of our states. That is so colossally horrible to comprehend, Dad, I'm still having trouble believing it's the most plausible solution your entire brain trust can come up with."

The threesome spent the better part of Thanksgiving night and the early part of Black Friday discussing how and when to announce to the country. Keaton and his mom leaned toward sooner, even saying Black Friday sure sounded appropriate. The president wanted more time and told them about a secret meeting he was pursuing with Palestinian leaders. He still waited on an earnest assessment of the Palestinians' financial well-being to see if they could swing it, and he felt like the Israelis would pay a huge sum to kick the Palestinians out of their backyard.

At 2:06 a.m., Chief of Staff Graham Blair knocked on the president's door. "I'm sorry to bother you, Dan. I wanted to alert you to a very specific situation developing in Austin that will affect the White House."

Blair described a hostage situation, where an ex-IRS agent went over the edge, shooting up the United States Federal Courthouse on 5th Street in downtown Austin. The crisis started when he exploded several large propane tanks to set the building on fire, then drove a block to 6th Street, where he shot into a crowd of partiers, killing at least fifteen. He now blockaded himself on one of the rooftop bars on 6th Street, holding several hostages. He was organized and tossed a stack of printed flyers over the wall of the rooftop to spread his manifesto to the world.

The Crowley trio listened to the rest of the story. "His platform is disturbing, Dan." Blair handed over a copy of the manifesto emailed by the FBI as soon as it had hit the street. "By breakfast, everyone in the country will have read this."

Final Answer Manifesto — What's Left?

185

I'll tell you —Nothing! The country is crumbling and the evidence to this is the destruction of our way of life. There is no America left! My family has abandoned me, calling me a "tragic" personality. I was good at my job with the IRS, but good, unfortunately, meant I had to tear lives apart and destroy the financial structure of others. But my faithful service helped the country. Then, without warning and with little explanation, those elitists fired me. FIRED ME!?! Cutting and cutting. If I'm not on watch at the IRS, who is? There is no hope for the country. It's on the president's hands, this blood spilled today. You have not moved to fix the situation, Dan Crowley, and so I'm on watch to help. I'll help the IRS cut expenses by eliminating some locations. And I can cut down the workload by eliminating some taxpayers until the president figures this out.

Dan Crowley looked at his son, who said, "Dad, don't you get this kind of blame all the time? It's just some wacko, right?"

The president clinched his jaw and looked from his son to his chief of staff. "It's what Blair will say next that makes this one different, Keat. He wouldn't have come into the White House Residence at two in the morning just to report a nut job with a flyer."

"Your dad knows his job very well, Keaton. Dan, about twenty minutes ago, three separate devices exploded inside IRS buildings in Denver, Phoenix, and Dallas. The devices were incendiary and have caused significant fires. He located them near the front-end servers in each location, so damage may be severe. And there is a loss of life—"

"On Thanksgiving night? The IRS staff was working on Thanksgiving?" asked Denise Crowley.

"They're dedicated and they have an enormous job to do. We expect to learn more about the death toll and the ripple effect of the damage to the economy soon."

Crowley heard the FBI's plan to sweep every IRS building in the country, piece together a background on the bomber, and trace his travel to see where and when he could have planted the other devices and explore the involvement by anyone else. The conversation turned back to the president three or four times, Keaton seeing firsthand how much stress one man can bear. The men made plans to profile the bomber as a wacko and distance Crowley's policies from being the true source of his demise. Sympathy, along with firmness and logic, would guide the country through this event, even if more buildings blew up.

The stream of details slowed or repeated around five thirty a.m., so the president decided he needed to grab a nap, knowing he would have a long day ahead, including a press conference. As Blair stood to leave, he made a joke about white guys always being the ones who wrote crazy manifestos before they blew stuff up.

The president said it was a white thing and Blair wouldn't understand, continuing the running gag on both sides of the color line between them.

Keaton started toward his room, down the hall from the president's, but stopped to say, "Dad, I knew you had a tough job, but I did not understand it could be this crazy. I am so proud of you, and I love you. Good night."

The First Lady smiled and said, "This is a Black Friday, and that was very, very nice of you to say, Keat. We love you too." She pushed the button to close the drapes and darken the room, just as the sun was rising. "I know you know this is not your fault, Dan, but I also know that knowing that won't stop you from carrying the guilt."

"You know me well, D."

83

AIR FORCE ONE

DUBAI, UNITED ARAB EMIRATES

A week had evaporated since the IRS explosion incident. The damage to the IRS network of servers in the three buildings that had been destroyed or heavily damaged brought the service to its knees, freezing many functions of tax collections and enforcements. The press had gleaned every detail about the shooter from social media, old yearbooks, public records, and nosy neighbors. His motivation was clear in his manifesto, and in writings scrawled on the walls in his apartment, his van, and even hidden tattoos. Every president had been in his sites for years, which had diffused the spotlight somewhat on Dan Crowley.

A second secret trip by a president to the Middle East in a few months frustrated the national press core because it was a true secret, with the president departing without notice or press attendees. The cost of this level of secrecy was a spanking by the media that the White House would not counterpunch. The press had started wild speculation about the sale of Montana theory, but the IRS bombings actually stalled those stories for a few days. Charges of "running scared" and "ill-timed vacation" popped up at once, with most charges connecting the trip to the domestic terrorist incident in Austin, which the shooter had blamed on the president.

"It's OK, Blair," said the president to his chief of staff aboard Air Force One. "What else are they going to say when we leave them behind and don't tell them where we're going? I don't blame them. Besides, I gave them enough. After that nut job blew up, I held daily press conferences, sit-down interviews, and more for a week. I've addressed their concerns up front."

The president had been clear that the destination and reason for this trip were to remain a secret. He wanted to negotiate from a position of power and could not dash about the world hoping to find a buyer for part of his country in a fire sale. Thinking in those terms shook the confidence of the most powerful man in the world. And thinking about that phrase made him smile at the irony—Dan Crowley felt anything but powerful at the moment.

Air Force One landed at Dubai International and taxied into an area protected by US troops. The local guests, all high-ranking officials or royal family members from four of the seven monarchies comprising the United Arab Emirates, had agreed to meet aboard the president's plane for the hastily organized meeting. This protocol avoided the pomp and high-jumping of an official state visit, simplifying the struggle for stature or potential security problems.

Blair watched the arrivals through a window and commented to President Crowley about the line of lavish cars approaching the plane, including a glimmering sedan leading the pack. "They covered that Bentley in solid gold. It's got to be worth a million dollars, easy," said Graham Blair.

"Don't act impressed," said the president. "Remember, it takes a thousand of those million-dollar cars to equal just one billion and a thousand of those billions to make one trillion. And we're looking for twenty-one of those."

"So, we need to find one of these princes to buy Montana for the low, low price of, well, so much money that we can't even put the amount in terms that a normal person can understand? Piece of cake."

The guests honored the request by the president to keep their entourages small. The party of nine joined him in the conference area of Air Force One, where, after warm greetings and service of strong Arabic coffee and Karak chai tea, the discussion turned somber. President Crowley knew the president, who was from Abu Dhabi, and the head of state from official functions. He had also met the ruler of Dubai, who served as prime minister of the UAE; however, he did not know the other two main players well and did not have his full staff to help him with the normal prompting when needed. One of the lesser rulers did most of the talking for the group, and Crowley could not recall his name without stealing a peek at his notes.

The UAE contingent shared a collective poker face during Crowley's telling of the dire situation in the United States. Crowley knew that there would be no sympathy. Although modernized, they still enforced Sharia law for various offenses in the UAE, and an offender could expect severe punishment for drinking alcohol or committing adultery. These rulers answered protests by large crowds with swift and certain punishment. They remained stoic as the president continued to divulge his plan.

The US and the UAE had been in difficult meetings in the past and dealt with equally serious matters. President Nixon oversaw the departure from the gold standard in 1971, and it was only the UAE's guarantee under OPEC to accept the US dollar as the global standard for oil purchase that kept the dollar safe. The secretive cost of the commitment had been a pledge of military support by the US to protect the UAE from all aggressors, in a very volatile region. It was a solid partnership that helped both countries thrive for decades.

The consequences of those historical events paled when compared to the agenda of the day. The group remained indifferent when Crowley dropped the bomb about the willingness to sell Montana. He looked at Blair to get a visual read on the situation. Blair shrugged a bit and turned back to watch the group. Nodding and discussing among themselves, the Emiratis reached a collective silence and turned their attention to their leader.

"We will buy Montana," said the president of the UAE, as if he had just ordered another strong coffee.

Crowley, almost losing control of his bodily functions, confirmed what he thought he heard. "So, you will . . ."

"We are the buyer you are looking for. This is not news to us. I was notified a few months ago that you had approached some other Middle Eastern parties, who would never have come up with the money and would have made terrible neighbors, but we have been patient, waiting for our turn at the dance."

President Crowley assumed Emirati spies had intercepted some internal discussion of his proposal from Israel, and covered, "I should have started here first: you are correct. It would have saved some time. I'm sure you understand our commitment to Israel, and we first looked for a partner that could help our allies if possible."

"President Crowley, are we not allies as well? Have we not supported each other in the past and are you not here today asking for our help?"

The president looked sheepish as he nodded a bit.

"While our Saudi and Yemeni neighbors curse you at every opportunity, we have remained a dependable friend and supporter to the United States, but still, we get lambasted by your press for our religious and age-old customs. Perhaps, we will win your press over if we are neighbors. But we must agree to a few important details before we can confirm this deal. Your price is agreeable. It is high, but I understand how you arrived at that number. So, the total of twenty-one trillion dollars is acceptable, but we must adjust the terms. You will not find a partner anywhere in the world who can hand you twenty-one trillion US in currency or gold—not at one time, not in gold, not in labor, not in anything that you can use to save your country. That partner does not exist unless you want China to complete their takeover of the world through your backyard."

"What terms do you have in mind?" said Crowley, hoping his poker face was holding up.

"Oil. Specifically, oil and natural gas now and oil and natural gas futures. And gold. Despite showboating with electric cars and some solar successes, your country is still oil dependent and will be for the next fifty years. Your country was heading toward oil independence, but re-regulation has stifled your progress and once again, you cannot meet your needs. Your politicians can rant and vote otherwise, but their demonstration won't change science or physics. The US and the world are inextricably connected to fossil fuels. Our offer is to provide all of your oil needs and resuscitate your economy.

The president scratched his chin a minute and said, "The UAE produces a lot of oil, but the amount we import each year varies. We are much more energy independent, thanks to new technologies over the last decade, but new environmental regulations threaten to put many of our own reserves out of reach. How will your plan turn our economy around?"

The next half hour involved notes, whiteboards, large numbers run on computers, and a bit of conjecture. If the UAE pledged its total oil production to the US for the next fifty years at a price locked in today—a rate below today's market value, it could equal more than $10 trillion in savings over the next five decades. The guarantee would bring incredible stability to the UAE and to the US, inoculating both countries from the radical swings in price caused mainly by political maneuvers. It would also allow the US to become an energy exporter to Russia and China at an incredible profit. Imagine the impact on the economy of the United States. And then imagine the impact on the world's oil markets when the second largest consumer of oil locked in a long-term price for such a huge part of its demand. The deal would destroy OPEC and any successor, but the UAE will face the music on that. With energy costs running constant for half a century, industry would bounce back and both countries would thrive. Transportation, including American-made cars and trucks, would see a huge resurgence from lower oil prices, and steel production would increase, along with many other related industries. The decreased production pressure on America's energy companies would free them to pursue aggressive development of alternate sources of power generation, creating jobs and a brighter future.

"In addition to the oil reserves and price lock, the UAE will transfer seven trillion in gold reserves to the United States so you may invest in programs and lower the national debt. This transfer can happen as soon as we execute the agreement, with the final caveat being the US create a permanent increase in military presence in our country—a significant increase, to help us defend from enemies outside our country and from within. You can call it training for our forces, if need be."

They enjoyed more chai after the group admitted that Arabic coffee was mostly for show. They toasted the initial idea at hand, and the president asked, "So, why? Why would you mortgage your future to help us? I know you're a dependable ally, and I see this arrangement would elevate the UAE to our most trusted friend, but there has to be more in it for you."

The prime minister signaled to his delegation that he would handle this one. "First, we love your country. Most of our children attended college in the United States. I graduated from Yale the year before you started your grad work at Princeton, President Crowley. We respect your country, even though we are devout Muslims and don't agree with all the choices you've made as a society. Freedom is tricky, but that is a debate for another time.

"Second, we are spending a lot of our treasury as our down payment, but not everything we have. Gold from across the world, from ancient times to present day, has found its way into our coffers, putting us into a position to make this move. We seek stability for our people and our families, which means we need enhanced protection from your military in these increasingly dangerous times. And not all of our enemies are external. Between us leaders," he said as he scanned everyone's face in the room, "the UAE and Dubai, in particular, are home to many organizations that have committed themselves to strike fear into the hearts of many. These organizations flourish, recede, and then reappear, including Hezbollah, the Taliban, Al-Qaeda, and others whose names are not even made public yet. We share some values with these groups, yes, but often, they disagree with some nuance of our culture, and people die because of those differences. Over fifty thousand Emiratis die in events of terror caused by these groups every year. And every year, the number and intensity of threats targeting us as rulers and our families increase. Too much Sharia law, too little. Too much Western influence, too little. And in our country, these threats are not empty threats, my friends."

Crowley and Blair looked at each other and nodded. Their small smiles were affirming, not an acknowledgment of a joke.

"So, we will buy Montana like we build billion-dollar islands that look like palm trees. We will explain to our faithful that Montana offers new trade opportunities to our friends in the United States and Canada. It will be our grandest resort for Emiratis to go fishing, hiking on glaciers, and skiing on real mountains. We will use it to educate our students abroad, and since you have invited us into your country's business, I believe I can trust you with this. The real story, the real motivation that should not leave this magnificent plane is . . . if things get bad at home, if one of the terror groups gains a significant foothold and we have to flee, can you think of a better place to hide than Montana? I am not Saddam. I will not squeeze into a rat's hole. I want to have a lifeboat the size of Montana to paddle around in the rest of my days."

* * *

The flight home was short. Crowley and Blair made plans on how to bring this deal in for a landing, establish a timetable, and create the short list of whom to tell what. Word could not leak out, lest the world oil and gold markets plummet, taking the global economy into a spiral. The Emiratis had given their commitment to pursue the deal—but had not agreed to the final closing date. There were questions, and the president knew the sale was still a long way from being a done deal. At least he could rest his head on the hope, like a pillow, as he drifted into a well-deserved transatlantic nap.

84

NEZ PERCE RIVER, MONTANA

Hump and his crew had not heard a sound, besides their own chainsaws, for days. The blanket of thick December snow dampened any noise and discouraged visitors in the gorge surrounding the Nez Perce River.

Dark set in early and the guys settled around the fire, with blankets pulled up to their chins. Redge was on his second can of Dinty Moore Beef Stew when Hump broke the silence. "What'cha want for Christmas, Redge?"

After a slurp and a chin wipe with his blanket, Redge said, "I want a hunnerd more trees. Yessir, that's sure enough everything on my list. Christmas at my house is always the same. My mom and sister will go in together and order me a shirt and some socks that I won't wear 'cause I don't go nowhere. I tell them that every year, and they say I should go out more, meet someone nice, but I don't. We always end up in a fight, so I think I'll just hang up here for the next week and keep at it. We can make a bunch of money with these trees, and spring's around the corner. My Christmas gift to myself is to keep working and make some *stupid* beer money."

The guys talked about how ugly their Christmas traditions were at home, and all agreed with Redge that they would rather start a new tradition in the woods making a bunch of money stacking logs. The count was over three thousand already staged and ready. They loaded the riverbed with them, going back almost a mile. They could see millions coming their way if they stayed at it.

Hump cemented the sentiment. "OK then, Christmas in the gorge it is. I'm glad to be here with you boys. Thanks, Redge, for the idea. I'll get you some Dinty Moore for your stocking and that hunnerd logs for your Christmas gift. And for me? I'll have two hunnerd."

85

VIRGINIA CITY, MONTANA

Austin. Phoenix. Denver and Dallas. IRS offices. The explosions and resulting fires that destroyed or disabled IRS complexes in each of those cities seemed to be all anyone could talk about at the Placer Gold Café for the last three weeks. Mona poured coffee for Morris and Hitch, just as Evan joined the Community Table. Mona bent over and collected her kisses.

"It's interesting how everyone talks about that IRS bomber guy," said Morris, as if he were an expert. Half the country hates him for being a terrorist, and half the country thinks he's a hero for knocking down the IRS and giving that idiot Crowley a black eye. The president needed to be put in his place, but I don't think the guy's a hero."

Evan pointed out something that had not occurred to the others. "You know, that terrorist incident was a big help to our movement."

"How's that and good morning to each one of you shiny people," said April.

Evan passed on asking what a *shiny person* was and continued, "Morning, April. I think half the country's sentiment that this guy is a hero bodes well for our cause. They seem to be ultrasympathetic to the message that government can't run over people . . . people like us."

After a few more sips and nods, the table agreed that Evan was correct and that their nation was perhaps closer to being established.

Cheers went up from the Community Table when the cold breeze signaled Bullseye Magee's arrival. Evan thought her red cheeks could have been caused by the cold or from embarrassment at all the attention. Most of the guys stood to hug her as she scooted to her regular seat. Evan reached out to hug her, but she allowed only a quick lean in and pat on the back.

"It is colder than a witch's thorax out there, ain't it?" she said to no one in particular.

Mona laughed at the whole greeting scene and said, "It's a little chilly in here too, sweetheart. Glad you're back."

The food arrived at the table, and Bullseye told a story or two about being busy at the mine and explained that she was just passing through to check on the ranch and pick up more supplies. Her tablemates turned the

195

spotlight off her and tried to piece together the puzzle of secession. They discussed the timing of their announcement, and most still agreed that they couldn't make the new nation of Montana public until the president announced his intention to destroy their way of life, for fear of looking like the aggressors.

They crafted the announcement in preparation, should President Traitor make his move. In the meantime, they reviewed a list of the groundwork required that Governor McLemore sent over and mobilized their resources of items they could provide.

The Secession team agreed that they should all head out for Christmas and visit with family and friends in other states, to prepare them for what was coming. Sweet sentiments and well-wishes for safe travels permeated the goodbyes.

Bullseye hugged Evan as they rose to leave and said softly in his ear, "I'm sorry I've been so busy, Evan. I do think about you now and then."

Evan smiled and let his eyes do most of the talking. He added, "I've been running too, Bullseye. I think about you all the time."

The warmth of his comment caught Bullseye by surprise. No, her reaction to the warmth of his comment caught her by surprise. She grasped both of his hands, gave them a squeeze, then leaned in for a closer, more connective hug. She whispered, "Thank you, Evan. I hope to see you soon."

April cried about everything and passed out candy canes wrapped in little purple ribbons.

86

WASHINGTON, DC

All was quiet. During a typical year, Christmastime at the White House heralded good cheer and decadent celebration. Instead of a gift, the economy had delivered coal and ashes to the president, so he canceled all yuletide events and told the staff to stay home with their families.

Dan Crowley loved meandering through the White House hallways in the late-night silence. After descending the small marble stairway to the entrance hall, he weaved through the main hall. Crowley knew every inch of the White House and had studied the history, architecture, and the artwork of our nation's greatest living museum—including the seventy-four painted portraits hung throughout the various hallways and rooms, long before he became its main resident. On busy days, he addressed them by name, in his mind, every time he passed them on the way to meetings. Now, on Christmas Eve with a near-vacant White House, Crowley talked to his favorites out loud. He preferred to address the portraits of the First Ladies by a nickname, some genuine and others that he had coined as terms of endearment. "Looking sassy tonight, Gracie," to Mrs. Coolidge captured in a lower-cut red dress, posed next to her hound, with one provocative foot dangling in the air. "Why the long face, Angie?" to Angelica Van Buren, painted with an elongated noggin. "My Jackie," "Sweet Anna," and "Oh, Claudia" (never Lady Bird, like everyone else called her) were all silent friends, who had kept watch over the men he admired most in the world, the presidents of the past.

Crowley had discovered the technique as a cry for help, while trying to keep it together during his grad school years at Princeton. His affable personality helped him make fast friends, but he never felt connected to the institution itself until one bitterly cold afternoon when he darted into the Princeton University Art Museum to avoid the chill. He was alone, prepping for finals, and his friends had all scattered for Thanksgiving. Most other spots on campus were closed.

With nowhere to go, isolated, and on the edge of losing his sanity, he started talking to the portrait of a dead white guy, famous for something or other, named Elkanah Watson. *Elkie didn't answer, but he was a good listener*, Crowley joked to himself. Each portrait's backstory served as a diversion from the pressure of studying, and before long, Dan Crowley had become the foremost expert on the art personalities at Princeton University. He felt connected to the school on a deeper level, once his research unveiled quirks in the lives behind the portraits that paralleled his own. Studying with focus became easy. When friends asked about a coping mechanism, he introduced a few of them to Elkie. His circle of painted confidants soon increased to cover many buildings on campus.

After greeting his gal pals inside the White House hallways, Crowley stepped outside, inhaling the sharp December air, then crossed the colonnade toward the West Wing. Negotiating the hallways, he saw the glow of the desk lamp from his chief of staff's office.

"I see that 'go home' order I issued doesn't apply to you."

Blair took off his readers and wiped his weary eyes, then glanced at his phone to check the time. "I was just about to head home in . . . three more years, except we're going to win reelection, so that's really seven more years, I guess. I'm just wrapping up."

"Nice. Graham, I still don't hear you talk about your dad much. Does he still live in Montana?"

"I think so. We don't speak; something about him beating the snot out of me as a kid and nearly killing my mom."

Crowley and Blair had discussed this situation years before. He gave Blair a few seconds to add another thought, but Blair was finished.

"How long has it been since you've spoken with him?"

Blair touched his phone, as if checking the clock. "Let's see, about fifteen years, right after my mom died. I just don't have anything else to say to him, and he hasn't tried to call me."

Crowley gave him more time, but Blair still added nothing more.

"Here's some advice from me to you, old friend. Call him. Tell him to get out of Montana. Help him get a jump on all the madness. And in the process, forgive him for all that horrible stuff. Be the bigger man. Here's the real secret. That forgiveness is for you, not him. Just let it go. Help him while you can, and you will free yourself for the rest of your life."

The corners of Graham's mouth turned up. "Thanks, Dan. You're a good friend. That sounds like a good piece of wisdom, but let me kick it around. Meanwhile, say hi to Shelly for me when you walk by Michelle Obama's portrait on the way back up."

"Man, I don't have any secrets from you, do I?" said the president as he hugged his friend.

87

DES MOINES, IOWA

"You guys don't have to leave," pleaded Benny. "Serious, dudes, it gets much cooler after you're in-world for a while and take over a country—"

Spanks (real name Nash) cut him off. "Look, man, I just can't get into your game. You're spending all your time and money on this stupid world resettlement game. You need serious help, my friend!"

The other two tagalongs, referred to in tandem as Will and the Geez, nodded agreement and took off, leaving Benny alone in his virtual world. *Real adventurers must often suffer shortsighted fools and simpletons.* Amanuel (as Benny was known in online global domination circles) preferred to run solo when heading into his international spy ring.

The fit of his virtual tuxedo was superb. The line of his jacket revealed the bulge from his Beretta. Hair—perfect. Skin—clear. No one dared mess with Amanuel. At least, until Benny's mom called him up for dinner.

Madonna's "Vogue" thumped and rumbled through a blown speaker, vibrating long after the beat had passed. Her powerful song drove Amanuel deeper into his trance-like world of online espionage. As Amanuel, he needed every tool available. Even a blunt instrument like disco.

As master of his domain, Benny had ruled every type of online gaming platform he had tackled: MMOs, adventures, construction, mystery, simulations, stimulations, stealth shooter, whatever. He had farmed, *Sim*'d, tanked, blasted, and puzzled through every game he could find, always purchasing the maximum advantages in ammo, clues, armor, scenery, weapons, cars, fuel, or whatever else was available.

He really loved being a character that could extinguish—he let that word roll out of his mouth like he was stretching taffy—extinguish others for any reason he chose. At a moment's notice, Benny could escape as Amanuel.

His one unreachable goal, the brass ring he had not been able to grasp, was an impenetrable game of *GloDom* (that's *Global Domination*, as he had explained on his Twitch channel). This was a gamer's game—hard to find, harder to join, and impossible to master. It existed only by rumor, with no central authority claiming responsibility. Myths and legends circulated about who played and won these games. Whoever planned and launched

199

these games was clever. It was Nakamoto and Banksy rolled into one new breed of online chaos challenge master.

These gamers thrived on irreverence and disrespect. Multiplatform jumps from social media to classified postings, coded news articles, blog posts, and into the role-playing world of live events made them near impossible to follow. Whispers in the industry dubbed their surreptitious new category "environmental gaming."

From the moment he first heard about *GloDom* on Reddit, Benny knew he had to seek and destroy this game, but he couldn't find enough information to feel prepared. He read a few articles with historical information about some of the legendary games, then articles about those articles that swore they contained the clues to get into the next game and a dissection of every crumb, sliced to an absurd level. Amanuel knew that accuracy in any article would cause the planners to change the path in a blink to avoid a bright light shining on their underground enterprise.

"Vogue," stuck on repeat, had shown no signs of giving up. Benny had only a couple of minutes before his mom called him up for mac 'n' cheese. Real life—and a substantive second life—required a massive amount of carbs.

For months, he'd checked message boards as he waited amped up for his mission. Then he found it—a clue on one of the Game Fan pages. His triple-tasking, code-breaking program had picked up something, and all the keywords matched up. There was a correlation between a message and an ad, no doubt targeted at him through some SEO program based on his numerous searches about finding a way in the game. Two words comprised his tip: *You're* and *In*. He clicked over to his code-breaker screen and entered the two simple words in the two spaces that he could see floating at the bottom. A nervous click on "enter" transformed his desktop into a pure white blur; a series of small gears appeared, whirling. They multiplied to create a massive, super-secure door that slowly creaked open . . .

"Benny, dear, can you come set the table?" called his mom down the basement stairs. *A hemisphere's fate was hanging in the balance!*

"In a sec, Mom."

A small panel emerged from center screen. The instructions were clear: You have 60 seconds to read the objective.

Not a second more.

You may not copy or save it to any computer or camera.

Erase your tracks.

Start Now!

Benny wiped the sweat from his palms onto the legs of his jeans, just as the code popped up. His eyes blinked as he struggled to bring the cacophonous mess into focus. He wasn't ready, but the game had started.

There was a clicking sound, pounding out the seconds, while a bold-faced timer positioned in the upper right-hand corner of the screen ticked down the seconds. Flashes emanated from the sides of the monitor, while words and numbers swam across the screen to build the full code, his clue. The combination overwhelmed Benny, even with help from his inner Amanuel.

"Benny, dear, your dinner's getting cold," sang his mother, from upstairs.

"Mom, I said—" Benny yelled in agitated response but froze midsentence. The counter hit zero, and his entire screen spiraled down a black hole.

A tiny hand appeared with a lone skeletal index finger indicting Benny. A small disembodied voice escaped from his speakers: "That's all you get."

And his chance faded. They locked him out. Months of searching were out the window. *What demon concocted this no-recording rule, anyway? Who relied on memory alone today, with all the tools available?*

Benny twirled his finger over his mouse, bummed that he had been closed out and conflicted that he had created his own back door into the game.

"They would want me in, right? They need a player like Amanuel, and this 'no recording or writing down the code' crap is just a test. Of course I should try everything possible to make it inside," said Benny, shifting to Amanuel midsentence.

He clicked the screenshot icon. During the blitz of the on-screen images and after a very split-second internal struggle over the ethics of whether he should grab a screenshot of the code, he snapped off a keyboard shortcut, knowing it would be there if—and only if—he needed it. He needed it.

Benny opened the image and leaned back to take a draw on a warm PBR that Spanks had left behind, expecting to see a screen filled with words and numbers. The screen filled full size with the code—but, to Benny's dismay, the entire right half of the screen was buried under a white blur from one of the pulsing lights programmed into the distractions of the code frame. It had flashed on the same frame it captured in the screenshot, hiding half of the code! The PBR hit the concrete floor of the basement and shattered. He couldn't believe his eyes. Even cheating, Benny couldn't break into this game.

"Benny, dear, are you all right?"

"No, Mom, I am definitely *not* all right!"

88

YUMA PROVING GROUND, ARIZONA

Yuma felt like home to the Hock crew. Their Autonomous Flying Cars had now withstood a barrage of fifty-six tests over the previous three months, ranging from endurance "fly 'til the battery drops" marathons, which had cost the team yet another prototype vehicle; rough-weather takeoffs and landings; and precision navigation, which included aerial highway adherence and simulated grocery store parking access. The vehicles had held up well under the increasing pressure of the test constraints.

Starnes had tossed everything she could think of at the AFVs as the test escalated. Hock understood that she wasn't trying to defeat him but hoped to fast-track the approval process. Lunches and evenings "shooting the soy sauce," as Starnes called it, made Hock come to appreciate her detailed approach to the test process, even if her rough edges had cost him a few vehicles.

During a night off base, Hock's team had invited Starnes to join them in Scottsdale for some Rehab.

"First of all, I'm pissed that you all have been talking about going to 'rehab' for months, which I thought was great because you are the sickest group of individuals I have ever met," said Starnes, as she bit into her PBJ-and-bacon burger from the corner of two tables pulled together at the Rehab Burger Therapy location on East Second, "and now I realize that you have been off at a bar called Rehab, having these amazing burgers. You all suck, every one of you, for not inviting me sooner."

"Au contraire, General," said Dr. Hock. "I know I've said on more than one occasion that we should get that woman some therapy." There was more debate, which Hock lost when a jalapeño pepper hit him on the cheek, and he turned to see General Amy Starnes complete a demure lick of her middle finger, smiling.

After the last bite of burger, Hock offered some business for dessert. The navigation tests had gone well, and he hoped the results would release them from having to include the backup nav system in the cars for the long-distance test.

"You know, General, if my cars can fly most of the course without stopping to change out batteries, it will be a huge boost to our marketing . . . I mean, the industry. I know they can do it safely with our onboard sat system. I just need the leeway on the backup system."

"You're still seeing the small picture, Hock. I can help you the most if I provide the independent safety verification of your AFV and confirm the data on every inch of the flight path. If I do, they can't accuse us of skewing anything. I can boost your marketing by showing how *on-target* your path was"—she smiled at the peacenik assistant, who was now used to getting the "target" jab at least once a session—"and how safe your vehicle is."

That ended the discussion about the backup navigation equipment for Hock. He couldn't argue against her looking out for his interest while she made certain the country's skies would be safe. They still had a couple months to fine-tune the cars, while waiting on the northern winter to lift, and to complete eight more test trips around YPG to strut their skills. Spring would keep them all busy.

Dessert arrived, to a chorus of oohs and aahs. Hock had ordered it without asking the others, and it made his evening feel like a party. Even if the discussion had not been all good, he would try to fix it with chocolate.

89

LAS VEGAS, NEVADA

"You boys are dipping into this kinda heavy," said Kip, the default Driven Gang accountant, because he worked at a bank on the outside. Shank had pulled out of Montana after the stampede test, less some living expenses with $85,000 cash in his saddlebag and no plan for the winter but a party. Instead of stopping in Seattle, he turned left and led the gang down the coast, through San Francisco, over through Sacramento, Tahoe for a crazy tubing session at Heavenly Valley, bowling in Reno, and finally Vegas for cards and warmth.

They had arrived in Vegas mid-December. Shank reckoned they had adequate funding for three or four months until they ran back to Montana and picked up the next saddlebag full of cash. Living expenses, habits, hangers-on, and hospitals chewed up their cash much faster than expected.

The Bi-Cycle Motel in North Vegas, which had a sign that tried to connect biker lore to the playing-card brand, had become base of operations for the crew over the last month and a week. It was not in rival territory and was cheap. The owners, Amanda and Brian, a sweet senior couple from Houston, joked with Nikki and Shank that they wanted to sidecar out with them when they left. They were honest folks with a full motel and big smiles.

"So, what does 'spending pretty fast' mean, Kip?" asked Shank, in front of the council, trying not to look too concerned as he ate a corn dog.

"A few weeks . . . maybe a month," said Kip.

Shank tossed his corn dog stick toward the trashcan. "Dudes, it's been fun here in Vegas, but I'm ready to live extra-large. We need to tag up with Bullseye. I know she's itching to go and won't let a little snow stop her." He smiled at the prospect of speaking with Bullseye again.

The trick to remaining the leader of a biker gang was to stay out front. Shank knew that no one joined a gang just to get by. He had to show them a great time and take them places. If he didn't, the next guy would. Bullseye's test stampede had been large money for work that felt more like a party. They got to tear stuff up, chase things, ride wherever they wanted, and celebrate with the spoils. A snowpack would make it tougher, but so what? It was a helluva lot better than shooting up a rival gang over territory rights, which would happen sooner or later in Vegas. They would either end up dead or dead broke. Vegas had been fun, but it was time to ride.

90

DES MOINES, IOWA

"Vermin, die," sneered Amanuel as he blasted a furry alien life-form.

"What's that, dear?" sang Benny's mom from upstairs.

"Nothing, Mom, I'm talking to my game."

"I'm worried about that, Benny. I think sometimes you spend too much time with your little game."

"In a minute, Mom," said Benny, making her point.

He had to find a way into one of the more exclusive role-playing games soon, or he would go nuts. As Benny, he was trapped in his mom's basement. As Amanuel, he grabbed the world by the biscuits and held on for the ride— extinguishing anyone who stood in his way. "Extinguish . . . exxxtinguish . . . extinguissshh," he practiced in a maligned Russianesque accent.

"Would you like more macaroni and cheese, dear?"

"Yes, I will extinguish another bowl," Amanuel replied.

Another hour drifted away with no progress. Congealed mac 'n' cheese sat next to Benny as he grew more despondent. *I should have done more to get in the game!* Once the initial contact sequence from Facebook started, he took the simple two-word code and the requisite sixty-second period to memorize his access key number and passwords, just like everyone else. Four words, that looked like German. Twenty-seven digits—no obvious sequence. That was a lot to swallow in one minute. The bold-faced timer, burned into the corner of the screen, added tension to the process as it pulsed and pounded down the time, partnered with an annoying sledgehammer sound effect and a laughing clown poking into the screen. So not cool.

All he got was "44°TUN . . . ," a fragment of a code on the screenshot, with most of the screen blurred white, hiding the full answer.

I don't need this . . . then an idea hit Benny so hard that he dropped his half-eaten Jack Link onto the keyboard. This was a test! Part of the game! *Sure,* he told himself. *Of course, that's what I would do if I wanted someone to prove their worthiness in a game of this caliber. They want me to break in.*

He would keep searching. There must be a "friendly" willing to talk— straight up, one op to another.

44°TUN. It was a start. *Is it a code, or a key?*

It would be a delicious moment when he cracked their code. Dinner would wait—a few minutes, anyway. He pinched the stub of his Jack Link and kissed it like an elegant cigar. *Now, how can I get Amanuel noticed?*

The plan played out simply in Benny's mind: Create a backstory for his Amanuel personality and post excerpts everywhere. Proliferate the story with keywords that would catch a gamer's eye, so they might recruit him for the next round of *GloDom*. Stop at nothing to get Amanuel noticed on Facebook.

Undercover . . . master of disguise . . . ability to blend in with indigenous . . . deadly problem solver . . . brilliant negotiator in all Middle Eastern matters and languages . . . smuggle . . . devastatingly attractive . . . seeking Global Domination.

With the help of his community college SEO marketing class tactics, Benny posted his story in a few blogs worldwide and, after three days of tweaking, spied his story on page three of Google when he searched *spy, intrigue, agent, undercover,* or any of fifty other terms he had curated for his online fable. Now he would monitor everything, waiting for them to take the bait and invite Amanuel into the game.

"Benny, dear, would you take the trash out when you finish playing?"

"Sure, Mom." *Playing?* He would show her what *playing* was from his control perch, while steering the political underbelly of the entire northern hemisphere—right from her basement.

91

LAS VEGAS TO LAME HORSE CREEK
BY TEXT

The layers of fabric on the cave entrance to the Sultan's Retreat fluttered in the breeze as Bullseye cracked the outer door to the mine and emerged above ground. There was no hardwired giga-anything this far up the valley, but the broadband card in her truck helped with Wi-Fi calls, and text messages slipped through, sometimes underground, when nothing else did.

>Need to check-in. Shank

A biker gang wouldn't get cold feet, so she imagined he was out of money.

>>NO service today. Need to text. What's up?

After a pause, he responded . . .

>My friends and I are ready for this little journey of yours. How soon can we launch?

>>too cold & snowy right now.

>we don't care. We don't care.

>>It's not about you. It's the animals. They won't move until it's warmer. Hang on just a few more weeks.

>OK...

Three circles kept blinking, letting Bullseye know that Shank was searching for what to say next. She beat him to the punch:

>>I can float 20k more your way if you need it.

Shank shot back:

>YES!

>>Just be ready when I need you. I'll head down the hill and wire it tomorrow. Stay out of jail.

>YES!

Bullseye imagined the parties the gang had with her money. She was about to do the same with Stubblefield's cash, and gold from some sheik or prince from the tunnel, so she couldn't blame Shank. Her party was a few million down a beach somewhere, with no bikers, no animals, and no snow.

92

VIRGINIA CITY, MONTANA

Governor McLemore utilized Evan in a series of Google Hangout sessions to fire up some big ranchers and to calm down others. Evan always brought bits and pieces of Secession progress to the Placer, where he found the company to be comforting.

The meatloaf had been eighty-sixed by the time he arrived at the café, along with the crowd. He just wanted some company and a salad, to which Mona said, "Of course you do, honey, and that's why you're all gorgeous and slim and not like these beefy ranchers."

Mona served him the Mondorf Salad, which she named after herself, although the recipe included making a Waldorf and replacing the walnuts with sunflower seeds. The diner was slow and the last two patrons scooted out as Mona served Evan's meal. She looked perplexed as she wiped down the table next to Evan.

"You doing OK, Mona? You look a little worried."

"Oh, I'm fine, Evan. I mean, other than the obvious: losing our homes or fighting the government and all. I've just been wondering about something for a long time. You're the only one I know that can help me, but I've been a little shy to ask. It's the silliest thing, but . . ."

"Well go ahead, girl. We know each other pretty well, and we're starting a new nation together. You can ask me anything." Evan had fielded lots of difficult questions during his tour with the governor and had become well versed in national matters, Montana history, and economic issues.

"All right. It's silly, like I say, but I was watching one of your movies the other day, *El Camino Good-Bye*, and I was just thinking, is there a difference when you kiss someone on the screen? I mean, does it feel different from a real-life kiss? I'm sure it doesn't mean anything, right, because you're just acting?"

No one had asked Evan that question on the recent tour, but he had thought about it back in Hollywood. "You know, Mona, I will say that I put my whole heart and soul into acting. When I used to make movies, I dove into whatever part I was playing, so sure, screen kisses count. There are lines I didn't cross, at least, while we were working, but I still wanted the intimate scenes to look real. They didn't have any lasting meaning, but for that moment—wow. So that's the difference."

Mona set the coffeepot down and leaned against the table, which slid a little under her significant weight. She blushed and recovered. "So, a romantic kiss and a screen kiss are the same?"

"Well, yes, and no," said Evan, not catching on very fast. "You want to look like there's a lot of movement, but you don't flex as much. Here, I can just show you. You don't mind, do you?"

"I would find it most fascinating," said Mona, after pulling out a tube of ChapStick and giving herself a quick glossing. She had pretty, full lips.

"Well, in a stage kiss, it's like this . . ." and he stepped close to her, reached his hands up to her cheeks, then slid one of them down around her neck and let it continue down across her shoulder to the small of her large back. As he did this, he drew her closer until their bodies pressed against each other for their entire length. He tilted his head and guided hers in the opposite direction with his other hand and engaged her soft lips with a slow movement of his mouth settling against hers, massaging her lips with his. He swiveled his head in a slow rotation from side to side.

After about twenty seconds, Evan eased away from her—but stopped a nose-length from her face. Their hips still touching and their embrace intact, Evan whispered, looking deep into Mona's eyes, "See—you can always tell a stage kiss. It just doesn't have the same stuff as a romantic kiss."

"R-r-right," said Mona, stuttering.

"Mona, you are a beautiful woman with the sweetest of smiles. You have always made me feel welcome here, even when others wouldn't. You are kind, and you are a special friend and one of my favorite people in the entire world, Mona, dear."

After speaking from his heart, Evan pulled her hips even tighter against his, closed his eyes and leaned in to show her how consuming a romantic kiss could be, even between good friends.

The difference in the kisses was Evan's heartfelt whisper, which caressed a sensitivity inside Mona and connected on the deepest of levels.

Evan felt her release a soft, pleasing moan as he kissed her.

When the kiss was complete, Evan held her close for a full minute. Sixty-four seconds, to be exact. He watched the big clock on the wall tick around, but he didn't want to be the first to let go. He enjoyed the safety of the embrace and could tell by her boa-like squeeze that he was not alone.

93

WASHINGTON, DC

"More dead, sir," said the chief of staff as he barged in the Oval Office. "Pockets of fighting have flared up all over, and I recommend we evacuate you to Camp David this afternoon, sir."

"No one is shooting at the White House, although I would understand if they did," snapped the president. "We're staying put. I have a lot of people to communicate with and hiding in the woods sends the wrong signal. Thank you, Blair," said Crowley as he dismissed his chief and addressed the others. "How are the people holding up in Montana?"

Fowler opened his notebook, revealing a list of names and stats. "Mr. President, we have it on good authority that the Secession movement has overwhelming support among Montanans and is mixed in polling in the other forty-nine states. Governor McLemore has recruited help from the wealthiest statesmen and the high-profile Hollywood-types who've settled up there.

The head of the Senate Energy Committee gave the president a concise, twenty-minute update on the world energy situation, as requested. Recent busts in major Russian and Chinese oil field exploration would increase OPEC's value, and the UAE's share should show a huge increase in their near- and long-term value. This confirmed the report he had received from Wall Street speculators whose information was sometimes ahead of his own intelligence folks. The president hoped this would keep the UAE's offer to buy Montana moving, with an earlier closing date.

The president updated the group on the UAE's due diligence. They had deployed undercover parties to Montana to do a site survey of the state and the assets as they prepare the contract. Fowler said, "Dan, I hear that they're using different excuses for their scouting, like university visits, factory relocations, and hunting trips. I'm sure the Secession folks will see through that, and it will make good fuel for their movement."

"I agree, Bill, but don't think we can avoid it. It's not like the whole thing is a big secret now anyway, right," said Crowley to Fowler.

The two ranking House members delivered the best news update of the meeting, giving insight on the legislative process required for Montana's sale to the Emiratis. Speaker Pazdan delivered the news:

"You'll be happy, maybe shocked, to hear that a huge majority of the representatives are voicing support for a bill to put Montana on the auction block, Dan. The Judicial Committee is crafting the plan to streamline the process and make this possible. It's still an uphill battle legally, but I think having a sweeping bipartisan majority from the House may get this thing done."

Crowley made some notes before speaking. "I'm not surprised that they voiced support for severing their fellow state, in order to save their own turf. It sounds worse when you say it like that, doesn't it? I think that's the reality, and we'll hear a lot about that as we go forward. Let's all remember that this polling was done under a secret scenario, and opinions could change under the light of day."

94

LAME HORSE CREEK, IDAHO

Bullseye's tunnel tenant would have to exercise patience. Transporting contraband between Idaho and Montana would be possible by carrying, rolling, or dragging; a large vehicle would not make the twists and turns. Regardless, it was much nicer than most of the tunnels that the drug lords used in and out of Mexico. *Call those drug guys in Mexico*, thought Bullseye.

She shut down the excavator for the evening, grabbed her laptop, and got swallowed by a huge, musty beanbag chair. The long Ethernet cable rigged to her broadband card up on the surface had been working well to extend the internet down into the mine shaft to her computer. When not digging, she had scoured online sites, trying to find a willing agent.

Bullseye started slow, not sure how to search for help. She tried phrases like "agent," "smuggle," and "covert," and kept stumbling on the name "Amanuel." No last name. Just *Amanuel*, along with descriptions like "capable," "deadly," "well connected in the Middle East," and "44°TUN." On top of all that, this Amanuel guy was smoking hot, as if that mattered.

Bullseye felt a little stupid running this search. A true smuggler would have connections to the underworld. A search on the net was not prone to just poop out a pirate, but she had run out of ideas and this Amanuel guy seemed like a good place to start. Bullseye posted a cryptic message, hoping to catch his attention with a little cat and mouse. The 44° reference seemed to relate to latitude (at least half of it, anyway) that was close to Lame Horse Creek. She had no idea what the "TUN" reference was, but she already had half a tunnel, so why not connect the dots?

"Intrigued by your intrigue. I am at 44°," began the message. "Amanuel—contact sought. Discreet." She gave an email address that ended in .md and used her VPN to route from Moldova through China and then to Bullseye's Gmail account. It would be troublesome to trace. China had seen to that, but the Moldovan leg was a taxing, confusing touch.

She stared at the screen, wondering what time it was in his part of the world. After deciding he was not likely to respond right away, she curled up in the beanbag chair, pulled one of the fabric panels off the wall for a light blanket, and drifted off for a nap. Tearing into the cavern walls had made her bone weary and dead tired.

DES MOINES, IOWA

This had to be it! After sorting out a few prank responses, Benny had spotted the short listing. No fluff.

INTRIGUED BY YOUR INTRIGUE. I AM AT 44°
AMANUEL—CONTACT SOUGHT. DISCREET.

Concise. Right to the point. This is how real international dominators would talk. No superfluous language or colorful picture-painting." *Contact sought.*

Benny put on his Amanuel swagger to create the response. He must get it right—too eager and they could bounce him from the game. Too evasive and he may get ignored. Benny got up from the keyboard and walked a circle, staring at the screen. He gathered his bathrobe, retied the frayed belt around his large waist, and sneered as Amanuel, "Yes, I'll accept your global espionage project." He lunged at the keyboard and pounded: Intrigued. I am the one you seek. Respond to . . .

Benny laid out steps for the solicitor to respond without using email. By breaking it up into phrases and posting it on three different job-site bulletin boards under the company name Bond Adhesives, he felt sure that no one could decipher the total message by mistake and proved Benny's prowess for the clandestine gaming world.

He would have time to ponder his next move as Amanuel and monitor any response from his smartphone, while he worked the overnight shift at the Taco Palace drive-thru window. He pulled on his orange Palace uniform shirt, which stretched to cover his expansive stomach. He wrestled his company bolo tie over his head, then slid the small metal taco clasp into position. Gazing into the mirror for a second, he lost focus . . .

Amanuel adjusted the bowtie and brushed his tuxedo jacket lapel with the back of his fingers. Attractive women stepped closer to Amanuel as he slid through the casino. He swiped his hand across his chest to feel the security of his gun under his tuxedo and realized . . .

"Mom, have you seen my name tag? I'm gonna be late for work!"

96

LAME HORSE CREEK, IDAHO

A series of dings from her phone cut Bullseye's nap short. The phone shook in her hand as she followed instructions to craft and deliver her responses. **SHALL WE SAY, 'IMPORT' GOODS UNDER THE RADAR TO THE NEW COUNTRY? THINK OF IT AS A 'TOLLWAY' FOR ITEMS THAT CERTAIN INDIVIDUALS WOULD NOT WANT OTHER INDIVIDUALS TO KNOW ABOUT . . .**

This was the third of her three posts to the Bond Adhesive employment bulletin board that afternoon. The first two described, in a brief and cryptic fashion, the sale of Montana to a foreign power and the opportunity to access the new country from the United States (and vice versa).

A few more posts and Bullseye would have her client. She wasn't sure what interested Amanuel the most—drug running, technology secrets— whatever; she didn't care. Her tunnel was the gateway in and out of the US to a state that she used to love but had been taken away, so the toll would be steep. Bullseye hoped to bank at least a million before she moved to her island.

DES MOINES, IOWA

Benny stood at his computer in the corner of the basement, still wearing his Taco Palace apron and name tag. He'd worked a long night at the drive-thru window, but now, looking at his ticket into the game of *Global Domination*, he had a hard time containing himself. He had to show them he was a worthy candidate, the middleman they needed. This was no doubt a dangerous, but key role for an international dominator.

But something nipped away at his confidence. Was this a sucker role? Was he the sacrificial lamb that every game needed so that the pros didn't have to die first? *Doesn't matter*, Amanuel encouraged his weaker host. *This is our gateway into the game, and we're gonna take it.* Benny sat up taller and allowed Amanuel to drive.

As the go-between for a smuggling operation . . . *cartel? . . . group? . . .* What was the correct term for this organization? "Concern" would cover it. As the interceder for the smuggling concern and a foreign country, Amanuel could demand his price.

A foreign country in Montana? Who creates this stuff? This game was too far-fetched for reality, but he didn't make the rules. He was just happy to do his part for global domination.

He would have to pay the concern a toll to use the tunnel to sneak stuff in and out of a new country that used to be Montana and America, then turn around and collect money from those hoping to use the smuggling route. The next part of the game must involve locating those who played the underworld folks in the new country and convey the opportunity to swing in and out of the US. *This game must have hundreds of players*, thought Benny. *Cool.*

Before he could locate those folks, he would have to give a number to the concern. An amount that let them know he was the man for the job. Benny hadn't learned of his currency allocation for this virtual world, but he assumed that would come soon. His twenty-five-hour-a-week paycheck at Taco Palace would not serve as a good reference for this decision. Besides—that was real money, and he had to make a bid with virtual funds. He looked inward to Amanuel.

With a different voice from inside his head, Amanuel slapped Benny twice and reprimanded, *You wuss! Ante up. They must not stop us.* Benny licked his lips and wiped the sweat from his forehead. Amanuel was right. He *was* a wuss! History would mark this moment as the merging of Benny and Amanuel. He would toss out an offer to grab their attention and then work to reinvent himself in real life—to be more like his game persona, Amanuel. There was no reason Benny should call the shots. Look at the miserable hole he had worked them into after all these years. It was time for Amanuel to lead. He sneered and typed the post:

I WILL PAY A FEE OF ONE MILLION U.S. PER MONTH FOR THIS DANGEROUS JOB. I WILL COORDINATE ALL INTERNATIONAL PARTIES TO USE THE SERVICE.

He exhaled long and slow as he hit the "send" button. It was only play money anyway, but the wrong amount could get him bounced from the game. And just like that, he was out there. If they bit, he would have to deliver at a level he had not ventured into for other games—as Benny *or* Amanuel.

Benny climbed the stairs, two at a time, with a newfound resolve. If his meal wasn't hot enough, he would command his mom to heat it up. He was a new man: Amanuel rising.

98

LAME HORSE CREEK, IDAHO

One million dollars a *month* to use her tunnel! The mother lode! There weren't enough tourists to drag on trail rides to equal that much money. Bullseye didn't know whether to drink, spit, swear, or just start digging in celebration. She reread that part of the message again and again . . .

. . . ONE MILLION U.S. PER MONTH . . .

A million a *month*! She could milk this for six months, maybe a year, then head south and not just lie on a beach but *buy* the beach! That would take planning. Payment had to be in gold, and the sheer weight would require a large-capacity truck. Or maybe it would be bitcoin, and she had to learn how that worked. Her mind swam with the list of logistics, when a thought—a chilling thought—crossed her mind: *I have to finish the tunnel.*

What will this Amanuel want to smuggle? Drugs? Tanks? Nuclear weapons? Truckfuls of terrorists? Who is he connected to? Regardless, he would expect a bigger thoroughfare than the one she had carved out. It was game on. Forget the tourists scratching at her walls; it was time to gear up. Bullseye wasn't afraid to spend a few hundred thousand now for the future. The first hundred thousand would go for a new front-end loader that could double her progress.

She sprinted outside into the snow to the hand-painted billboard that read, "Bullseye's Ghost Town—Trail Rides, Mining for Famous Montana Sapphires and Gold Panning." She took a bucket of white paint and dipped a broad, stiff brush in the liquid, then crossed out the "OPEN YEAR-ROUND" part and painted over a huge "CLOSED FOR GOOD." Stepping back to admire her work, she added one final phrase. "KEEP OUT!!!"

99

VIRGINIA CITY, MONTANA

Evan kiss kissed Mona and settled at the Community Table. After returning from another blitz tour with Governor McLemore, he had promised an important update to the team.

About three minutes later, Bullseye followed him in, to the cheers of her friends. "Bullseye, you sweet thing, we have sure been missing you," said Mona, as she helped Bullseye take off her scarf.

"Well, I've missed you all. My schedule has been crazy. With all this sell Montana thing, I guess the boys from Washington are trying to squeeze in a few more hunting trips before their playground goes away." After protests and outbursts of "How can you work with those state-stealing scoundrels?" Bullseye defended her decision. "Look, no one knows what will happen, so meanwhile, I will take as much of their money as I dang well can. What's the news from up here?"

"I missed you, Bullseye. You look fantastic," said Evan, as he gave up his chair for her and leaned close.

She looked a little embarrassed. "Oh, Evan. I've had my hands full with all sorts of things, but I should have called. I'm sorry. I will call soon, maybe on my way back to Idaho."

Evan smiled warmly, then held his hand up to the table and said, "Listen, I've got something more current to bring up and it's not good news." The entire table hushed after Evan's dramatic beckon. He leaned forward. "I was with McLemore and Senator Hepburn on this last trip. They cut Hepburn off from official contact with the president, but he still has plenty of friends on the committee who are keeping him posted on new developments, and there's been a big one." Evan took a sip of his coffee while the entire table waited, holding their collective breath.

"I've been told the president has a buyer. Somebody in the Middle East is interested in buying our state and turning it into their country."

"Son of a . . . ," gasped April. No one else generated a sound. Bullseye nearly choked on her coffee.

"Can you believe somebody has enough money that they could help the United States by buying a piece of it? How rich are those people?" added April.

218

A-million-dollars-a-month-to-use-my-tunnel rich, thought Bullseye. "Mona, I need to grab that to go, sweetie," she said, slamming a long slurp of coffee. All her friends at the table protested, saying her cheeks were still red from the cold.

"I know and I'm sorry. I just thought of the gear I have to grab at the farm, and I should hightail it back to the Lame Horse to keep working." The group whined as Bullseye collected her scarf and coat while waiting on Mona to bring her breakfast. April took control of the setting.

"So, if they have a buyer lined up, shouldn't we be ready to announce our secession?" asked April, which launched a discussion about where they should hold the press conference. They did not notice when Bullseye moved toward the front door or that Evan had followed her.

"Listen, Bullseye," Evan said as he helped her with her coat, "you're a hard one to read, but if you're leaving because I haven't called you, or you're still mad about me dropping in on you and the vice president, I'm sorry. I don't have any idea what's going on with you."

She pushed her arm through her sleeve, almost punching him in the mouth, maybe by accident, then said, "Oh, Evan, honey, this is not at all about you. You are a good-looking man and you cast quite a spell, but there are bigger things in my life right now. I'll tell you what's going on in my world. My business is at a critical juncture, and a couple of very powerful people are investigating a merger with my operation. I've got to run by the farm, pick up some explosives, run back to Idaho, take off all my clothes while I'm working in my sauna-like mine shaft, let the sweat trickle down my well-defined abs and down to . . ." She paused her description and her slow-moving index finger tracing the path at her belly button, to see if Evan might fall over, then added, "Down to the ground so I can work carefree and focus on the merger. Take care, Evan." As she finished, she reached up and tweaked his nose with her thumb and index finger, then slipped out the front door.

He didn't move until the cold air slapped him.

100

WASHINGTON, DC

The eight months since the Camp David brainstorming session had been the longest of the president's life. The two months since the leaders of the United Arab Emirates agreed, in theory, to buy Montana had slowed to a crawl. Updates showed limited progress, and he could feel the financial crisis hurtling in around him.

"Mr. President . . . Dan . . . ," said Vice President Fowler as if he didn't want to disturb his quiet train of thought.

The president turned from a distant stare out of the window of the Oval Office and said, "Yes, thanks, Bill. Sorry. OK, it's time to tell. We need to announce our intention to sell Montana," said the president, matter-of-factly.

"Are you sure we're ready?" was the foremost response heard over the rumble of questions from the senators, Fowler, Stubblefield, and Blair, seated on the couches opposing each other in the Oval Office, with the president behind his desk. The president stood and circled, grabbing his stick on the way, and leaned against the front, clasping his hands with the stick protruding like a wand.

He had picked up a simple wooden stick with a small burl at Camp David during their first meeting about Montana. The president seized it, swished it, jabbed, thrust, and slashed with it, and carried it around during the brainstorming. The stick made the trip home from the Montana meetings, and every night he left it on his desk in the Oval Office or in his private study next door, never taking it into the Residence or out in public. It was not for national consumption and only close staff ever saw the president carrying or waving the stick. It was a *thinking stick*, and he secretly wished he had a more powerful one—even a real magic wand.

He used a quiet tone to indicate this decision was nonnegotiable. "It's time. Too many leaks have developed. My office has gotten calls from corporations, big donors, even politicians asking what is going on with this Montana thing. Panic will set in soon if we don't confirm something."

"But, Mr. President, we don't have all the answers yet and haven't finished the legal foundation for eminent domain claims . . . ," said Chief of Staff Blair, looking over his long list of items to accomplish in the short term.

"I know. I know. We can at least squelch rumors and build some confidence that we will try to be fair with everyone—even though what we're doing is not fair, people need to know what they're in for."

"When, Dan?" asked Bill Fowler.

"In about two weeks, I'll call a press conference after I line up a few more details and lock down the vote in Congress as best I can. I would say I want that to be a secret, but based on past performance, I won't expect much," said the president, looking right at the VP, who turned to look at Graham Blair. "I won't be announcing anything specific about the potential buyers—we're still ironing out the deal with the UAE, and I don't want to screw it up, but an announcement about our intentions may help our negotiations."

Secretary of the Interior Alan Stubblefield said, "I hope this doesn't create a wave of panic and profit-seeking in Montana, Dan."

"Who says it hasn't already started, Alan?" said the president, pointing his stick at Stubblefield.

101

CORVALLIS, MONTANA

Shank led the Driven Gang up highway 93 into Corvallis and then east. The *e*-less Dud Ranch sign was a welcome glow on the horizon after the long drive from Vegas. Nikki had called ahead, and the owners said the place was all theirs. Corvallis had an official population of nine hundred, plus a few, so the 150 bikers in the Driven Gang were a significant addition to the local scenery. Vegas was fun, but the money had leaked like an old man's diaper, so Shank led them back to a spot where they couldn't spend much to wait on the stampede.

The food at the Dud Ranch was OK, and the motel was quiet unless the gang wanted otherwise. They could almost all fit in the restaurant at once, and Shank convened the meeting as they all gathered.

"I know it's colder than Vegas—quit your whinin'," he said to kick off the meeting. "The snow will be gone soon, and we'll launch our little rodeo. Until then, we can make our own fun, right?"

Everyone cheered, talked, and deferred as gangs do when a strong leader lays down the law. The music started back up and the meeting splintered into little groups. Shank met with Chaz, the Dud Ranch owner, at the end of the bar and plopped down their last $12,100, with the plan: Chaz was to host one helluva party, keep track of the tab for the rooms, the food, and the booze, and when the money dried up, the gang would take off on their "rodeo." Shank hoped that at off-season rates the end of their party would coordinate with the snowmelt and Bullseye's animal alarm clock, so they could ride on to their next fortune.

102

EUREKA, MONTANA

By the time the governor's plane climbed out of Eureka, banking right to avoid Canadian airspace, Evan Morris already had his boots kicked off and a bourbon in hand. Their series of meetings around the state continued to be emotional and successful. The last two, at a stunning castle manor on Shelter Island in Flathead Lake and in the hills above Lake Koocanusa, near Rexford, at the largest log home Evan had ever seen, included a roomful of the state's wealthiest and most influential citizens, which helped build Evan's confidence that the Secession team had developed a critical mass of support with deep connections all over the United States.

"Well, Governor," said Evan to McLemore and the four others on the plane, "when do we go public?"

"That's the hard part, Evan," said the governor. "I still don't think we can announce anything until the president shoots first. If we're premature in our move, we'll look like we're trying to steal all the national park land for ourselves, and that won't work. Meanwhile, the rumors are spreading, the media is following all sorts of wild story lines, so real estate prices have dropped to zero, tourism is down, crime is up. It's crazy, but I'd rather the president just announce that he wants to sell our state so we can stop this slide."

The governor's phone buzzed, and Senator Hepburn's name popped up on the display. After a brief conversation, the governor announced they had their answer: the president was likely a week away from making his big announcement.

The news focused their conversation. They parsed their plan as they flew over the Little Bighorn and landed on the Northern Cheyenne Indian Reservation to meet with members of the Cheyenne, Sioux, Crow, and other tribes to see if they would make one last stand, this time with their Montana neighbors.

103

SCOTTSDALE, ARIZONA

Yuma felt like molasses to Dr. Hock's flightrepreneurs. The heat was oppressive, and their craft was restricted to running tests around the same YPG courses. Hock was ready to fly cross-country and show his investors and the world that his Magic Carpet could transform transportation forever. He maneuvered to Scottsdale for the evening, inviting Starnes to join him for another burger at Rehab.

With a dab of ketchup in the corner of his mouth, Dr. Hock pleaded with the general, "We've done everything you've asked. We've passed test after test at Yuma. Our cars are ready to fly the distance, General."

"They may be ready, but now I'm not sure the course is ready, Hock. I'm still waiting to wring out the install on a couple of navigation pods way up north. I don't think it will take too much longer, but we're crossing some tall mountains and need the snow to melt a little to have clear access, and now, Congress is woofing about cutting the funding for this program altogether."

"So how about this? What if we run half the country, just to let us stretch our wings? Yuma to Southern Utah. Then back. You can pick the turn. Could you do that quickly, under existing budgets?"

The chatter in Rehab escalated, so Starnes leaned closer to Hock. "That'll give a good read on the distance, but not push it too far out of the chute." Starnes rubbed her chin. Then bit her burger. Then wiped her chin. Then said, "For God's sake, wipe the ketchup off your mouth, Hock. You eat like a high schooler."

He wiped both sides of his mouth, around his smile.

She continued, "OK, I'll give you that shot. Yuma to Utah. Southern Utah, most likely, so you won't be running over too many mountains and no urban areas. I'll work it up and get my guys to run the beacon line to make sure everything checks out quickly and try to beat this budget cut."

Then the general handed him another napkin.

104

DES MOINES, IOWA

Benny lapped the basement. For a week straight, when not *may I take your order-ing* at the Taco Palace drive-thru, he was scanning sites for the final confirmation from the gamer with the handle "Bullseye." *Great username.* This Bullseye sounded serious, and Benny knew his character Amanuel had to keep an edge, to prevent elimination from the game.

OK, MR. AMANUEL, I THINK IT'S TIME WE MET FACE-TO-FACE. IF YOU'RE SERIOUS ABOUT THIS GAME, FIND YOUR WAY TO THIS COUNTRY, TO IDAHO, AND I'LL GIVE YOU THE GRAND TOUR.

The other posts that followed provided a longitude and latitude right on the Idaho/Montana border. The posts said he should come as soon as possible and bring a deposit to seal the deal. He would have to dress the part. A tux would do, as he had described himself as a man of international distinction, coming from "somewhere in the Middle East."

Confused, Benny dropped sweat all over his keyboard. He couldn't decide if this was real—not the money part but the travel and actual meetup part. Was the game leaving the virtual realm and going terrestrial into some cosplay-acting thing? It sure sounded like it, and the prospect spooked him. What if this was a hoax—a bunch of dudes luring him out to the woods to kill him? What if this was . . .

I know, what if this is your coming-out party and by happenstance you grow some marbles? said Amanuel, to himself, inside Benny's head.

"It could be a sucker move. They do this all the time to weed out the nubes," said Benny, guessing, out loud.

What if you're just afraid that your diapers will fill up and you'll run out of breast milk? You wuss. I can't believe we live in the same body. You are hopeless. How can you expect to make it on a steamy night in Morocco with a she-spy when you can't even stretch your umby cord a couple of states away? "You disgust me," shouted Amanuel at himself.

"What's that, dear?" asked his mom from the top of the stairs.

"Nothing, Mom. Just talking to myself," said Benny.

And playing with yourself, like always. How about you just reach down and take inventory, and if you find anything that resembles marbles, use them to answer this Bullseye character, who's offering the adventure of a lifetime. Tell him we're on our way. Get your worthless friends to come if you need backup, scolded Amanuel.

He typed the post as Amanuel guided his fingers on the keyboard:

I WILL TAKE YOUR CHALLENGE AND COME TO YOUR LITTLE TUNNEL. I WILL BRING MY MOST TRUSTED CONFIDANTS AND THE EVIDENCE YOU SEEK. I WILL ADVISE OF EXACT ARRIVAL BUT ANTICIPATE TWO WEEKS' TIME.

He exhaled again as he hit the "send" button. Amanuel called him a *wuss* as he retreated into the background. Benny clicked his window closed and headed upstairs. "Mom, I've been thinking of taking a little trip."

Benny jumped as he heard the mac 'n' cheese serving bowl shatter against the floor upstairs.

105

THE WHITE HOUSE
NATIONAL TELEVISION/INTERNET

The East Room of the White House had been transformed into a dramatic television studio, chosen to look expansive and formal, but not opulent. The presidential seal hung on a substantial, polished wood podium, which rested on a low stage, flanked by a tall American flag, carefully pleated to reveal the stars plainly in view, in front of a dark-maroon velour curtain. A single camera and prompter, with a minimal crew, including audio and makeup, worked quietly, preparing to capture and circulate the announcement to the outlets in the press pool, waiting downstairs. The floor director spoke softly to the president as he received his final pat-down from the makeup specialist, then turned to count the crew in to the broadcast. She did not need to hush the room as the red tally light blazed on the camera.

"This is a difficult night for our nation," said the president, taking his first beat, as practiced. "Your family, every family in our country, has felt the oppression of the nation's impending financial disaster. You have raised your collective voices, crying, 'Enough is enough.'"

The president paused again, without blinking, still peering into the lens.

"As your president, I have not steered you clear of disaster. Congress has failed you. I apologize for my role in this catastrophe. As a Congressman I helped get us into this position by voting to approve higher and higher levels of spending money that we just did not have. Your family is required to stick to a strict budget, and yet for years, administrations and Congress have failed to follow that same simple principle that your grandmother and Dave Ramsey have always said: live on less than you make. As your president, I have not been bold enough to stop the spending, nor have I addressed the many other issues that are conspiring against our way of life. Tonight, I am announcing an aggressive plan to retrieve our country from this dangerous precipice."

Round sweat beads formed on the president's powdered brow, but he dared not wipe his face.

"The first part of the plan involves a massive restructuring, or I should say, *resizing*, of government. Through executive orders and legislative proposals, I am asking Congress to expedite my plan on slashing over one trillion dollars from our budget and more than twenty trillion dollars from our deficit with radical organization and policy changes, as well as shedding some entire programs and assets. The details on these cuts in government will be available in the next few weeks, but understand that life as we know it in our great country has changed and must change again to survive."

The president leaned over the podium, ignoring his notes. "I can't believe I just uttered that phrase: life as we know it in our great country has changed and must change again to survive. To *survive*. That is the cost of decades of over spending and it stops now." He straightened up and paused to take a sip of water.

"The plan requires the understanding and support of all Americans. But saving America and the second part of the plan requires the sacrifice of a special segment of our population. Tonight, I'm alerting the citizens of Montana that the United States government will exercise the eminent domain transfer of land from their state, with the intention of selling this property as an asset to a sovereign foreign people."

Crowley blinked twice as a fat drop of sweat trickled past his right eye. He covered the difficult process in methodical fashion: how his administration had selected Montana over other states, some of the discarded ideas they had investigated, and a sad reminder of the tragedies, along with the death toll, that had precipitated such a radical move. The president felt the First Lady's emotional support, without looking in her direction. Denise's proud-of-my-husband look—lips pursed, slightest wrinkle in her chin, cheeks grinning—had been his favorite reward over a long political career. That look always reassured him, and feeling her just off camera encouraged him to make it to the closing paragraph.

"I'm sad to confirm the rumors that have been rumbling around about this radical step. I have been working with members of Congress to prepare legislation allowing us to move forward quickly with this action, and there is widespread, bipartisan support. There are thousands of details to tackle, but let me address the two thoughts uppermost on everyone's mind. Number one—we will provide fair compensation for all affected Montanans, and number two—I promise the full strength and loyalty of the federal government and our military to ensure a peaceful transition through this plan."

The president had not intended to pound his fist during the last sentence. He feared how that would play in the press.

"I will unveil the detailed plan for this transition over the next few weeks but want to add one important point this evening. All of you will feel the pinch of shrinking government services as an inconvenience or, at worse, have to replace some benefits. But it is the citizens of Montana who are being asked to make the biggest contribution. It is not fair to ask Montanans to surrender their homeland and pioneer a new life elsewhere. Every citizen in every state, including Montana, must realize that anything short of this extreme step could result in a complete failure of the American way of life. Thank you for your understanding and thank you, Montanans, for your sacrifice. And God bless America."

The red tally light on the main camera went dark. The silence in the East Room was thick and sticky. Video crew members, always busy at a broadcast's conclusion, froze in place and gazed down at the floor, stealing glances at each other. The First Lady gave the supportive look to her husband, who scooped his notes into a neat pile and smiled back.

Chief of Staff Blair broke the tension with, "OK, good rehearsal. Let's do one for real? Maybe funnier this time?"

106

LAME HORSE CREEK, IDAHO

The phone hanging from the safety cage in the excavator buzzed. Then again. And again. Bullseye ceased slamming away at a boulder and reached up to look at her phone. She wiped her face, grabbed the phone, and walked toward the surface, heading through the door to the fading daylight.

Her phone vibrated again, which announced a new text. A picture of Morris Evans's horse showed up on the screen with his text:

>Get you carkas over here right now!!!

Just as quick, a picture of a horse's ass flashed on her the small screen, showing an incoming call from Hitch Jenkins.

"Bullseye, did you talk to Morris?" Hitch asked and added, without giving her time to answer, "He's bad off. Worked up worse than I've ever seen him."

Bullseye chuckled a little. "Here we go again! I'm down at the Lame Horse, so you have to calm him down yourself."

Her calm attitude shocked Hitch. "Didn't you hear the president's announcement just now, Bullseye?"

"No, I was digging away. What'd he say?"

"He said it! He announced that he was selling Montana. It's official, and now everyone knows it. You need to watch the broadcast on Twitter, so you can see how he laid it out. He's a smart guy, and I think he may have convinced the rest of the country pretty good and that's bad for us. Check it out, Bullseye, and I'll go calm down Morris."

The vice president had warned her face-to-face, but she still didn't believe it would happen. A new owner was coming to the Montana side of her tunnel either from the Middle East, China, or from right there in Montana. But, either way, she and her pals would no longer be Americans if they stayed in their homes.

107

VIRGINIA CITY, MONTANA

Hitch fast-stepped across Wallace Avenue toward the County offices, but Morris waved him over to the café. Mona had the lights up and the coffee on for this blustery February evening and within minutes, Morris and April led a delegation of others to process the president's remarks.

"We knew this day was coming. Now it's official," said Commissioner Morris Evans, struggling for control. "We have a plan, and now it's time to launch. The president wasn't even that good tonight on TV. Nothing's changed."

"Everything's changed," said Actor Evan Morris as he blew into the café from the night air. He kiss-kissed Mona and brushed back his thick blond hair. "I've been on the phone with Governor McLemore, who thinks we need to move fast, or we'll lose the battle for public opinion. Did you all see the president? His delivery was impeccable."

Morris ran his hand through his thinning hair, sensing control slip away.

Evan continued, "The governor wants to have a final planning session with all the main players in the movement tucked away where the media can't find us. We met with some militia groups, way down on the Idaho border, at a place called Lorae. Those militia guys know how to hide. The governor wants to sneak down to a dingy little restaurant called the MooseTracks there in two weeks."

Hitch jumped in. "Hey, that's Bullseye's backyard! Lame Horse Creek is next door, across the border in Idaho. She eats there all the time."

Evan said, "Well, that will be the site of our planning session for our official announcement. Let's keep it under our hat."

Morris stepped back in with, "OK, everyone clear?"

After a short silence, April spoke. "Why no, Morris. I'm not clear on anything. This is all teetering so precariously on the edge of chaos. I am not clear or comfortable or happy or . . ." and the starlet erupted into a fountain of tears.

Evan shuffled around to April before Morris could offer any help. "Thank you for saying that, April." He squeezed her, and she snuggled deep into his shoulder with arms surrounding the star for security as he continued addressing the group. "I bet we're all scared. Fear is natural. Even though we planned for this scenario, we didn't dream this day would arrive. How in the world can a few thousand Montanans confront the president of the United States?" He grabbed April by the shoulders and separated her from his side, looking her square in the eye. "But we can, April. We are few but mighty because we are defending our homeland. Truth and virtue are on our side, and the rest of the United States will come to see this massive injustice for the offensive crime it is—and stand with us!"

April said, "Oh, Evan, that was beautiful. You always say the perfect thing."

"I'm glad you liked it, April. It's from my 'face of Montana' speech that I'll be delivering to the press when we make our announcement, and I've been practicing. I want it to sound sincere. One of McLemore's people wrote it."

Everyone in the room nodded; they were believers.

The planning lasted late into the night, but no one seemed in a hurry to head out after they had exhausted their Secession talk. They all looked beat up, like the president's announcement had knocked the wind out of them. Mona dusted off two bottles of whiskey, and the planning meeting turned into a "lovely little whiskey-fueled soirée."

LAME HORSE CREEK, IDAHO

Organization. Make lists. Bullseye utilized the smoother sections of the cave walls as her canvas and children's sidewalk chalk to scribble expanding to-do lists up and down as high as she could reach. She lacked artistic skills, but her chalk list showed a hint of flair as she incorporated the white quartz veins running throughout the gray granite walls of the caves into the scrollwork of letters on the list. This evening's list was pointed and written in a large, stern hand showing urgency, with no time for artistic flair:

Call Shank and put the gang on standby
Call Stubb and find out what the hell is next
Finish the deal with Amanuel and get some money!
Finish this dang tunnel, girl!

Retreating four steps, Bullseye leaned on her small yellow excavator to ponder her priorities. She lunged back in and scrawled:

Pick out curtains for my new home on the game preserve
Google Mexico vacation!

With fatigued flair, she punctuated the last item with a smiley face. A cloud of chalk dust hung in the cave from clapping her hands as she hiked up to the entrance to get better phone service and called Shank and the Driven Gang. She wanted them on standby, out of jail, and somewhat sober whenever the snow allowed them to go.

109

WASHINGTON, DC

"One thing you never were is patient, Da-an," said the First Lady, mimicking his old girlfriend to get his attention. "It will take a little time for this to play out." She hugged him like they were dancing as Chief of Staff Blair knocked and walked in the Oval Office.

Crowley broke their embrace and said, "What do you hear?"

"Well, it's amazing, Mr. President. The House and Senate have kept quiet or been positive. No one has said you're off the deep end . . . yet. But the most incredible part is the rioting has stopped cold. Overnight, everywhere, it just stopped like the whole country wants to give your solution a chance."

"Or they're afraid you'll come after them next," added Denise Crowley.

Blair said, "Whatever the reason, the hiatus has bought us a little peace."

"Well, that's the good news. We have to keep positive stories in front of the press, so that if the Secessionists announce their plan, they won't capture everyone's sympathy. Graham, I have to meet with the Montana folks. Have we figured out when we can make that happen?"

"I'm sure Governor McLemore, who is heading the movement himself, would be open to meeting anytime, Dan."

"I think we need to look for an opportunity that is broader, something that will involve a whole group of their organizers. I don't want my appeal to be to one person, so we live and die by what he says. We could make him a martyr or a rock star, and he could twist my words to motivate his folks."

"Yes, sir," said Blair. "We are keeping a close eye on Montana. I said that it was peaceful everywhere, but Montana is an exception. There isn't rioting, but there are widespread reports of looting and vandalism on federal property. Post offices and railroads have been hard hit with 'go back to DC' and 'traitor' graffiti spray painted on rail cars, bricks through windows, and people stealing anything they can convert to quick cash, like museum pieces, glass, and aluminum."

"Something tells me this will get more complicated than a recycling war before this is all over," said the president. "At least the rioting is contained for now, so let's focus on getting a group of Secessionists together for a secret meeting. I want to do that soon."

CORVALLIS, MONTANA

"One thing I know," said Shank, as he looked around the Dud Ranch restaurant at his fellow bikers, "is that last night Mr. President gave us a big fat get-out-of-jail-free card. He told the whole country he doesn't give a crap about Montana or anything in it, so it's ours for the picking."

Nikki held up her beer bottle and shrieked, "Hell yeah!" as she slid her jacket down off her shoulders to reveal a large tattoo of an American flag on her bicep. "And here's what the prez thinks about Montana," she yelled as she grabbed the long knife from Shank's leg sheath and drove the tip into one star, sending a fat dribble of blood down her arm and a spurt across her shirt, onto the table. With a twist of the knife, she shrieked again, "Take that, Montana!" They met her stab with a chorus of hoops, hollers, and whistles.

Under the blood and rowdiness, Shank leaned over to others at his table and said, "But I'll tell you, we need to move, snow or no snow. All hell is sure to break loose in this state, and I want to be on the front edge of that wave."

Shank cleared a pool table and directed Kip and Fleet to spread out a mesmerizing logistics profile they had crafted by studying the terrain with topographic maps, the snowpack, long-range forecasts, and other factors, under the bright table light.

"Whatcha learn, boys?" said Shank.

"I think we can take off from here," said Fleet as he pointed with the tip of his beer bottle to a spot just west of Darby. "That will give us a shot right up the valley here and use the West Fork of the Bitterroot River, then merge with the Nez Perce River on the left to keep the animals on track as we head south and up to that alpine meadow Bullseye pointed us to. To cover it all, we'll run bikes on top of both ridges and keep the herd down in the meadow and moving through that gorge as it narrows near the drop zone. They'll run right where we want them."

Shank studied the plan. "That doesn't look very far, guys. Are you sure we can grab enough animals?"

Both bikers looked at each other. They pulled out a Droid tablet and showed the "Wild Game Density Per Square Mile" charts they had calculated for the valley, contrasted with the distance of the test stampede conducted a few months earlier, the analysis of the aerial photos from the drones, and other hunting records for good measure. The analytics from the stampede equipped Fleet to run simulations on the new route, which they presented on their final three spreadsheets. The guys had done their homework to show the gang had every opportunity to locate and stampede thousands of deer, elk, moose, black bear, and who knew what else during their twenty-plus-or-minus-mile run up the valley from Darby to Lorae and into Idaho. "Boss, we're looking at a few million bucks' worth of animals on this route," said Kip, calmly.

Shank was pawing at the start line but couldn't argue when Fleet and Kip presented the snowpack regression model they had prepared, recommending a few days more melt time. Shank asked Fleet and Kip to spread the kickoff date to the gang. While they were toasting the upcoming launch, Shank approached the Dud Ranch owner/bartender. "Hey, Chaz, can you slow down a little on pouring for us? Looks like I have to make that twelve grand last another two weeks."

Chaz loosed a spacious smile and hissed between his few remaining teeth, "Shank, with rooms and food and the way you vermin have been drinking, that money evaporated long ago. Remember, there's a hunnerd and a half of you here. But don't worry none. We'll make it work. Keep on partying until I run out of beer, and then you just bring me back a piece of something from that little stampede of yours."

The motel owner's generosity moved Shank. "That is fantastic of you, Chaz. I'll make sure you're taken care of when we're done."

As he reached out to shake hands with the sweet old man, Chaz clamped down his vise-like grip and opened his sweater with his other hand just far enough for Shank to see a .357 Magnum snorkeling up from his belt. "And, Shank," he said, "I ain't talking about no antlers or souvenirs. I'm talking about a big pile of cash, or I'll turn your butt over to some dudes that will make you wish it had just been the Feds." Shank tried to escape the old man's grip but couldn't. He kept a forced grin with clenched teeth so anyone around would think they were just shaking hands. The old man locked an icy stare on the biker as he tightened the grip even more. "I'm old, and the president just said he's selling the state out from under me. I don't know what I'll have left, so I'm looking to you for a slice of my retirement. Now, party all you want, and I'll stockpile your food and beer for the trip. But in case you had some crazy idea about cutting me out, keep in mind these folks on standby know where to go and who to tell every little detail that went on with your little band of banshees here"—he leaned in closer—"and to be extra clear, Shank, I'm talking about dudes that have killed wolves with just a knife. Big wolves, Chaz, with huge knives. They make your gang look like kids playing dress-up, and they're losing their land too, so they'd just as soon shoot anyone messing with Montana. Now, I'm counting on you to make a fortune like you're telling your folks, and all I want is a Chaz-sized chunk of it. So just keep partying, like the leader you are, and in a couple weeks, go get that money and drop off a big fat pile of it right here in front of dear old Chaz."

Chaz gave back his hand, and Shank rubbed it, as the little man closed his sweater and turned to clean up the bar. Shank grinned and said, "Chaz, not only will you get your money, because I respect the hell out of that move you just pulled and the way you've taken care of us, but I wish you were riding with us." He leaned back over the bar and took Chaz's hand one more time and added, "And between you me . . . I hope someday I can be that badass."

111

NEZ PERCE RIVER, MONTANA

The parade of Pacific storms roller-coastering through the Bitterroot Valley in February can spread a blanket of snow one day and fifty-five-degree sun the next. This warmer-than-expected year brought a rapid melt to the mountain snowpack. Trickles became streams and after a few sunny days, the level of the Nez Perce swelled—a month earlier than typical.

Hump and Redge read the thaw. They had rolled over seven thousand logs into the creek bed during the winter, waiting for the rising water to take them away. A few of the smaller ones slid down the river at its lower level during the last month, beating the rush. Hump hired a downstream crew of two greenhorns to collect the logs when they floated down to Idaho. No milling, no trucking—just drag the logs out of the river with a giant mechanical claw and stack them on the land Hump bought just across the border.

Hump and Redge crossed the bridge, looking for a better vantage point to see upstream and walked into the MooseTracks Diner. Hump hung his cap on the first pair of antlers he passed as he headed for a booth by the window.

"I see one coming now," whispered Redge under his breath, "and she's floatin' right along just fine."

Claudia brought their coffee, set the mugs down, and then put her fist on one of her boney hips. "What do you think about this sell Montana thing?" she asked after she finished taking the rest of their order.

After some puzzled looks, Hump explained that they had been trapping for a few weeks and had not seen the news. She filled them in on the president's announcement and, after she found out they were from the Montana side, told them about the Secession movement.

Redge and Hump didn't speak much through the rest of their meal. They finished, paid, and headed back up the gorge to their camp to cut more logs. In the truck Hump said, "I guess that senator was shooting us straight. I hope this water comes up quick. We need to warn these greenhorns to get ready, get our moola, and get out of here!"

* * *

Johnny Andsager was trout fishing upstream from the MooseTracks as a log came around a bend and bounced off rocks on the eastern bank. Johnny was reeling in as he watched the log float by.

The raft of logs with the large green orb stenciled with "US Army" in large letters swayed in the current until the top-heavy raft hit a deeper pool and flipped over, just before the final bend where he was fishing, near the deck of the MooseTracks. The pulsing blue lights continued to run around the edge of the orb, as the raft wedged against a couple of other logs near the bank of the creek. Another log washed over the top, burying the orb deeper in the creek and farther from view.

Johnny landed his fish and headed up to the MooseTracks. The orb had stopped a hundred yards short of the diner.

112

DES MOINES, IOWA

He reread the post, trying to decide what to do:

OK, MR. AMANUEL, I THINK IT'S TIME WE MET FACE-TO-FACE. IF YOU'RE SERIOUS ABOUT THIS GAME, FIND YOUR WAY TO THIS COUNTRY, TO IDAHO, AND I'LL GIVE YOU THE GRAND TOUR.

The trip was real, and that had caused the game to gain an odd texture of virtual and reality. It was one part cosplay, one part Dungeons & Dragons, and two parts Bond or Maden's Clancy, with variables yet to be defined; Amanuel was ready and dragged Benny out from under his pillow to prepare for the trip. Five days and they would be on the road to *Global Domination*. Five days and they would most likely be dead.

Amanuel said to himself, *Benny, don't pack your fears, my weak friend. Leave them tucked under your bunk bed with your little pretend monsters.*

"It's a very long way. I don't know what to expect. I'm not sure I—" said Benny out loud, before being cut off by Amanuel, who demanded Benny slap himself rapid-fire, three times.

Wuss. Wuss. Wuss. "You disgust me," shouted Amanuel at himself.

"What's that, dear?" asked him mom from down the hall.

"Nothing, Mom. Just scolding myself," said Benny.

"OK, have fun, dear. I'm folding an extra pair of undies for your trip and those nice warm socks Aunt Michelle got you for Christmas."

Benny sensed Amanuel losing patience, so he listened. *We are ready, young Benny. So, finish your packing, gather your game clues and your tuxedo, grab yourself by the eggs, and let's make this trip. This is our moment. We shall settle for nothing less than epic.*

His voice cracked as he said "epic."

113

NEZ PERCE RIVER, MONTANA

Local fisherman Johnny Andsager waded up to the MooseTracks for breakfast, hung his waders on the pronghorn rack by the door, and took his regular seat at the counter. "Claudia, have you noticed a lot of trees floating by early this year?" Johnny asked as his favorite waitress brought his coffee with three creamers.

"Naw. I think we always have some when the water first rises."

"This seems a little different," Johnny shot back. "I've been seeing prepped trees—limbed and cut to length, all floating by in a row. It's crazy."

"It's them Army guys doing something up on the ridge," Reuben shot from the kitchen, right after Claudia rang the bell to put in Johnny's order. Reuben started his order and continued, "They were hanging around last fall for a day or so and had lots of gear with them."

Claudia added, "And they sure didn't tip worth a durn, so I didn't spend much time talking to them. I was glad to see them go. If you ask me, they were setting up some spy stuff. You know—like watching who's paying taxes."

"Claudia, you always think someone is spying on you," floated Reuben, from the kitchen.

Johnny added, "And if it ain't someone spying on us, it's some alien or Sasquatch dude trying to take advantage of you."

Claudia folded her arms and said, "That's the last time I tell you boys anything. We'll see who laughs when they come wagglin' them probes in your direction." She froze.

"We love your stories, Claudia," Johnny said, as he looked at her and noticed her blank stare. He whirled around to see what had caught her attention. "What the . . . ," was all he could say.

Charging down the river, right toward them, was a half-submerged UFO. A blue halo, rotating around and around a large metal disc, caused the crystal-clear water to cast an eerie glow with each pulse. The Army orb raft floated free and bounced off the rocks in the river, toward the restaurant.

"Oh, God, here they come again!" exclaimed Claudia, as she dropped the coffeepot, shattering it all over the counter, floor, and Johnny.

The bobbing ring of lights was big enough to drag on the bottom, which made the speed erratic. It surged ahead in the depths and popped up and down in the shallows.

"Well, would you looky there?" exclaimed Johnny.

The heavy unit rotated in the water, presenting the words "US Army" painted across the green metal shell in stenciled letters.

"I told you. I tried to warn you. They's coming for us and that thing is just the first wave!" shrieked Claudia, taking her apron off like she was going somewhere.

Johnny said, "I have no idea what that thing is, but it sure explains those trees floating by. Don't nobody say nothing until it rounds the bend and heads to Idaho."

No one else spoke as they wandered to the downstream side of the coffee shop to watch the amphibious weapon float out from under the deck and bob its way toward the Idaho, glowing as it went.

* * *

The orb bounced and bobbed around the first bend, passing out of sight a few yards downstream from the MooseTracks, its frame wedged between two large boulders. Two trailing logs washed on top of the orb, shoving it deeper toward the bottom. By evening, seventeen logs had joined the jam, obscuring the lights from view, except in the darkest of night.

114

CORVALLIS, MONTANA

The last thing Shank saw before he set out on Highway 269 was Old Man Chaz patting his waistline with the .357 tucked under his belt. It relieved him to ride out with his gang.

A ribbon of steel and rubber consisting of a hundred bikers snaked along the highway, two abreast. A decoy posse of forty-two bikers ran the other direction to be loud up the road toward Missoula then back into Hamilton to keep the county sheriff distracted. Most of the local authorities and even the National Guard were busy in the towns and cities, dealing with the escalating looting.

The Ravalli County sheriff picked up the line of bikers as they drove south on 93 out of Hamilton and followed them into Darby. The cover story, when asked, was a few days hiking and camping at Rombo Campground. To pour it on even thicker, they said there were rumors of a rival gang from Seattle, headed toward the Lolo National Forest to stir up some mischief and encouraged the sheriff to just shoot 'em because they hated those weasels. That brought a laugh from everyone—cops and bikers.

The gang screeched into the Mercantile on Main Street in Darby to stock up on supplies. The Merc was a Montana wonderland, with more crap stacked per foot than any trapper/camper/shooter could ever need. Shank loved the taxidermy on the wall and spread the word to learn about the animals they would be stampeding. Stuffed-animal action scenes depicted a mountain lion poised to kill a goose, black bears ready to grab a bee's nest, elk heads with antlers wider than a bike with a sidecar, and an entire wall covered in pelts from every trap-worthy species in Montana. The display was stunning, and Shank let the girls pick out which varmint they should be on the lookout for to make coats after the stampede.

Below the pelts was a photo display of livestock damage, ripped to shreds by wolves. Ranchers and hunters held up huge carcasses of dead wolves they had shot to protect their land. Shank tried to stand in front of these pictures, so they wouldn't see how large these wolves were, and worse, how vicious the ranchers looked with their guns and snarls. Shank hoped they could avoid both species during their run in the woods.

The Mercantile's staff appeared nervous to Shank. Wherever he took a large group of bikers, people stayed on edge. Shank approached the large dude with a leather biker vest who worked the gun counter and asked, "How you doing, Brother? This sell Montana situation is a helluva thing, right?"

The clerk didn't smile but picked up an odd-looking muzzle-loading pistol that Shank guessed had been handmade and rubbed it with a polishing cloth. "You bet your bike it is. You boys got plans to leave the state?" he asked Shank.

That was code for "Get the hell out of my store." He responded, "I think we're just like you—trying to figure it all out. We're going camping for a few days to plot our next move. I was hoping Montana could be home for years to come, but who knows now?"

A nod and a fist bump fell in Shank's direction. "Well, I hope you get it figured out, dude, and then I wish you'd ride to Washington and help straighten out those idiots." He leaned over the counter and lowered his voice. "I'll tell you something. If you're looking for somewhere to be free, and I mean really free, there's something cool ready to happen here in Montana. You might catch wind of a new country starting up. We won't let the president sell us off without a fight, so join us."

Shank smiled and nodded back. The clerk kept talking and kept polishing the old gun, flipping it to point across the counter directly at the biker.

"But, Brother, let me warn you. If you're not interested in being part of something new, then my advice is to ride on. People are sleeping with their guns since their homes are being taken away, and they'd just as soon shoot you as talk to you. Word to the wise—and I can tell you are the wise one in this pack of wolves."

Shank sent word to mount up. He gave one last nod to his new friend at the Merc and strode to his bike. He took the words as sage advice, not a threat.

Rombo Campground was a short twenty miles down 93 and 472, tucked between towering ponderosa pines on the West Fork of the Bitterroot River, the staging ground for the stampede. Patches of snow speckled the shady spots along the way. The stampede would have been more fun in the summer, but it was go time. Shank heard earlier in the day that there could be a new country being formed by Montanans. All hell could break loose, and the lead biker didn't want that to disrupt their own hell breaking loose.

Shank checked his phone as they arrived at the campground. He opened an email from Bullseye while the rest of the gang circled and started their setup. It read:

Shank- I helped you over the winter in Vegas and now I need one big nasty favor. On your route, a few miles up the valley after Painted Rocks, there's a place called the Flying B Bison Ranch with a huge bison herd. About 5,000 head last time I checked into it. Get 'em all. Just tear the place down and grab every last one of them in your stampede and drag them along with you. Buffalo are easy to stampede, and they'll run if you get them pointed the right way.

I don't care if you burn down the ranch house. Why? I won't say much, except that the guy that owns that ranch, Hank Rogers, used to be my neighbor in Madison County. I was in serious trouble once as a little girl, and I ran to his place for help. Instead of protecting me, he brought me right back home to the demon that was trying to kill me. I want him to taste some of that terror. I was nine, and he probably thought going home was the safest place for me, but I tried to tell him. I tried to tell him. But he liked my father, and no one believes a nine-year-old, so screw him. Get 'em all. Get him.

There's an extra $50,000 in it for the gang if you can take care of him for good.

Bullseye

A smile crossed his face as he slid his phone in the rib pocket of his black leather vest. Shank liked this Bullseye chick, and he loved revenge as much as cash. He gathered his council to prep them for the morning stampede kickoff, delivered the target for Bullseye's request, and, heeding the warning from the Merc clerk, spread the word to keep their firepower close since it might take some persuasion to handle the local ranchers.

115

VIRGINIA CITY, MONTANA

Evan had exhausted the week answering questions on Google Hangout, Skype, Slack, and in meetings around the state, via the governor's plane. The morning after his return to Virginia City, the crowd inside the café pulled, hugged, questioned, and encouraged him all the way to his seat. Since the announcement by the president, people in the state had gravitated toward public locations to discuss the travesty. During most of his speaking engagements, Evan had mentioned the Placer Gold Café as his "home info spot," and more and more people had traveled there to seek answers face-to-face and to find comfort.

Evan felt his popularity changing. His new status grounded him, not because of his old movies, but on the hope people pinned on him to help save their homeland. He wore that like armor.

"I'm just trying to bring a modicum of calm in these stormy times," Evan said aloud as he sat down with his friends. Mona gave him a huge squeeze during the double-kiss routine.

April complimented Evan, "Oh, I loved that line . . . was it called *Calm Before the Storm* with Glenn Close?"

"Well, I think it—"

"Sure, I remember, you were standing on the deck of that burning sailboat, people were jumping, and there was a shark, but you took off the last life vest and put it on Glenn. I'll always remember because I had to go look up the word *modicum*."

Evan felt small for getting caught in a movie quote to state his emotions and was glad when Morris started the agenda.

"Listen, everyone, I've got a lot to update you on this morning, so if it's OK, Evan, let's dive in. There's been a bunch of news since the president's announcement, as I predicted—"

Hitch jumped in, "There are reports of more looting in Missoula, and they burned down the main post office in Bozeman. That presents the question of whether we'll need to prepare for fighting within the state to root out dissenters as we formally declare. It could get ugly."

April joined the announcements. "But there has been a modicum of peace in the rest of the country"—she smiled at Evan, who smiled back at her fabulous word use—"since the president's pitch, which I have to say doesn't bode well for us."

Morris said, "Well, I heard about those items, sure enough, but we need to be concerned about the Secession movement convention. We head over there tomorrow, and I want to make sure we're ready." April raised her hand right in front of Morris, so he called on her. "April, did you want to say something?"

April stood and said, "I have an update concerning the convention. I let the governor's assistant know that I will bring a prototype of the new Nation of Montana flag, for approval, along with our official Secession ribbons. And I'm making matching scarves in our nation's colors out of satin for the women, or for anyone on the committee who wants one. I won't judge whoever wants to wear it. We should be scarf-neutral."

"I don't quite know what to say, April," said Evan, who captured the sentiment for the table. "The flag will be inspiring to see. You are the Betsy Ross of the new nation."

April blushed and straightened the collar on her snow-white fleece vest as if she had just done some heavy lifting. She sipped her steamy tea and said, with pacing, "Why, thank you, Evan. Are you ready to be unveiled as the face of the new nation?"

Morris added to her question. "Yes, Mr. I Am Montana, are you ready? It's almost game time, right?"

Evan felt the table lean forward, toward him. The crowd hushed and he turned his head to find the entire restaurant peering his way. Actor Evan could read a moment—he lived for moments like this. While everyone waited, he took a long draw on his coffee, then set his mug down and stood while he began to speak, as if his words lifted him out of the seat. This time he spoke from his heart and not a movie script.

"The question is not: Am I ready? No, no. There is no question about that. The question is: Are *they* ready?" He pointed to what he thought was south, to indict the other forty-seven lower states and continued. "We're from Montana. We're ready for whatever comes our way. We have carved out a life that we're proud of even when it wasn't easy. And when I say 'we,' I don't mean just you and me in this café." He gestured all around the room and raised his voice as he continued. "I mean people that called Montana home, if only for a short while, going back to Lewis and Clark, from Sitting Bull all the way to Ted Turner, Huey Lewis to David Letterman, Ansel

Adams to Evel Knievel, and Calamity Jane to John Mayer. And I'm talking about the millions of people who have stood in amazement at the wonders of Glacier National Park, zoomed downhill at Big Sky, studied at Montana State, cast a fly in the Ruby River, rodeoed in Bozeman, lumberjacked in Darby, or joined any of the spectacular activities that Montana offers. Each of those people has a little piece of Montana inside of them now, and I know they are ready to stand with us as we face this president and his desire to sever our ties." Evan sauntered around the café and grasped every single person on the shoulder as he passed. "Montana has touched all of us in ways we can never forget. And now, Montana needs that touch returned. Americans—real Americans—always do what's right. This may be about money to President Crowley, but it's about right and wrong to us. The rest of America is ready, I'm certain, to stand with Montana to pursue the only option we have to do what's right. Americans always stand together for freedom."

Evan, who had transfixed the crowd at the Placer, had one piece of business left. He spun around and grabbed the arm of one diner recording his speech on a cell phone. He looked right down the barrel of his lens and said, "Am I ready? You're damn right I'm ready! Are *you* ready to do what's right, America? Are *you* ready to help the New Nation of Montana?"

Raucous cheers and applause broke out in all corners of the Placer Café. Mona put down her coffeepot to clap and said to the woman next to her, "I kissed him," to which the woman replied, "Me too."

Evan's passionate plea, captured on a single cell phone, had been seen live by 472 people on Facebook. By the time Evan sat down, they had shared it to others in the café and posted to Vimeo and YouTube hundreds of times around the country. And *liked*. And *starred*. And forwarded. And forwarded.

"OK, Mr. Face of the Nation, I can see you are ready. That was some speech, Evan. If you get the country half as fired up as you just did this room, we won't have any trouble," said Morris.

"Thanks, Morris. This has come into focus for me; I said I'm all in. It could have been better, though. I wish Bullseye were here. She's the one who challenged me to dive in deeper. I hate that she hasn't been around very much."

Mona smiled a flat smile with taut cheeks, then turned and headed back to the kitchen.

On the way back to his ranch, Evan called Bullseye to tell her he missed her. She didn't answer, so he left a short, cute message. The next day, he called back before he left for the convention in the hills and left another message, just to make sure she had received the first one.

116

BITTERROOT NATIONAL FOREST, MONTANA

Shank found his way back to his tent at the Rombo Creek campsite around six a.m., after a wild night that had turned into a wilder early morning. Most of the group ended up naked for an icy plunge in the West Fork of the Bitterroot River after midnight, followed by a group streak back to the campfire. The first night camping and preparing for the stampede had been fun, but the late night and the cold spring morning made getting cranked up difficult.

After the slow start, Shank led the line of a dozen Harleys right out of Rombo and south down 473 toward Painted Rocks State Park. They stopped on the dam so Nikki could take a picture of the marauders. She said it would be famous one day, like the Hells Angels pic with the Rolling Stones at the Altamont rock fest sixty years prior.

As he headed higher into the hills, Shank wondered how much longer he could do this. He wanted to get out when the getting was good. He worried about slipping, thinking back just a day when he had gotten his butt kicked, even if it was metaphorical, by a dried-up old dude named Chaz with a stronger grip. Things were upside down.

He looked behind the group, just exercising old habits of watching his back. With the caution of the Mercantile dude about ranchers with rifles swimming in his head, Shank pushed the start of the stampede even higher up the valley, so most of the run would be on national forest land. There was just one large ranch on the edge of the national forest—the Flying B Bison Ranch.

They cruised past the Alta Campground and then veered south. Shank spread the word for the group to fan out and start the stampede. He headed up to the edge of a bluff overlook while the bikes took off, roaring around the edges of the valley. Pine trees speckled the large, open meadows on the valley floor and appeared to be lifeless. Shank fixed his stare on a group of large ponderosa pines downrange. After the test run last year, he knew there were thousands of beasts hiding in these trees over the next few miles. In just five minutes, a cloud of dust entered the valley on the right side, coupled with a low roll of thunder that didn't stop.

Nikki started to say, but froze midway through, "Holy—"

The gang pointed and whooped, but no one heard over the deafening rumble of bison, charging the valley from the edge of the woods. Hundreds of magnificent animals circled up and halted near the middle of the meadow, as a circle of bikers paused near the edges of the valley. Thousands more bison roamed farther down the valley.

"That's our starting point, boys. We get these fellas running in front of the bikes and they'll rally our herd for us," Shank yelled, pointing the way down the bluff to his lieutenants. "No mercy now, hear me? No mercy! Let's ride!" he shouted and revved his engine.

The gang responded with hollers and donuts in the dust. Shank read the Flying B sign two hundred yards away, carved into four massive logs stretched across the driveway. He thought about Bullseye's note, which charged him to "take care" of the owner of the bison ranch for old times' sake. "I've got a little stop I need to make as a favor for Bullseye," he yelled to Nikki.

117

LORAE, MONTANA

Evan crossed the short bridge by the MooseTracks and slid to a stop. The road was still a little icy from winter's overnight gasps, but the morning sun had melted the exposed parts, confirming spring's early arrival. Morris jumped out of the passenger side of Evan's Tesla to take the lead into the MooseTracks.

Claudia greeted the group with menus and a smile. "Hey, fellas. Welcome. Take any table you want. Can I get you some coffee?"

"That would be great," said Evan as he flashed a smile, hoping she would recognize him. He tipped his hat back more, then took it off altogether, hoping to aid her recall.

"Say, wait a minute. I met you a couple of months back with my friends in the Brotherhood and the governor. And after you left last time, I saw you on TV," Claudia said, elbow on hip.

"Well you have, darling. I was here with the governor, and I'm the face of----"

"I knew it. You're the face of that Liberty Life Reverse Mortgage ad, right? They play that thing every day during my story. My mom thinks you're a real biscuit. It's nice to have someone famous around here for a change." She dropped off the coffee and spun back around toward the kitchen. Over her shoulder, she hollered, "Hey, mortgage guy, autograph our antlers before you leave," and pointed to several sets of antlers hanging over the entryway with caps, beads, and little hoops made of dollar bills hanging over them.

Evan glared at Morris and hoped he was smart enough not to say a word. Even Morris should know not to kick a man when he was this far down.

"At least that confirms this place is far enough up in the hills for our Secession meeting," Morris said, applying a little salve to Actor Evan's wound.

After Claudia returned with their order, Morris said, "Claudia, are you all set for the big meeting tomorrow? How many people can you handle comfortably?"

"Darling, I'm uncomfortable with three, if they're idiots."

They laughed, and Evan knew that was a truthful response.

Morris, Hitch, Evan, and April spent the afternoon helping Claudia clean out the extra room inside the MooseTracks, to make room for all the Secessionists to gather. They set up two large paper pads on easels and a whiteboard, and April organized her items on a table up front, ready to greet guests and color-coordinate the entire effort.

After the team set the meeting up for the next day, they walked across to the Lame Horse Creek operation to invite Bullseye to dinner. She had not answered the texts, but they saw her truck in the parking lot.

The friends went to the Lame Horse Gift Shop and found the door unlocked. Evan pushed his way in first, and after Bullseye didn't answer their yells, Hitch led them toward the tunnel entrance to check on her. They grabbed flashlights from the tourist-miner bin and descended the steps into the cave.

The Sultan's Retreat stunned the team! It looked like a palace, with massive columns, pots spilling over with jewels, and colorful bursts of fine fabric flowing in warm breezes—all dramatically lit from below by vibrant fixtures buried in the display. "She sure has been busy," said April. "Oh, my, would you look at this setup?"

"Pretty fantastic . . . it's like a movie set," said Evan, looking at the elaborate dressing shimmering in their lights. "I bet her clients love coming down here. What fun." He pointed out the light behind the tapestry on the far wall. The team pushed open the carpet door and ventured deeper down the tunnel.

They entered the Dome Room and across to the feeder tunnel. "Just incredible. Who would've thought all this was under here?" said Evan. Morris stopped for a rest in the Dome Room while the others carried on for another ten minutes of walking and yelling Bullseye's name, reading the chalk list hieroglyphics on the cave walls along the way. The tunnel grew warmer and warmer as they continued deeper.

They reached a fork in the tunnel, and April suggested they split to help the search. She and Hitch went left, and Evan wandered alone into the tunnel to the right. The temperature was at least fifteen degrees warmer in this part of the tunnel, prompting Evan to strip off his coat as he cornered a sharp bend. The tunnel glowed ahead and after rounding a rock outcropping, Evan stopped and dropped his flashlight!

Under the soft glow of an amber lantern lay Bullseye Magee with her eyes closed, laying peacefully in a trickling pool of steaming, warm water, wearing only a pair of headphones.

The dropped metal flashlight clattered on the rock floor and caused

Bullseye to sit up and scream, yanking off her headphones. "What the heck?"

"Bullseye, it's me, it's Evan. I'm so sorry to scare you. I was looking at you; I mean, looking *for* you. Bullseye, wow . . . you look amazing." He stepped closer.

Bullseye splashed a little water on her face to help her snap back to life, then stood up, dripping. Unashamed, she lowered her arms to her side. The lantern to her left cast soft shadows that accentuated her sculpted body, glistening as the water drained off her shoulders and down her back. Stepping out of the warm flowing puddle, she landed right in front of Evan.

He reached down and picked up the towel on the rock next to the pool. She stood still in front of him, but he couldn't pull his gaze away from her mysterious green eyes in the subdued cavern lighting. He reached around her, opened the towel behind her back, and gently wrapped her in it as he hugged her, then dabbed a few drops off her cheeks with a corner of the towel.

"How many laps did you swim today?" said Evan, glancing at the tiny puddle in the trickling stream where she had been lying.

"That's a good one, Actor Boy. I've got my own personal mineral spa here with a never-ending supply of hot water, and these smooth rocks fit my aching body just right. It's one of my favorite places when I don't have a parade of tourists tromping through here."

"I'm sorry to interrupt your quiet time. I miss you, Bullseye. I'd love to have you join us for dinner over at the MooseTracks. There are important details to talk about . . . but mostly, I just miss you."

"Thank you, Evan, and I'd love to. The way you just said that . . . is just about the nicest thing any man has ever said to me." Bullseye smiled at Evan, then reached up with both hands to pull his face close to hers. The kiss she initiated so mesmerized him that he didn't notice her towel drop to the ground. Or, at least, he ignored it and focused on her kiss.

"Should I dress up or come as I am?" she said, pulling her lips away from his.

Evan smiled and squeezed her hands. He heard their other two friends stumbling back up the tunnel and said, "I think I'll go catch up to Hitch and April while you decide. Unless you have a bigger pool, we'll wait up front."

She smiled and waved him away. "Y'all go on. I've got to take care of something that will tie me up for a couple hours, then I'll meet over at the MooseTracks. Hey, thanks, Evan."

118

BITTERROOT NATIONAL FOREST, MONTANA

Deep snow patches still dappled the shadows from the big Douglas firs, and a few flowers peeked out of the brown soil where the snow had retreated, but the landscape still looked in winter's grasp.

Shank and the Driven Gang ripped across the high alpine meadow. The bison herd scattered as soon as the bikers revved their engines, circling and regrouping while trying to escape the noise. Kip, mindful of his early fence-tangling defeat months before, took the eastern point and started the herd down from the hills. Once the gang spread 110 Harleys across the valley, bison, deer, or elk would have no chance to slip back through the line. "Get along, little hog-doggy," screamed Kip.

The Flying B Bison Ranch stood at the mouth of the beautiful valley, pointing straight to Idaho. A few of the bikes zoomed ahead to cut the first couple of fences and drag off the heap of barbed wire. The other fences gave way under the pressure of a charging herd of buffalo, who also knocked over most of the farm buildings and the kitchen addition of the ranch owner. Shank waited to see if the stampede flushed him out. He had decided he would shoot him, plain and simple, for what he'd done to Bullseye when she was a little girl. That would be his gift to her. He waited until the entire herd ran past the house and kicked in the door but found no one at home. *Lucky day for that dude,* thought Shank as he emptied his pistol into the headboard of his bed, just because, then moved up the valley.

Bullseye had mapped out a plan to create some targeted holding areas along the route. There were box canyons they hoped to corral the animals into on the first two nights, and the third would require some temporary plastic fencing they carried aboard some four-wheelers. To encourage the herd to stay through the nights, Bullseye had arranged an aerial assault of round hay bales by helicopter and flew with the pilot for the first few runs. She promised to wave to Shank as she would have the pilot dip low over the stampede to help the effort, just past the Flying B Ranch. She had set up an airdrop of three hundred bales around the canyon floor in each of the three stopover areas. The local rancher she hired had been overjoyed to get the $55,000 rent for him and his helicopter, so he threw in the hay for nothing. He'd had a few questions about the activity on the national forest land, but Bullseye had explained that a large payment like fifty-five grand was to make certain there were no questions. Shank remembered her smiling when she told of his reaction. Shank found it interesting that something about her liked pushing men in whatever direction she thought they should go. His experience with her had all been good, probably because he was already leaning in the direction she was pushing.

From his vantage point high above, Shank was awestruck at the number of animals they had "convinced" to join their journey by the end of the first day. Hundreds of beasts from several species ran shoulder to shoulder, trying to stay ahead of the thunder generated by the two-wheeled machines and the bison herd. And that was after just one hard day of rustling. After a rugged but uneventful run during the day, the animals careened into the box canyon with high rock walls on three sides that Bullseye had identified and settled in for the first night.

Shank pulled into the campsite after helping Fleet figure out how they would handle the overnight security on the herd. He yawned from a long couple of days—well, a long year and a hard life. All he needed now was a few good days to guide these animals into Bullseye's little playpen in Idaho.

119

WENDOVER, UTAH

The Army personnel looked nervous, gathered around the general in the mobile command center on the edge of a huge salt flat in Utah. The abbreviated test plan to fly the AFV from Yuma, Arizona, to Wendover, Utah, had taken several intense weeks of preparation but only a few hours to execute. A Hock staffer reported, "General, our monitoring truck is reporting a hiccup in the car's primary navigation system."

"Just how are we supposed to get this gall durn magic car to find us way up here in Utah if the navigation system doesn't work?" queried Starnes. "Cardillo," came the shout from the general, to which an assistant named Cudzillo stepped forward. The general read his name tag and thought he was smart for not correcting her pronunciation.

"Ma'am, it looks like the nav system worked fine when the craft cleared Yuma airspace. All systems were A-OK over the corner of Nevada and into southern Utah," Cudzillo added. His permanent rosy blush, always an endearing quality, made him look guilty, as if he were hiding something.

Test Supervisor Andi Calton stepped up, flipped her auburn hair over her shoulder, and said, "But trouble set in just north of Lake Mead. The LiDAR processor blinked, General. The malfunction appears to be computer-related because of heat buildup from the massive amount of data being processed from the NORM mainframe program."

"So, did we lose her?" Starnes pressed. "Did she crash?"

"No, ma'am, our default safety settings brought the AFV down easy once it lost its bearings," said Calton, "and we're double-checking the Ground Coordinate Transmitter beacon backup system for possible malfunction. I don't anticipate any further trouble, General."

"Well, you can't imagine how comforting that is to me. Tell me one thing, missy," Starnes challenged, "did you anticipate the last problem we had?" Feet shuffled in the gravel.

After a nervous pause, General Starnes eased up on the team. "Listen, I can see that the GCT didn't override the LiDAR when it went offline. I'll need answers on how the LiDAR flight path computer went down and why my system didn't kick in. It's important that you guys get this fixed before we fly again. I'm telling you, if this screws up, you will be the losers. Someone else will figure it out and jump ahead of you. I can only do so much to help you get off the line first, but it must be safe. So, let me translate, in case you didn't hear me. Make sure my GCT backup nav system is working before you take off again so we can always navigate off our beacons during testing. Period."

The team looked at Dr. Hock, who spoke without looking at anyone but General Starnes. "I hear you loud and clear, General. It shall be so."

Starnes squinted and said, "Listen, Hock, I'm not supposed to tell you this, but the president wants to come watch this test. He feels the advance in technology could be some upbeat news for the country for a change and actually boost our economy. It's on his schedule to attend if I was comfortable with everything, but so far, I'm not. We need to be ready in case he insists on dropping in. I don't want him waiting on us."

Hock was near speechless. "I . . . I don't know what to say, General. Having him witness our flight would be the validation we need. We'll do whatever it takes to get it together, Amy . . . General, and we'll be ready. I promise."

120

NEZ PERCE RIVER, MONTANA

Unknown and unseen, two old-growth Douglas firs—over forty-eight inches in diameter—had snagged on the same large boulders and smaller trees that had jammed the log raft with the Army's orb, only ten yards around the bend from the MooseTracks. New trees skimmed along and landed on top, hiding the blue glow from the lights, pushing it deeper. Rising water helped big logs crisscross and lodge deeper into the crevasse. In a week, over four hundred logs had stalled behind them, turning into a rather efficient dam. Water was still passing through the jam, but nowhere near as fast as it came down from the valley above. As the water level rose behind the dam, more logs released and floated down, compounding the problem.

* * *

Downstream, the two greenhorns enjoyed the break from the constant workload, and neither thought to call Hump and ask why the trees had all but stopped coming. In their mind, raising an alarm just meant more work.

121

LORAE, MONTANA

Pickups, SUVs, and a few cars lined the narrow road twisting along the Nez Perce River, and could be a dead giveaway that something important was brewing this late morning on the first of March. As it was, no one saw the cars, since this road didn't go anywhere except Lorae, some old logging and mining operations, and Bullseye's Lame Horse Creek Tourist Trap across the line in Idaho.

April sat pert and pretty behind a table with a small sign that read, "Welcome Secessionists!" anchored by a tricolored curlicue ribbon in the corner. The Montana flag included the state seal and many colors, so she settled on dark blue, gold, and silver, based on state iconography. She handed everyone a name tag and an "I'm with Montana" T-shirt, which featured a logo she had developed personally, as explained to each recipient, personally. A band of gold, silver, and deep-blue ribbons, with the ends curled, held each shirt in a tight roll. She tucked the new Montana flag under the table for presentation at the proper moment and smiled when Evan commented that she had prepared a tidy Secession.

Governor McLemore and Evan Morris sat on the deck in the crisp, early-morning mountain air, while a few of the governor's handlers fussed about. "I think we're up to a hundred on the list for this gathering, and I'm not sure we can hold that many inside this little diner. We'll have to split up and maybe have our big meetings out here on the deck," said McLemore.

"I'm not sure all hundred will be able to find us way out here," said Evan Morris. "But you wanted to be free from distractions and in a place that would welcome our more controversial parties to attend. This is the right spot."

They planned the convention to be a three-day event, but the agenda included approval of the official announcement and strategy for its release, ratification of a preliminary constitution, as well as final contingency plans if things got ugly with the US government, making it obvious this would take time. They didn't plan on much sleep.

The Secession plan had seeped into all corners of the state, and most Montanans seemed on board. Reports from people in the other forty-nine appeared mixed. Social media rants revealed that many still refused to believe that the United States government would—or could—claim the land as their own and sell it off to foreigners, despite the president's explanation.

"The president was smart to position the sale of Montana as a 'sacrifice' by us locals to save the rest of America. Polling says most Americans view any rumors of secession by Montanans as a betrayal to the greater good since they need our sale to keep the country from tearing itself apart."

Evan leaned against the deck railing and echoed the polling chatter, "Afterall, the president offered fair compensation and resettlement help to everyone who was being displaced, right? I'm a little sick of hearing that."

"But then there was your little video bombshell they call 'The Plea.' That could not have been any stronger, Evan."

One visitor to the Placer Gold Café captured Evan's four-minute passionate rallying cry to his fellow Montanans and labeled it *Sell Montana? Evan's Plea* on Facebook Live, and posted everywhere, then shared. And shared. After jumping platforms and millions of views in the first week, "The Plea" was the viral launch the movement wished for, albeit a little premature. It introduced the notion of secession to Americans. Evan had represented the concept in a powerful and personal fashion, as it pinged from one phone to the next. Many Americans calculated the cost of what the president had decreed, based on the video, and even sent vows of support through Facebook, Vimeo, Twitter, and YouTube, labeled *you gotta see this* and *are we next?* A crowd-sourcing account got attached somewhere along the way with a Venmo address, and #SellMontana raised more than $4 million, mostly five dollars at a time.

"Well, it helped, and I believed everything I said. My fear is, the truth is that most Americans were just relieved that someone else would bear their burden, and it will only cost the rest of the country a couple of national parks."

The circle around Evan and the governor grew wider. "We have our work cut out for us. We better finish setting up inside and look around for more chairs to bring out here," said the governor. "Whatever happens, it's going to be something we'll remember for the rest of our lives."

122

BITTERROOT NATIONAL FOREST, MONTANA

Crossing the state line to Bullseye's Game Preserve was about eight miles away, as the crow flies. According to Kip, the route they would run to keep most of the herd together would be closer to twelve miles. Shank knew the most difficult terrain was still ahead—the last two or three miles, where the valley closed to a narrow gorge through a mountain pass. This last bit of the journey ran right through the town of Lorae and a diner he'd been to before called the MooseTracks. The gorge walls soared on either side of the valley, which would funnel the herd through the little town, maybe taking down a building or two in their path. That was still twelve miles away, and he had a day or two to figure that one out. It had been a productive day and Shank felt the herd growing.

In the old days, cattle drives could average ten to twelve miles a day across open ground. The bikers were dealing with a herd they couldn't see for the trees, steep canyons—some still covered in deep patches of snow— a few fences, downed timber from past forest fires, loose rock, and who knew what else in their path. Shank told Fleet his goal was to drop the herd in two days.

No resistance from authorities had materialized. The National Guard was on standby, but the popularity of "The Plea" video challenged the loyalties of Montana members of the Guard—making it unlikely that anyone would come looking for a bunch of cycle-riding deer rustlers on national forest land.

"Home stretch, you buzzards!" shouted Shank. "Two days, and I'll show you the way to the bank. Set 'em up for the night."

A few members of the gang riding ATVs circled wide of the herd so they wouldn't scare the animals, and hauled out rolls of tall plastic netting, threaded with an electric fence line. It was quick work to string up the netting using cable ties and trees throughout the forest, creating a perimeter. The fencing was dark green with small white ties flapping in the evening breeze, making the barrier barely discernable for bikers and beasts.

The stampeding bikers slowed, allowing the animals to break stride and walk. A few of the fastest animals ran into the netting and struggled, until a few of the bikers circled round and scared them back toward the center of the enormous holding area. As the animals folded in, the marauders used a long rock outcropping as a back wall and completed most of the circle with the flexible fencing, covering an area almost a half mile wide and longer than two miles deep in the alpine meadow and forest. Forty bikers filled the last quarter mile and took turns overnight stoking small fires and revving their engines to keep the animals away from that edge of the pen.

It was a cacophonous night: moaning and roaring, bellowing and snorting, revving and shouting. Fights broke out every few minutes between nervous animals. Huge round hay bales scattered around the pen by the helicopter provided food, and a place to sleep for the smaller animals who furrowed inside. The moose, elk, and bear segregated near their own species, while sentries monitored the other breeds.

Shank took in the amazing scene and smiled as he dispatched guards around the perimeter to light smudge pots, hoping the flames and the scent of burning kerosene would keep the herd off the fence line. He rode over to the camp, grabbed a warm place by a fire, and spread the word that there wouldn't be any party tonight. Everyone was to stay in the zone, either working to secure animals or resting. The security team would leave early to build the animal pen for the last night, a couple miles down the valley before it funneled into a steep gorge.

His tent looked inviting after the hard ride through the woods, even though the sun was just going down. This night and one more. Two more days circling a bunch of wild animals as restless as he was. The day after that, he would be through with this life stampeding these animals and leading his wild bunch.

Regret seeped into his last thoughts before he succumbed to sleep. He wished he could have shot that guy for Bullseye. He must have been a real scourge to that nice woman.

123

WASHINGTON, DC

"We have confirmed the location of the Secessionist secret meeting, Mr. President," said Commerce Secretary Wayne Redmond. Stubblefield and Fowler, among the four others gathered alongside the president for the impromptu walk-through in the East Room for an upcoming White House ceremony, listened with interest.

The president thought of several questions, then asked, "So, if I were to sneak up, so to speak, on this little town of Lorae, you think I could run into the main players in the Secession movement, including Governor McLemore and Evan Morris from 'The Plea' video and talk them down from the ledge?"

"And, Mr. President, there's the added benefit of having no national press involved. It's supposed to be a complete secret," added Redmond, "because the Montana press views the national guys as traitors. They've been very tight-lipped about everything so far on their end."

Blair offered, "Dan, we can use the flying-car test as a cover. That would put you in Utah, near that corner of Idaho or Montana, with a good excuse. Then we can cancel at the last minute and head to Montana." President Crowley pulled Redmond to the left side of the room under the massive Lansdowne portrait of George Washington, created by Gilbert Stuart, to ask him a private question.

"Redmond, this whole thing started with you. So, give me your God's honest opinion . . . is there any way you see this working? Do you think these Montanans will sacrifice their land for the sake of the other forty-nine states? Because I gotta tell you, I don't think I would if I were them, and I'd be ready to fight."

Redmond said, "Mr. President, I don't think they'll happily give their land to you, but I think you can make taking it from them a little more palatable, if that makes sense."

They posited a few more thoughts, after which the president put his hand on the secretary's shoulder and gave him a reassuring squeeze. "Thanks, Wayne," he said, then turned to the others and announced, "Gentlemen, grab a change of clothes. We're going to Montana first thing tomorrow morning, and I want you all to join me."

124

WENDOVER, UTAH

The Army had dotted the landscape with land-based navigation beacons for the AFV test from the Yuma Proving Ground in Arizona to the Canadian border, near Malmstrom Air Force Base. They hid beacon units in the most remote areas imaginable, including extreme rock outcroppings, restricted Doppler towers, and skyscraping trees.

The trail of beacons snaked along the west side of Utah to avoid dense populations. A series of towers circled an immense salt flat near Wendover, creating the perfect vantage point for viewing the AFV test. Overnight, Starnes, with help from FAA Director Chris Minucci, had put her best foot forward since the president had accepted the invitation to visit Wendover for one hour to witness the test.

In a flash, Starnes had used the US Army and private contractors to transform the barren salt flats into a hospitality viewing suite and AFV museum. They had trucked in sanitary facilities, bleachers, a presidential box with solar-powered air-conditioning, video viewing screens with long-range lens packages on the cameras to herald the approach, catering tent, and more. The area had all the accoutrements of a viewing suite at the Preakness.

Getting the AFVs ready to fly with the correct versions of the general's GCT navigation backup and putting together a dog and pony show for the president stretched the Hock Industries team thin. They had erected a shapely, pointed, tent-like structure borrowed from Cirque du Soleil's warehouse in Vegas to house five added AFVs for the president to survey up close.

The inside of the tent looked like a new-car showroom. Each vehicle was painted a different color and displayed a different body style and interior. Two of the AFVs spun on large turntables. A series of graphics and logos, a little reminiscent of a NASCAR team, made sure all press photos paid homage to those supporting this technological marvel.

Minucci's phone rang, and he hurried to answer, having seen the White House office number pop up. "Go for Minucci."

"But" and "I see" were the only words he squeezed in edgewise. Not even a goodbye. Whoever was on the other end was in a bigger hurry than he was.

"General, I've got some bad news. The president has now decided to skip our AFV test tomorrow because of a more crucial issue," said Minucci.

"More pressing than redesigning the entire transportation system of the United States? I bet it has something to do with that dang Montana situation."

"They wouldn't tell me, General, and I'm in his inner circle of advisors, so it must be something top secret," said Minucci. "The way this country's going, who knows what will happen next?"

It took just four phone calls for Starnes to find out the president's plans. His trip may have been a secret from the press and the rest of the world, but the military still carted him around, and General Starnes still had enough connections in the service to eke out a little intel.

"Director Minucci, the president may not want to come to our test, but I think we can still take our test to the president," said Starnes. "Crowley is flying into Malmstrom and then heading to Lorae, Montana. It's a tiny town right on the Idaho border, and we planned our test to fly over the Continental Divide, right near there. We have a series of beacons slicing right through the valley he'll be in."

"Yes, that's right," said Minucci, who pretended to understand. "That man's got some nerve pushing into Montana when the whole state is ready to bury him."

"I think that's got something to do with his visit if I hear correctly, but that only helps us. If we put the AFV test overhead right when the president walks in, he will see it, and bingo—we got him."

"General, I think you're onto something there," said Minucci.

"And to make sure he sees it, let's put a few more vehicles in the air. How many of those cars under the tent will fly?"

"The crossover wagon is just a concept shell, but Hock told me the other four are good to go. That's four on the ground plus the one in the air, so we could fly five cars in a formation up there, I imagine," said Minucci, running through a myriad of logistics as he overpromised.

"That's it then. Five in the air and we'll program a little dip-n-flip to show the president how we can fly these things," said Starnes.

"I better get the Hock Industries folks on the line. It's going to be a long night."

125

I-90 IN WESTERN SOUTH DAKOTA

Amanuel would not be caught dead on a bus unless the job demanded it. He convinced himself he had to submit to the humbling nature of interstate bus transit to slip from Iowa to Montana undetected as a cover—and to save some of Benny's drive-thru wages.

GloDom was an expensive game, but Benny felt he was closing in on the final stages and would finish in style. The mix of online and live role-playing was an unexpected twist, but when asked to meet face-to-face with the Bullseye tunnel character, he had answered the bell. Epic!

Benny had convinced the gang to take the bus trip with him to see Bullseye's underground palace once they saw the amazing pictures of the cavern. To secure a warm welcome, he convinced Bullseye that he was bringing some representatives of the "client" and would forward the money ASAP, following a positive tunnel preview.

The weekend promised to be an epic journey for these five friends. It had been years since their last endeavor on the road, to Comic-Con. They had milked those memories as long as possible, but the stories had grown stale, even with new lies woven in the retelling.

Benny skipped his prom years ago and had never wasted money on frivolous endeavors like dates or activities with friends, other than movies and the one trip to the Comic-Con Road Show that blasted through Chicago five years prior. To save money, the four of them slept in a parking garage underneath Grant Park in an old minivan borrowed from Spanks' mom. They spent little on food—and none on hygiene. The entire trip set each of them back less than ninety-four dollars, including the sixty-dollar admission to the event. The trip had attained instant legendary status.

Des Moines to Missoula, Montana, was a little over thirteen hundred miles. The trip by bus, with stops, translated into twenty-nine hours of beautiful scenery, one mile at a time, along with a day and a half of bus smell and no shower.

Benny's mom packed a series of sandwiches with color-coded labels, organized by likely condiment expiration. Mayo-anything versions were red tagged/first. To make sure he stayed on the narrow path, she had also included a handwritten Bible verse on a piece of paper towel placed under each sandwich.

Before Benny realized there was a verse attached to each snack, he had swallowed a big piece of Philippians 4:8—*Finally, brethren, whatever is true, whatever is honorable, whatever is just, whatever is pure, whatever is lovely, whatever is of a goo . . .*

As a kid, Benny had earned reward money from his mom to buy video games by memorizing Scripture—and he had gotten pretty good at spotting the different translations, which earned him bonus cash. Benny assumed he was digesting *good report—if there is any virtue and if there is any praise—think on these things.*

He knew the King James Version would have been much harder to swallow.

After four hundred miles, Benny had a handful of verses, some stained with mayo, which he planned to read again later when the guys weren't looking, just so he could think of his mom.

Benny caught a reflection of himself in the window against a black night sky and snapped out of Bible verse/mealtime and got back on task. He would use the remaining eighteen hours of the bus trip to rehearse his role as Amanuel.

To maximize his character and his chance of winning the game, he had recruited the services of Missoula's finest limo service to take him to the secret rendezvous point. The limo and a rental tux seemed critical to his first impression. The guys grumbled but agreed after some adventure-shaming. "This adventure-cosplay stuff isn't cheap if done right," he explained.

He relaxed and watched South Dakota slip by the window throughout the night. He would be ready to make this the legendary trip that they would talk about for years to come. *Benny's crazy,* his friends would say.

As the sixth sandwich and the drone of the bus tires pushed in on his senses, he settled in for some sleep. The seat on this Nation-Cruiser bus was comfy, but not as nice as his gaming chair in the basement. The last thought before he fell asleep came as he glanced at the half-eaten Bible verse clutched in his hand. Amanuel didn't even have a mom, but Benny did . . . and he missed her.

126

WENDOVER, UTAH

The general had thrown the checklist together, with the help of Director Minucci and Dr. Hock, hoping to get a parade of flying cars to show off for the president during his visit just up the road in Montana. Last on the list was to alert the Secret Service, so they knew the test was coming and didn't freak out as the cars hovered close enough for the president to see the vehicle's capabilities. First on the list was to make sure the cars could fly safely and not crash on top of the president. Hock got off the phone with his team down at Yuma and joined the general for an update.

"Four of the five cars that you see here under the tent were just for show, but they can fly. These cars have our LiDAR system and can have your backup nav system installed tonight, but we won't be able to test it until we fly in the morning. We're confident with our nav system and can rely on the backup if it's necessary. Remember, General, the only trouble we've ever experienced was because of the conflict between your system and ours, so it may be safer to go with just our system in a pinch."

"You get ready, get those cars up there, and make sure the LiDAR and the beacon system are on board. I'm OK leaning on your systems. They've been improving, and we've had only one mishap in over three hundred tests, correct? Just get ready. We're leaving here at four a.m. to convoy up there, and we have to be on time."

127

ANDREWS AIR FORCE BASE, MARYLAND

Air Force One was lighter than usual, with half the normal press corps and staff along for the ride, at the president's direction. The press was told the trip would be a quick turn to Denver for a financial summit and memorial for the victims of the recent protests, so the members of the different media tucked themselves in the rear section of the gigantic fortress, near the tail, to work on their computers or nap during the sunrise takeoff.

After slipping out of the senior staff meeting room near the front of the plane, to a quiet corner of the dining room, Stubblefield asked Fowler in a covert voice, "You want the good news or the bad news?"

"Let me see; we're with the president, on his plane, headed to the state that he's selling out from under its citizens, which is the same state where you and I have at least fifteen major felonies in progress . . . ," Fowler said.

"Settle down, Bill. Everything looks to be in good shape," said Stubblefield. "The bad news is not all that bad. I talked to Bullseye last night, and her biker boys have started the stampede already."

"So why is that bad news, Alan?" asked Fowler.

"That's not the bad news. They might have five thousand head in the herd they're pushing, and they just started. They said it was amazing."

"OK . . . and that's bad because . . . ?" sputtered Fowler, like he was still waiting for the other shoe to drop.

"Because, my friend, there will be so many animals in this stampede it will cost a fortune to pay that girl."

Fowler agreed with Stubblefield that their friends would pay several fortunes for a lifetime of trophy hunting on their new preserve. A few million dollars up front to Bullseye was only a temporary setback. Stubblefield smiled at the volume of good luck flowing their way, while Fowler took a sip of breakfast.

"I'll tell you one bad news item that could crop up," said Fowler. "We're heading into this meeting with the president and a lot of pissed-off locals in Lorae, Montana. You realize that Bullseye's place is just a couple hundred yards away, and, unless I miss my guess, she'll be involved with these Secessionists."

Stubblefield looked out of the window of Air Force One somewhere over middle America for a second, then hoisted his breakfast of Jack on the rocks, and said, "No worries, my friend. If there's one thing Bullseye has in spades, it's discretion. She's made half her money by telling stories and the other half by knowing when to shut up. She won't say a word about us, and unless I miss *my* guess, she won't be tangled up with those Secessionists unless it pays a lot of money. I know that woman too well."

DARBY, MONTANA

Redge used his day off to drive into town. He pulled the frayed blue tarp over the Army's big green disc with pulsing blue lights, wedged into the rear of his truck bed. "That thing'll get you arrested, that thing'll get you arrested," he said, mocking all four people who had told him the same thing.

After he sent the first pod floating downriver toward Idaho, Redge decided he could make big money by selling the second Army UFO unit he had found, mounted high in the trees, for scrap. It had a bunch of steel in the housing and a ton of copper inside. Thing was, he had spent the morning traversing the valley to a couple of small towns to pawn the disc, and each one had the same response: *arrested.*

Even Buz Castle, the auto graveyard/parts guy who would buy anything short of a kidney, wouldn't touch it. A night in county jail now and then wasn't a big deal, but these folks were talking about federal this and that. That's hard time, no matter how you slice it. Redge knew it was time to dump the disc.

He swung around the back of the People's Harvest Food Store in Darby and noticed a fancy van with a large electronic-looking dish strapped on the top. After some spray paint, he could not read the US Army stencil or tell the disc had been green. One big ratchet strap later and Redge had secured the disc to the spare tire mounted on the back of the van. It almost looked like it belonged there, except for the hand smudges in the fresh paint job.

Redge was happy to get rid of the bad omen and drowned his sorrows in a cold can of Dinty Moore before he drove back up the hill. *Thank God for pop-tops,* he thought. He thought it again eight miles later, when he popped the second can.

129

DARBY, MONTANA

News Videographer Scott Kirkpatrick came around the front of People's Harvest Food Store just as an old lumber truck pulled out of the parking lot. He tossed the bagful of car cleaning supplies and snacks onto the seat and hopped back into the *Action News* van. With a lot of downtime in the news business, Scott liked to keep his little satellite truck looking showroom new.

The tip he received about the governor kicking off the Secession effort at a secret convention could be a gold mine, if he was the only news guy to toss up to a live satellite signal. The buzz from "The Plea" video had everyone in the media and on social platforms wondering when the movement would go public. He had his local affiliate and the Fox network plugged into his favorites for quick dialing.

As he pulled out of Darby onto Highway 93 and headed south to find his way to the border town of Lorae, he noticed the van felt sluggish. He started to pull over and check the tires when his iPhone screen flashed "Boss."

"Friday? Sure. I should be back by then. I love cat stories, but I gotta warn you, if I can find the governor today and get an exclusive on the Secession announcement, I'll be moving to DC for the network."

Scott talked to his boss about scheduling some remote shoots for another fifteen minutes, until he forgot all about the sluggish operation of the van. He turned west on 473 and followed the West Fork of the Bitterroot.

It might have been possible for other cars to see the pulse and glow of the lights on the disc under the spray paint as he drove into the highlands, but there was no traffic behind him on the tiny mountain road.

SALMON, IDAHO

The convoy left at four a.m. on the dot, according to General Starnes's watch, and had not stopped for five hours as they drove up Highway 93 from Wendover, Utah. When they rolled through tiny Salmon, Idaho, they made a scheduled detour to take a leak and grab some grub.

General Starnes looked at her screen and said, "There's another beacon coming up soon as we leave town, on the backside of the forestry sign for the Salmon-Challis National Forest District, and I'm reading it loud and clear. Sometimes the Army gets it right."

Two hours later, the convoy approached the Idaho/Montana border and pulled into the empty parking lot of the Lame Horse Creek Ghost Town and Mining Operation. They peered down the hill to find a long line of cars parked along the road and glimpsed the bridge that crossed the Nez Perce River to the MooseTracks Diner.

"OK, here's the plan," said Starnes, who took a knee in the Idaho dirt and grabbed a small pine stick to sketch out her thoughts. "Today they are starting their meeting and will jam a bunch of Montana folks into that café down there. The president will land at Malmstrom this afternoon and do some business at the base. First thing tomorrow morning, his convoy will make the five-hour drive to Lorae, approaching from the north, so we'll see him come up that road in a parade of SUVs. We'll have only from the time he gets out of the car near the MooseTracks, crosses the bridge and steps inside, which should be about twenty minutes with hellos and whatnots. That's OK—we'll only need two if our timing is right."

She continued, "Calton, program an impressive parade of all five cars flying three circles around the perimeter here, so we all get the idea. Nothing fancy, no figure eights or loops, little missy." Calton scribbled notes about the tasks and left off the demeaning part.

"Does the president know this will happen?" questioned Wendell, the assistant tucked behind Calton.

"The president's boys and the Air Force will know this is coming down, so we won't scare anyone. I'd hate to see them shoot us down." The general laughed, but only for a second. "He will use this as his excuse for coming to the area to talk to these people. It's good cover."

The group returned to their cars for the drive down the mountain and back up the Continental Divide to the hotel at the Lost Trail Pass Ski Area on Highway 93, right on the Idaho border. It was the closest available lodging since the Secessionists had grabbed everything within an hour's drive of Lorae. Tomorrow would be a long day, made longer by the hour-plus drive from their lodging. *Why in the world did the president pick such a remote corner to meet these folks?* Starnes thought.

As the convoy turned around, Starnes had her jeep turn wide, running right next to the river. She looked upstream toward the MooseTracks but didn't notice the massive pile of logs or the pulsing blue LEDs in the pile's bottom. Although underwater, the beacon was still transmitting. The general had been right: *sometimes the Army gets it right—these beacons worked in any condition.*

131

LAME HORSE CREEK, IDAHO

Bullseye peeked through the curtains of her gift shop. She had come up to check the arrival time for the prince and Amanuel and instead found an entire platoon of Army folks in her parking lot. Her thoughts spiraled:

-*The Army tracked my smuggling activity with Amanuel.*

-*The Army discovered I was the source of the Secession.*

-*The Army heard about the Secession convention and is going to take out the entire brain trust at once, putting a quick end to the squabble.*

While she figured out her next move, the circle of folks around the general sketching out plans in the dirt mounted their vehicles, then took off down the mountain toward Idaho, out of sight.

Bullseye checked her messages and found no updates from Amanuel. The only thing she could think of was to warn her friends across the river at the MooseTracks. She found the horse's ass icon and wrote a quick text to Hitch:

< Get ready. The Army is snooping around on my side of the hill. They're gone for now but might be back.

She hit "send" and looked over toward the MooseTracks. Last night's dinner had been fun, laughing more than she had in months and even stealing a kiss from Evan under the antlers by the restrooms when no one was looking. She wanted to run over and help them get ready. "Well," she told herself, "it was fun, but the real truth is I need to take care of me. No one else will. My million-dollar-a-month prince is coming, and I still need to polish up some things underground. They'll figure it out."

Bullseye turned to plunge back into the tunnel but carried the thought of her friends close. She truly loved her little group of rogue patriots; they had been everything to her for years. She allowed a sweet memory or two of Morris and Hitch to float by. And another thought or two of Evan. "Oh, that man," she whispered, before descending back into the mine.

* * *

Hitch's phone rumbled but went unanswered. His phone sat in Evan's SUV, where he left it charging while their meeting continued inside.

132

MALMSTROM AIR FORCE BASE, MONTANA

The long runway at Malmstrom afforded Air Force One plenty of room for a gradual deceleration, and those on board didn't notice the landing. The president had stopped in Denver earlier in the afternoon, which was his "official" filing for the trip and a dodge for the press. There, he met with disgruntled leaders from labor unions and community groups, followed by a private memorial for the families with loved ones killed during the protests.

The president's team billed the meetings with the unions as "secret working sessions" to keep up the smokescreen for the entire trip. The attendees in Denver posted about their meeting as soon as the president departed, helping him to appear proactive and engaged with the people of the country. He was "rolling up his sleeves and digging in," according to one secondhand report in the *Denver Post Online*, but most of the coverage shifted by late afternoon to the touching memorial service that seemed to transcend politics, universally breaking the country's heart.

President Crowley sobbed with the family of the little girl shot in her stroller, as the mother handed him a picture of her taken two days before the murder, smiling and playing in their yard. The president didn't hesitate when the young mother asked if he would pray over the event. "There are no words, Lord, only questions. Why are there angry cries and sorrow when little Bethany should be here, giggling joyfully? Sad, vacant expressions, when all of the deceased Americans from that day should be home, hugging on their families? We know there are difficult things about this life, but we can face those—it is the times that pure evil lifts its veil to show its ugly reality that we simply cannot fathom and should not tolerate. Oh, come, Lord Jesus! But perhaps that is for another day, Lord. Today, I just grieve over the loss of these precious children of God."

The solemnity of the event quelled the protestors on the edges, and after sincere hugs and encouraging wishes to the president, Air Force One taxied out of Denver and made the brief hop over the Rockies to Malmstrom Air Force Base in Montana for the evening. The press entourage on board were escorted to accommodations on the base, with no knowledge that dinner and the next day's schedule did not include them.

The president kicked back in his office near the tip of the plane, reviewing notes with Blair. "That was a powerful day. I understand the importance of having dinner with our military folks here in Montana tonight, but I am wiped out after that memorial service."

His chief of staff tried to protect him from himself. "It's only a small dinner on the plane with the base commander and a few of his core staff to assess the situation there in Montana. It would be fine, Dan, if you cancel. I will make certain they understand why you just weren't up for it. No one would be after that day."

Dan Crowley rubbed his eyes with his fists and nodded, while Blair continued. "And I don't think they'll mind because, much to my surprise, several of the lifelong Montanans on the base asked if the dinner invite was optional, preferring not to eat with someone who would betray their state and country. They don't exactly hold you or your plan in high regard at this particular moment in history."

The president stopped rubbing his eyes, but kept his fists clenched. "What time is dinner?"

The dining area on Air Force One comfortably accommodated the twenty-five service personnel from the base during dinner but grew uncomfortable after the meal, when discussion elevated to shouting. Raising one hand to quiet the guests, while still holding his banana pudding in the other hand, the president asked them to suggest alternatives to save the nation's economy. The limitations or problems of every idea brought down the volume of discussion. He had been through them all in his Camp David sessions and at every turn since and lost patience with some of his replies.

As the president crawled into bed, his mind ached. He had spent the evening arguing with armed forces who reported to him as commander in chief. In the morning he would meet with the Secessionists, who despised him even more. How would he handle a group that had financial and emotional investment in the state? Tomorrow would be his most difficult day as president.

Another thought crossed his mind, as he tossed and turned, that was both comforting and disturbing. He hoped tomorrow *would* be the most difficult day he had to face as president. If he got through the day with these Montanans and then somehow made the answer work for the whole country, better days would be ahead. God would have answered his prayers.

The president prayed over a lengthy list daily but had quit praying for himself to become smarter or stronger or for others to fail. All he prayed for was that God's will be done and maybe a little help to get out of the way if he was the one screwing up everything. He fell asleep while praying over and over for God to intervene with something earth-shattering.

133

MISSOULA, MONTANA

The long bus trip had relaxed Benny. After wriggling around a bit, his curves conformed to the seat, and the every-other-hour scripture-laced snacks held out until hour twenty-eight. At the final stop he hopped off the bus, duffle in one hand, thirteen and a half Bible verses in the other, and headed for the terminal restroom and a hot shower.

After securing a handful of quarters, Benny walked into the pay stall as a dirty, bus-riding basement dweller. With one shower and the aid of the steam from the humid restroom to press the rental tux he had rolled up in his duffle bag, he emerged as Amanuel, international man of intrigue.

He double-checked his metamorphosis in the bus station mirror. Shaving his sparse barely-beard was a bold concession to the game, but a necessary step to draw closer to his Amanuelness and one step farther from his old life.

A shiny black limo pulled up to block the main entrance of the Missoula bus terminal. The driver, dressed in full uniform and dark glasses, held up a small handwritten sign that read, "Amanuel—International Operative."

Benny took a deep breath and strode out of the terminal, putting on dark glasses to accent his tuxedo. His entourage followed behind in their tuxes and soaked in the few admiring glances sent their way. As they approached the driver, Benny said, "I am Amanuel," and lifted his glasses back on his head. The layer of extra hair gel lubricated the path of the glasses and helped send them sailing over his head and off his back. Will and the Geez reached out and caught them together, almost pulling apart the glasses like a wishbone.

"Allow me, Mr. Amanuel," said the driver as he jumped to open the door and grab his duffle bag.

"Thanks," started Benny, then quickly dropped an octave and added, "you indulge me, my good man."

"Will there be any stops before we proceed to your destination, sir?" continued the driver, in a professional, almost distant manner.

Amanuel drank in the full effect. "I am on a mission of international importance, and by my calculations, we have a little over two hours of driving ahead of us . . ." After a quiet few seconds, Benny leaned forward and directed, "But before we get on the interstate, proceed through a McDonald's." Will and the Geez high-fived, while Spanks fist-bumped Amanuel.

Benny had a feeling that this was likely his last weekend in the *GloDom* game. He would win or be eliminated. Even if there were another level, he had spent every nickel to his name on a bus ticket, a tux, tubs of snacks, and a pricey limo rental for a full day. This was his big shot, and he had to savor every second of the day. His progress with the game bothered him, however. There must have been a clue that escaped his watchful eye. He had failed to discover the method of currency they would give him for the negotiations. For more than a month he had been stiff-arming the tunnel owner, Bullseye, promising to wire the million-dollar deposit as agreed. Bullseye had become insistent, and Benny's excuses, which bought him time, did not feel like a successful strategy in the game. To triumph this weekend, he had to find a code for his virtual funding.

The account number that Bullseye had provided did not help. Somewhere along the way, he had missed a critical clue for the virtual funding source, and his fee for that miss would be a shame-laden trip home. At least he would make sure the team made as many memories as possible before the GameMasters punched their tickets home.

Benny tried to smile sly and slow, slipping into his deeper, slimier Amanuel character. "Gentlemen, the mission is to enjoy the cavern to its fullest, allowing one of Idaho's slickest operatives to wine and dine our group. To imagine what it would be like to be a sheik or a prince and have someone court us like this man is doing in the game." He paused, noticing that they seemed to enjoy his performance. Leading them farther down the road, his accent grew more Middle Easternish.

"And so, to maximize our fun, we need to act like we can take his little smuggler's roost—or leave it. Behave as though we could eat him for breakfast and not even burp," said Benny, acting like he had a toothpick and sucking through his teeth, "and when we're done with the discussion—and only then—will I decide if he lives or dies. That is how Amanuel rolls."

At the precise moment, Benny grabbed his iPod and paused their favorite Pantera track, a go-to for over fifteen years. He glared at his compatriots and, with great daring and flare, launched "Vogue" like a missile through the booming speakers of the limo. He reached into his duffle bag and pulled out four pairs of matching sunglasses. Heads started bobbing to the beat as they each put on their glasses and adopted the same sinister scowl that Amanuel displayed. One by one (except Will and the Geez, who came in together) they joined him in the zone.

134

NEZ PERCE RIVER, IDAHO

"Don't you jackasses think you should have called?" scolded Hump Mankin. He and Redge boarded the small boat and left the greenhorns on the shore. Having caught wind of the Secession convention from Stubblefield, Hump decided he better drop in to make sure nothing became too obvious while the president was meeting above the very river that their illegal logs were floating down.

According to the greenhorns, the trees had flowed with the spring melt but stopped *a while ago*.

"There must be a jam upstream somewhere. We staged a bunch of trees this winter, and there's a lot more water flowing up there than we're seeing right here. I know it's a lot deeper before the MooseTracks," said Mankin.

"So . . . that means?" questioned Redge.

"We gotta keep running upstream to wherever that jam is. We're almost to the MooseTracks, so we may see a person or two there. No one runs a boat up this little creek, so if we saw someone fishing, they'd think we was crazy . . . but I think we may have bigger problems." Redge turned around to see a mass of people—maybe a hundred—gathered on the bridge and the deck of a restaurant. "That's the MooseTracks, Hump. I guess they started their Secession meeting already."

They rounded the bend and saw the base of a huge logjam caused by their timber, below the MooseTracks. The accumulation of logs looked as solid as any beaver dam and allowed only random chutes of water to punch through.

"I don't think they can see it from up there because of the rocks," said Redge.

"Right, Redge," said Mankin. "We'll just slide by and see what it'll take to bust up the jam." Just then, a loud laugh trickled down the streambed from the crowd above. "On second thought, it might be best to wait until the party's over, so we don't get asked a lot of questions." They turned the boat and gunned the motor.

135

LAME HORSE CREEK, IDAHO

White dust from the gravel road caked on the limo as it snaked through the edge of Montana. Amanuel may as well have packed Benny in the trunk. He had seized control and would not relinquish it to a naïve, taco-pushing non-spy. These were dangerous waters only a skilled operative could navigate. Sean leaned against the limo windows as they cruised past the Moosetracks Diner and across the state line into Idaho to the Lame Horse Creek parking lot. The Gift Shop door swung open and Bullseye walked out toward the limo, while Madonna stayed on repeat.

Bullseye had her hat pulled down and her game face on. She wore snug-fitting black pants, boots with a heel, and a River Annie's Cold Shoulder shirt, flowing open to reveal a tank top underneath. The outfit and her walk toward the limo showed off her muscular physique.

"Follow my lead, fellas, and I'll show you how to master this game," lectured Benny, just before he dropped an octave and added, "and when it comes to gorgeous women, you may have my leftovers."

"That's good because she's pretty hot," said Sean, who rarely spoke.

"She . . . ? Holy crap, Bullseye's a hot girl?" said Benny, with his voice wavering, then dropping lower, said as Amanuel, "Hot like molten clay that I will mold into the vessel of my desire."

That earned him a shove out of the limo as the driver opened the door. Benny had spoken with only a few women as beautiful as the one standing in front of him, and all of those conversations had been at the drive-thru window. She appeared older than girl gamers Benny met online. And then he realized that she was likely a black widow—the beautiful antagonist who lured a young player into her embrace, only to suck out the life and cast him out of the game. It would take craftiness to avoid her web.

Amanuel wondered if the lineup would pass Bullseye's muster. A quick gaze at the group left him hopeful, as long as no one spoke. They all appeared to be midtwenties, each in matching sunglasses and dressed tons nicer than he had ever seen them back in Des Moines, respectively wearing some version of a tuxedo—but that's where the similarities ended.

The one introduced as Hakim, the nicest dressed of the bunch, was sporting

Chuck Taylors with "Spanks" written in Sharpie on the side, to contrast his formal attire. His sidekick, introduced as Sean-tu, had a few tattoos peeking out from his collar, written in English. Will and the Geez—who had not adopted an alias—had neglected to take off their class rings, which proudly proclaimed their graduation from Des Moines Tech High School five years prior.

Bullseye's expression morphed to mystified. These fellas didn't look like a group of terrorists or Middle Eastern billionaires or, well, anything other than a bunch of twerps. "I'm Bullseye. Are you supposed to be Mr. Amanuel? What's going on here? I'm confused, Mr. Amanuel. I mean, I see a fancy limo, but I didn't expect a bunch of vandals. I thought we were ready to do business, and it looks like some sort of game to you fellas."

Will and the Geez laughed at the game reference.

Benny panicked. He knew he was getting bounced out of the game soon, but he didn't want it to be in the parking lot before they got to see the cavern. He needed to be bold but didn't know what to do—until he felt Amanuel step up and take over.

"Tut, tut, Miss Bullseye, and we did not expect a female naysayer named Bullseye. I guess we are both guilty of a bad first impression," Amanuel said, while he shook a finger at Bullseye, then adjusted his sunglasses. "One second, please." He turned to his friends and with his back to Bullseye, he said, "A thousand pardons, Your Excellency." He paused long enough to execute a deep bow with both hands placed palm to palm in front of his chest but peered over his sunglasses and winked at his friends.

Spanks, reacting to the clue he had just become a prince or something, said, "This infidel has much to learn about our kingdom and our customs. May her tunnel collapse and her camels contract a rash." He sneered in an indefinable accent, as he stormed off to the limo. The others followed.

Bullseye kicked the dirt once Amanuel turned toward the limo. She said to herself, *OK, girl, hold your pissed-offness in check. I know it's against your nature to let anyone push you around—especially a guy. But it will rub you even more raw to pass up a shot at a million dollars a month. So, suck it up, bow when you have to, laugh at their jokes, and grab their gold, just like you do on hunting trips. They look like twerps, but they could be princely twerps from some kingdom in the Middle East, so let's keep a grip.*

Amanuel slowed his pace, and Bullseye could tell he was giving her time to take the bluff and call them back. They drew closer to the limo until finally the driver reached over to open the back door for Amanuel and the boys to load back up, first the Geez, followed by Will, Spanks, and Sean.

136

LOST TRAIL PASS SKI RESORT, IDAHO

"OK, are those cars in the air?" questioned General Starnes from her team, and the Hock Aviation techs gathered around her in the ski resort's rich, wooden interior of the grand lodge, which was empty this time of year.

"Yes, ma'am, the cars have left Wendover and they are headed our way, averaging ninety-four miles an hour, and should arrive in three hours and forty-eight minutes," said Test Supervisor Calton, with complete confidence.

"Alrighty," said Starnes to the rest of those assembled. "Calton, you track those things and let us know when they're ninety minutes out. We'll make our way up the hill to the Lame Horse again and stage until the cars are in sight. This little air circus will be a nice surprise for the president."

137

BOZEMAN, MONTANA

The Bozeman airport handled a large volume of private aircraft with high-dollar hunters heading north to shoot or higher-dollar fashionistas heading south to ski, prance, and sit by a fire in Big Sky. Once the president confirmed the rumors about the sale of Montana, the real estate market collapsed and most of the jets were outbound, filled with priceless artwork that residents salvaged from their Big Sky condos.

The arrival of the Dassault Falcon was of special note. The jet was larger than most, and the passenger manifest listed royalty from the United Arab Emirates, which prompted a secret call from the tower to the local press. Even though the alert was against protocol, the rulebook had gone out the window with the president's announcement. "The Arabs" were rumored to be potential suitors, so alerting Secessionists when a wealthy entourage from the Middle East arrived was a sign of loyalty to the new nation.

Responding to a welcome by the tower and a casual question about who was on board, the pilot answered with "The prince and his friends are coming to look around." When asked who it was, the American pilot responded to the tower he wasn't at liberty to give names, "but they're dripping in gold."

The traffic controller sent a message to a local reporter, who forwarded to Morris Evans's phone. Morris poked out a text to Bullseye, wanting her to get the news from him:

> Press confirms Arab prince and gang landed in Montana a while ago just to "look around." Pull the rug out from under us is more like it...

A large compartment lowered from the bottom of the Falcon, and two well-equipped SUVs with darkened everythings descended to the tarmac. The contingency from the UAE deplaned and stretched, making gestures like they were soaking in the fresh, cool air. They boarded the SUVs and took off past the hangars and off the airport property toward the east.

138

LAME HORSE CREEK, IDAHO

The text alert from Morris about the Arabs buzzed on Bullseye's phone. She pulled her phone out of her tight pocket and glanced at it as she watched Benny and the kids load up the limo, still not knowing what to make of them.

She dropped her phone and shouted to Amanuel before he bent over to enter the limo, "But, wait . . ."

Her voice was enough to stop Amanuel in his tracks. Bowing toward the limo he raised a mischievous eyebrow and a finger, mock-begging for an additional minute of their patience. He spun on his heels, still bowing, and circled back toward Bullseye.

"I didn't mean to insult your friends, but they don't look like they mean business to me," stammered Bullseye. "I'm just trying to sniff out any phonies, but I can see you are serious players."

"Miss Bullseye, the gentlemen in that limo represent a serious player indeed. His Majesty," Benny said, bowing again, "has been authorized by his father to enter whatever arrangement he may find suitable. Money, my friend, is no object."

Bullseye rubbed her chin, then slid her fingers into her tight pockets, leaving her thumbs sticking out. "And you've known this feller and his daddy for a while?"

"I have traveled far and wide and met a great many people," sniffed Amanuel. "While I cannot confirm or deny my relationship with the king, I will admit to having completed military training with the prince. He is a dear friend, and I would, without hesitation, absorb the thrust of a saber to prevent his demise."

Bullseye started to believe Amanuel's words, but had trouble trusting her eyes. Amanuel's tuxedo shirt was half untucked, with his generous stomach lapping over the waistband of the rented black pants. One clip-on side of the bowtie had pulled off the collar, leaving it dangling like an ornament off to the other side. A smear of chocolate up his sleeve made this man-child look like his military service came from Xbox rather than a battlefield, but he sounded committed to the prince.

NOVEL BY STEVE GILREATH

"It matters not anyway. You have insulted a royal prince, and he is not a forgiving man. I am sorry we have wasted your time and devastated that you have wasted ours. Goodbye, Miss Bullseye." After one more awkward bow and a quick spin back on his heels, Amanuel pointed toward the limo.

"OK, Mr. Amanuel," surrendered Bullseye, joining in the awkward bowing ritual, "I'm sorry for what I've said if it was offensive, and I appreciate you making the trip all the way out here. Please, let's just get the others and head over this way and let me show you around before you make any rash decisions." She motioned toward the cave entrance, then tried to sweeten the deal: "I have beer and ice cream sandwiches inside just waiting on you fellas." She gambled that ice cream had an international appeal, even for a group of rich twerps like this.

Amanuel said, "I will beg, but I do not anticipate favorable winds of grace. You may retire to your antechamber, and if I can persuade the royal prince to forgive your insolence, we will join you inside. Please prepare the ice cream, just in case."

139

LAME HORSE CREEK, IDAHO

Benny jumped in the limo and screamed, "So hot!"

"You were an awesome prince, Spanks!" Will and the Geez said together.

"Guys, she's so hot," uttered Sean.

Benny said, "She's so into the game. I guarantee they'll give us extra points for acting like we would walk away. Now she's gonna give us a chance to see the cavern. I told her Your Highness would consider the offer if she gave us free ice cream and beer."

Spanks lunged at the door. "One prince, coming right up."

Amanuel shoved open the wooden door to the gift shop and informed Bullseye that he had convinced the prince to give her one more chance. They tried to look stern as she did that funny little half bow and led the entourage down into the cave, each grabbing two ice cream sandwiches and a bottle of beer from an old gold pan plate before disappearing underground. They descended two partial flights of steps that were a little slippery from condensation, then passed the sign that read, "Sultan's Retreat." On cue, Bullseye said, "This place is fit for a king," and pulled back the first two musty curtains, revealing two soaring, fake-bronze columns framing the entrance to the bedazzled room.

"Jachin and Boaz . . . ," whispered Benny, frozen in place at the sight of the biblical-scale pillars.

Bullseye asked, "Is that some kind of Middle Eastern phrase of delight?"

The faux splendor of the draperies and beads, plastic palm fronds, and gurgling waterfall, all lit from below with dark, moody shades, overwhelmed Benny—but what truly captured his attention were the two massive columns near the entrance. *Jachin and Boaz* . . . he tried to remember which was which.

Years of intermittent concentration during Bible studies led by his mother swirled through his head. Benny had poured over much of the Old Testament like a video game. He loved the violent parts, the detailed sex, and the cool palaces—all of which he found in abundance throughout the Bible. King Solomon had the triple play.

Benny's mom had seen fit to include I Kings, chapter 7 under the "Hour 14 Salami Sandwich" for the bus trip. She placed the entire chapter there, knowing he hovered over the description of Solomon's temple, and had even built a scale model out of Legos in Sunday school. And to her, *salami* sounded somewhat like *Solomon*.

He set up the pillars . . . He set up the pillars at the vestibule of the temple. He set up the pillar on the south and called its name Jachin, and he set up the pillar on the north and called its name Boaz. And on the tops of the pillars was lily-work. Thus, the work of the pillars was finished.

Snap out of it, puss, came the reprimand ringing in his mind from Amanuel. They had suffered a day-and-a-quarter bus ride, spent a year's worth of drive-thru wages on tuxes and limos—all for the sake of the game. Focus! He must allow Amanuel to dominate, leaving no room for Benny and his Bible-based sightseeing excursions.

Bullseye took a cautious step around his entourage, moving closer to Amanuel, as if she didn't know how to evaluate his silence. She repeated, "Mr. Amanuel, is that OK? Are you ready to see my tunnel?"

Amanuel, realizing that he must have appeared in a trance during the previous minute, glared into Bullseye's eyes and said, "I will look at your tunnel. But know I very much like your columns, too. All the boys giggled like pageant finalists and poked elbows in each other's ribs as Bullseye pulled open the next pair of drapes.

Benny was beside himself. *What is this game all about? These guys are overboard! A real tunnel? I was expecting a cardboard replica or maybe a spare room decked out to simulate the route. Too cool!*

The room echoed with the sound of trickling water tumbling from stacked clay vases as if they were never-ending sources of life. The shimmering waterfalls bathed the walls of the cave in pulsing waves of light from tiny LED fixtures buried within. Beams of light refracted off trunks filled with chunks of glass and beads, twinkling like a nighttime sky. A warm breeze blowing from deeper in the cave choreographed walls of hanging fabric in a slow-motion ballet, beckoning the visitors forward. A ghostly soundtrack of Middle Eastern standards flowed through the room and carried the theme forward.

"This will serve as a good cover for whoever would enter from the United States side," said Bullseye, laying out the tunnel benefits for the gang, "and you hide the smuggling route behind these carpets over here." She tugged back two large carpets that appeared plastered to the walls, hinged to swing open like wide barn doors. The long tunnel glowed to life, with the yank of a tasseled gold rope—a switch that activated a meandering string of lights that crawled along the ceiling and wall of the tunnel and zigzagged out of sight. "It's only a fifteen-minute walk back into Montana—or whatever country they'll call it," said Bullseye, selling harder, "and there's enough room to run small vehicles through here. Just a little more work will turn it into a full-on road."

Trying to keep up with the game, Spanks the prince said, "And what of all this water? There seems to be an abundance leaking through this passage."

"Yeah," added Will and the Geez, in unison.

"It is a cave system connected by tunnels, Your Excellency," pleaded Bullseye. "It is natural for clean water to run through cracks in the limestone throughout a cave like this. In addition, the Nez Perce River flows along or, perhaps, over this wall," she said, pointing to the green, slimy wall on her right, "and some water will always filter through in the springtime. It will dry up again in the summer and winter."

The entourage looked satisfied with her answer.

"What'll you be pushing through here, if I might ask?" asked Bullseye.

Amanuel took a secretive tact—because he did not understand the question or the next step of game. He offered the raised eyebrow and a sly smile toward his friends, who all mimicked his eyebrow lift in Bullseye's direction. She smiled as if impressed even more with the surreptitious reaction.

As the tour weaved through the tunnel toward Montana, Bullseye provided specs on completion dates, moisture control, and more. Benny was a tad overwhelmed, wondering which of these factors would be clues for the next step in the game.

The tour gathered for a break around her favorite little hot-spring pool, illuminated by a soft amber lantern. "You should all touch this water. There are geothermal springs flowing through here and this freshwater spring always runs at 102 degrees. I love to come down here when no one is around, take off all my clothes, and lay right down in the pool. It fits my body like a glove, and the sulfur content in the water will heal just about anything that's ailing."

Benny could imagine every single move Bullseye had described, in luscious detail. Will and the Geez both swallowed hard as Bullseye brushed passed each boy and touched their shoulders while she described her natural spa. Bullseye led them the additional hundred yards to show where the egress into the backside of the hill and out into Montana would be once she punched through the mountainside. Amanuel was still focused on her hot-spring bathing ritual and had no questions.

"Well, if there are no further issues, then, I believe we're ready to sign a contract and start the wire transfer," she said, staring at Amanuel. "Here is my offshore account number, assuming everything is to your satisfaction. I have all the papers back in the Retreat, so let's wander back up there and get it rolling." She handed him a card with twenty-four digits on it.

Benny's heart jumped; a code! The reason he had traveled all this way—why the game creators had put him through the ruse. He must have proven himself worthy and would now sail through to the next layer of the game. This was fantastic!

"Sure, Ms. Bullseye," said Benny, dropping his accent a little. "I haven't gotten the code thing figured out to see how the money works in this world, but this should help."

"It is to your liking, Mr. Amanuel, isn't it? If so, you can push through the first payment. I think one month—the first million—should be enough to lock it up."

Benny looked at the twenty-four-digit number on the card. "One million will be no problem."

Bullseye sighed and smiled, then locked him in a firm embrace that connected from his cheek all the way to his knees. She reached up to rub the grinning Benny on the shoulder, spun him around, and pointed him back down the path they had just followed.

Benny fished around for his sunglasses as they prepared to head up to the surface. He said, "Imagine what this would be like if we were talking about real money, Miss Bullseye, or, what is your real name?"

Bullseye looked mystified. "Son, I don't know what in the hell you are talking about. All I know is that I got a hundred thousand worth of excavating into this tunnel, and your prince here better be good for it, or I'm gonna make things ugly for you all!"

140

LORAE, MONTANA

The crowd outside the MooseTracks splintered into smaller groups, as the third day of birthing a nation bared some nerves. The warm morning sun allowed them to expand the meetings alfresco, and the sound of trickling water under the bridge encouraged them to exhale. The governor had cobbled together one ensemble of the most optimistic committee members, who perched on the bridge about twenty-five feet above the water level, with their legs dangling over the edge of the deep gorge, chattering about a brilliant future in the bright sunshine.

The optimists talked about how the other states would absolutely rally behind them, knowing they wouldn't want the president to choose them as his next victim. If the Feds could take Montana, why should anyone else feel safe?

A dour, pessimistic bunch huddled in a dreary corner of the MooseTracks lounge and whispered about leaving the effort altogether, fearful of military intervention. Conspiracies laced their discussion. "I hear the Feds spiked the drinking water in Missoula, and a full Army brigade is camped right across the border in Idaho," said one panicked Secessionist.

Actor Evan Morris slid back across the bridge and back inside the MooseTracks to find this group and said, "You've heard too many of Claudia's stories. A battalion of soldiers will not come flying over the hill. Stop being so paranoid."

Governor McLemore bounded from one group to another, gauging the collective pulse. He joined a very intense constitution group sequestered on some boulders along the bank of the river, under a cluster of shady cottonwood trees just sprouting their leaves. "We owe you all a heap of gratitude for the extensive advance work on the new constitution."

The state representative leading the committee made a mock toast with his coffee mug and said, "Sure, Gov. Now all we have to do is create a few critical mechanisms, like how to control future change. Shouldn't take more than a few minutes, right?"

During a break, the team congregated around the snack table Claudia had supplied near the bridge railing. Evan Morris added carrots with tiny dollops of ranch to his plate, while Morris Evans nudged by with a cascading display of sugar and chocolate in various forms filling up his plate. "Evan, the success of this whole Secession movement comes down to how persuasive you can be. When you talk to the rest of the country, sell this thing. Let 'em know what we're all about."

"Well, that's a lot to put on one man," said Actor Evan. "I'll do what I can."

The governor joined in, "I can't wait to see . . . *the president?*"

He stopped short as President Crowley marched around the corner and onto the bridge, which was still about half full of the optimist group, dangling their legs. Secret Service flanked him by a couple of steps, all dressed in rugged hiking gear. The Montanans froze, but the president didn't hesitate and walked right into the middle of the gathering, toward the governor.

"Well, if it ain't the Scoundrel in Chief," spouted Hitch Jenkins.

141

OUTSIDE LORAE, MONTANA

The phone on the dashboard of Starnes's vehicle buzzed and bounced. She clawed at it to engage the "answer call" button. "Go for Starnes."

"General, this is Andi Calton. The fleet is right on schedule and is one hour out from the maneuver in Lorae."

"Atta boy, Calton. Give me another heads-up at thirty," the general said before she hung up and continued sharing her plan with the rest of the van. "Two more turns and we'll be at Lame Horse Creek. I want all the vehicles staged in a semicircle in case the president wants to come over and watch the display. I know these things fly themselves, but I want us to put on a show."

The troops signaled their compliance while Hock's team looked at each other in the back seat, like they were trying to figure out where that left them.

"Hock, you stick with me. We'll skip over to the MooseTracks together in exactly thirty-two minutes and confirm the president is in the middle of that brouhaha. I'll call for the cars to fly right over his location. If things go as I plan, I'll introduce you to the president right after we dazzle him with our little demo."

Hock and most of his team clapped like they were breaking a huddle. They pulled up the radar signal and locked on the tight grouping of flying cars, in the middle of Idaho, heading north, across the Salmon-Challis National Forest. Hock pulled a handful of tissues out of the overstuffed pocket on his lab coat and blew his nose, then cleaned his glasses and shook his head.

LORAE, MONTANA

The springtime sun warmed the mountains throughout the morning and caused the wind gusts to surge and whoosh across the meadow, up the valley, down from Montana, toward Idaho. As the valley narrowed at Lorae into the gorge where the MooseTracks hung over the edge of the river, the velocity of the breeze picked up and pushed the tall Douglas firs side to side.

Evan Morris faced north to make sure the breeze blew his blond hair straight back when he took his hat off during the impromptu meeting with the president of the United States, the governor of Montana, Vice President Fowler, Interior Secretary Stubblefield, the lieutenant governor, and their inner-most council of Secession movement officers on the large deck area of the MooseTracks, all dressed in some version of plaid flannel shirt. Evan noticed four bighorn sheep bound along the rocks of the gorge just above the water, then followed Stubblefield's gaze, locked on the opposing rock wall, watching a huge herd . . . or was that a gaggle or a clique . . . regardless, it was a bunch, maybe eighteen or twenty whitetail deer traversing the wall of the gorge.

As the president tried to defend a passionate point, an eagle screeched as it soared just over their heads. The shadow was so large and the noise so piercing that it caused some on the deck to take cover. Crowley, McLemore, and gang broke off their conversation and pointed off to the side of the gorge. Evan noticed a steady stream of animals, large and small, running along both sides of the river surrounding them. He also saw Stubblefield pull up Bullseye's name on his cell phone and wondered if there could be two Bullseyes in this world.

"Something wrong is going on with these animals," said one of the Northern Cross Militia members, hand on his pistol.

143

BITTERROOT VALLEY, MONTANA

Shank's Harley acted as tired of him as he was of it, but the end was in sight—only a couple more miles—and he'd cajole over five thousand head into the preserve and tuck the reward into his account. The Driven Gang had pushed these animals across the Bitterroot Valley and toward the gap in the Continental Divide, near the star on Shank's map, called Lorae. They would cross into Idaho there and over into the preserve set up by Bullseye and some Washington dudes.

The whole gang jumped on the last few miles of the drive, creating a hundred-bike-wide fan spread out across the alpine meadow and up the ridge on both sides through the spacious forest. The motorcycles swarmed closer together as the topography of the valley narrowed and the walls became steeper, kicking up a dense curtain of dust.

About forty members of the gang dropped their bikes and took off running, in boots and full leathers, through the rocks and patches of snow, shooting, sliding, and screaming like teens at a water park, to scare the mountain goats climbing the sheer walls back into the fray.

Shank pulled up Bullseye's contact info and dropped a message in her window.

< ready or not, here we come. There's a bunch of animals knocking on your door, so I hope you rolled out the welcome mat.

LAME HORSE CREEK, IDAHO

Bullseye kept a close eye on Amanuel as she steered him, the prince, and the entourage back toward daylight at the tunnel's entrance. He had given her some mumbo jumbo about a code and his offshore account, not being accustomed to some of the wiring practices in this country and avoiding international monetary limit restrictions. Bullseye guessed it sounded plausible enough to keep talking as she scuffed along. She diverted the group into the Dome Room, and the boys became more animated. They called out every detail with wonder and approval: the treasure chests of beads, the baskets overflowing with brass vases made to look like gold, the old pottery pots filled with dollar-a-pound gems and minerals. She told them that this was where she imagined they could store tanks . . . or camels . . . or . . .

The prince picked up on the exercise and said, "Or rockets."

She smiled, believing she had stumbled on an answer to part of their smuggling desires.

As the tunnel became shallower, her phone buzzed as text notifications caught up to her in the Dome Room closer to the surface. Each message made her more nervous. She saw Stubblefield's name first, then Shank's name popped up.

"Gentlemen, I need to see about something topside. I'm going to let you poke around some on your own. Here's where you can start." She pointed at the stream of water under the pallets on the ground. "You just follow this little trickle here if you want to go back to the place in the stream where I love to lay naked. After a long day, I take off all of my clothes and I ease into that little tub-like area of the rock," she said as she slowed her pace and fanned her hand across her shoulder and down the front of her neck, allowing her fingers to disappear behind the top section of her shirt, "and let the warm trickle of mineral water roll over every inch of my sore muscles . . . oh, I already told you about all that, didn't I?"

"Uh-huh," said Will and the Geez, together.

"You must be tired from all your travel. Head back there, take your clothes off and enjoy the hot springs. No one will bother you. There are some towels down there, so just go relax for a while. Or, you can follow the water this way back to the Sultan's Retreat, and chill in the soft beanbag chairs and enjoy another ice cream from the freezer in there. You gentlemen make yourselves at home. I'll join you in short order," said Bullseye, directing the last word toward the exit as she turned and bounded up the tunnel, looking down at her phone.

Sound traveled a long way through the tunnel as the entourage talked over each other. She heard the boys as she rounded the next turn and prepared to exit. The bits and pieces were confusing: "You think she'll join us?" ". . . naked?" "You think that's part of the game?" "Dude, I saw her first," "She wants a prince," and "Benny." It was hard to figure out. Her phone buzzed again, and she rushed up the stairs.

When she got closer to the surface more texts loaded, first from Stubblefield:

< What the hell? Is the stampede today? I'm here with Pres and I see animals.

A second later, Shank's text landed:

< ready or not, here we come. There's a bunch of animals knocking on your door, so I hope you rolled out the welcome mat.

Bullseye crashed through the door of the tunnel entrance, past the gift shop, and stumbled into the parking lot, while looking down at her phone. She skidded to a stop as she slid around the ticket booth and looked up to see an entire platoon of Army vehicles staged in a semicircle.

She gasped and ducked back behind the ticket booth. *What the fat is this?* she thought to herself. *They could have tracked the prince and are on to me now, ready to arrest me for treason. But they aren't aiming their weapons at my tunnel—they're facing the wrong way, toward Montana, and must be ready to squash the Secession plot before it even gets started. The government takeover has begun!* She had to warn Morris, Evan, and her friends.

Her mind raced as she snuck back around the gift shop, down the bank of the Nez Perce, out of sight from the road, and moved toward the MooseTracks.

She carefully navigated the slippery rocks by the river, when a huge buck, followed by a panicked parade of four does, almost ran over her. Bullseye fell on her butt and looked at her phone. She didn't know what to do. A few million dollars' worth of wild game was about to tear through their meeting, and if Shank didn't get anyone to funnel them in the pen, she would lose everything.

At the same time, she was about to close the deal for a smuggling route with a specious prince, who was waiting for her with his boy-band backup, down in the tunnel; but the Army was camped outside her cave door, waiting to smoke her out, costing her millions.

Help Shank wrangle and make a bunch of money or help Amanuel hide and make a bunch of money? If they caught her doing either, she'd likely see nothing but prison the rest of her life and could forget about the money. If she was wrong and the Army dudes were there to step on the Secession, she would never forgive herself for not warning her friends. It was just a bunch of old codgers, but they were the only people in the world that she cared about. And the only men who had ever treated her fair.

Bullseye pulled her hair and squealed in frustration. She knew what she had to do and picked up her phone, hoping to have at least enough bars in the gorge to make one call. She pushed her contacts and then . . .

A mountain goat, scared by the noise that rose from the valley, brayed with every leap from rock to rock and butted Bullseye hard, causing her to fly off the rocks and headfirst into the river. Her phone hit the water just before she did, lost to the current. A pool of blood formed in an instant on the boulder where her head had slammed. She dragged herself to the edge of the river just before she passed out, still bleeding.

145

LORAE, MONTANA

Scott Kirkpatrick thought he saw several large animals darting along the small two-lane road as he snuck the *Action News* van closer to the MooseTracks Diner. He leaned forward with his elbows on the steering wheel just as a massive gray wolf landed right on the hood of his van, snarled, then leaped off, tearing the metal of the hood with its claws. Scott grabbed his camera and hit the "auto calibrate" control, setting the satellite dish in motion on top of the van. He looked across the river in time to witness a parade of animals—very large creatures—careen past a huge crowd cowering on the deck of the MooseTracks Diner, the animals stumbling on rocks, crashing into the deck's railing, crossing the bridge, and scattering into the woods.

Scott grabbed his sat phone and texted the station:
< Get this all. Go live. Don't miss. Call network. I think President is middle of group on the deck. More...

He hit "send" on his phone as he pushed "record" and the "live feed" buttons on the video control panel, then switched to the roof-mounted camera and used the joystick to bring the MooseTracks into focus. Under a human canopy formed by two Secret Service agents, he spotted the president, Governor McLemore, and Evan Morris. Everybody screamed.

Scott powered up the GoPro on the dash and hit "record," spun the dash mount toward himself and started a rapid-fire narration, trying to describe the scene. After a fast series of disjointed images involving the president head-to-head with Montana's Governor, attacks by killer wolves, and herds of wild animals run amuck, he paused and shook his head. He took a deep breath, and in a much slower, more deliberate cadence, told his family he loved them in case he didn't make it out.

* * *

In the control room of *Action News* in Missoula, the technical director for the morning news show was cleaning up some video packages for the next day's programming. He noticed a feed coming from their regional van, next to the Middle Eastern satellite feed. He popped it up on the large preview monitor and clocked the digital address of Scott Kirkpatrick's truck. The chaotic image showed wild animals and people scrambling over each other. He grabbed his headset and clicked on the producer's office. "Hey, Matt, you gotta see this. We may want to go live with whatever it is. I think it's . . . wait a frickin' minute . . . we got a live shot of the governor, squatting next to the president, who's bending over so far to hide from something that it looks like he's trying to kiss his own butt."

* * *

On the back of the *Action News* van, the spray-painted orb that Redge had cut down from a tree and attached to the tire mount glowed and whirred. The bright midday sunlight revealed the "US Army" logo clearly, through the white spray paint.

146

LAME HORSE CREEK, MONTANA

Starnes grabbed Hock and pointed at the third group of animals she had seen gallop by Bullseye's parking lot past their trucks. "OK, Hock, it's time to go get the president ready for our debut. I don't know what all these dang animals are doing running amuck, but they better not screw up my demo."

She stared down Andi Calton and yelled, "Calton, you got those cars close by yet?"

Calton issued a crisp response. "They're right on target, ma'am. Five minutes out, as planned."

"OK, I want you to do a little re-programming. Let's send them around the valley, then swing them back down this way, so the first time we get a good look at them here will be from the north, coming up the long meadow and the river. I can see everyone tucked up under the deck at the MooseTracks, and they won't see them if they come from the south like we had planned."

"General, the battery levels have reached a dangerous level on three of the craft. I'm not sure they can handle much more. The climb to the extra altitude has been a drain."

"There's no time to stop and swap now, sweetie. You just keep your foot on the gas."

"General, I'll do as you command, but I'm telling you, the car diagnostics are calling for immediate battery change and—"

"Calton, I don't want any screwups, and we can't charge these cars right now, so let's flip off the primary LiDAR nav system and save as much power as possible. When the chips are down, I'd rather depend on the Army than a bunch of hippie developers. We don't have to worry about other traffic flying by anyway, so let's use our beacons."

Hock stepped forward and began the protest, louder than the others gathered. "General, that's not smart. We haven't wrung out the system in these show vehicles. Our LiDAR is much safer."

"The president is standing there, so it's my butt on the line," said Starnes. "I have to go with my gut and use what I've seen work for years. OK, Calton, switch those beacons on and light up the path. We spent a fortune putting beacons all the way to Canada. I want those cars guided off our Army pods. They need to be reading something anchored to the ground."

Calton answered, "OK, General. Working on the land-based GCT nav activation now. I've entered the flight path, and you should hear the vehicles buzz by your nine in about fifteen seconds."

"Nice jargon, Calton. Let's go see the president." The entourage moved toward the bridge to cross over to the MooseTracks. As promised, they heard the buzz of their vehicles off to the left as the cars headed out west before making their entrance for the president from the north. The rumble grew lower and louder as hundreds more animals bounded out of the woods, followed by a pack of thirty-five bikers. The animals ran past the Army platoon who came face-to-face with the bikers. One biker saluted and squeezed the throttle to throw up more dust, leaving the group of Army trucks in the rearview as the bikes dove into Idaho.

147

LORAE, MONTANA

The Driven Biker Gang had done the job. They had terrorized almost twenty miles of countryside by pushing thousands of animals into Idaho. Kip and about thirty others had circled wide and rode ahead to open the entrance to the pens. There was a tense moment when the group ran face-first into an Army platoon, but Kip had saluted, and kept riding.

Stubblefield's team had left about a half-mile-wide gap in the fencing on the end of the compound. A noisy funnel of motorcycles helped the animals find their way into the pen while Fleet activated the auto-count game monitors.

Shank relocated to a bluff farther south to drink in the action as they neared the only real bottleneck in their path—the MooseTracks Diner, about a hundred yards away. He pulled up his binoculars and wiped his eyes to make sense of the scene.

First in his field of vision was an enormous number of elk, sheep, deer, martens, and even a black bear running for their lives. A massive herd of stampeding bison followed the road and bashed cars, knocked over small trees, and tore past the bridge to the MooseTracks. Many of the animals tried to cross the river on top of the logjam that had formed an impromptu bridge.

Shank focused across the bridge and saw a terrified crowd, cringing on the deck at the MooseTracks, holding each other and the deck railing, pointing at impending danger all around. It was chaos—but it got worse. A loud, electronic noise surged up the alpine meadow, toward the gorge.

In a burst of buzzing, five flying cars whisked overhead, just above the treetops, hovering. The wind and sound from their fans were deafening, masking the roar of the bikes' engines. The animals scattered in every direction—over the ridge, into the Nez Perce River, right back through the bikers themselves, over the meadow, and toward the woods.

A gigantic, terrified moose sidestepped the chaos on the logjam and dashed across the bridge, into the crowd of people gathered outside the MooseTracks, sending a waterfall of humans off the bridge on the downstream side to avoid being trampled. Everyone and everything made a noise, but the flying cars hovering overhead were the loudest.

The Secret Service grabbed the president and dragged him inside the MooseTracks, out of harm's way.

148

NEW YORK, NEW YORK

"This Fox News Alert is happening now. President Crowley is under physical attack today in Montana. There is no audio with this clip, so we can't explain why the president is in Montana, but we know that Crowley, along with the vice president and secretary of the Interior, are squared off in a secluded meeting with Montana's governor and some of the state's leading citizens who have threatened to secede.

"The president's party is apparently under attack by a notorious group of bikers, identified by their jackets as the Driven Gang, who have fired shots and stampeded a herd of wild animals toward the president. Flags and patches on other people shown here indicate involvement by several different militia groups from the northwestern United States, but it is not clear which side they are on.

"Meanwhile, Fox cameras spotted an aerial assault by a squadron of flying cars . . . that's right, I said flying cars . . . and, well again, we just don't know at this time if these cars are weaponized . . . wait, I'm being told that there is confirmation that a contingency from the United Arab Emirates has arrived in the area. Reports confirm the team from the Middle East landed in Bozeman yesterday and may have something to do with this insurrection. Please stay tuned to Fox for more developments on this extraordinary story."

149

LORAE, MONTANA

Starnes pulled her pistol and shot a charging buck right between the eyes, dropping him less than ten yards from where she stood, then pushed through the last hundred yards to reach the bridge. She looked down at the river and saw Bullseye Magee, trying to recover from her concussion. Starnes sent two staffers down the rocks to retrieve Bullseye while she yelled at her satellite phone for Calton to get the flying cars out of the area.

"Why are they just hanging there?" she yelled. "We didn't program that."

Calton clenched her phone and controller pad as she avoided the charging animals behind an Army truck back in the Lame Horse parking lot. "General, we programmed the cars to freeze in place if there's a conflict in your beacons. You didn't test your CGT beacons this morning and there must a problem with their locations. Those cars will stay frozen until we override the issue."

"Girl, don't give me some fast talk about the Army screwing this up. Now get those cars out of the air, and I mean now, before these animals kill someone or the cars run out of power and fall out of the sky on top of the president. Do you hear me, Calton?"

She answered, "But, General, the conflict is your beacons. The vehicles don't know where your antenna pods are. If I override our safety protocol, I can't guarantee what will happen."

The general held the phone straight in front of her reddening face and roared into the mouthpiece, "Well, I can tell you what will happen. I can tell you that if you don't override your damn safety system, and I mean right now, I will ride one of these planes up your butt so far, you'll taste it. Now do what I say and make these cars fly according to the Army nav pods; do you read me?"

"OK, General, but the outcome is on you. I'm turning our system off, and I want everyone who can hear this to know that the consequences are on you."

With the flip of a switch, the flying cars shimmied. The AFVs' onboard tracking systems grew more confused as they recalibrated, using the Army pods from the beacon disc spray painted and mounted on the back of the

Action News van, and the beacon now buried under the logs in the river. The flying five-car parade hovered for a minute straight overhead the MooseTracks Diner before two cars dropped straight down about twenty feet, then slammed into each other, recovered, and soared straight up. The other three zoomed off in several directions.

I hope the president didn't see that, thought Starnes, as she scrambled for a place to hide.

Three of the cars then sought the beacon leading to an emergency landing site, programmed as a safety measure, right next to its pulsating orb on top of the ridge. The cars dove at the disc, now buried under the water. One by one, the AFVs plowed into the logjam with a tremendous, escalating explosion.

Two other flying vehicles skidded out of control through the water and slammed into the dam. The logjam weakened, then jarred loose, sending a massive wall of water and logs cascading downstream at an incredible velocity. The two forty-eight-inch Douglas fir logs that had started the jam bobbed in the deep rapids now racing toward Idaho.

The two giant logs joined side by side and crashed, full speed, into the rock wall of the gorge underneath the MooseTracks. The force of the water blasted the logs right through the thin rock wall and exposed a cavern—the Sultan's Retreat great room of Bullseye's tunnel! In a flash, the river diverted into the tunnel, sending millions of gallons gushing throughout its hallways.

Benny and his gang had just taken their clothes off and were wading through the hot springs of Bullseye's tunnel when the force of the rushing water picked them up and slammed them against the walls. They coughed, swam, and surfed the current up the tunnel toward the stairs leading to the gift shop, bruised and bleeding. Spanks grabbed Benny's arm as he thrashed by and then grabbed a beanbag chair floating by and paddled toward safety. Spanks screamed like he was on a mechanical bull. Benny cried.

The scene above ground was just as chaotic. Most humans on the bridge or deck sought refuge inside the MooseTracks as the animals terrorized the area. Vice President Fowler scrambled toward the diner but slipped in the process and shoved Stubblefield over the deck railing, into the rushing river. He did not even turn to watch him wash away downstream on a massive wave.

And then the ground began to shake.

150

LORAE, MONTANA

"I'm pretty sure this is in one of my sandwich Bible verses!" screamed Benny, between sobs. "First a flood, now an earthquake?"

The boys flailed, swam, and floated past the Dome Room, up the main entrance tunnel, and crawled up the steps, hoping to get out of the cave before they drowned. The icy water rose almost an inch a second. Will and the Geez were the last of the boys out of the tunnel and vaulted off the final step, just as the rushing water swallowed it. They foraged for a towel or a T-shirt inside the Lost Horse Gift Shop to cover up their pasty-white naked bodies.

This was not an earthquake. The logs blasting into the tunnel at high velocity had slammed into the last couple of columns that Bullseye left standing. To make room for her smuggler tenants, she had carved away too much support from the large Dome Room, not realizing she was right next to the Nez Perce River and just below the MooseTracks. As the logs took out these two main supports, a few smaller support pillars crumbled, along with some thin walls between the abandoned shafts from a hundred years ago. The remaining layer of ceiling rock quivered under the eroding support.

The crash was catastrophic but surprisingly efficient. Most of the rock sheared along the ceiling lines of Bullseye's Dome Room and the feeder tunnels, which allowed a massive rock island almost sixty yards across to fall as one huge section into the hole, with nominal crumbling. The water, which had filled the tunnel through the colossal holes blasted in the walls by logs, cushioned the collapse like an immense hydraulic pad tucked under the rock island that held the MooseTracks, along with a hundred citizens, some elk, bikers, a section of road, the president, and some trees!

The pressure created by the sudden collapse of this massive weight forced water to shoot into every side tunnel and crevice at a high velocity and blast open several large blowholes around the area. Rocks, dirt, fake jewels, fabric, and water gushed out of geysers everywhere as the MooseTracks sank thirty feet below ground, with the entire Secessionist movement riding it down below grade. The hydraulic effect of the water underneath allowed the entire island of rock, including the restaurant, to settle with a soft landing.

The collapse had buried Bullseye's Sultan's Retreat forever.

151

NEW YORK, NEW YORK

"This Fox News Alert is live from tiny Lorae, Montana. Our expert Montana Secession Correspondent Scott Kirkpatrick at our Fox affiliate in Missoula has been sending us amazing live pictures, and we now have audio. This incredible scene shows President Dan Crowley, Vice President Bill Fowler, and Interior Secretary Stubblefield meeting with Montana's Governor McLemore and many others in the Secessionist movement, including the new face of Montana, Evan Morris, to discuss a solution to the sale of the state."

The B-roll footage on the screen showed each of the players mentioned cowering in a tight ball of arms and legs, clawing to get underneath the others, while an elk charged across the shaky wooden deck.

"Just five minutes ago, in a bizarre and unexplainable series of events, the building in which the parties were meeting simply vanished! In this stunning video, again, shot just minutes ago, the president, shown here, rushed inside the building as the entire structure disappeared inside a sinkhole, followed by these ballistic geysers around the edges." The video continued to track with the announcer's words, bearing witness to the incredible series of events. "A series of explosions, a crash involving five flying vehicles, a flash flood, and a stampede of wild animals preceded the collapse. There is instant speculation that these geysers or explosions on the perimeter were part of an elaborate plot to kill President Crowley, as one member of an unidentified area militia can be heard yelling, 'Sent him straight to hell.'"

"During the chaos, it appears a few citizens, including Secretary Alan Stubblefield, was shaken off the deck and swept away with the flood." A small circle illuminated on the video clip of the deck shaking, highlighting a person identified as Alan Stubblefield as he was clearly bumped overboard by the vice president and seen waving furiously in the rapids while carried downstream. "His whereabouts are unknown at this time. We're waiting for word on the president's condition and will not cut away from our main live shot, but until we have more, let's hear from wild animal behavior expert Denson Daluga and see what possible explanations for this herd activity . . ."

152

LORAE, MONTANA

The rescue began even before all the water receded into the main river channel. The flood had washed a few people downstream, but most paddled to shore after the force of the initial deluge dissipated. A group above ground quickly mobilized with ropes and makeshift ladders strung together for victims to crawl out of the massive hole that had swallowed the MooseTracks Diner. The entire rock island holding the MooseTracks, about sixty yards across at the widest point, came to rest nearly forty feet underground and slightly on a tilt. The walls of the hole were sheer, carved and scoured by the descending granite monolith.

"We need five or six stretchers down here to lift out some of the injured folks. I think there are some broken parts here and there, but we're doing OK, aren't we?" said Evan Morris, looking up from the hole, having climbed on top of the MooseTracks to survey the entire scene and trying to cheer everyone up before spotting Bullseye and climbing down to help her.

The flood had extinguished the flames from the crashed AFVs. Their mangled remains lay twisted on the rocks in the streambed in clouds of white and black smoke. The collisions killed a few deer and bison as the logjam broke loose, but that seemed to be the worst of it. Despite the massive damage, no one had died during the chaotic scene, although there appeared to be more than a dozen broken legs and arms, a few concussions, including Bullseye's, and lots of scrapes.

The muddy vice president crawled out of the opposite side of the pit from the president, who yelled, "Fowler—anything you want to explain about all these trees?"

Fowler looked around for Stubblefield and said, "Sir, it was Alan—"

"Save it, Bill. We've been tracking this since you first spoke with Mankin months ago. You, my ex-Vice President, are going to jail for trying to rape the people of Montana during one of their most difficult situations in history." He signaled the Secret Service to restrain him.

Scott Kirkpatrick caught the entire interaction with his remote cameras. The president gave the camera a thumbs-up, while Morris Evans shot a dripping one-fingered salute behind the president's head, all streamed live to the entire country.

310

LORAE, MONTANA

After two hours of sorting out the mess and assisting triage for the injured, Claudia crawled back in the hole to find her purse. The entire structure of the MooseTracks Diner was standing upright in the center of the gigantic forty-foot-deep chasm. The walls on two sides had split open, and several large pieces had severed and fallen off, some covering two of the cars that had been gobbled up by the hole. The kitchen was exposed, with boxes and jars of food still clinging to some of the metal shelves that were all screwed together. Claudia entered the fragile structure through the shed attached to the back of the kitchen that held firewood and other supplies, now covered in gooey mud, water, and rock debris. She slid through the slick shed, taking in the devastation they had survived, and moved past the colossal walk-in freezer, which seemed to be anchoring the entire structure in place. She grabbed her purse off a hook and scurried back out into the cold mud. In the setting sun, a twinkling reflection about ten feet up the wall of the pit caught her eye.

Intrigued by the sparkle that danced on the east side of the rock wall, she picked her way through the mess in the pit, squinting when the light reflected into her eyes. Claudia grabbed a muddy chair from her former diner and wedged it between the wall and a huge dead elk crushed in the collapse. With a little prodding from a dining room fork, the shiny rock popped out and dropped, bouncing off the elk's bloody shoulder and into the mud.

Claudia jumped off the chair with a splash. She reached into the shallow mud puddle and picked up a beautiful red gem about the size of a marble. She understood right away that she had unearthed something precious. "Would you boys looky here?" she exclaimed.

"That ain't no Montana sapphire," said Morris Evans, noticing the gem was reddish and not blue. "What you got there is a big ole ruby. I bet it's worth . . ."

Before he could finish, Claudia rubbed the color off the stone, realizing the red was blood picked up on the bounce off the dead animal. She stood back up after she washed it off in a trickle of water and could not speak.

"Is that . . . ?" was all Morris Evans could say.

Everyone nearby snuck in a step or two to gawk at what appeared to be a rough but beautiful diamond pulled fresh from the rocky crack in the wall opened by the collapse.

Bullseye, her head wrapped in a bandage, made her way down the ladder into the area to see what remained of her tunnel and pushed to the front of the small crowd. She yanked the clear gem from Claudia's hand, while fishing a jeweler's loupe from a little chain around her neck, and wedged the magnifier into her right eye, the one the medics had not covered with a bandage. She rolled it over and over in her fingers while everyone waited for her "expert" opinion.

"Claudia, what we have here is a big fat diamond, all right," Bullseye declared.

"Diamond? You mean there are diamonds just stuck in the ground around here?" questioned April Lear, squeegeeing mud off her legs and arms.

"You betcha, April. Ain't you heard of Ekati and Diavik?" said Bullseye, putting her know-it-all-tour-guide hat on. "Most folks think all diamonds come from South Africa, but fact is that the two largest diamond producing mines in the world are right up the road in Canada, just a few hundred miles north of right where we're standing. They produce about five million carats a year, between the two of them . . ."

April fainted into the mud, starting a small scramble by Morris and Hitch to revive her.

Bullseye continued, "And the land we're on here in my mine ain't all that different. There's kimberlite here and there—see that blueish rock strip that runs down the side of the pit there? That's it, and sometimes it holds diamonds. It was just a matter of time before I found a big diamond. I've been telling you boys I could smell 'em for a long while now, haven't I, Hitch?"

"So, I need to go check my ranch for these kimberlite rocks and see if I've got diamonds in them?" said Actor Evan Morris, to a chorus of nodding heads, apparently wondering the same thing.

"Now, don't go rushing off and crushing every rock you find. A diamond needs a bunch of factors to form. That vein that cracked open in the flood must have been part of a volcanic vent . . ."

Bullseye enjoyed telling stories around the campfire to her hunting clients but found this setting a little more intimidating. Not only were there over a hundred people hanging on her every word, but one of them was the president of the United States. They destroyed her tunnel and were about to sell her ranch out from under her, and she wasn't sure if she'd see jail time because of the stampede thing, so she maximized the opportunity to lecture. "Kimberlite is formed during volcanic activity by ultrabasic magma, which is alkali poor, but full of H_2O and CO^2 and a bunch of trace elements. Diamond xenocrysts, transferred from host rocks, get caught in the kimberlites, or long vents"—she looked at Evan, who smiled sweetly, as if she were singing to him, which caused her to flash a schoolgirl smile— "as they move to the surface through the mantle at velocities of ten to twenty miles per hour by this thing called the 'crack propagation process.' They're big ole volcanic vents that formed between cracks in the other, harder rock. And where you find one . . ." She splashed a bucket of water up on the crack in the rock wall, which washed away some mud and crusty lava rock and revealed a lustrous trail of sparkling clear and amber diamonds—thousands of them—running for several yards before plunging back underground. Bullseye couldn't catch her breath. "Oh my!"

The crowd gasped at the waterfall of diamonds protruding from the wall of rock in front of them.

"And it's right here in your mine, Bullseye," shrieked April, after she caught her breath. She did her best to glue her hair back in place as she saddled back up to Bullseye. "And she's my very best friend in the entire world!"

"Pardon me, Mr. President," interrupted Scott Kirkpatrick. He pulled up the *Action News* app on his iPad. "I think you might like to see this."

The president, grabbing a towel from an aide, said, "What do you have that could be so important right now?"

Kirkpatrick made his way into the inner circle formed around the president and spun his iPad around, making sure he noticed the *Action News* logo first. He turned the president a little to the west, so the camera up on the truck could pick them up in the live feed. "As you may know, I'm Scott Kirkpatrick, Chief Montana Secession Correspondent for *Action News Missoula* and also a geologist and—"

"And, the point?" said the president.

"Where we're standing—and—where that diamond vein starts, appears to be just inside the boundary line of the Nez Perce State Park in Montana."

"And not on Ms. Bullseye Magee's land?" pleaded April Lear, to their collective defense.

"What the . . . ?" was all Bullseye could muster.

Puzzled looks played all around as the news guy continued. "And there's no telling which way the vein runs, but if it follows that crack, it might just head off a few yards into Idaho, and then west, which is national forest property."

"What the . . . ?" Bullseye repeated.

The president addressed Bullseye, "Are you OK? Your head looks pretty bad."

Bullseye nodded and started to speak, but the president cut her off.

You're Bullseye Magee, right, the Mother of the Secession movement, I think they call you, right?"

Bullseye adjusted her bandage with two mud-covered hands and blushed. "I don't know about all that, Mr. President. I just know when some man grabs me by the throat and tries to steal my ranch, I'm likely to come up with all kinds of crazy ideas."

Bullseye's friends circled close behind her, with Morris putting his hand on her shoulder.

The Secret Service team tensed up as the president stepped a little closer toward Bullseye. "I don't blame you, Bullseye. This whole thing is outrageous, and I only started this Montana thing because I was trying to stick up for the rest of our land and no one had a better idea. How in the world can it come down to this?"

The flowing river and a few animal noises were the only sounds heard, as the crowd froze in place and watched the showdown.

The president reached over and said, "Can I see that diamond? How big are those kimberlite things up in Canada? Are they worth billions and billions of dollars?"

Bullseye buffed the rock on her bandaged head, then handed it to Crowley. "No, sir. It ain't billions with a *b*. It's trillions, with a *t*. Lots of them."

"Ladies and gentlemen," said the president, adopting a press conference tone to his voice and looking up into Scott Kirkpatrick's camera, "are you still live? Let's make sure everyone is safe, and then I want this area sealed off until we can find out what happened here and who owns what."

As they crawled out of the hole, Bullseye splashed a bucket of water on her face and when she bent over to put the bucket down, she scooped up a few diamonds that had come loose and slid them in her pocket. Her head throbbed from the concussion, but opportunity proved to be a great antidote.

DOWNSTREAM

Secretary of the Interior Alan Stubblefield dangled twenty-one feet above the rocky shoreline, snagged on a dead western red cedar limb that tore through the back of his coat when the wall of water carried him downstream. Stubblefield tried to rescue himself by grabbing anything that floated by, but tree limbs had plucked him from the flood. The wave roared passed, leaving him stuck up a tree.

The water receded in a few minutes, which took away his fear of drowning, but replaced it with a more vivid fear of falling, being crushed, or trampled by stampeding animals. He peeled off a pile of black fabric that had clung to his arm during the flood, which turned out to be a tuxedo jacket with a plastic bag holding a handwritten note sticking out of the pocket. Dangling from the tree, the secretary read the note out loud:

"Jonah 2:3—*For thou hadst cast me into the deep, in the midst of the seas; and the floods compassed me about: all thy billows and thy waves passed over me. 2:4—I am cast out of thy sight; yet I will look again toward thy holy temple. 2:5— The waters compassed me about, even to the soul: the depth closed me round about,* (something was smudged out by the water, then . . .) *yet hast thou brought up my life from corruption, O LORD my God.*"

"Please, somebody help me. Lord, help me. I promise, Lord. I'm going back to church. I'll be a good politician. This time, for real, Lord, if You'll just get me back on solid ground. I know I said this before when You got me through Baylor and when I won my cabinet appointment, but I mean it this time. I know this verse is straight from You!"

As Stubblefield started crying, he wiped his eyes with the paper on which the verse was written. He did not notice on the back, in matching handwriting to the verse were the instructions: "Hour 12—Pepperoni and Pesto. Your favorite, Benny dear. Love, Mom."

155

WASHINGTON, DC

"Thank you and God bless the great state of Montana and these magnificent United States of America."

"And we're clear," said the floor director, who stood next to the prompter on the camera in front of the president. The bright key light went dark.

"Yes, we are indeed clear," repeated the president, smiling at his wife, who stepped around the camera to give him a hug.

It was the president's fifth prime-time announcement to the nation in the two months since the event in Montana. The news had improved each week and canceling the sale of Montana was the answer to his prayers. His opponents had called him a bigger crackpot for announcing that God had delivered an answer to his prayers and saved the country than they had when he announced he would sell Montana in the first place, but he didn't care. There simply was no alternate explanation in his mind. God had provided a literal earth-shattering solution.

Everyone in Washington applauded him for having enacted massive departmental cuts created, which reduced the size of government by 16 percent! It was not the ultimate answer, but a tremendous leap in the right direction. These bold moves set the pace for legislation containing further cuts and restrictions from Congress, not to mention a balanced budget amendment—with the first bill co-sponsored by the representatives from Montana with broad bipartisan support.

"Oh my gosh, Crowley, I can't believe you made it to this moment. Two months since that day in Montana and now, think about what this represents," said the First Lady, as she squeezed her husband. "You've figured a way to reshape government without having to sell Montana, and the entire country is responding. You know, I think there's a chance you still may reach your full potential."

"Well thank you, Mrs. President," he said as he pulled out a huge diamond ring and slid it on her finger. "It's a genuine Montana diamond and I think I earned it. Now the question is, did I do good enough to get a kitchen pass for some cookie dough?"

She gasped, then smiled as she kissed her husband and said, "I'll sign an executive order, just this once."

156

VIRGINIA CITY, MONTANA

The Community Table at the Placer Gold Café had been buzzing for two months since the Secession convention and the Lame Horse Discovery, as they called the diamond vein. Misgivings and mistrusts toward the federal government oozed from the committee, which included the governor and the local Virginia City constituency, but all agreed to the president's call for a moratorium on secession while he sorted out the new diamond discovery. In the interim, a triumvirate of forces from the United States Army, the Montana National Guard, which included some militia members, and mine-owner Bullseye Magee, with some help from her friends in Madison County, guarded the Lame Horse Discovery. They watched each other more than outsiders.

President Crowley's announcement to call off the plan to sell Montana had rewarded their patience.

Geologists required more time to evaluate the field, but the fissure appeared to run hundreds of yards, very near the surface, before diving deep into the earth. It fractured into several dozen additional threads, with anyone's guess on how deep they ran until they finished analyzing core samples. It looked to be chock full of kimberlite, with conditions suitable for an unfathomable diamond harvest like the Diavik mine to the north in Canada and could contain millions of carats of diamonds.

A majority of the diamond find resided on Montana state property that would soon bear the name *Save Montana State Park*, since it had done just that. The rest of the find lay under a national forest, which gave the US government claim to much of the mine's yield. The government would need time to calculate the exact value, but guesses ran in the trillions, with some estimates in the double digits of trillions. Interest by all four of the world's largest diamond mining companies made it obvious this find was big enough to save Montana and allow the United States to catch up on its promises to the citizens and keep out of trouble, as long as Congress did not go back to spending like coupon-wielding moms on Black Friday.

Several of the Community Table regulars took jabs at Bullseye to remind her of what could have been. The site survey ended up proving the

317

main chutes of kimberlite ran right around the edge of her property. As she cleaned out her tunnels, she ran across a few sizable stones blasted clear in the hydraulic pressure of the collapse, which helped pad her pocket. There was never any actual proof that she could smell diamonds, as claimed.

The fact that Bullseye's tunneling escapade helped create the financial opportunity for the country in the first place brought leniency from the administration and the courts. Her agreement to cooperate with state and federal officials during the cleanup, along with her testimony against Stubblefield and Fowler, earned her immunity from any jail time for the stampede charade. She told officials everything she knew. Her friends chalked up the stampede as just one more wild-but-harmless attempt of hers to create a lifetime of crazy stories to reenact around the campfire with her hunting clients.

"Don't you forget, I still own a hundred and forty acres right next door to that big diamond mine. Whatever they do, they'll have to go through my place to do it. Or at least buy T-shirts on the way out," said Bullseye, licking her wounds, "and did I mention that I own the trademark to the name Lame Horse Mine? And did I also mention that we open the Lame Horse Hunting Lodge next weekend? With all those animals running around, we have the best hunting in ten counties—guaranteed. Sounds like 'whatfer' with zeros on it to me."

After some snickers and a mock toast with coffee mugs, Bullseye leaned in a little and said, "And did I mention how sorry I was . . . I am? Sorry for taking advantage of the state that I love and friends that I love even more? The best I can figure is that I got eaten up by the past and caught dreaming about the future but didn't realize how amazing the present is. I really do love you all."

Evan put his hand gently on Bullseye's back and said, "What was the worst moment for you, Bullseye? Can you even narrow it down to the point when you thought you were going to die or knew that you might lose everything, or the Army may shut you down—holy cow, this sounds better than any of my movies!"

They all laughed, except Bullseye. The tears in her eyes gave away the depth of her feelings, something they had not seen in all the years gathered around that very same table. They grew quiet and leaned in to hear her speak.

"I know the moment. My worst moment was also my best. I was on the rocks, by the river, literally torn between those twerps in my tunnel, thinking that millions of dollars were waiting for me, then the stampede, knowing if I didn't get the pen open, I could lose millions, and of course, right over the hill, knowing the Army was coming to grab all of you and squash the Secession. All those millions sitting a few yards away and all I thought about was helping my friends. The money just didn't matter." She took a sip of coffee and wiped a tear from her cheek. "OK, well it mattered a lot, but not enough to stop me from choosing to help save you bunch of worn-out ranchers. I've never felt anything like that in my entire life, and it was absolutely the best moment I've ever felt. I've never loved anybody like that before. You fellas . . . and Mona, April, have changed me."

Warm smiles prevented any talking. After another sip, Bullseye finished, "And then that dang bighorn knocked my lights out and next thing I know, everything I had put together was underwater or gone, except my friends, who were still there with me. And the president, of course."

Everyone forgave Bullseye but didn't make a big deal about hugging or anything, other than April. One more mug toast was enough. Mona swirled in from the kitchen with two coffeepots and said, "Did anyone hear what happened to those poor little naked boys from Iowa?"

Bullseye said, "I got a few emails from that Benny twerp. He hit on me for two months, trying to get me to Skype with him from my hot spring. He lost his video game, but he sure struck gold. That little faker is the keynote speaker at some big cosplay convention, or whatever they call those role-playing, dress-up, immerse-yourself, video-game gatherings. And his Twitch account has gone off the charts. I think he's done at the drive-thru for now. And his mom got an endorsement deal from some gourmet mac 'n' cheese outfit."

Bullseye turned her attention to Actor Evan Morris and asked, "Evan, are you sad that your career as Montana spokesmodel is over? You had a few million views on your 'Plea' video. I have to say, it was some of your finest work."

Actor Evan rose and tossed a twenty-dollar tip on the table for Mona. "Well, it's not over yet. I've changed the venue and added some big plans, so I hope you'll excuse me." Evan smiled at Bullseye and said, "Someone I respect a great deal once asked me what I was all about. Guys, I came to Montana to hide, but after all we've been through, I've decided to accept the offer from Governor McLemore to become the permanent spokesman for 'Our Montana,' and we start today by shooting a few spots around the state. I want the whole country to know how great our state is and what we almost lost. We're going to weave in a few messages about being free while we invite folks to come visit. McLemore is leading the tour and is flying down to pick me up."

The tablemates looked around, impressed. "Shoot, Evan, I'll support you. It's almost like voting for my name anyway," said Morris Evans.

"Thanks, Morris, I'm glad I can count on you, but I'm not really running for anything. Either way, I'll make sure to mention weed control whenever I can." His friends laughed.

Mona said, "Evan, you've crawled all over this state asking for people to help with the Secession. What was your favorite part?"

Evan turned around toward Bullseye and said, "That's an easy one; she's right here." He extended his hand to pull Bullseye up from her chair, then moved toe to toe with her, slid two fingers behind her belt buckle and pulled her close. She didn't blink as he gazed right into her green eyes. "I'd love to spend some time at your ranch to see if we can figure something out, Bullseye. You know, I've never met anyone like you—not even close. Is there any chance you'd come with me today on this little excursion? The governor's got a nice plane, and I'll have you home by dinner."

Bullseye's green eyes warmed as she squinted just a little. "Naw, Evan, you go get your campaign rolling. It sounds perfect, and people will love having you invite them to Montana for a visit. I'll be at my place when you get back and believe me, that's something I've never said to any man. I like the idea of you running all over, talking about Montana. Just make sure you save a little time to lie on a beach somewhere, will you, handsome?"

"I was thinking more than a little time together, Bullseye," said Evan as he eased down to one knee and slipped a beautiful diamond ring out of his pocket and held it in front of her. "Will you? I love you, Bullseye. Will you marry me?"

With both hands, she caressed his tan face, then stroked his beautiful blond hair, standing him up and bringing him closer. He smiled a little as he moistened his lips, just before engaging in a deep, passionate kiss that lasted even longer than the hoots and hollers from their friends. Before the kiss ended, Evan realized that his list only needed one name.

THE END

EPILOGUE

A few months after the story ended, Hank Rogers, the old man who owned the Flying B Bison Ranch slammed and latched the trailer door, then thanked Bullseye for helping him round up a few more head of bison. Most of them had scampered off into the woods but wandered back to the meadow as summer made its way up the valley. Bullseye brought a few friends who had made a game out of running the strays. None of them were on motorcycles.

Besides her agreement to testify against the high government officials, part of her public service was the restoration of as many animals as she could recover, along with some long-term conservation work. She unloaded her last trailer load of bison for the day and put her hand on Old Man Rogers' back. "Hank, I'm sorry about this whole thing. I don't know what got into me."

Hank spit, then said, "Bullseye, it's all right. Having a few buildings destroyed is nothing. I'm just glad I got out of the way. They would have killed me if I'd been at home or anywhere near the stampede. You know what saved me, right? Whoever left me this note sure was my guardian angel." He held out a piece of paper with some hastily written words on it: *A biker gang is coming to destroy your ranch later today. Save yourself. Run somewhere safe. Go now. Run.   — LB*

"Well, I'm glad somebody warned you, but it's still a shame you have to rebuild everything."

The old rancher took off his hat and looked down for a second. "Bullseye, I owe you the apology. A long time ago, when you were a little girl, you ran to me. You were in trouble and came to me for help, but I just didn't understand. I didn't know that side of your pappy. And I did the worst thing in the world; I took you right back to him. I thought a little girl was always safest at home. I am so sorry for not helping you, Bullseye. I heard later, from your momma, what a scoundrel he was, and I am just so very sorry, sweetheart. I'm just so sorry, Laura Brennan. I'm so sorry, LB."

Bullseye cried and hugged the sobbing old man. "It's OK, Hank. It's OK. I didn't think you'd remember since no one's called me LB in forty years. I've had to rebuild my fences too, and I think I'll be OK."

Forgiveness did that.

NOTES FROM THE AUTHOR

For Montana Purists: I created a river. My *Nez Perce River*, if real, would start high in the hills in the southwest corner of Montana, somewhere west of the Lost Trail Ski Area, but east of the Lost Horse Pass—likely due south of Painted Rocks Lake—and head west and south through a dip in the Continental Divide, which I made up as well. It is named after a tribe of Indians that helped Lewis and Clark traverse the Bitterroot Mountains in 1806. There are passes through the Continental Divide, and I flattened one out a little in order for water to run downhill through an alpine meadow and into Idaho. I have driven and camped all over this area—Rombo, Alta, Painted Rocks, Lost Trail and Lost Horse, logging roads, fire roads, and all along the border between Montana and Idaho. There are some areas that are pretty close to what I've described, although maybe just not quite flat enough to have a river run out of Montana to Idaho. Go with me here—it is a novel, after all.

I've also created a small town right on the border of Idaho. I'm sure you understand that it had to be the correct size (minuscule), correct location (on the border and on a river, over a cave), and out of the way. This town is called Lorae. Thanks, Denise, for loaning me your middle name. I won't tell anyone that it came from a lounge that your dad liked in Harvey, Illinois. I saw several places that looked exactly like the MooseTracks—with the bridge, deck, wooden siding, just as I described, on Highway 473 on the Connor Cutoff Road.

The town of Virginia City, Montana (especially Wallace Street), is charming and close to what I described, although I did make the town seem smaller and slower than it is, just to fit the story. I moved the County Offices into the old courthouse because it's a beautiful old classic historic building with creaky stairs, etc. I created the Ole Gold Rush Days festival, but many of the names in the territory's history are factual. All of the people I met there are sharper and bear very little resemblance to those I described in the book. It's a great town/county!

There is a Bitterroot Wildlife Management division, but I turned it into a state park for my purposes. Almost all of the roads and routes are real, and I enjoyed driving most of them. Maybe one day I'll make it out to that stunning estate on Shelter Island in Flathead Lake, if I'm invited.

Think this is all too far-fetched? I took some political liberties, but the principles are solid. I tried to keep most things anchored in reality—economics, law, geology, and physics. The diamond mines at Diavik up the road in Canada are very real—and are as big as I describe. The flying car technology is real and there are various versions rushing to market. It will likely be online well before the time frame set out in my book. Thanks to Michael Gallagher for the informed discussion on LiDAR technology. It was difficult to weave that technology simply into the flow, so I dumbed it down and made it my own, likely maligning it in the process.

The government seizure of land—both small and large—is documented and used from time to time by our politicians as a solution to problems. Several Supreme Court and lower court rulings regarding eminent domain and "takings" rulings are easily searched and are the basis for my plot, which I believe makes it plausible, although admittedly unlikely for an entire state. Still, if you can't suspend belief a little to enjoy a book like this—it's on you, not me. If you still think this is too crazy—check out the action taken in the early 2000s by the Barstow, CA, city council! It makes me look almost clarevoyun . . . clairvoyen . . . smart!

The economics of this book are too real. While employment numbers go up and down, there are many other drivers of our economy, and *all* of them will be wrecked by overspending (along with other variables: size of government vs. GDP, etc.) Congress should be required to take a Dave Ramsey course, or better yet, let's elect Dave to straighten out this whole mess! Alex Pazdan was a savant-like sounding board on economic issues and a good friend to propel me forward.

I used a lot of names, borrowed from friends and family. You know those disclaimers you see all over about "actual people/events"? This is it. There's no correlation between the character and your name, unless you're flattered, then, of course, I intended it as such. I would hope that most of you never live up to the image associated with your literary namesake.

Tim Smith and Michael Nolan have been good discussion partners. Jared Sullivan guided me with substantive comments as my first editor, and I will be forever grateful to Barbara Carpenter for her editorial care and wisdom during my middle draft. Erin Young provided expert guidance, experience, and thought provocation with her editorial services. The superb proofreading service I received from Lynn Post/PostScripts

Editing was a true gift! Thanks to Reedsy for making those connections very simple.

I've had several wonderful research trips through Montana, and I met many nice people, including the rangers at the Bitterroot National Forest and Salmon-Challis National Forest in Idaho. Special thanks to Charity Fecther in the Madison County Planning Office, for the kind help and advice. I'm sure Hayden and Graham will back me up for more research, as long as I drop them in Big Sky for more snowboarding! Camping at Rombo Campground on the West Fork of the Bitterroot River was a spectacular base, from which to explore most of the locations used in the book. I also loved the Kootenai, Lolo, Bitterroot, and other national forests and could spend more days hiking through Ross Creek Cedars park. Incredible! Darby, for Logger Days, and the Mercantile are very much as described and full of nice folks.

I created the concept for the cover a decade ago, and Thom Schupp brought it to life. All he got was a "senator's aide" character for his work. My daughter-in-law, Andi Gilreath, loaned her creative graphic prowess to my "FriendStarter" campaign Flipbook, website, and other critical areas along the way. I borrowed her name for a tech in the flying car group and made the character almost as smart as she is.

I am very grateful to a close group of friends who stepped up during my FriendStarter campaign to help me launch this thing. I could not have done it without Ken Clarke, Bob Starnes, Brock Starnes, Dan & Kim Lynch, Amy Houk, Claudia Wadzinski, Cindy Austin, Al Denson, Amanda Thompson-Reilly, Marion Seaton, Fred & Maralee Laughlin, Wayne & Fran Kirkpatrick, Katie Bomar, Mary Berndt and Melissa Trevathan at Daystar Ministries, Amy Grant, David & Cissy Fleet, Phil Madeira, Tad Yoneyama & family, the Scott family, the Patten family, Dan & Sue Daluga, Derek Daluga, Steve & Janice Minucci, Graham Hepburn, Jennifer Sage, Gregory Roman, and Connie Thurman.

This book took a year to write, which I was careful to space out over the course of a decade. In addition to the above, I was encouraged by many friends at various times, and it means the world to have these friends cheering for/challenging me: Tim Crowley, and Zach Cudzillo at the beginning; Dan Johnson, David Mastran, Abby Frazier, Chaz Corzine, Allen Gilreath, Grant Barbre, Mike Maden and others toward the end. As thanks for their roles in my life, some of their names have been attached to a VP, a president, an aeronautics assistant, the FAA chairman, and others. Not a bad ascendancy!

I also owe thanks to John Patton, Bill Reeves, Lonnie Castle, Keaton Wadzinski, Mark Buente, Sean Selvig, Austin Baggett, Kelsey Bastian, Chris

Halleen, Will Redmond, Matt Nelson, Nash Fleet, Blake Wilkinson, Eric VanZee, Lib Gilreath, Betty Hock, Renee Wilkinson, Michelle Riggins, and others who encouraged me at various stages.

I offer very special thanks to Johnny Musso, my mentor in life, who offered peace and wisdom, rarely using the word "I." John McLemore helped me find peace in dark times.

In a strange dedication, I will mention Coach Ray Bonanno. He was my PE teacher and coach in sixth grade. I was his Bullseye. This part of the story indicates my pursuit of forgiveness towards him and hope that others who had a "Daddy Magee" in any form may find peace. Suffering and surviving sexual abuse as a child creates a haunting that permeates adulthood with dark pockets full of fear and questions. I've looked for answers when none exist, so forgiveness will have to do. I've cried rivers as I've shaped Bullseye around my nightmares. No kid should face that evil. Pray for me. If that was your life growing up, I'd be honored to pray for you. If you read this and realized that you are the abuser . . . stop it. Just stop. Tell someone what you've done and save two lives at once. I am glad to help you find your way.

Alex, Hayden, Graham, and Andi helped in the sprint to the finish. They really made this endeavor fun, and I love having them cheer for me. I am blessed to have such great kids and fully expect them to surpass all my creative efforts.

I started this book two months before the very first iPad was introduced in 2010. It is set in the near future, and the world changed mightily during that decade. I was forced to refine the tech scenarios constantly and to revise my economic forecast downward time after time. Government overspending was the constant. My final flurry of writing came amidst the threat of a closing window. I started "wanting to have written a novel." I ended "wanting to have written a novel while they are still printed on paper." I barely made it.

The first review I received is the only one that matters—and that's from Denise. She stood close during this long process and anxiously, but patiently, waited for the result. Having read the book aloud during a series of car trips, she declared, "It's good." She has always been a great judge of talent. Love you, dear!

Enjoy!

Visit *stevegilreath.com* **for updates, book club materials, and discussions.**

REFERENCES;

Chapter 3 <u>Caner, Mehmet, Thomas Grennes,</u> and <u>Fritzi Koehler-Geib.</u> "Finding the Tipping Point: When Sovereign Debt Turns Bad," in *Sovereign Debt and the Financial Crisis: Will This Time Be Different?* <u>(World Bank Publications, 2010).</u>

Chapter 47 ". . . even though the Supreme Court ruled about a hundred fifty years ago that it wasn't legal to secede. Now, that doesn't mean we shouldn't try. Our situation is different." Reference: <u>Texas v. White,</u> 74 U.S. 700 (1869).

Chapter 125 Bible Verse-New International Version © 1984.

Chapter 153 Bullseye's diamond speech referenced: Kjarsgaard, Bruce. (2007). Kimberlite Pipe Models: Significance for Exploration. Proceedings of Exploration 07: Fifth Decennial International Conference on Mineral Exploration.

Chapter 154 Jonah 2:3 King James Version.

Additional Canadian/Diamond References:
Janine Mundt Supervisor: PD Dr. Thomas Seifert (Department of Economic Geology and Petrology, TU Bergakademie Freiberg, Germany)

Additional National Debt Resources:
All historical numbers used in *Sell Montana* are accurate and as dire as I said—and potentially as disastrous as foretold. Future predictions are from actual economic models, not just for dramatic purposes. If you think my scenario is crazy, look at the chart below, created before the pandemic. Our debt curve is even steeper now.

I found TheBalance.com a helpful resource with clear illustrations of the national debt and deficit discussions.
<u>https://www.thebalance.com/national-debt-by-year-compared-to-gdp-</u>

and-major-events-3306287

https://www.thestreet.com/politics/national-debt-year-by-year-14876008

https://www.usgovernmentspending.com/debt_deficit_history

CPSIA information can be obtained
at www.ICGtesting.com
Printed in the USA
JSHW040440221120
9702JS00001B/2